PRAISE FOR

THE MONSTROUS CITADEL

"Intricately crafted and exhilarating, this is a worthy continuation of the series."
—*Publishers Weekly*

"A fun and fast-paced read full of so much action and intrigue that I felt like I was sitting on the edge of my seat all night long."
—*The Arched Doorway*

PRAISE FOR

CITY OF BROKEN MAGIC

"An enjoyable, anime-influenced romp."
—*Locus*

"A fascinating debut . . . Readers will be antsy for the next installment."
—*Library Journal*

"With complex characters, political intrigue, and discussion of feminism and the caste system . . . readers will enjoy *City of Broken Magic* and its fresh spin on the fantasy genre."
—*Booklist*

"A fast-paced, exciting ride. And an entertaining one."
—*Tor.com*

"*City of Broken Magic* shines most brightly in the interactions between the three Sweepers, and fantasy fans will hope for more exploits in Amicae."
—*Shelf Awareness*

"Incredible attention to detail."
—*BookPage*

"Terrifying shadow monsters haunt a vividly rendered working-class present with the sins of generations past. A thrilling ride, with promise of deeper mysteries to come."
—Max Gladstone, Hugo Award finalist

"*City of Broken Magic* explores what happens after the familiar heroes have gone, and the importance of those who remain to begin again."
—Fran Wilde, Hugo and Nebula finalist,
award-winning author of the Bone Universe series

ALSO BY MIRAH BOLENDER

City of Broken Magic

The Monstrous Citadel

FORTRESS

OF

MAGI

MIRAH BOLENDER

A TOM DOHERTY ASSOCIATES BOOK · TOR · NEW YORK

FORTRESS OF MAGI

Copyright © 2021 by Mirah Bolender

Edited by Jen Gunnels

A Tor Book
Published by Tom Doherty Associates
120 Broadway
New York, NY 10271

www.tor-forge.com

Tor® is a registered trademark of Macmillan Publishing Group, LLC.

The Library of Congress Cataloging-in-Publication Data is available upon request.

ISBN 978-1-250-16931-0 (trade paperback)
ISBN 978-1-250-16930-3 (ebook)

Our books may be purchased in bulk for promotional, educational, or business use. Please contact your local bookseller or the Macmillan Corporate and Premium Sales Department at 1-800-221-7945, extension 5442, or by email at MacmillanSpecialMarkets@macmillan.com.

First Edition: April 2021

Printed in the United States of America

0 9 8 7 6 5 4 3 2 1

DEDICATED TO MY EXTREMELY SUPPORTIVE SISTER,

WHO KEEPS ASKING ME TO SIGN HER BOOKS BUT NEVER

ACTUALLY BRINGS THEM TO ME TO BE SIGNED.

NOW *ALL* OF THESE BOOKS ARE MADE OUT TO YOU.

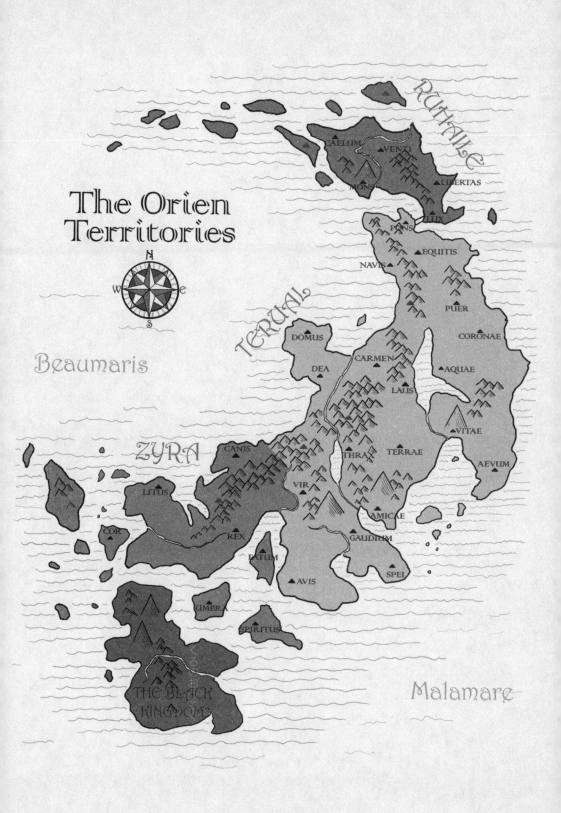

The Orien Territories

N
W   E
S

Beaumaris

TERVAL

ZYRA

RUTAILE

AELUM
VENTI
MONS
LIBERTAS
ILIX
PONS
EQUITIS
NAVIS
PUER
DOMUS
CORONAE
DEA
CARMEN
AQUAE
LAUS
VITAE
CANIS
THRAX
TERRAE
AEVUM
LITUS
VIR
COR
AMICAE
REX
GAUDIUM
FATUM
SPEI
AVIS
UMBRA
SPIRITUS

THE BLACK
KINGDOM

Malamare

FORTRESS

OF

MAGI

PROLOGUE

"I can't believe you got to write a letter to *the* Laura Kramer."

The Laura Kramer, Colette mouthed nastily as she closed her neighbor's door. Her longtime friend, Ellie, and a coworker who might've been named Dot stood behind her on the sidewalk chattering about Sweeper business. Colette squatted down and cupped her hands around the scruffy little head of the neighbor's dog.

"It's another one of their idols," she muttered. "Just another thing I'm left out of. You don't care about any Laura Kramer, do you, Noodle?"

Noodle wagged his tail and licked her hands, because he was a good boy who didn't talk over her head. Colette cracked a smile. She pressed their noses together (instant regret; his was cold and wet), before straightening and gathering up his leash. Noodle sprang down the front steps to race about the others' legs, and their conversation died into laughter.

"Okay, I'm set!" said Colette, hopping after him. "That's an hour of free time. Where are we going, Ellie?"

"The park," Ellie replied. "There's an ice cream stand that has the weirdest flavor. It has pieces of chewing gum inside! Ice gum. It'll be great."

"Ooh, I want to try that!" said Dot.

Colette gripped the leash tighter. This was supposed to be her day with Ellie.

For almost nine weeks now, Sweepers had been on high alert. Even apprentices like Ellie had been activated, pulled out of school and placed in one of the Sweepers' many magical bunkers across the city of Gaudium for easier deployment. It made sense: the feared city Rex had launched one of its habitual crusades to the lower island. That had always caused trouble for everyone else, but Sweepers seemed to think this crusade was different. Colette couldn't go a day without being smothered by gossip.

Did you hear, a classmate would say over her shoulder, *ERA shut down all trains to Zyra! What are the cities down there going to do?*

I heard that Cor and Litus are totally cut off! Sucks to be on islands, doesn't it?

No way, I heard Canis was trading with them by boat and reporting by telegram.

Don't you know? Canis's telegram operators keep disappearing from the gatehouses! They've lost thirty operators in eight weeks!

Nobody can even say if Rex still exists. There's too many monsters for anyone to get close and check.

What city is going to fall? If things are this bad, one has to fall, right?

Colette would suffer it all in silence, stomach churning. Did everyone come to gossip by her because she was friends with a Sweeper? She didn't know any more than the rest of the class did! Once she would've been able to open her bedroom window, meet Ellie on the fire escape, look out at the bay and the distant glimmer of Amicae beyond it, and talk past midnight about anything and everything. But Ellie wasn't there anymore. Until today, Colette hadn't seen her since the alert was raised. She was scared for Ellie's life . . . and also scared that she was being left behind. Ellie spent so much time now with Dot and other apprentices, and Colette was just normal. She didn't understand what they were doing or what they were talking about, and wondered if Ellie found her boring now.

That's a part of growing up, her mother had said. *Sometimes people grow apart.*

Colette did not want to grow apart. Dot had hogged Ellie for more than two months. It was Colette's turn.

"Don't you want to spend time with your own classmates?" said Colette, barely polite.

Dot shrugged. "Most of them are apprentices, so I see more than enough of those losers."

"Then maybe you want to go back to the painting studio you liked? Miss Hunter never lets you go in there on duty," said Ellie.

Dot gave an exaggerated frown. The two of them looked at each other for a while. Colette didn't know whether to be glad Ellie wanted to spend time alone with her, or distraught that these two could hold a silent conversation when she'd never managed such a thing herself.

"Going to the studio takes me past the park anyway," said Dot. "I'll walk with you on the way over."

Ellie rolled her eyes as if this were the best option they could hope for, and they all set off with Noodle prancing before them. Currently they walked on one of the Second Quarter's thoroughfares, the Outer Rim, which gave good views of the surrounding countryside if the light was good and you picked a spot without too many tall buildings in the way. Dusk gathered heavily over them, and streetlamps flicked on to illuminate the many walkers and the occasional vehicle. Colette's eyes tracked a couple on the other side of the street: their arms linked, a picnic basket hanging from one hand, and quiet laughter meant only for this little bubble of existence. She wished she had that right now, but with Dot along, she was sure she'd only be stuck with Sweeper talk. She was right.

Dot started again on some tangent about how all the Sweeper-Rangers of the wilds had retreated back into their cities, and rumors of monster activity they'd brought back with them. It felt like more fearmongering. Morbid. How could they still talk about that when danger hung over their heads enough already? Didn't they ever get tired of it? No, she decided, when Ellie joined in about some man named Basil Garner. If you couldn't beat them . . .

"Have you had to deal with many infestations yourself?" Colette asked. She wanted to hit herself. Now she sounded scared.

"No!" Ellie said, to her surprise. "Not even one. Usually you can find monsters all over the place, *especially* in a spike like this, but even if the southeast is getting hit hard, all the monsters on the east coast have disappeared! The head Sweeper thinks it's a trick, but you know how little threat there is right now?"

She gestured grandly at her hip. Colette stared, completely confused before realization hit. Dot wore a heavy supply bag around her waist. Ellie carried no Sweeper equipment at all.

"Isn't that dangerous?" Colette gasped.

"It is," said Dot, unsurprised. Was this the real reason she was tagging along? Because she was worried about Ellie being unarmed?

"We haven't had a single infestation, though!" said Ellie. "It's been weeks of all of us just sitting around and picking our noses. It's fine! Let's just be sixteen today, okay? Just two best friends—"

"And a chaperone," said Dot.

"—out to get ice cream."

"Are you sure?" said Colette.

"Yes." Ellie draped her arms over Colette's shoulders and said, "I never get to see you anymore! The Sweepers will still be there when I go home tonight."

"Still—"

"You want to know why the infestations aren't here?" Ellie pointed. With the dusk and the buildings, the bay and the wilds outside couldn't be seen very clearly, but Colette had seen such a point so many times, she knew Ellie was pointing at where Amicae must be. "We're right next to the Sweeper city, and *Laura stinking Kramer.*"

"Who?" said Colette.

"Amicae's head Sweeper," said Dot. "She's not much older than us, if you can believe it!"

"And she's amazing!" said Ellie. "She was the mastermind behind the Wrath of God incident last year. Do you remember that light show? Monsters had totally taken over the city and she killed them all in, like, three hours, single-handedly. I heard she's shot Rexians in the kneecaps. I heard a Puer criminal tried to kill her in the train depot and she said *no thanks.*"

"You're getting her and their last head Sweeper confused," Dot laughed.

"They both fought Rex and won! The point is, Sinclair Sweepers are tough as nails. They scare off Rexians, and they scare off infestations, too. They don't have any more monsters than we do."

"Yeah," said Dot, nodding along with Colette's obvious confusion. "Amicae doesn't understand it any better than Gaudium does. They've been writing back and forth with us to compare what's going on. And someone"—she cast Ellie a jealous look—"got put on correspondence duty and wrote out our head Sweeper's response to them yesterday."

"Laura Kramer will see my handwriting," Ellie said dreamily.

Colette couldn't fight a smile. "Are you sure that's a good thing?"

Ellie squawked, delighted and indignant in equal measure, and tried to mess up Colette's hair. "That's big talk, coming from someone who cheats and uses a typewriter!"

Colette slipped from her grip and ran ahead. Noodle had been inspecting a fence, but his ears perked up as she dashed past him. When Ellie passed too, he yipped and bounded after them. The dwindling passersby sidestepped them, but the strangers looked amused rather than annoyed. Ellie caught her around the middle as they reached a line of shops with large glass windows. She heaved Colette up off the ground and spun her, with Noodle nipping at her raised heels, before setting her back down. By this time the leash had tangled around them almost as effectively as a net. Colette had to unwind them, which was hard to do with Noodle still excited and herself giggling almost too much to breathe.

"I don't think you two are going to make it to ice cream," said Dot, jogging up after them. "Even if you do, you'll just get into an argument and drop it all. I'm sure Noodle would like that, but—"

Colette raised her head to reply, but the words died on her tongue. She went rigid in Ellie's arms, and Ellie said, "What's wrong?"

"Didn't we pass people?" said Colette.

The street over Dot's shoulder was empty. On the opposite side of the road, a picnic basket lay abandoned on the sidewalk. Colette looked the other way—surely other walkers here would be just as confused—but no one remained in the direction they'd been heading, either. They were alone. In all her sixteen years, Colette had never seen this thoroughfare empty. Ellie's grip tightened on her. Noodle went still and began to growl. Dot spread her stance, hand going for her bag.

"We had a whole crowd of people just a second ago," she said quietly.

"Hello?" Ellie called. "Is anyone there?"

No one replied.

"I don't like this," said Dot.

"I-is there some kind of event going on?" said Colette. "Maybe something happened on another street?"

"We'd have heard it too, wouldn't—" Ellie's head turned sharply toward the shops. "Who's there?"

The store window was big, showing off mannequins draped in the newest fashion trends. Past the colorful dresses Colette couldn't make anyone out, but Ellie leaned toward it as if someone were there.

"What?" she said again.

"Nothing's there, Ellie," said Dot.

"But there is! Can't you hear it?" said Ellie.

"I don't hear any—"

But then Dot paused, too. Ellie let go of Colette, and both apprentices inched toward the window with wary expressions. Colette couldn't hear anything. No voices, no footsteps, no approaching vehicles. She held Noodle's leash tighter and tried to tell herself everything was okay.

"What are you hearing?" she whispered.

"Someone's talking," Ellie said quietly. "They're asking us about something. *Do you know the wrath.* I don't understand."

Dot sucked in a breath. "It's not a voice."

"Of course it's a—"

"If it was a real voice, Colette would hear it."

Ellie stepped back, trembling. "Magic?"

"Anti-magic."

Noodle squealed. The leash wrenched so hard Colette was pulled off her feet. She landed hard, and was dragged three feet into the street before the leash's handle slipped off her wrist. She looked up in time to see the leash slither over the opposite sidewalk and up, into an alley filled with shadows so dark they looked physical. No. They *were* physical. She pushed herself up on skinned palms and choked, "Monster! There's a monster!"

"Two of them?" said Ellie, hurrying to her side.

"More than that!" said Dot, looking all around them. Colette couldn't see anything else, but she didn't know what to look for anyway. Dot's panicked gaze rested on them again, and she said, "Get Miss Hunter."

"You can't be—"

"You don't have anything!" Dot snapped. "I can at least do something! Now go! Run as fast as you can!"

"What are you doing?" said Colette. To her horror, Dot charged for the alley. "Wait! Dot, stop!"

She was pulled again, this time by Ellie's grip on her wrist. Ellie had trained for this, to run and fight, and she was fast. It took all Colette had to keep up without tripping as they dashed away down the thoroughfare. Light flashed over them, coupled with a loud bang from some kind of weapon, but she couldn't look back.

They didn't come across any other people. More things were dropped on the sidewalk for them to jump over: purses and canes and grocery bags, all lost when their owners had been snatched away into the darkness. One of the streetlights had been knocked over by a still-running vehicle with no driver. They'd all been taken like Noodle. She'd walked silly little Noodle since he was a puppy. She wasn't able to do anything, and now he was dead, and how could she ever tell her neighbor? Would her neighbor even still be there to tell? No, no, she couldn't think like this, she had to concentrate on running! But her fear only increased, because Ellie was shaking her head.

"Shut up!" Ellie cried as they crossed over Twenty-Seventh Street. "Go away! I'm not listening to you!"

Was that anti-magic—the infestation—following them?

"Where's Miss Hunter?" Colette panted, both to direct herself and to bring Ellie back from whatever she was hearing.

"Close!" said Ellie. "There's a bunker nearby. She and the other Sweepers are there on standby. Why aren't they out here already?"

Because such a huge disappearance of people must've alerted them that something was wrong . . . unless any reporters were gone, too. What if the Sweepers had been caught? Just as quietly, just as quickly? What if there was no help?

Ellie stopped suddenly, and Colette crashed straight into her. They'd reached another crossroads, and the road ahead of them churned black like the waves of a deep, inky sea. All the air left in Colette's lungs disappeared. She looked around. The crossing street had the same swell of darkness. When she turned, she saw more of it pouring out of the alleyways and into the road they'd come from. There was no sign of Dot. No sign of Sweepers. Just the unnatural, incoming tide.

And then came the noise. A horrible, grating thing, heavy like a sound could never be, settling in a way that made her whole body—head, ribs, breath—feel like it was being crushed. She tried to cover her ear with her free hand, but that was useless because it wasn't real. It wasn't a voice, but the feeling or impression of one pressing her down toward the ground.

Do you know the wrath, it said. *The Wrath of God. Wrath of Amicae. Disgusting thing that it is. Tell me.*

But Colette didn't know anything.

Useless.

That word felt incriminating. Colette fisted her hand in Ellie's shirt and said, "What do we do? How do we get out? Is there a signal?" The black waves crashed toward them from every direction, faster than an automobile, swirling like something out of a nightmare. "Ellie, what do we—"

Ellie turned and hugged her. Colette froze. She could hear the wheeze of Ellie's breath next to her ear, feel the tremble of her every limb, and realized that there was nothing they could do. Ellie had nothing to break them out with. They couldn't contact anyone for help. They were going to die. Colette choked out a sob and hugged Ellie just as hard. If she hadn't been so insecure, maybe Ellie would've met her with proper equipment. Maybe if she'd tried harder to understand, Ellie could've made it out of this. It was her fault.

Take pride in the fact that I ate you, said the voice. *Of all possible children you could feed, it was instead myself.*

"I'm sorry!" Colette wept. "Ellie, I'm so, so sorry!"

Ellie held her even tighter, but had no chance to reply.

The waves thundered over their heads and ripped the ground away. There was no warmth, no cold, and no Ellie. They were lost to the black sea.

1

DEBT REPAID

"Gaudium's quiet today," said Laura Kramer.

She leaned close enough to the cable car window to make a mark on it with her nose. Currently she was descending from Amicae's Fifth Quarter to the Sixth, and the cable line jutted out just enough that she could glimpse the speck of Gaudium in the southwest.

"Is it?" said Okane Sinclair, her coworker and the only other current passenger.

"Do you think something's wrong?" said Laura.

Okane hummed. He moved to the same window, sat on the uncomfortable metal bench to angle himself the way she did, so he could look out with his unnaturally silver eyes. Honestly it was impossible to tell anything about Gaudium at this distance, but he always humored Laura's moods like this. She glanced up to give him a grateful smile.

"Do you sense anything?" she asked.

"No, but Gaudium's far away," said Okane. "I'm not able to sense anything across the bay."

"You were able to sense something happening way underneath Amicae, back during the Falling Infestation," said Laura.

"I was standing on top of it. - - -'d notice a hornets' nest if - - - stepped on it, too," said Okane.

"I get it," said Laura, turning back to the window. "I'm just worried, is all." They were supposed to have infestations around every corner, with the size of Rex's crusade. The further an infestation was from its hive mind the longer it seemed to take for the hive's anger to reach it, but they'd had more than enough time to roll their way northward. "We should be in the middle of a catastrophe right now."

"I'm glad we're not. We have too few people to handle a catastrophe," said Okane.

He and Laura were the only officially active Sweepers in all of Amicae. Sure, there were mob Sweepers in organizations like the Mad Dogs and the Silver Kings, but they were loose cannons at best, and the Mad Dogs had actually initiated one of the worst monster swarms in the city's history; it was a wonder they'd made it out of the Falling Infestation alive. They weren't equipped for a catastrophe in the least.

Laura picked at the seal on the cable car window, brow furrowed, before saying, "It's kind of selfish, but I keep hoping Gaudium reports something. They're south. Whatever comes up will hit them first. If we can get any kind of forewarning . . ."

"And you're worried about Ellie."

"Wh—But—Of course I'm worried about Ellie! But it's not like I'm playing favorites!" said Laura.

Okane raised his brows, as if to say, *Oh, really?*

"Maybe I've got a little favoritism," Laura admitted. "But you saw that letter, didn't you? She signed it at the end herself! She used about twenty exclamation points to postscript how much she admired us!" When she'd first opened the letter, she'd hardly dared believe it. She was used to Amicae's newspapers publishing trash about her, and their ongoing attempts to link her to the mobs. And to hear such praise coming from a Sweeper, even an apprentice, was precious validation. She'd kept checking it all through the day yesterday and come away giddy every time. "Do you have any idea how long I've wanted to get something like that?" Okane eyed her a little more closely, and she said quickly, "Don't answer that honestly."

"A long time, anyway," said Okane. "I understand being acknowledged can be good for figuring out where - - - are - - -rself. I'll admit, though, I'm not fond of attention from strangers."

He turned to look out the window again, and one of the markers of his discomfort was made more obvious as a result. Two months ago, Rexian forces had tried to attack Amicae through the mines, and Laura and Okane had been the first on the scene to hold them back. Laura had emerged with branching discoloration up the length of her arms, but Okane's injury was more obvious. A kin-infused gauntlet had missed his eye but left five welted burn lines where those fingers had been. The old money-shaped scars on his arms he could at least hide under his sleeves, but the new one on his face pulled attention everywhere they went. Okane still tended to associate attention with future pain. It wasn't a good combination.

"You don't have to be, right now," said Laura. "It's probably for the better, here in Amicae. If you did want the Council here to praise you, you'd be disappointed at every turn."

Okane snorted. Outside, the roofs of the Sixth Quarter eclipsed what little of Gaudium they could see.

Amicae's Sixth Quarter held no residences but the outer barracks of the military, the emptied Ranger district, warehouses of the fields, and, of course, the trains. The cable car station was wider and cleaner than most, considering the traffic—even First Quarter citizens had to use this landing if they went traveling—and when the cable car drew even with the dock, an attendant on the outside not only opened the door, but offered his white-gloved hand to help them disembark.

"I'm good," said Laura, and hopped out of the car with Okane quick behind her.

The attendant accepted this with grace, and simply said, "Good day, miss."

The Union Depot rose high before them with many spires, a clock face above its massive doors reading 9:10 A.M. They were running late. Laura hurried her pace, and Okane fell into step beside her with his head down to hide his face from the passersby. There wasn't anywhere else to hide; with so many restricted operations in this Quarter, walls had been built to funnel everyone straight from cable car to depot to keep anyone from wandering. By contrast, the inside of the depot was wide and loud and open. Travelers and peddlers crowded around the pillars, the ticket stalls rattled, and the steam of arriving trains mixed with the smells from wheeled food stalls. Voices echoed high overhead among the arches and the hanging clocks. Simply put, it was chaos.

"More people than usual today," said Okane.

"There are some big film stars coming in about now," said Laura.

"Which ones?"

"Barnaby Gilda and Monica Reeves."

Okane gave a low whistle. "The biggest film stars there are these days."

"Exactly. That'll give us plenty of cover to meet Byron," said Laura.

"Platform six?"

"Exactly."

Perfectly timed, the doors of the train on platform three opened. The crowd that had been milling before now surged toward it, and the shouting increased tenfold.

"Mr. Gilda! Mr. Gilda! Please look over here!"

"Miss Reeves, you've been nominated for the Golden Bough! Do you have anything to say to your fans?"

Camera flashes popped amid the clamor. Laura thought of her last visit to the depot, thought of Juliana MacDanel pointing a gun at her face, and practically ran to avoid the influx of attention. Unluckily for her, the uninformed people on surrounding platforms were hurrying in for a look at the commotion too. She fought her way upstream, and by the time she found some calm behind the pillars of platform six, she was panting from the effort.

"Okay. So. I may have underestimated the sheer amount of fans," she said.

One of the actors must've said something, because the crowd shrieked with delight. Okane winced at the noise.

"Do - - - think Byron can even find us in all of this?" he asked.

"Are you doubting my skills already?"

They leaned around the pillar to find PI Byron Rhodes leaning against the opposite side. He wore his usual bowler hat, with the ever-present pipe stuck between his teeth. He didn't look very threatening, but he had once been part of the police's MARU task force, and Laura had seen for herself just how good his information gathering could be. He gave them his usual tired smile and said, "Thanks for coming on such short notice."

"You've never called us out like this before. We knew it had to be important," said Laura. "If you called us directly, it must be Sweeper business, right? But it can't *actually* be Sweeper business if police haven't roped this place off. There's no infestation here, is there?"

Would one finally be here, come in on the trains? Laura automatically fell into a wider stance, looking around for hiding places and emergency exits for the crowd. Okane did the same, but his brow was furrowed in confusion.

"I haven't sensed anything," he said. "Has a hibernating one been delivered to Amicae?"

"There's no infestations involved, so I wouldn't say that it's exactly a Sweeper problem. It's more of a . . . Sinclair-Kramer problem," said Byron.

"A Sinclair-Kramer—" The only thing related to them personally that Byron would be involved with . . . Laura's eyes narrowed. "You don't mean there's a mob connection here, do you? Have you finally found a lead on the Falling Infestation?"

That would be worse. Laura could take on a monster easily, but she wasn't so keen on being shot at by actual people. She was also sure she'd be a terrible detective.

Byron shook his head in amusement. "Do you really think the Mad Dogs are going to slip and expose their ties to that this late in the game?"

"Everyone says they're cocky, and they've got most of the northern Fifth Quarter on lockdown," said Laura.

"They didn't lock down that area on luck or brute force alone. They're clever. We're a long way from proving anything on the Falling Infestation."

"Then is there another mobster plan in the works we should know about?" said Laura.

"The situation here has nothing to do with mobsters, and it's not an infestation."

Laura and Okane shared an uneasy look. "Really? Then I've got no idea what you'd need us for."

"It's a bit complicated, but rest assured, you are exactly the professionals I need right now," Byron replied. "Come with me this way. I'll show you."

He led them still farther from the cameras, almost to the end of the depot itself.

A small, square building stood between platforms eleven and twelve, bearing a door marked EMPLOYEES ONLY. Presumably it housed a break room or office for station workers. Byron knocked twice. After a moment it opened a crack. A woman in the depot's red uniform peeked out. She took in Byron and the two Sweepers behind him with suspicion.

"We're expected," said Byron.

"If you're looking for the timetables, you're in the wrong place. Go back to the ticket booths," said the worker.

"You don't recognize the detective you personally called?" said Byron.

"*You're* the ex-policeman?" The worker deliberated a moment, then opened the door further so they could enter. "Fine. I trust you can pick your company well. Come in, but do it fast."

They entered without further ado. As she passed, Laura noticed that the worker held a rifle under her arm, and her eyes flicked back and forth in such a nervous way that one would expect a cavalry to appear in pursuit of her. She closed the door and bolted it once they were all inside. Another depot worker stood deeper in with a matching firearm; luckily the muzzle wasn't pointed at them, but at three people who sat around a small break table. The three seated people all had ash smeared across their cheeks; not the by-product of mining, but more as if they'd swiped the remnants of a campfire to mask something on their faces. Likewise, their clothes weren't anything like a miner's, or even the depot workers'. Two of them wore heavy uniforms with the shadow of a ripped-off crest, laden further with straps, buckles, and bags of supplies, and most importantly, long sheaths at the belts to hold familiar magical blades. The last member of the group was probably the roughest-looking—where the others had obviously prepared for a long trek, she wore regular civilian clothes, tattered and dusty from a journey that had certainly not been by train. Despite her shabby appearance, this last member clapped her hands in delight at the sight of them. Laura recognized her immediately.

"Zelda?" she gasped.

"How sweet!" Zelda cooed. "The dream team remembers me!"

How could Laura forget? Zelda had led them through Rex on their ill-planned rescue. They'd parted outside the city limits, and despite the mention of a reward, Zelda said she had another task to attend to. Laura hadn't expected to see her again. Come to think of it, she'd seen the man sitting beside Zelda too: Ivo had aided them in Rex's Sweeper headquarters. The third member, slight and blond with painfully green eyes, was a total mystery.

"They said they knew you," said the worker at the door. "Mr. Rhodes, they mentioned you by name."

"Yes, you mentioned that much over the telephone," said Byron, striding closer. He stood in the very middle of the room to eye them all. "This fits into the situation as I understand it already. It appears they're also familiar with the Sinclair *family*."

Laura shot a glance at the station workers, but they didn't seem at all intrigued by the mention.

Zelda grinned. "Isn't that Sinclair a *shining* example of manhood? I gave him a *glowing* review."

"It was *crystal clear*," Byron said dryly, and Laura groaned at the awful joke.

"But why are - - - here?" said Okane. "Why would - - - come all the way to Amicae and then let - - -rselves get caught?"

Because they had. Zelda was a Magi, but while most Magi could temporarily boost their speed, strength, balance, or sensing, she could erase herself. Anyone not specifically looking for her or the people beside her wouldn't pick up on their presence at all. She could've walked to the Cynder Block and knocked directly on Laura's door, but no; here she sat in a train office, mashed between a pair of possible invaders and the depot switchboard, with guns pointed at her and an investigator watching every move. She looked quite pleased with herself.

"I'm here for my reward," she said.

"Is it true that she assisted you in retrieving Amicae's magic supply?" said Byron.

"We never would've escaped if Zelda hadn't led us in and out," said Laura. "I already told you about this."

"You did, but it would be remiss of me not to double-check. It's one thing to know someone helped you, and another to make sure we're talking about the same person."

"Well, it is. She risked her life. She's our friend," said Laura, with all the conviction she could muster.

"It's good to see - - - again," Okane said quietly. "When - - - stayed behind, I wasn't sure - - -'d escape Rex's notice."

"I'm an expert," Zelda replied. "Really, I'm more impressed that - - - two made it. I guess the Fatum station really helped?"

"It's a long story," said Laura.

"Let's focus on the here and now," said Byron. "You're all Rexians, and you want something from Amicae."

"That makes it sound so calculating," Zelda grumbled.

"It very well could be," said Byron. "What are your demands?"

Zelda spread her arms. "Sanctuary."

For a moment silence filled the small room.

Byron slowly took the pipe from his mouth, as if he needed all his teeth to deal with this. He certainly sounded clearer that way, and it gave him something to gesture at Zelda with when he said, finally, "Sanctuary? You're telling me that you came all the way from Rex, cut through the wilds on foot, to ask Amicae for *sanctuary*?"

"Exactly." Zelda piously folded her hands but wore a too-smug smile. "As an informant, having secured Amicae's interests, I'm a traitor to Rex and would be killed on sight. In keeping with the Act of 1186, I seek asylum in Amicae with my family."

The two other Rexians looked absolutely nothing like her. Neither of them had her dark skin or curls; Ivo looked Wasureijin, and the other woman—whoever she was—shockingly Zyran. This last addition unnerved Laura the most: she sat with her back ramrod-straight and ready to spring, eyes menacingly focused on the train attendant. She looked like Rex's ideal walked off an assembly line. Only her Magi-bright eyes belied the image.

"Allow me to introduce them," Zelda continued. "Ivo should be familiar already—he pointed us to Amicae's magic in the first place—but this is Bea. She's a stick-in-the-mud."

Ivo inclined his head. Bea didn't move.

"And you're all here for . . . asylum," Byron said slowly.

"We don't wish to be a drain on - - -r resources," said Ivo. "We've already supported Amicae, and will continue doing so. Bea and I are Sweepers. We can lend our strength and experience to Amicae."

Dread filled Laura's stomach. Amicae's last attempt to bring "expertise" to the Sweeper department landed them with a pair of violent traitors; ex–head Sweeper Juliana MacDanel had been deported to Puer awaiting punishment, and her brother Lester had been kidnapped and killed by Rex. Zelda had proved her mettle, but the other two?

"As if we'd trust our city to you!" The second station worker hadn't spoken until now, but spat her words as if she had a personal grudge. "Your people are the ones who attacked us. Rex tags all over in November, and the mine invasion in January? You're just here to spy on more weaknesses! We don't want you here!"

"We're not the ones who attacked Amicae," Zelda huffed. "At least aim that bravado at the right—"

"You're Rexian!"

"Wait a moment," said Byron.

"They're invaders," she snapped.

"They're informants," Byron corrected. "Spies. We need to know what Rex is thinking if we want to stay a step ahead of them."

"Well, they're not useful to us if they aren't back there getting the damn information!"

"That isn't our call," said Byron. "We'll turn them over to the city guard. The Council can decide what to do with them."

"We had a deal," Zelda insisted.

"A deal in no way authorized by the city," said Byron.

"So they should get the hell out," said the depot worker.

"You can't just throw them into the wilds!" said Laura.

The depot worker sent her a scathing look. "Of course you'd defend a threat, you Mad Dogs trash."

"Excuse me?" Laura hissed.

"This is above us," Byron said firmly. "I wanted the Sweepers here to verify their story. There's no guarantee of anything—whether they'll stay, whether they'll work—and this should be determined by our highest authority. The Council will hear their story. The Council will pass judgment."

"They're Rexians," the depot worker said again.

"Refugees."

For a tense moment they stared each other down. Finally the depot worker averted her gaze and grumbled, "I'll trust the MARU."

MARU? For a moment Laura hesitated. The Mob Action Resolution Unit had been disbanded years ago, and the "enlightenment" had dispelled any notion that Sweepers were their heirs. There was no MARU left to trust, but then again, hadn't Byron once been a member?

"Thank you," Byron said anyway. "Laura, Okane, are you armed?"

"As armed as Sweepers can be," Laura replied.

"Splendid. You'll assist me in escorting them to police headquarters. They'll need to be under observation until the Council can make a decision."

Laura suspected there should be phone calls first—to alert the Council, at the very least to arrange a cell—but no one made any move toward the telephone.

Instead they ushered the Rexians up and out the door.

Outside the crowd hadn't dissipated. If anything it had grown. The film stars held court somewhere near the main entrance, so Byron made for the depot's side doors. Laura followed along, feeling on edge and foolish. The Rexians followed easily, heads down but strides sure, and Zelda glowered as she mashed an ugly hat on her head.

"I did everything - - - told me to," she grumbled. "I contacted Byron. I pulled - - - in for backup. I thought I was supposed to be welcomed!"

Laura winced. "You have no idea how much I wish it were that simple."

"Isn't it?"

"My first plan had you coming in with a massive bargaining chip. They wouldn't have turned you away if you showed up with us and all the magic in tow."

"So just making sure - - - didn't die in the first place isn't good enough?"

"No," Okane said miserably. "We may be the only Sweepers left, but the Council hates us. We seem to undermine everything they do. Overthrow the wall policy, ruin their MacDanel publicity stunt, ask for funding—"

"They keep looking like the villain," said Laura. "It makes sense, because they've lied through their teeth for years, but politicians don't really like it when you confront them with their own bullshit."

"Who knew," said Okane.

"Hell, it might even be worse for you if we're brought in," said Laura. "If they think we're on your side, they might just reject you out of spite."

They emerged into sunlight. Byron sighed at the straightaway—there were no such things as side entrances or secrecy in the area between depot and cable cars—but the stars had bottlenecked almost everyone else at the depot doors, so Byron gestured for the six of them to walk tall and strode toward the landing. The celebrity arrival was so interesting, the car attendant didn't fully notice them; he held out his hand mechanically as if to help them inside the nearest empty car, but his eyes were fixed on the crowd. You could've sent a parade in front of him and he wouldn't have noticed. Only Zelda took the offered hand, and seemed thoroughly displeased that she was being ignored against her will this time.

"Good day," the attendant said distantly, so late that the door was already clattering shut and autolocking. The gears above them ground into motion, and they left the dock. Now well away from prying eyes, Byron stuck his pipe back between his teeth and set to work lighting it. He looked like he'd aged a year in seconds.

"You do know if I turn you in to the Council, it'll be a mock trial and execution waiting for you?"

"Execution?" Laura was horrified. "If it weren't for Zelda we'd never have gotten the Sinclairs or our Gin back. They helped us—helped Amicae—at risk to their lives!"

"They're still Rexian. They can be paraded as prisoners, so the Council can pretend they're doing something about the attack."

Laura rubbed at her temples. "We can't just let them die! Can't we sneak them out to a satellite town?"

"I don't want a satellite town!" said Zelda, affronted. "They've got no defense against infestations! Besides, I didn't risk life and limb just to live in some shithole with the Rangers and farmers."

"Satellite towns are more on edge about Rex than the cities proper," Ivo agreed. "We avoided them as much as we could on the way here, and were still almost shot near Avis."

"Can't we just vanish into the rabble Quarter?" said Zelda. "The extra Quarter is what Amicae's famous for! If the Council never knows—"

"- - -'d still never survive without city-issued identification," said Okane.

While they spoke Byron finally got his pipe lit and took a pull of sweet-smelling smoke. He held this for a moment, then said, "I'd rather not send you all to your deaths."

"Thank you," said Laura.

"But if you want to stay in Amicae, we'll have to do this through at least semi-legal means. Heather is our highest authority who'd understand the risk you took and what it means to our city. We'll appeal to her."

Heather Albright, Amicae's chief of police, was waist-deep in the latest mobster-related catastrophe but made time for them anyway. They crowded into her office and Byron related the entire situation. Albright looked over the Rexians with a critical eye, attention lingering on their ash-smeared faces.

"Sweepers," she said slowly.

"They are, anyway," said Zelda, gesturing lamely at her companions. "I'm nothing of the sort."

Albright drummed her fingers on the desk. Every tap of nails to wood was slow, loud, and sharp, like the ring of individual gavels. Everyone was silent under the sound. Laura, the subject of her judge's scowl, began to squirm. After almost a minute of collective discomfort, Albright brought all her fingers down at once and stood.

"Laura, step outside with me for a moment."

Laura winced but did as she was told. Everyone left behind looked anxiously at Byron for answers, but the door closed before the investigator could do any more than shake his head. Albright led her directly into a neighboring meeting room.

While Laura gravitated to the table, Albright leaned against the closed door, peering through the window to ensure the hallway outside was clear. Once she'd confirmed it, she turned to give Laura a downright acidic look.

"You know, I used to hope that you'd learn from your old boss's mistakes, but you seem determined to outshine him in every way."

Oh, ouch.

"I'm sorry," said Laura. "I know you've got a lot on your plate right now, but we can't just abandon them to the wilds or even to the Council—"

"They're Rexians," said Albright. "You have brought *Rexians* into my office today."

"Good Rexians!"

"Whether they're good or not is irrelevant! How did they get into the city?" said Albright.

Laura honestly didn't know, but admitting that wouldn't be good. "I . . . well . . . I suppose they must've gotten in the way Okane and I got out, on our way to Rex?"

"Which was?"

"Hobo style."

Albright inhaled deeply. She took off her glasses and pinched her nose. "So they've already presented a security risk."

"What? No! They turned themselves in!" said Laura.

"They've thwarted our border guards, which have been significantly bolstered after the last attempt to attack Amicae—a *Rexian* attack, need I remind you," Albright said icily.

"Would the border guards have let them through if they tried entering normally?" Laura challenged. "People have tried to shoot them on sight! It wasn't an option for them!"

"And what else will they think isn't an option?" said Albright.

"Nothing, if we can treat them decently," said Laura.

Albright pinched her nose even tighter. She dropped into one of the chairs and kept her eyes squeezed shut, as if telling herself this was all just a bad dream could make it go away. Laura gripped the back of another chair and leaned over it to continue, "If these people wanted to hurt us, they would've done it already. Zelda had every chance in Rex to turn us in and didn't. They had all of Amicae's Sweepers in one spot down in the depot today, and all the way here, and they didn't do anything."

"You're not all of Amicae's Sweepers, though," said Albright.

"We're the only ones the public or the Council acknowledges!"

"Rex's purpose isn't silly little smear campaigns. They want to take out entire cities. You alone are too small a target for them. If manipulating your kindness will bring them to a bigger target—"

Laura huffed with annoyance. She dropped into the chair so she faced Albright properly across the table. "I'm not claiming that they don't have ulterior motives. The thing is, Zelda's motive *is* sanctuary. Remember, I'm the only one who's been to Rex, and I have—" She hesitated. "I've got insight you don't. Not just on the city, but these people, too. Zelda and the others, they'll do anything it takes to escape Rex. They know how bad it is. They wouldn't come all this way otherwise."

As much as she hated to admit it, Albright's doubt came with good reason; Rexian Sweepers didn't value themselves. In their city she'd almost been killed by a Sweeper ready to put herself over the Quarter wall in the process; another Sweeper had killed himself without hesitation to fulfill some obscure rule; in Amicae's mining tunnels, they'd fallen and been crushed by their own fellow Sweepers. It was a hallmark of Rex to not care about their own well-being, beyond completion of a mission. But because she'd seen those self-destructive Sweepers, she could see the clear differences between them and Zelda. Zelda was too much of a person to let Rex manipulate her, and Ivo had been desperate enough to escape it to assist traitors to the city.

"I find it hard to believe they came all this way alone," said Albright.

"Okane and I made it to Rex alone," said Laura.

Albright's fingers moved to rub at her temple. Her brow remained furrowed, but it was less out of annoyance and more from weariness.

"I understand that you trust them—"

"With my life."

"But I wanted to trust Juliana MacDanel, too, and she had all the recommendations we could hope for," said Albright. "Your word is all I have to go on right now."

"Is that not good enough?" Laura grumbled.

"It's idiotic to place so much trust in something with only one source," Albright retorted. "You Sweepers might have the luxury of following instincts over facts, but my job is to keep the civilians of Amicae safe. I can't afford to buy into a single girl's impulses."

Laura leaned back sharply. Albright could be terse at times, and had shown clear irritation with Clae once upon a time, but she'd never been outright insulting.

Albright took another deep, slow breath. "That was unprofessional. I know that you're just as invested in Amicae's safety as I am. Instinct and magic go hand in hand. It's part of your job. I have no right to nitpick. I'm still used to working with other police, and even Clae Sinclair. We've all had to examine the big picture, rather than have the freedom to focus on a specific issue. We have too many people to please before we can work on anything, and none of the people I need to please would be happy with this. You have to admit, it doesn't look good to anyone outside your Sweeper department."

Laura deflated some, but kept her hands fisted in her lap. "I'm aware."

"The Council has placed a lot of time, effort, and publicity into the re-inforcement of our gates and guard stations," said Albright. "If it becomes known that a trio of outsiders thwarted all those measures, and thwarted them so easily that they got all the way here into the Third Quarter and were only discovered because they arranged it—that would be a catastrophe even if it were a trio from proven allies, like Gaudium or Terrae. The pub-lic's peace of mind would be utterly shattered. If word got out that we were infiltrated by *Rexians* again . . . that makes three times in the past year. Confidence would erode on every level."

"They tried to come here as legally as possible," said Laura.

"And even if they had followed every legal measure, we would still end up with Rexians here in the Third Quarter. We'd be promoted as fools and traitors for allowing them so deep into the city that they could stage another attempt on Amicae's structure," said Albright.

Laura threw up her hands. "But that's not why they're here!"

"Frankly, Laura, the truth doesn't matter," said Albright.

Laura brought her fists back down on the table and seethed, "Then what does matter? What's the point in anything if we're going to reject the truth?"

Only now did Albright open her eyes, and Laura realized just how dark the bags under her eyes were.

"The Council's been trying to remove you ever since the MacDanel in-cident," said Albright. "I've been trying to downplay your recklessness so they'll keep you on even after they get a new head Sweeper . . . but this is spitting in the face of everything they're doing. It would be the final straw. If you propose having *Rexians* on board, you will cross a line. I can't bring you back from this."

"What's the Council going to do, fire their head Sweeper?" Laura scoffed.

"They fired MacDanel."

"And I was there to take her place. They don't have another me around to pick up the slack. They've got a hard enough time trying to hire regular Sweepers right now, let alone a boss. Where are they going to get anyone with any experience? I guarantee Okane would quit as soon as I'm fired, and you can't think anyone can tempt the mobster Sweepers into going straight, so there's no one left here in Amicae. What other city is going to send us any extra Sweepers in a spike like this?"

"A spike with no monsters," Albright said dryly.

"For *now*," said Laura. "But no other city is stupid enough to risk it. The Council has no other options than me."

"You can't hide behind the numbers forever," said Albright.

"I know, but I'll use it as long as I can, if it helps me do what's right."

For a moment they were silent, simply glaring at each other over the table. Laura understood Albright's point—of course she did—but this wasn't something she could compromise on. She knew Zelda and the others were here to escape Rex, and as far as she was concerned, they'd earned their safety. Laura took a deep breath of her own, folded her hands to look a little more proper, and schooled her tone back to evenness.

"Look at it this way," she said. "We've been trying to hire new Sweepers. Today, three professionals have come to us: at least two fully fledged Sweepers, and one expert in what happens behind the scenes. It would normally take months of negotiations with other cities to get someone with even an iota of their experience transferred over from another city. You want competence? Rex has the strongest Sweepers in existence. Low budget? They're not asking for much. A lasting investment? There's nowhere else for them to go. Loyalty? They've already proved that, and saved our city once. They wouldn't hesitate to do it again. Accepting them is the best choice for Amicae."

Albright shook her head slowly. "You really think these people are a benefit?"

"Yes."

Albright pursed her lips. "I don't approve of this. I can't. It would be the end of my career."

For a moment Laura didn't believe her ears. Albright had been the Sweepers' supporter through a number of incidents already—she'd kept Clae's secret, of all things—and she hadn't really thought she'd be turned away this time. What would happen to Zelda and the others now? She swallowed thickly, opened her mouth—

"But." Albright slowly slipped her glasses back on. "The reason I took this job in the first place was to help as best I could. You're the expert on Sweeping. If you say this could help us, I trust you. I'll trust these people based on your trust."

"Thank you," said Laura, the relief making her sag. "Thank you, thank you—"

"This goes no higher than me," Albright said sharply. "The Council will not know, and neither will most of the police force. You'll tell no one the truth of this. These Rexians . . . they'll need a cover. You were familiar with Rangers recently, weren't you?"

"Y-yes," said Laura.

"Then that will be our cover. Rangers aren't citizens of the cities, and have no records to be researched. While you were in the wilds—or perhaps while repelling the previous Rexian invasion of the mines—you met them and recruited them. Rangers handle beasts and danger on a regular basis. It's not a big jump for them to switch jobs like this."

"Right!" said Laura. "Although, the, um . . . the tattoos? What should we say about that?"

"There's a division of Spiritualism that puts their teachings into numbers," Albright replied without pause. "The tattoos will correspond to a weave. I'd visit a church to confirm what their particular numbers equate to and come up with a story for them all to defend why they were tattooed with that sequence."

"You thought that up quick."

"I can't afford to be slow on the uptake." Albright stood again. "Are you sure this is the path you want to follow? You can't turn back after this."

"Absolutely," said Laura.

"On your own head be it," said Albright, and left the meeting room.

Thank god. Laura followed a step behind, just in time to hear Albright announcing to the Rexians in her office that they were accepted as Sinclair Sweepers. Zelda clapped her hands in delight. Okane had kept his distance from them, and now moved toward Laura to whisper, "We're clear? They can stay?"

"We've won Albright over," she replied. "For now, at least."

"This won't be as easy as handing you badges and letting you waltz into the city," said Albright, leaning against her desk. "Like it or not, you're from a city that's tried to destroy Amicae multiple times. Double agents exist, and I can't dismiss the possibility that one of you could be one. You'll be on probation."

"What's that supposed to mean?" said Zelda. The words might be wary, but she'd apparently tuned out as soon as they were approved; she currently paid far more attention to the torn cuff of her left sleeve than the semantics of their stay.

"It means that we'll treat you as a person of interest." Albright held up a hand and began ticking off fingers. "We'll create your documentation, find you housing, and place you in new employment as if you were in witness protection, to help you blend in and keep from making a scene. You'll also have a strict curfew and may only visit designated areas. If you're missing or sighted outside those areas and your guard or boss can't give a good reason for it, you'll be detained as enemies of Amicae and handed over to the Council after all."

A slow smile curved over Zelda's lips, even while her eyes didn't leave her sleeve. Of course, she could slip past any guard easily.

"And how exactly will this be monitored?"

Albright took one of her paperweights and brought it smacking down on the corner of her desk. It wasn't a true paperweight but a manacle, formed of a metallic material inlaid with lurid purple designs. The magic inside it hummed slow and steady. Laura recognized it as a Gin amulet even before Albright explained, "You'll wear those. The amulet is unable to be removed except by those with the correct key, and it reports your every movement to the main stone here in the precinct. If you 'disappear,' we can use it to hunt you down."

The smile slid off Zelda's face.

"Amicae's tattoo," Ivo murmured.

The idea made Laura want to argue, but she kept her mouth shut. They were getting a pretty good deal, all things considered. It wasn't unreasonable for Albright, risking so many things by even allowing them inside the city, to want to keep an eye on where they went. Laura's problem was that these were manacles. No matter their use, the shape felt criminal—as if Zelda and the others were arrested mobsters awaiting punishment, or worse, somehow owned. To be slapped with this right after escaping Rex's thumb . . . that had to feel like a betrayal. No one seemed any happier than Laura, but it was the only compromise they had. The Rexians allowed Albright to clap the manacles on them, and with each snap something inside them seemed to shutter. A police team, comprised of two burly men with thunderous expressions, was immediately assigned to them. Byron looked over them with a critical eye before leaving the station.

"Remember, if anything's wrong, call," he told Laura. He pointed his pipe at the newcomers and added, "That goes double for you three."

He'd done more for the Rexians than any Amicae citizen would feel the need to, but Laura still felt a little abandoned.

"I need to place calls for their living arrangements," Albright said next, sitting at her desk and already reaching for the telephone. "It won't be fast, so in the meantime, bring them to see your offices."

That, at least, Laura could do. She bid Albright good-bye, and she, Okane, and the Rexians left the stuffy police station. She didn't expect any conversations to be easy, with the manacles and their new guards in tow, but the Rexians seemed determined to keep their mouths shut the entire way. The more she walked, the more anxious Laura became. Were they uncomfortable? Were they mad at her? Were they regretting ever coming to her for help? By the time they turned onto Acis Road, she felt like a nervous wreck.

"Well," she said, trying to sound confident, "here we are! Sweeper central."

The shop stood crushed between a pawnshop and a bookstore, all three businesses bearing peeling paint jobs that really should've been attended to a year ago. The windows were dirty, the concrete of the front steps was eroding, and the faded, near-illegible sign creaked ominously in the wind. The only way for it to be any more underwhelming would be for that sign to fall entirely. For a moment Laura really thought it would.

"This has to be a joke." Zelda looked at the nearest glowering policeman and said, "Tell me this is a joke."

"Is this a satellite office?" Ivo asked.

"If it isn't, send me to one," said Zelda.

"We don't have satellite offices," Laura sighed, as Okane fit his key into the door. The shop had always looked shabby, but now that she was showing it to someone she actually wanted to impress, it looked unsalvageable. "Okay! First thing to know about Amicae's Sweeper program: do not under any circumstance use Clae Sinclair's reputation as an indicator of the city's quality."

Okane turned the knob but the door stuck, refusing to open. Obviously the city was dead set on giving the worst first impression imaginable. Face burning, Laura kicked the door, and it jolted open. The wind chime rattled, and she gestured grandly.

"Come on in."

They entered as if expecting to be attacked. Of course, there was nothing to be afraid of here: just the counter, the stools, the infamous black drapes, and the back door. Laura sat on a stool, watching them survey the space.

"Please stay on the first floor," Okane told them. "The second floor is my home. We had a problem with the last head Sweeper on that matter."

The MacDanels had held them at gunpoint in his own home and later changed the locks. Laura swallowed down that bitter memory and continued, "So long as you respect his privacy we won't have a problem."

"Even while we have no privacy of our own," Zelda laughed, waving her manacled hand at the policemen. "That's not ironic in the least."

Okane glanced at the guards and knit his fingers together nervously. "- - - have a point, but I can't see any way this could've gone better."

"No," said Zelda, looking pointedly at his new scar. "I suppose not."

"I'll keep working on it," Laura said firmly.

"I think that's enough for one day," said one of the policemen. He and his fellow had watched the whole exchange with furrowed brows, and seemed to think now was the best time to intervene, before Laura started giving them any ideas.

"We will introduce the . . . *recruits* gradually," said the other.

"By now the living arrangements will have been made," said the first policeman, checking his pocket watch. "We'll take them there and return with them in the morning."

"*Will* they be back tomorrow?" said Laura.

"They will," the policeman said gravely.

"Or maybe we won't," Zelda said bitterly. "We'll see how trustworthy the 'friendly city' is after all."

The Rexians were shuffled out onto the street and ushered away. Laura stood at the window to watch them go, wishing she had some clever alternative plan. For the life of her she couldn't think of anything.

"I don't like this," Okane murmured, coming up behind her.

"That makes two of us. The idea of Zelda with that manacle makes my skin crawl." Laura sighed. "At least we're able to keep them. What did you think of the other two? Ivo and—what was her name, Bea? We know Zelda, but never got the chance to interact with them much."

"I don't know what to think of them. Ivo wanted to deescalate the situation earlier, but whether those are his true feelings or an act to ease their transition I don't know. As for Bea, she didn't look pleased with anything."

"No." Laura wrinkled her nose. "She looked more tempted to burn it all down. But Zelda's there to presumably keep them in check. Besides, we handled the MacDanels, didn't we?"

"If - - - call that 'handling.'"

"The fact is, we have some experience with shitty coworkers. So long as we keep our guard up, we should be able to handle this."

"I wish I had - - -r optimism."

She reached for the cord on the blinds, and rattled them down to cover the window. "I'd say it's late enough for me to get going, too. Wouldn't want Morgan to think I've been waylaid by Charlie or something. I'll get here early tomorrow to help figure things out."

"I appreciate it," he said, moving to the opposite window and pulling the blinds. "Say hello to her for me. Her latest try at the cookbook is coming up soon, right?"

Ever since his Underyear introduction and brief stay at their apartment, he'd grown fond of her aunt and cousin. As they slowly closed up the shop for the night, Laura laughed and shared the latest in Morgan's culinary escapades: how she'd most recently catered to a spoiled thirteen-year-old's birthday party in the Second Quarter and cake had miraculously ended up on the ceiling. The chatter made things feel normal. At long last she picked up her bag and bid Okane farewell. The shop light clicked off as she stepped onto the front stoop. The only light came from the streetlamp, but this was enough to cast a glow over the figure on the opposite side of the street. Laura froze.

"Haru Yamanaka," she ground out. "I haven't seen you in a while."

Haru laughed like her annoyance was genuinely amusing. "Business is booming." He tipped his hat; his Mad Dogs mob tattoo was barely visible on his wrist between sleeve and glove. "We did so want to contact you, but the boss's attentions were pulled elsewhere."

"Fine by me. If this is about your proposition at Underyear, my answer is still no," said Laura, adjusting her bag and carrying on her way.

Haru followed. It was another reminder of just how strange her life had become, to be mildly uncomfortable at a mobster following her instead of fearing for her life. She wondered if Haru was involved in whatever had Albright so stressed.

"I like your new recruits," Haru said casually.

"What's that supposed to mean?" Laura snapped.

"I mean Clae Sinclair never would've allowed a Rexian to cross his threshold. It gives us some hope that you're not cut from quite the same cloth."

"What, because I'm not doing this by the book?" Laura scoffed. "The police chief is aware of them. Or didn't you notice the police escort?"

Technically she wasn't supposed to talk about that, but if the cat was out of the bag already, she wanted it to be useless as leverage. If the Mad Dogs took her word, they wouldn't investigate, and might just leave it alone.

"Rexian all the same." He shrugged. "You know, they bring such lovely business prospects with them."

"We're not having this conversation. Why am I even talking to you?"

"Perhaps because you've realized the Mad Dogs aren't the big bad threat you imagined?"

She rounded on him and glowered. "You assholes are the reason no one listened to us in the first place. You're the reason we got in trouble with the Silver Kings, and you're the ones who didn't stop that first Rexian Sweeper before he corrupted the MacDanels."

"And we're the ones who kept Miss MacDanel from shooting you in the face in the middle of the depot," said Haru. He didn't flinch away from her, but his smirk grew sharper and his tone lower with irritation. "So quickly you forget. This isn't a meeting of hostility, Miss Kramer. I'm just here to get your answer."

"I said no," said Laura. She turned to continue on her way, and stopped short when he moved to block her.

"But did you put any *actual* thought into that decision?" he drawled. "Or are you just playing the part of the Council's goody two-shoes? Even you should know that won't get you very far."

Laura fisted her hands. She wanted very badly to push him aside and keep walking, but that was an idiot idea. Saying no to mobsters at all was dangerous territory, though, and she hadn't been punished for it yet. If she did shove him, would he even retaliate? Or would he just take it and keep hatefully smirking? From what little she understood, he was taking these recruitment orders straight from the Mad Dogs boss—an ex–Sinclair apprentice, but otherwise a complete mystery of a person.

"What do you want, really?" she asked, picking her words carefully. "Not just you, but the Mad Dogs in general? What do you have that I could want?"

Haru only shrugged. "I thought I made it clear. We want to absorb you."

"But what does that actually mean?"

"The future plans of the Mad Dogs aren't for the ears of nonmembers," he hissed. A moment later he recomposed himself, smirk widening into a wider false smile and tone sunny as he continued, "Rest assured that our motive is to spread awareness of infestations and protect the city from those who would do it harm. We have a heavy emphasis on the Sweeping aspect."

"Because your boss was a Sinclair apprentice."

"And therefore privy to the terrifying nature of the beast. Don't you want support in your fight?"

"That's the problem here," said Laura. "I don't know what 'support' means from you, or what you'd demand from me, and I'm not willing to sell my soul. I see what you're doing to the rest of Amicae, and I want no part of it."

Haru snorted. "Trust me, Miss Kramer, you haven't seen what the mobs can do."

"Is that a threat?" said Laura.

"Call it what you will." Haru finally stepped away, and turned to head in the opposite direction from the trolley station. He kept talking even without looking at her. "Keep thinking on this. We'll give you one more chance to change your mind, but if you don't . . . then you might know too much."

2

SEEING RED

The next day, Laura kicked everything off by asking, "Rex worked with Amicae's mobs once, right?"

She regretted it as soon as she asked it. Yes, Haru had mentioned *lovely business prospects,* but she didn't need to start the Rexians' first actual day on the job with another massive problem.

Ivo blinked at the papers in his hand for a moment, digesting the information before actually looking up. "Excuse me?"

It was too late to take back. Might as well roll with it.

"Mobs. Criminals." Laura waved her hand, hoping she looked at ease.

Okane frowned halfway through handing out another faded instruction packet. "Do we really need to ask that right now?"

"It's not supposed to be an accusation," Laura said quickly. "The Mad Dogs prey on Sinclair apprentices, and they're not exactly subtle about it anymore. I think it needs to be addressed as soon as possible."

"We're focusing on too many bad things," said Okane.

"Hello? We can hear - - -," Zelda said flatly.

"I know," Okane said quickly. "I just—I really am sorry about all this."

"Amicae's less the 'friendly city' and more the city of chaos these days." Laura glared at the police guards, challenging them to argue, but they stood unmoving by the door.

"Rex has connections to many cities and their crime syndicates," said Ivo, setting the papers on his knee. Thankfully he remained unruffled. "Through these contacts Rex seeks to disrupt the cities, inspire chaos and make it easier to take them out. This has backfired in the past, such as in the case of Carmen. In those cases the criminals run the government, tightly and securely enough that Rex has few openings. Other cities aren't so lucky."

"Anything specific about Amicae?"

"I wouldn't know." He shrugged. "Rex has specific task forces. A separate force for every city, which learns the ins and outs of said city. They are specialized, and share nothing with those not involved. Rex fears spies as much as anyone."

"So you don't actually know anything."

"Only the most general information available. I was a Sweeper of the main city and nearby wilds. My work didn't overlap with invasion forces of any kind."

"There aren't any real invasion forces left anyway," said Zelda.

Okane shuddered. "Our experience last month says otherwise."

"That piddly group?" Zelda laughed, reclining with her elbow atop the counter. "I heard about that. A bunch of idiots led by a bigger idiot with a grudge. If Rex really wanted to do damage, there would be more than a few scars in the mines. That group played nice. Rex proper would've taken out a Quarter or two at the very least. When Rex moves, they move en masse."

"They didn't count as an invasion force?" said Laura.

"Rex pooled all its forces for the crusades into Kuro no Oukoku, including invasion forces." Zelda smirked. "That wasn't shared with Sweepers—they never give the Sweepers any real information—but I could walk around and hear everything I wanted. Anyone who doubled back into Terual was moving against orders, because all the mobs have been dropped."

"Rex no longer thinks in the long term," said Ivo. "All focus is on this last crusade. It will make or break the city and its creed. Of course, they don't consider anything but victory."

"That seems very Rexian," Laura muttered.

"Why the concern about mobs? If they've already identified us as Rexian, they'll know we're not easy targets. Do they believe we're an invasion force?" said Ivo.

"I don't know what they know or what they want, but I know they've got horrible methods," said Laura.

To emphasize this, she held up the newspaper with today's headline: HOSTAGE SITUATION RESOLVED: 100,000 ARGENTS PAID TO MAD DOGS. The accompanying picture showed the hostage herself, a six-year-old heiress who'd been dumped in the emptied Ranger district with a broken arm as soon as the ransom was paid.

Bea took in this image of a child's tears, shrugged, and flipped the page of her manual. "We can handle mobs."

"Hubris," Okane muttered.

Bea sent him a surly look, but before she could speak the door opened. Laura stood quickly and said, "Hello, this is Sinclair Sweepers, how can we—Oh! Grim. It's been a while."

Grim was not a human, though he made a very convincing likeness. He was entirely pale as porcelain, and moved like a ghost who knew he didn't quite belong. He took off his wide-brimmed Ranger hat as he entered and said gravely, "Good morning. I don't wish to bother you, but—"

He stopped short in the doorway, expression carefully blank. Laura barely had time to register this strange reaction before the Rexians reacted much worse. Zelda leapt from her stool fast enough to knock it over and backed into the counter. Bea went for her blade; Ivo moved in front of her as if to block the motion, and she shoved him away to draw it fully. In a flash the policemen had guns in their hands.

"Put down the weapon!" one barked.

"Everyone stop!" said Laura. "We clearly have a misunderstanding."

"There is nothing to misunderstand," Bea spat.

"Quite," said Grim.

"You're in a city, you don't have to be afraid of Rangers," said Laura, going to stand by Grim. "Everyone, this is Grim. He's our friend, and he's saved our lives multiple times."

"It's good to see - - - again, Grim," said Okane, without batting an eye; Zelda looked at him as if he'd grown another head.

"What is that thing?" she hissed.

"It's Grim," Okane replied.

"That doesn't explain anything!"

Too late, Laura remembered her own first reaction to Grim: both she and Okane had been plagued by a feeling of familiarity, and couldn't figure out why. Okane once described Grim's presence as the inversion of an infestation. Like another instrument playing the same note. That would only be amplified for a Magi onlooker. Of course seeing him without an explanation would be scary.

"He's . . . like Clae," she offered.

Ivo's eyes widened and he backed up another two steps.

Zelda groaned and buried her face in her hands. "Where does Amicae find all of this bullshit?"

"- - - can put down the blade. He's a friend," said Okane.

Bea didn't move.

"Bea," Ivo whispered, glancing from Grim to the police.

Bea set her jaw. She sheathed the blade but kept her hand on the grip. The policemen lowered their guns but didn't put them away. *Ooh*, this was shaping up to be a *fantastic* morning.

Grim gestured at the Rexians and said simply, "Why?"

"They're Sinclair Sweepers now," said Laura. "Zelda and Ivo helped us escape Rex, back when you found us—"

"They abandoned you in the wilds?"

"No. Look, they only had power in the city. We agreed to go into the wilds alone. They're nice, Grim, I swear."

Grim didn't seem remotely convinced, but he'd been born in Thrax, and Rex *had* destroyed that city a century or so ago. The Rexians here might not have done the deed, but they had the city's unmistakable mark on them. It must be a sore point.

Luckily Grim was mature enough not to make a scene. Instead he fixed his pale eyes on Laura and said, "I've come with a job for you."

"The greatest headhunter in Terual wants our help?" Laura joked. "Sure! What do you need?"

"To stay inside Amicae, Cherry and I have had to put aside our role as Rangers for alternate employment. We've taken positions at a club called Toulouse. One of my new coworkers has made some strange observations in the workplace that sound to me as if they are infestation-related."

Grim knew infestations as well as any non-Sweeper could hope; he wouldn't come to them with a suspicion unless it was well deserved. It was a real monster. The first infestation they'd had in a solid month. Laura sobered immediately, and in the corner of her eye she saw Okane stand straighter.

"What kind of observations?" she asked.

"She says that the shadows move, for one," said Grim. "Other coworkers have heard strange noises. One said she saw an eye, and couldn't move until another worker pulled her from the room. There used to be stray dogs in the alley, and their numbers decreased until none are left. I believe they have been eaten."

"It must be a fairly big infestation, if it's using its eye so freely," said Okane.

"That goes without saying," said Bea. "Smaller infestations don't take such risks until they are confident enough in their own strength and hunting abilities."

Ivo glanced between them, worry clouding his features. "Will we accompany - - -, or remain here?"

"You're coming with us," said Laura. "I haven't seen Rexian Sweepers working, after all. I want to know what you can do. What I can trust you with."

Ivo became uneasy again at the mention of trust.

"We are strong and efficient," said Bea.

"I suppose I'll just stay here, then," said Zelda.

"All of you will stay together," the first policeman growled.

"You shouldn't bring them out," said his partner. "These people aren't trustworthy."

"How can you tell that if you don't even know them?" said Laura, crossing her arms. "If Chief Albright could make the choice to trust them, I'd say that speaks enough. Or don't you trust Albright?" The two of them became quiet and surly; like the rest of the police they seemed to have a healthy respect for their chief, but that didn't play well with their biases. "These people are Amicae Sweepers now, and more importantly, they're under my authority. You're just here to make sure they're safe. If I say we go on a job, you two need to shut up and follow my lead. Got it?"

"The chief may have allowed them into the city, but she won't approve of exposing Amicae to them on a whim," he said meaningfully.

Expose Amicae to them, as if they were something dirty. Laura's lip curled.

"Then the chief can take it up with me later," she retorted. "Grim, what's the best time to check this out? What kind of place is Toulouse? Do we need to make an appointment?"

"Toulouse would prefer investigations take place outside business hours, so if you have time we could begin now," said Grim. "It isn't far. Just a short way past Water Tower Seven."

Laura raised a brow. "Right now is outside Toulouse's hours? Now is in pretty standard business hours."

Grim didn't bat an eye. "Toulouse is not a standard business."

That sounded sort of foreboding. But while Grim might be a vaguely immortal denizen of the wilds, he also had a good head on his shoulders and remained considerate of what might be dangerous for his human companions. If both he and his Ranger partner worked at this Toulouse place, it couldn't be that bad.

"I suppose you'll have to show me what's so special about it," she said. "Let's get going, everyone."

Water Tower Seven rose out of a twenty-foot radius of mosaic tile. The mosaic's swirling pattern echoed the carved sections of the tower looming thirty feet into the air, just higher than the cluttered surrounding buildings. Its elaborate detail looked fit for the First or Second Quarters. It was a holdover from the days when all Quarters maintained a similar economic level. The city had become increasingly stratified since its conception, and the fancier elements of the lower levels had fallen into disrepair or been demolished by "high-minded" persons to keep the classes distinct. Water Tower Seven's previously pearly sides and copper bands had worn down, its white sides now stained a brownish green, its spires weathered to roundness. Graffiti and posters plastered the base, advertising everything from Ralurian delicacies to brothels. Laura itched to scrape one of the brighter film posters off for her scrap collection, but now was hardly the time.

"You know, if I didn't know better, I'd think we were going into the red-light district," she said.

"It's pretty tame for a red-light district," Okane commented, pointedly not looking at a poster emblazoned with a naked woman.

"You say that as if you've been to a red-light district before," Laura said dryly.

"Well," said Okane.

"You *have*?" said Laura. "Since when? I thought—" She thought Frank Sullivan kept him locked up his whole life, but that wasn't something to bring up around the others. "—thought you were . . . excessively sheltered?"

"There's a smaller red-light district up in the First Quarter. Henry Sullivan brought me with him there once when his usual valet was out sick. It was. Hm." He looked off into the distance, going pink as if dredging up a truly embarrassing memory. "Most of it was as raunchy as - - -'d expect, but did - - - know some of these rich people get excited by watching a fully clothed woman eat potato chips? She had a full audience. I just don't understand. Maybe it would've been better to stay sheltered."

Laura's hand flew up to cover a smile. "Oh, Okane. You are sheltered."

"What?" he said sharply. "Do - - - mean to tell me that kind of kink is common? Grim, please tell me that's not where we're going."

"We have many acts, but that's not one of them," said Grim, completely unfazed by the conversation. "While we are close to the red-light district, Toulouse is not part of it. We sell a different sort of pleasure."

Again, foreboding.

Grim stopped at the water tower and peered down the many branching streets. Laura followed his gaze, but saw nothing out of the ordinary.

"Are you expecting the infestation to be moving in broad daylight?" she asked.

"I am more concerned by mobsters," said Grim. "Club Toulouse has been forced to pay a protection fee to the Mad Dogs. Their agents are always present, but that isn't always a good thing. Because the Mad Dogs are attacking other mobs, the others attempt to retaliate and we have become a potential target. Toulouse's employees don't move alone anymore."

Maybe it was good to have the police along after all.

Grim led them down one of the roads, and as they walked it grew darker. Buildings here had been painted earthy colors: browns and blacks and deep hues that threw odd shadows even in daylight. Alleys wound in and out of the streets, allowing for hiding places. Laura thought she saw a few silhouettes flicker out of sight. Her eyes narrowed and her hand gravitated toward her bag.

"Keep an eye out, everyone," she whispered.

Zelda nodded. She kept her head held high and her step sure, but her eyes flicked across available escape routes. Ivo and Bea switched gait as easily as breathing. They hadn't been slouching by any means, but now they straightened, shoulders back and hands moving to rest on the hilts of their blades. It wasn't much of a change, but it made them look suddenly untouchable and ready for danger.

Apart from glimpses and shadows, no one could be seen on the street. Maybe it wasn't a thoroughfare, but Laura found herself perplexed by the lack of people. On any other street she'd find at least a couple of stragglers, regardless of whether the businesses there operated at night. It was fairly early morning, so maybe even someone finishing their night late might have been around, but no. Either the businesses had really slim hours, or the Mad Dogs around here ran a tight ship. She was inclined to think it was the latter.

Wrought-iron lampposts lined the street, all of them shut off for the day save one. Where the others were bulky columns with a hooded square of glass set atop them, this one rose thin as a sapling and rounded like a great decorative cane, with a lamp hanging from it like a drop of dew. The lamp glowed red, muted by the sun. At night it must've looked downright sinister. Beside the odd lamppost, sunk into the side of a larger building, was a black door with red glass at the top. *Toulouse* was written just below in matching paint.

"What did you say this place was, again?" said Laura.

"A peculiarity," said Grim. He rapped on the door and called, "Yvonne, it's me. I've brought the Sweepers."

The scrape of a lock told them someone had been waiting by the door, and it opened to show a young woman with dark skin and an eye patch over her right eye. She gave Grim a shaky smile.

"Really? They're not—I mean, they're the ones you worked with before?" she said.

"Yes. I have all confidence in Laura and Okane," said Grim.

"And they don't have ties to . . ."

"No. They are not Mad Dogs," said Grim.

"Other mobs?" Yvonne checked.

"None," said Grim.

One of the police officers stepped closer. Yvonne quailed against the door, but when Grim leaned between them she forced herself to stay put.

"I hear that you pay the Mad Dogs a protection fee," he said.

"I—I—Ooh." Yvonne looked at Grim for help.

"Mob protection is an unfortunate reality these days," Grim said smoothly. "It is our only option, unless we want them to start attacking us themselves."

"And you haven't called for the police?" the policeman scoffed.

Yvonne looked steadily at the ground, and Grim replied, "Police presence does little to ease our customers these days."

"Are you running an illegal operation?" said the policeman.

"It is a gallery of eccentric art. Every piece is well within legal and moral bounds," said Grim. "But when someone comes to lose themselves in an experience, an armed guard at the door brings reality back to them. Besides, if a policeman were here, they would make Toulouse an even bigger target for the mobs. We would not risk our customers' safety that way."

"So you bow to the mobs instead."

"As I said, an unfortunate reality."

The policeman quietly seethed. He couldn't be happy, with mob "supporters" on one side and Rexians on the other. He turned to his partner and said, "We'll investigate the area. If any Mad Dogs are in the vicinity, we'll bring them in."

His partner glanced at the Rexians. "Is that really our objective?"

"If the head Sweeper is so confident, our absence won't matter." The policeman sent Laura a scathing look, then led the way toward the nearby alley. His partner shrugged and followed.

"Wait a second!" said Laura, starting after them. "What are you doing? Investigating is fine, but if you try to pick a fight with a mobster on their territory—"

"Laura," said Grim.

When she looked back at him, he shook his head mutely. Laura gave a frustrated sigh and stayed put while the policemen vanished.

"They're going to start another fight, Grim! The Mad Dogs will pull in reinforcements, and the police will pull in reinforcements, and we'll have another shoot-out. I thought you wanted to keep this place safe."

"The Mad Dogs know that as well as you do. They won't be caught here today," said Grim.

"W-why don't you come inside before we test that theory?" said Yvonne.

She stepped away from the door so they could all come inside. Laura hesitated, looking after the policemen again, but shook her head and gave up on them. Grim had good instincts. Besides, if those officers were out of the way, they'd finally have some breathing room with the Rexians.

Club Toulouse was much larger than its out-of-the-way door implied. It took up the entire block—other doors and signs served as a front to the massive operation. Walls had been knocked out, and a great mauve-carpeted floor stretched as large as a theater, crowded with tables and chairs until it reached a jutting wooden stage hung with red curtains. A small band section with a piano hugged the stage. Arching stairs curved on either side, leading to a second floor lost in darkness. Ornate birdcages of myriad shapes and sizes hung from the ceiling, glinting dully in the stage light. Laura stepped deeper into the room, turning slowly and squinting up at the cages. Something was up there. She didn't know what, but it felt familiar.

"You're right, she's very perceptive," said Yvonne, following them in. "Those are amulets up there. I'm surprised you could spot them, but I guess that's your job."

"Club Toulouse relies heavily on amulets for its business," said Grim.

"Of course! Our specialty is the liminal room!" said Yvonne.

Laura looked to Okane, and he shrugged; clearly he didn't know what that meant either.

Grim coughed lightly. "Yvonne, I'm afraid it's not a well-known concept."

"Oh! Yes, I see, I got ahead of myself," said Yvonne. "Well, Miss . . . Sinclair?"

"Kramer," Grim corrected.

"Kramer! I'm so sorry. A liminal space is one where it's believed the walls between this world and the next become thin, or even nonexistent. Those spaces are usually marked somehow. Like . . . fairy rings. Strange patterns in the ground. Places that seem odd or ungrounded. You try to go back but can't find it, so you wonder if it was really there at all. Supposedly spirits can appear in these places and reality is completely turned on its head. Here in Club Toulouse, we create our own. It's not a real liminal space. We use amulets to mimic the dreamlike quality in our galleries."

"The audience is drugged," Zelda clarified.

"Not drugged!" said Yvonne. "It has no permanent effects. As soon as you leave the room, the effect stops."

It was like no gallery Laura had ever heard of, but she could see the appeal. Escaping from the chaos of current Amicae would be a draw for anyone, so Toulouse must make a lucrative business. But even beyond the current crowd, a trove of powerful amulets would be plenty attractive to the mobs; by investing in this business, they had a good deal whether Toulouse succeeded or failed.

"How many amulets do you use for this?" said Laura.

"It varies depending on the performance. Some performers like Grim barely need them, but others . . ."

"How many are there total?"

"There are at least fifty in the building at any given time. Toulouse takes liminality very seriously," said Grim.

Okane eyed the cages with new appreciation.

Laura's lips pursed. Fifty infestation sites, possibly more? How did they expect her to inspect all of them? Okay. Narrow it down. Find the most likely site. A cause.

"You keep track of the amulets' magic levels, right?"

"As the club's secretary, Yvonne was able to prepare that information," said Grim. He took a sheaf of papers from one of the nearby tables and handed it over to her. "This is a listing of recycle dates."

Okane came closer to peek at it, but quickly drew back again; his reading had improved, but not enough to absorb such tiny text quickly. Laura gave him an apologetic look and flipped through the papers. This listed every amulet, with notations on each one's size, shape, rate of magic depletion,

and recent refill dates. If only all amulet owners tracked usage so meticu-
lously. Despite this, Laura found that all the amulets were around half full.
Any infestation must've been planted. None of these could be the source.

"My initial thought is that this is another instance of inter-mob warfare,
but I'm not well enough acquainted with Amicae's politics or city infestations to make a true determination," said Grim. "I hope you can shed light
on the situation."

Laura felt a swell of pride. Not long ago, Grim and Cherry had been the
ones guiding her and keeping her safe. Knowing he trusted her enough to
have her return the favor spoke volumes.

"Where did you say your coworker saw the eye?" she asked.

"Back in the alley. She was looking for the dogs."

"Then I'd like to investigate there first. If we don't find any infestation,
I want to work back through the building. Is that acceptable?" said Laura.

"Of course!" Yvonne drew herself up, bolstered by the confidence in Laura's tone. "If you need anything or get lost, just call. We'll help as best we can."

The back alley of Club Toulouse resembled the entrance, though not
so clean. A few toppled trash cans stood along its length, spewing rub-
bish across disjointed cobblestone. Cats perused the spillage, lounged on
cans, and observed the intruders with piercing eyes. Otherwise the alley
remained distinctly common. The Sweepers strayed through it, looking for
anything remotely strange. Laura decided nothing was here—Okane was
far too calm to be near an infected amulet—but said nothing, instead ob-
serving the others. Ivo and Bea seemed just as settled as Okane but they still
dutifully searched, scanning refuse and tapping at the walls.

"Wow, I'm so vital to this endeavor." Zelda leaned against a trash can.
The cat atop it hissed and sprang away just before the can toppled entirely.
It hit pavement with a crash, prompting all the other felines to flee. Zelda
stumbled before righting herself, blushing furiously. "I mean, really, this
many Sweepers is totally overkill, and I'm not even a Sweeper!"

"We don't have the option of leaving you behind right now," said Laura.
"Besides, I'd rather have you with us, in case anything happens."

"So, rather than subject me to members of the public, it's better to throw
a noncombatant into an infestation's range?"

"We're equipped for infestations," Laura defended. "Besides, I told you I
wanted to see your style."

"*Style,* she says. All Rex does is seek and destroy. How's that for style?"
Zelda snapped.

Laura looked at the other two. "Is that true?"

"We are not usually given background of the situation," said Ivo. "I suppose Amicae's style fosters better understanding."

"What need have we for understanding?" Bea asked, as casual as if she were commenting on the weather as she peered inside one of the trash cans.

Ivo sent her a look, the foulest Laura had seen him make thus far. "What need have we for anything? We, Rexian trash?" Bea blinked up at him in surprise. Ivo set his jaw and stepped up to Laura. "My magical sensing is not so refined as my brothers' and sisters', but it has proven sufficient on previous excursions. I sense nothing in this immediate area. If this were Rex we would keep looking to appease our handler. - - - have neither time nor resources to waste on such useless acts. I propose that we move on into the building."

His eyes were hard but honest. Laura nodded.

"Okay. Let's go inside, then. Anywhere you want to check first?"

He tilted his head in confusion. Obviously he hadn't expected her to agree. It took a moment for him to reply, "No. I have no preference."

"Then we'll go room by room."

She led them back inside. Ivo entered with something of a spring to his step; Zelda with an annoyed slouch; Bea as poised as usual, but with a tick of irritation pulling at her brow. As he passed, Okane leaned toward Laura and whispered, "What happened just now . . . that was very good."

"Isn't it?" Laura replied. She glanced up to be sure the others weren't paying too close attention. "Maybe it's stupid, but I feel kind of proud of Ivo. He's been with Rex all his life, but he wants to be his own person."

True, Ivo had been rejecting Rex even the first time they met him in the enemy city—he'd freely engaged with a runaway like Zelda, and not only failed to report the Amicae intruders, but pointed them to exactly what they'd come for—but he'd acted then with hesitation. She'd wondered how long it would take him to feel safe enough to show here what they'd seen in Zelda's magical protection.

"I'm a little proud, too," said Okane. "But also sort of jealous."

"What do you mean?" said Laura.

"It took me a lot longer to admit to things I felt," said Okane. His eyes looked far away again. Laura remembered how he'd been when he first became a Sweeper: how quiet he'd been, how he'd tried so hard to blend in with the walls. The man next to her was hardly recognizable as the same person. She knocked their arms together and said, "Hey. I'm proud of you, too."

Okane snorted. "I'm not looking for praise. Let's focus on the job before those policemen get back. I don't think they'll help the situation at all."

Ugh, no they wouldn't.

When they returned to Toulouse's main room, they found Grim and Yvonne drinking tea at one of the tables.

"Any luck?" said Yvonne.

"Not yet. We were hoping to check upstairs, next," said Laura.

"Oh, please do!" said Yvonne. "Either of these staircases will take you up."

"You'll need to use the third arch in, third door on the right to access the rooms on the second floor," said Grim. Laura gave him a blank stare of incomprehension. "They're connected in a maze. The more people walk, the further from the real world they are. The other doors are there, but they're sealed to keep the maze enclosed."

"That's right!" Yvonne leaned over the table, clutching the teacup with both hands as her eye twinkled; liminality must be one of her favorite subjects. "We've experimented with liminality before, and there are so many different *kinds,* so many different places and moods and—And we're trying to draw you away from this world. We found that it works best if there are multiple versions of liminality to experience. The array of locked doors, with the satisfaction of finding the single, correct one, that's a minor form of liminality. It makes the experience precious! A secret! The root, '*limen,*' itself means 'doorway,' so we're starting it on the right foot! Once inside, you pass through to the other world. We don't want anything disrupting that experience, so the other doors aren't able to open and interrupt you. All around the gallery rooms, too, we've got special muffling spells set up with the amulets to prevent the noise from spilling over too much. That way each gallery and each liminal space can stand on its own, without being polluted by the others, or by other guests!" She paused to take a breath, and seemed to realize both how much and how fast she'd been talking. She flushed. "I'm so sorry. I'm not on the floor much, so I don't get to talk to people about it."

"Don't be embarrassed! You being so passionate about it tells me it must be a pretty amazing experience," said Laura.

"That's what we keep telling her," Grim said quietly, but he smiled into his cup.

"I—well—You don't count, Grim. You're being paid to say it's good. *I'm* being paid to say it's good. We're really not good judges," said Yvonne.

"I mean, if I were an employee and I were off the clock, I'd complain," said Laura.

"- - - complain even on the clock," Okane murmured.

"Ha, ha," said Laura. "The point is, you're clearly passionate about it. The gallery must deserve it."

"We'll have to keep the threshold analogy in mind when we enter," said Okane.

"It won't be very impressive right now! The amulets are functioning, but so much of the interaction and the art is conveyed by our gallery workers, and none of them are here right now. You should come back later, when we're fully operational. But I hope—" Yvonne ducked her head. "I hope you'll tell me, at the end, which gallery was your favorite."

Laura would find something to like if it killed her.

The Sweepers took one of the curving staircases to reach the second floor. From here they could still look over the balcony's edge to see the stage and all the tables, but far more importantly, they found the doors. Laura had expected a simple wall of doors, but that would apparently be too obvious. There were multiple walls, their arched entrances all staggered so there appeared to be five different 'rooms' of doors, with enough space to imply that all of those doors were true entrances to some kind of twisting hallway. Some were surely fake, but the sheer number was off-putting. On Grim's instructions they went three rooms in. Inside this section there were only two doors on the left, and three on the right. The third door down on that right side was almost flush with the wall so it looked more like a trick door, but Laura figured that was part of the misdirection they wanted. She opened it up and a dark, empty hallway greeted her.

"Is this right?" she said, stepping in. "It's dingier than the mines."

"It has some kind of amulet influence inside," said Okane, following close behind.

"So, like the darkness is the liminality?"

"No. I think it's part of the threshold."

"Can you three feel it, too?" said Laura, looking behind her.

The Rexians all stood on the other side of the threshold, tense and perplexed. Zelda's mouth moved as if she were speaking.

"What?" said Laura.

Zelda raised a hand to her ear as if straining to hear her, and her mouth moved more slowly. Laura still couldn't make it out.

"It's blocking out *all* the sound," Okane realized.

Laura crossed back over the threshold. Immediately Zelda's voice became audible.

"—and if we were to, I don't know, *get ambushed in there,* that would be a sorry way to end things, wouldn't it? Without even being able to call for help—"

"Can - - - hear us?" said Ivo.

"Now I can," said Laura. "Hang on. I want to test something."

She screamed at the doorway. Okane looked vaguely disturbed—he could see what she was doing—but wasn't startled by the noise. He couldn't hear it at all.

"Is everything all right up there?" Grim called.

"Fine!" Laura shouted. "Just testing!"

"- - - couldn't have warned us?" Zelda grumbled, rubbing at her ears.

Laura winced. "Sorry. This is . . . I guess they take their liminality really seriously."

Okane leaned against the doorframe so he was half in, half out, and when he spoke, his voice sounded distant. It was like sitting in Laura's Cynder Block apartment with the window open and hearing something pass by in the street.

"I don't think the Mad Dogs are interested in this place for the business," he said. "I think they took Toulouse for the amulet functions. They're likely studying the commands that Yvonne's rigged to give them secrecy in other locations, and even if they don't want to move anything from here, the club itself may provide a secure meeting place as is."

It made sense. As far as Laura knew the mobs had multiple secure locations to hold their meetings and plot their movements, but any one of those could be found or trashed by the police or other mobsters; even the notorious Sundown Hill, previously believed to be the mobs' untouchable stronghold, had been attacked with an infestation back in December. Sundown Hill had never held the attraction of having an anti-eavesdropper spell.

"Do you think the Mad Dogs are here right now?" said Laura.

"No," Okane replied, so easily it had to be true. "Yvonne knows this place better than anyone, and she was wary about potential mobsters. Besides, there's Grim to think of. He'd be able to tell what's going on, amulet or not.

He would've warned us if there was more danger, or even come with us if there were a possibility."

"With this many amulets?" Laura said skeptically.

Okane glanced up, brow furrowing. "His body can't hold up under a lot of magic . . . but we saw him hurt by Anselm, that time. Nothing here is that powerful."

"And I do suppose he would've warned us," Laura mused.

"So - - -'re assuming we're safe just because one person didn't notice anything," said Zelda.

"Grim would know," said Okane.

Zelda groaned and rubbed at her face. "I shouldn't be surprised. - - - trusted me that easily in Rex. - - -'re just that stupid."

"I'm getting a little offended," Laura muttered.

"Regardless of whether the so-called Mad Dogs are here, we are expecting an infestation," said Ivo. "We will be moving cautiously anyway, correct?"

"Of course," said Okane.

"If there are Mad Dogs, we will see them while scouting for the monster. Infestations are cleverer to hide themselves than humans," said Ivo. "Is that not true, Bea?"

Bea had been grumpy since they came back inside. She didn't look at him but replied tersely, "That is correct. Humans would not normally escape our notice."

"Exactly," said Ivo. "We may move on without—"

Bea talked over him: "But humans using amulets may. We have already observed that the amulets in this building deceive and cut off our senses. This impedes all forms of investigation. We cannot assume that we are not simply sensing what an enemy wishes us to sense. We cannot be certain of safety or victory."

Ivo's confidence cracked. He pursed his lips in annoyance, closed his eyes, and settled on replying, "Safety has never been a certainty for us, but victory always has been."

Zelda's brows rose high on her forehead, but Bea seemed to settle.

"This is true," said Bea.

"Then why should we assume a single building and a single tunnel more dangerous or difficult than anything we have seen prior?" said Ivo.

"We should not," said Bea.

"Then we will move forward with caution, but certainty of success," said Ivo. Bea nodded. "Onward to the four corners."

She strode into the hallway with no further hesitation, expression blank but step lighter than it had been all day. Laura looked back and forth between Bea's back and Ivo's resignation, incredulous. She'd seen that slogan written on Rexian walls.

"Wait," she said. "Was that—"

"Is that - - -r plan?" Zelda hissed. "Spout Rexian propaganda at her when she gets stubborn?" Ivo motioned for her to quiet down, but it was useless; Bea was over the threshold and Zelda was in no mood to be hushed. "This isn't Rex! That's the worst—Do - - - have any idea what could happen here if - - - keep reinforcing that?"

"I'm not," said Ivo. "I'm *not*," he insisted, looking at Laura and Okane. "I despise Rex's ideals. I hold no love or loyalty for them. I only mean to remind Bea of her own proven talent, and what she has accomplished. It is more ingrained in her than it was in me. Zelda and I, we are not Rex's ideal in any way, but Bea passes by appearance, and the handlers—Her indoctrination was more intensive. The handlers rarely wasted time with those they considered unfit, such as myself. It isn't surprising that she associates Sweeping and confidence with Rexian policy. It will be difficult for her to work her way out of it. But she *will*. She wouldn't have deserted with us if Rex truly held her loyalty."

Doubt still wormed under Laura's skin. She met Zelda's eye, and found the same doubt reflected back at her.

"I trust you," she said, because she didn't really have a choice. If Bea wasn't here for the same reasons as the other two, she still had the police guard and the manacle to think about; and Laura wouldn't doom Zelda and Ivo over that kind of suspicion. Laura forced herself to look forward again, to look confident as she continued, "If she was one of the Sweepers' best over there, I'm looking forward to seeing her in action. Maybe I can pick up a few tricks."

Ivo gave a soft sigh of relief. Zelda crossed her arms, clearly annoyed by Laura's stupidly easy trust. Bea looked back at them from inside the hallway; she beckoned them to come, and with varying degrees of hesitation they followed her. Once inside the hall they walked slowly and took in their surroundings as they moved. As far as Laura could tell, there wasn't much to observe. It was almost supernaturally dark in here, like she'd crawled down a knuckerhole or entered the mines with all the lights knocked out. She shook an Egg and raised it for light, but the glow didn't penetrate far.

"Black mist," Okane observed. He drew a hand through the air, and smoke wisped and curled between his fingers.

"Infestation?" Laura checked.

"No. It feels different," said Okane. "I'd say it was amulet-induced."

"Why would anyone put black smoke at the beginning of an entertainment gallery?" Zelda grumbled, arms held close to her body. "Setting off an infestation scare is a shit way to start the experience."

"I don't think Amicae's citizens are educated well enough to know this is a monster indicator," said Okane. "Up until last year, I didn't know any warning signs."

"Amicae believed the city walls kept out infestations, so there weren't any kind of lessons about what monsters looked like or how to tell if one was near you," said Laura. "The Falling Infestation put a stop to that, but everyone's still far behind in what to pay attention to."

"The wall policy was a masterpiece," Bea said in the front. "It was an Amicae invention, but Rex's infiltration units assisted in supporting it. They hardly needed to do any work for Amicae to almost destroy itself."

Laura paused. "Rex used the wall policy against us?"

"Did - - - hear that from the handlers?" Ivo said quickly, as if desperate to prove that she hadn't been among the infiltrators herself.

"I did," said Bea, nonchalant and focused on the hallway ahead rather than her audience. "As I understand, Amicae's politicians were bought off to keep the policy in place, and they took the money rather than their safety. The weak and greedy don't need much to undo them."

Laura's blood boiled. She remembered all the letters she'd written to the Council as an apprentice, and all the responses she'd gotten telling her that she didn't know anything; she remembered Clae railing uselessly against the Council about supplies, pay, and stupid policies that pushed the city to the brink; she remembered the newspaper interviews with Council members dismissing the Sweepers as useless and destructive. And that whole time, they'd been bribed? They knew the danger, but decided to doom the future and make a few quick argents instead?

Both Laura and Byron had realized that the Falling Infestation had been the work of the Mad Dogs, but the reasons had been a mystery. *They bring such lovely business prospects with them.* The Mad Dogs had definitely known about Rexian bribery. She wondered if the mob, led by an ex-Sinclair apprentice, had been following the Council's actions and fighting them the way Clae had. She wondered if the Falling Infestation had been their way of putting their foot down: to create a contained catastrophe that would stop the Council's suicidal practices and wake Amicae up to the real danger. Their painting of a Rexian kingshound at the instigation site would be at once their way of staking a claim (a mad dog), and a way to stir everyone up against Rex. If it was true, she felt a stab of vicious vindication; the Council deserved to be stopped. They deserved to face some consequences. But as soon as she thought that, shame rushed through her. Regardless of the reasons behind the Falling Infestation, people had died. If Laura's new suspicion was true, then innocent miners, interior workers, and Clae himself had all died in a convoluted game for money. Losing Clae hadn't been worth it. There would've been better ways to confront the Council.

"Do - - - hear that?" said Okane.

Laura pulled herself out of her thoughts to see him peering ahead, hand still raised but eyes squinting.

"Hear what?"

"Shh. It's soft, but it's still there."

They all went silent.

Tick.

The sound was distant but harsh.

Tick.

The next one came louder, enough to make Zelda jump.

TICK.

It rolled over them like the source had rushed down the hallway to knock the sound about their ears. Laura ducked on instinct.

"Nothing is here," said Ivo, looking around them.

"Nothing that we can sense," Bea retorted.

The mechanical *tick* came again, loud like an overpowered metronome, and in its wake came more: *tick, ping, ding, tock, hiss, whirr, pop,* together and cascading over each other like an unruly chorus.

"What is it? A machine?" said Zelda, covering her ears.

"Earlier it didn't—" Okane's eyes widened in revelation. "Laura, block it out."

"What are you talking about?" said Laura.

"- - - can't hear my '- - -,' right? This might be the same. If it is, - - - can cancel it out the same way!"

Laura squeezed her eyes shut. *I don't need to hear it. I don't need to hear it.*

I know what's actually happening, and I don't need the magic on top of it. I only want to hear what's actually there, so anything else should—Oh. She lowered her hands from her ears, fascinated. She could still hear all of the ticking faintly, but when the others flinched under another loud stroke, her ears didn't pick up on it.

"You're right," she said. "This is amulet influence." She moved ahead with the revelation, and the further she went, the more she recognized the noise. "Those are clocks!"

The hallway ended in a red door, and she pulled it open without a second thought. The room beyond held clocks of all shapes, sizes, and designs, jumbled all together like a horrible collage upon crimson walls. None of them had been set at the same time. Their swinging pendulums and twitching second hands jerked and clattered and swayed in complete dissonance, fighting each other for both visibility and volume. The light source came from seemingly nowhere, since the ceiling was a solid black. A rumbling feeling took hold of Laura's chest; it was her only warning before the shadow of a giant pendulum passed over the room. The air moved with it, as if the physical object had just whooshed horrifyingly close to her. Laura stumbled with it, wrapped her arms around herself and looked back at the others to screech, "People *pay* to experience this?"

"It's—" Okane ducked at nothing. "It's—My god. It's ringing the hour."

"No, it just rang," said Zelda. "Just a tune without an hour. What's up with that?"

"What's up with any of this?" said Laura.

"Liminality," said Ivo. He and Bea were handling the sudden clock onslaught much better than the others; under the presumed hour chime he simply closed his eyes, as if against a headache. "If we are to assume that this is meant to draw us away from reality, the passage of time is key, correct? In many old stories, people meet the otherworldly and return to find that a hundred years passed in their absence; other stories, they are gone for years and come back as if they had never left. We are now in a timeless place. We may have all the time in the world, or otherwise no time at all."

"That's really poetic, but it seems a little too harsh in here for that!" said Laura.

"Exactly!" said Zelda. "Ugh, all this *tick tick ticking*. It's like I can hear my lifetime ticking away!"

"Let's move on to the next room, shall we?" said Okane.

Ivo nodded. "I don't sense anything malicious here, either."

As if it knew what they wanted, a grandfather clock swung open its door on the opposite wall. A narrow door was inside. They all happily climbed through it, and found another dark hallway. The clocks cut out immediately. Something told Laura that her favorite room to report to Yvonne would probably be these hallways meant to divide them.

Their next destination did not encroach on the hallway, and turned out to be much more innocent than the last gallery. Water filled this one: fountains and rocks crowded the room in heaps, creating pools and cascading waterfalls with countless drips from a masked pipe system in the black ceiling. It was peaceful. Laura doubted any amulets had been worked into this one.

Past the water room and another hallway, they found a dark gallery wrought with latticework. It was gloomy and indistinct, but the lattices looked like elevator grilles. Laura moved to a section surrounded in them, and marveled how it felt like she was aboard the familiar elevator in the interior. Yes, she was in transit—productive enough not to feel guilty about it, but nothing required of her at the moment. She was simply on her way. Where to? She didn't know. Where from? She hadn't the foggiest idea. But that was okay, because the lattices would take her where she needed to be.

"Oh, no," said one of the men outside the lattice. "Oh, that's dangerous. Laura, get out of there."

She looked at him blearily. He had such silver eyes, all alight with worry. Why was he worried? Why would an elevator be dangerous? And then she remembered the shrill feedback of a radio being beaten against an elevator door, a man jumping, the massive clutching hand of an infestation ripping elevator and shaft away from the interior wall. Clae had almost been trapped in an elevator. Clae. Yes. And that meant . . . the man looking at her was Okane. Her foggy brain sharpened as reality crashed back in, and she left the lattices so fast she almost tripped over herself.

"I forgot who you were," she whispered. "I forgot who I was."

"- - -'re sensitive to magic," said Okane. "Maybe for normal people it can lift their worries, but with - - -, or with any of us, it's too strong." He sent the lattices an anxious look. "We need to be careful not to let the amulets in here overdose us."

Laura felt tempted to make a joke about never having heard of magic overdoses before, but the scars on her arms and Clae's current crystal state were proof enough. Any potential humor died in her throat, and she followed meekly as they entered the next hallway.

Laura immediately knew that the next gallery was Grim's. It glittered like cracked quartz, and jewels of every color sparked from the walls. There was a weird, dim luminosity to this room. Grim with his glittering, scarred rock hands would look right at home. Most people would assume he was an amulet-inspired ghost, appreciate the effect, and walk right past.

"It's beautiful," Ivo whispered.

"Something's wrong," said Okane.

At that moment, Laura caught motion out of the corner of her eye. She whirled, but nothing was there beyond more gems. She took a slow step back.

"How many of these are amulets?" she whispered.

"I'm not sure," Okane replied. "I can sense some are active, but tracking it down further . . ."

"We're not accustomed to standard amulets," said Ivo. "They're hard to detect. It's like sniffing out the path of a breeze. They're no different from that which we usually comprehend. Infested ones are a different matter." He went rigid a moment before turning sharply and glaring at the wall. "Though I suspect this is one of them. I sense something here."

"It's moving," Okane whispered.

They all went silent and followed his gaze. His eyes tracked slowly up the wall, over the ceiling, but there was nothing there. Laura's heart pumped faster but she didn't speak. Calmly, she picked up a piece of sparkling rock. She checked Okane's attention—he'd focused on a point almost right above their heads and crouched as if ready to run, waiting for the movement of a predator. The ceiling remained blank and black as it had been in every other room. No sign of anything moving on it. Unless . . . Laura hefted the rock, then lobbed it at the ceiling. It didn't quite reach but spun in flight, catching the lamp's glow. The resulting flash vanished as an inky black hand lurched down and snatched it up.

The Sweepers leapt away, plastering themselves to the wall.

"Where did it come from?" Laura snapped as blackness bubbled on the ceiling. "The whole ceiling's bare!"

"It's not," said Bea, and pulled out her gun.

The glow of the gems dimmed as she squeezed the trigger. When her crimson bullet hit, it flashed higher than the ceiling. The plaster wavered before fading. The ceiling had been an illusion, hiding the open metal beams and rafters of the building. The infestation twined around a number of them like a great, slimy hammock held up by nineteen dripping ropes.

Its surface seethed like an anthill. One limb swayed, congealing around the rock before pulling that back into its body.

The infestation hadn't been hit by the bullet, or if it had it didn't do much damage. The creature made a burbling noise, its already roiling middle spitting inky, corrosive droplets, then twisted itself back into the rafters and retreated behind a walkway. In its wake, the beams were smeared black and smoking.

"We've got to get up there," said Laura.

Bea and Ivo made a sharp movement but stopped short. Ivo looked agonized. "May we go on ahead?" he asked.

"What, are you planning to fly up there?" Laura said skeptically.

"Something like that," said Ivo. His words were sure, but his ears went pink.

"Wait, really?" She paused, realizing they had their own amulets as well. "Oh," said Laura, feeling tremendously stupid. "Be my guest."

Ivo touched the amulet on his belt. A slight buzz rose, as if he'd activated some kind of electric device. He took three long steps toward the next wall, and the buzz intensified into an aggressive *zip* as he jumped. He went higher than he should've, and when his feet hit the wall they didn't slip. In another three steps he heaved himself atop the divide, before launching toward the beams. Bea followed.

Okane gaped at them. "What kind of amulets do *they* have?"

"We don't have time for that right now." Laura ran back toward the door. "We have to get up there!"

They rushed past the lattices, the waterfalls, and the clocks. Laura cursed every hallway, because the damn muffling spells prevented her from hearing any of the action. She had no idea if Ivo and Bea were doing well. As they hurtled out the final door, the floor shook from what must've been a kin blast. Laura ran straight into the rail of the balcony, leaned over it, and shouted, "Grim! Infestation in the roof! How do we get to the rafters?"

Down at the tables, Yvonne choked on her tea. Grim stood so fast he almost knocked over his chair and replied, "The furthest door on the first wall goes into a stairwell, leading to the catwalks!"

Laura doubled back and heaved the aforementioned door open. While she and Okane sprinted up, Zelda lingered at the bottom of the stairs.

"Have a great time! I'm sitting this one out!"

Zelda would be safer with Grim and Yvonne, so Laura didn't much care.

Above the maze of liminal rooms (no less than fifteen based on a glance) were the rafters, with a catwalk above. The metal walkway extended over the entire area, zigzagging in stark right angles so the staff could keep a close eye on their customers, their property, and coworkers' safety. It was lit by the glow of the rooms below and daylight coming from a line of windows, presumably the same windows that opened out to the alley. The infestation sped along the catwalk, roiling like a shadow before shooting out legs to grab on to the suspension cables, heaving itself up and over its pursuers in a delicate arch. It reached out more extensions to cage Bea, but in a flash Ivo was there with blade drawn. A foggy haze followed the track of the shining blade, slicing easily through the beast's feelers. With a scream the whole creature liquefied, dropping down the side of the walkway before solidifying again to catch itself. It swung away like a child on a playground.

"It's fast!" he called.

"Can you hit it?" said Laura.

Okane tracked the monster's progress with his gun but shook his head. "I'm not good with moving targets yet."

"Then we'll have to get closer."

Laura charged. She took a sharp right along the walkway and threw a flash pellet. It burst on the opposite rail and the infestation recoiled, redirecting at the last moment. Bea leapt to its destination, gun raised. Two more bullets burned into the creature before it squalled and vanished under the metal again. It spread along the bottom, using feelers for balance, and yanked. The metal under Bea's feet bent. The entire structure swayed. More feelers rose up, skittering across the ground and reaching for her shoes.

"It's eating the structure," she reported, before hopping lightly onto the rail and launching into the air with another *zip* of her amulets. She landed on the rafters below, turned, and aimed upward.

"Guns are proving ineffective," said Ivo.

"Still worth a shot," said Okane, and pulled the trigger.

Unlike the muted bursts of the Rexian bullets, the Amicae one smashed into the infestation's body and exploded with force enough to send blackness spattering along the rafters. Bea moved out of the way just in time. Ivo stared.

"Or, perhaps, ours were ineffective."

The infestation screeched. It lurched up again and onto the walkway, speeding along it upon hundreds of tiny legs. It went for Ivo first. He jumped one way and then another, but the creature warped its body to follow, stretching out its arms. It was inches from grabbing his ankle when

Laura clacked an Egg against her amulet and threw. The Egg flashed bright enough to wash the walls in glaring light. The infestation slowed in confusion, distracted enough for Ivo to get away before the Egg plunked into blackness like a fishing lure. This one detonated with a horrible roar.

The closest suspension cables snapped, and they all jolted. Laura had to catch the railing to keep balanced. The infestation could barely be heard over the shrieking kin, but it wasn't overwhelmed yet. It heaved itself up on smoking, crackling legs, and bulled toward Laura and Okane. Okane put another bullet in it. The monster's right side dissolved into ash and smoke. It rolled, sprouting arms at ugly angles to keep momentum. Laura readied another Egg. One more should kill it. As soon as the weapon left her hand the infestation slid under the walkway. Smashing on the metal, kin lapped up the rails and surged over the sides to burn the tarry trail, but the infestation had escaped. The walkway continued to shake, harder and harder as the infestation kept going.

"It's under us!" yelled Okane.

He dropped to his knees, looking to either side, trying to guess where it would appear. The infestation smashed up through the walkway behind Laura. The metal bucked, sending both reeling. The infestation pulsed with kin light, bleeding tarry black as it soared over their heads. There was a shout from the left and a Rexian Egg burst on the monster's side, accompanied by a round of bullets. The infestation didn't care. It seized the rails in slimy hands and plunged down on them. Laura rolled, grabbed Okane with one arm, and slapped her amulet with the other. The amulets in her shoes activated with a surge of heat. She kicked out and sent them both skidding to safety. The infestation hit with an ugly slapping sound and surged like water. It eddied near Laura's feet, but she'd already untangled herself from Okane and armed another Egg. The infestation tried to squirm away, but kin and glass latched on to the monster's tacky surface and spread with a triumphant hiss. The monster squalled and flailed. Too weak to form arms without them burning away, it fell off the walkway and hit the floor of the gem gallery. Ash, smoke, and golden sparks billowed up from it. Ivo and Bea dropped into the liminal room. They pulled masks over their mouths and noses and ventured into the smoke. A few more flashes of red, the smoke wavered, and a terrible smell rose with it.

"The infestation has been terminated," Bea called, muffled.

Laura let her head drop back onto the metal as she breathed a sigh of relief.

Beside her Okane held the gun in white-knuckled hands. "That was close," he said.

"No kidding. Good job, Ivo, Bea."

"It was our pleasure to assist - - -."

Laura sucked in another two fortifying breaths before getting to her shaky feet.

"What kind of amulet was it?"

The smoke was dying down. Ivo stooped and picked up the amulet. He held it aloft between two fingers. At first she thought he held a piece of infestation itself, but realized that no, it was simply a black chess pawn.

"Strange choice," Laura murmured. "A game piece like that implies a set."

"I don't sense anything else around here. Wherever the rest of the set is, I don't think it's in Toulouse," said Okane.

"Should we trust that, with all the amulet effects in here?" said Laura.

Okane nodded. "The air up here is clear. Look, there are no ceilings in the rooms, and - - - can't hear any more than what's actually happening. Letting the spells affect bouncers wouldn't be good, would it?"

"What is the amulet protocol?" said Bea.

"Let's go back to the main room," said Laura. "We can report to Grim and Yvonne."

"I suppose there is no one else to report to," Bea mused.

"We'll meet - - - there," said Ivo.

Laura gave him the thumbs-up before turning to help Okane. They skirted the hole in the walkway and descended the stairs. Zelda had seated herself at the table in the main room to sip loudly on a cup of tea; Yvonne clutched her own cup with shaky hands, and Grim had left his entirely to stand near the stairs. When he saw them the tenseness eased out of his shoulders.

"I trust the issue is resolved?" he said.

"You were right: you definitely had an infestation," said Laura. "It moved over the rooms on the walkway, and had access to the alley through the windows up there. It only appeared there at night, right?"

"I-I don't—" Yvonne gripped her teacup so tight she looked ready to break it. "But it's dead? It's gone?"

"It is, but we damaged some things." Laura grimaced.

"The walkway?" Grim guessed.

"And a bit more. It fell into the gem room and . . . well, you know as well as I do that infestations tend to stain what they touch."

"The stain is not necessarily harmful," said Grim, tapping his chin. "We could rearrange the props and utilize it for contrast."

Ivo glanced at Laura, giving only a slight movement of his hand. Laura gestured for him to come closer. He did so hesitantly, and didn't quite come level with her as he held up the amulet.

"Mr. Grim, this is the source amulet. The infestation took root here and maneuvered from it to attack - - -r business."

Grim looked at him. Once upon a time Clae had done something similar: simply stared at people with a completely blank face to either intimidate them or impress upon them the stupidity of whatever they'd just said. Laura didn't think this was meant to be anything so mean, but that was not a human gaze and it didn't hold any of the warmth she was familiar with from him. She edged closer to Ivo and said, "Grim?"

Grim stirred back into movement. His pale eyes blinked. "My business?"

To his credit, Ivo showed no sign of being unnerved. He answered coolly, "- - - arranged for the Sweepers to come. Is it not the case?"

Grim nodded slowly. "I understand."

Laura did *not* understand this odd little interaction, and she doubted Ivo did either. They were rescued from further awkwardness as Yvonne approached them to inspect the amulet.

"A chess piece? That's odd," she said.

"Do you recognize it?" said Laura.

"No, none of our coworkers—Actually." Terror caught her all over again, and she looked at Grim as if for help. "Don't the Mad Dogs agents play with a set like this?"

"Did you go close enough to see their game?" Grim said disapprovingly.

"I couldn't help it. They wanted me to bring them records," said Yvonne. "I couldn't just say no!"

"Did you at least bring a bouncer with you?"

"But then the floor would've been unsupervised . . ."

"I fear Amicae is a city of fools," said Grim. "Regardless, the situation is resolved." He turned to Laura and Ivo. "Thank you for your help."

"Wait, they're done?" said Yvonne, baffled. "There's no payment, or—"

"We get paid by the city, so there's no additional payment needed," said Laura.

"It still feels wrong to have you leave without anything," said Yvonne. "Surely there's something we could give you?"

"- - - might need those funds for repairs," said Okane.

As if to punctuate this statement, another cable snapped, and Yvonne winced at the sound.

"I could, um . . ."

She pointed at Ivo. He tilted his head.

"Could what, Miss Yvonne?"

"Your." She rubbed her face, exactly were the Rexian numerals were tattooed on his.

Zelda's chair clanged back onto all four legs and she looked around so fast she probably gave herself whiplash. "Seriously?"

"Only if you want!" Yvonne squeaked. "I've just—Mobster tags are very bad to have visible like that, so if you wanted to remove it, I know people."

Was it better or worse that a stranger's first impression of them was "mobster" instead of "Rex"? Thankfully Grim didn't correct her.

Ivo's eyes lit up. "I wasn't aware it could be obscured, beyond makeup."

"I have a connection through our owner who uses amulets to make a special treatment. It's supposed to ease scarring, but it works on tattoos as well."

"We would appreciate it very much."

"Well, I don't have that here." She looked flustered. "I'd have to get in contact with the source on the other side of the city, and he might have to make a special alteration, but I'll speak with him and see what we can work out."

"We'd be eternally grateful."

"Then I'll have Grim contact you when I get news?"

Zelda threw up her hands and cheered, "Fantastic! We won't be like *this* forever."

"This" obviously meant their numbers, but something about that enthusiasm made Laura wonder if she meant the situation at large. The manacle glinted dully on Zelda's arm, barely visible under her sleeve but still undeniably present.

3

LACKING

In all of Amicae, there were only two Sweeper properties: the shop itself, and the armory. There were Amuletories, of course, but those were considered a public service and operated outside Sweeper influence. Citizens had always frequented Amuletories to have their household amulets recharged, and the service supposedly didn't overlap with Sweeper paranoia, so the Council had never limited their work even while cracking down on the Sweepers themselves. The Sinclairs were forced to buy all their equipment to keep it from being disposed of. What had once been the proud, unbreakable Sweeper city was reduced to a single family, two buildings, and chronic stubbornness. For over a year of apprenticeship Laura hadn't realized the armory even existed, and she didn't want any other Sweeper stumbling around without knowledge. She was set on showing it off to the Rexians.

"I mean," she said as she hopped off the cable car, a week after they'd left Club Toulouse, "what's the worst that could happen? Rex has already broken into it once. It's not like they don't already know it exists."

Okane frowned down at a paper with the address of the Rexians' apartment. "Are we really sure about showing it to them? Zelda is one thing, but the others . . ."

"You're not too fond of them?" said Laura.

"I wouldn't say that . . . but I can admit I'm not very comfortable," said Okane. "What we first saw of Ivo the other day was hopeful, but then he started twisting Bea back toward Rexian ideals. I understand his argument, but that was still manipulation. And Bea fell into that so readily."

"We can't expect them to throw off Rex conditioning that easily," Laura pointed out. "They've lived their whole lives keeping their heads down to avoid getting killed by their handlers."

"But—" He fell quiet as they walked, following the directions on his paper. He pinched the page tight enough to wrinkle it as he mulled over how to word his thoughts. When he spoke again, it was slowly, carefully. "If - - - put me back into the Sullivan house, I could go back to what I was before. It was always the same routine, ever since I was a child. I could easily fall back into that rut and keep going through the motions. And maybe it would feel safe, to be back where things were bad but predictable. But I wouldn't be happy about it. Bea was happy to fall back into old behavior."

Laura frowned. She agreed that Bea's actions yesterday were unnerving, but this was really out of her depth. She wanted to think her gut reaction was wrong.

She wanted to believe that everything was okay. Was that stupid after the MacDanel debacle? Probably. But she wanted to believe, so badly. "Maybe she's still trying to figure out how to live in a strange environment. Maybe once she's more comfortable here, she'll be brave enough to climb out of that rut."

"Ivo offended her when he scorned Rex's search methods," Okane said bitterly. "Didn't - - - see her face when he asked - - - to move on? That wasn't the face of someone on uncertain ground. That was disagreement, plain and simple."

Laura hummed, trying to think back. She'd only noticed Bea's surprise at first, and the brooding as she'd gone back into the building. She didn't think that concluded anything.

"Don't - - - think it was suspicious?" Okane pressed.

"I think if I clung to suspicion, I would never have trusted you, either," Laura murmured. She felt a little guilty to say it, but . . . "There are a lot of people in my life that I'm so close to now, but at the beginning made a terrible first impression. You, and Clae, and Cherry . . . If I'd settled for the Okane as you were, on your way to crawling out of that Sullivan rut, I'd never have the Okane as you are now. I can't even imagine life without you anymore. Being friends with you has taught me a lot. So, I'm hoping Bea's like you." She looked up to meet his eyes. "Someone who's looking for a chance. Someone who wants to grow, even if they didn't think it was possible before."

Okane's mouth opened and closed. He blinked hard and averted his gaze to the street sign ahead.

"That's true," he said softly. "I'll think of her like that. Like I used to be."

"Exactly. Give her time, and give her security. She'll come around," said Laura. "They all will."

Albright had arranged an apartment in the Third Quarter for the Rexians. The building looked ordinary, even high-class: the red brick walls were perfectly aligned and unblemished by the weather, despite the historical plaque announcing the building to be almost as old as Amicae itself. Blindingly white trim wound around the windows and eaves of the gray-shingled roof. A window washer currently hung suspended at the fourth floor, cleaning with practiced ease. Laura and her family couldn't have gotten into this sort of place if they tried, and she felt a little jealousy for the beauty of it.

"It's a little underwhelming," said Okane.

"Underwhelming? The residents must be rich," Laura scoffed.

Okane snorted. "That's not what I meant. It's just, with the way those officers have been acting, I almost expected them to be kept in a prison."

"That's true. It's good to know that Albright's taking proper care of them," said Laura.

She sucked in a breath, shifted the box she carried under her arm, and strode to the front doors. They entered a lobby with white walls, high ceiling, and white, minimalist furniture. The only spot of color was the uniform of the receptionist behind a desk at the far end of the room: scarlet with gold buttons, similar to but more elaborate than the train depot's ensemble. The room felt enormous and crushing at the same time. Utterly impersonal.

"It's like an office building," Laura whispered, fighting the instinct to slouch as they walked deeper in. "Um, excuse me?"

The receptionist had tracked them all the way from the door—of course she had, there was nothing else here to pay attention to—and now gave a wide customer-service smile that was so fake Laura wanted to recoil.

"Good morning! How may I assist you today?"

"We've come to visit some of your residents," said Laura. "They're our employees. The, uh—" She leaned to check the paper Okane was still holding. "The Kingsleys." She frowned at Okane and said, hushed, "Seriously? That's the surname they've been assigned?"

Okane shrugged hopelessly. He hadn't been any more involved with the decision than Laura was.

"I'm afraid we don't have any residents with that name," the receptionist said sweetly.

"Is this not the Kent apartments of Savio Street?" said Okane, holding up his note.

"It is," said the receptionist, "but I'm afraid we have no Kingsleys here."

"Really? Because we've been told—" Laura pursed her lips. Maybe this was on purpose. She pulled out her ID with its three stars—signifying access to anywhere in the city she wanted—and said, "We work with the chief of police. I'm sure you've got some kind of list of who can come and go here freely, and both Okane Sinclair and I should be on it."

"I'm afraid I don't know what you mean," the receptionist simpered, but she eyed the ID with far more attention than her words implied. When she looked back up, her smile was blinding. "If you're here for the Kingsleys you are unfortunately out of luck, but if you're visiting anyone else, the elevators are behind me and to your left."

Laura took back her ID, unsure whether to count this as a victory or not. She and Okane followed the directions to find the elevator: its gold-plated grilles boasted a dial at the top indicating the floors, which only enforced the feeling of being in an office as far as Laura was concerned. Who needed that kind of feature in an apartment building? The push of the button brought it down. When the grilles rattled open, they found a man in uniform just like the receptionist's, standing beside the rheostat. A dedicated elevator operator. This place really was rich.

"Good morning. Which floor did you need?" said the operator.

"Third floor, please," said Laura.

"My apologies, but the third floor is off-limits due to construction," said the operator. "If there's any other floor you'd care to visit—"

"We just covered this with the receptionist," Laura said tersely. "We know the third floor's not under construction. We know who's on the third floor. We have clearance for the third floor. Do you want to see our IDs, or can we move on with our lives?"

The elevator operator sagged with resignation. "Very well. Come aboard, miss."

He pressed the third-floor button. The door closed, the grilles rattled back into position, and the operator turned back to the rheostat mounted against the wall. The operator must be talented, because the jostling was minimal as they slowly rose up the shaft.

Laura leaned close to Okane and whispered, "This level of secrecy is kind of excessive, isn't it?"

"I suppose it means Albright's committed to keeping the, er, Kingsleys safe," said Okane.

"Yeah, but you'd think they'd be able to acknowledge us, of all people." Laura fiddled with the lid of her box, unable to ease her nerves. What if they weren't going to find the Rexians after all? They'd shown up on time every day to work with no complaints, though Zelda certainly complained about everything else, so she wasn't worried about them having a roof over their heads. She just worried about Albright laying so many false trails that Laura couldn't find them when she needed to. "I'm guessing the apartment building has a list of who can access, or the receptionist wouldn't have sent us to the elevator, but to not acknowledge it at all . . ."

"Third floor," the operator announced.

He stilled the rheostat dial, pulled open the grille, and opened the door. Before them lay a long apartment hallway, painted in more white, with solid wooden doors labeled with brass plates. On any other occasion Laura would expect all ten visible rooms to be full, but between the building employees' performances and the two police guards, she doubted any beyond the Rexians' were filled.

The guards in question were the same two who'd followed the Sweepers around on Albright's orders for the past week. They positioned themselves down the hallway—the farthest one from the elevator sitting in a chair with a book, the closest one leaning dourly against the wall near the elevator. Mr. Dour was the officer who'd been so eager to look for Mad Dogs; when he'd returned to find their business finished in Club Toulouse, he'd been very upset that they dared move without him. In the meantime he had, predictably, not found any Mad Dogs to bully. Laura quickly had come to the conclusion that his bad attitude that day wasn't due to any supposed slight to policemen at large, or irritation about his lack of success. No, these two were just assholes. It was a personality trait. They'd even refused to introduce themselves. They both had name tags—B. DOWS and X. RIDLEY, respectively—but Laura was set on calling them Mr. Dour and Mr. Sour until they behaved like normal, courteous people. Okane had warned her that this wasn't very mature of her, but she honestly couldn't care less.

Today Mr. Dour pushed himself up off the wall, put out a warning hand, and growled, "No one's allowed on this floor."

The *nerve*.

Laura reached out to slap his hand back down and snapped, "Excuse me? You know full well who we are. We're more than allowed to be on this floor!"

Mr. Dour planted himself firmly in the elevator's entryway and said, "We have orders. No one in. No one out."

"I happen to know those are not your orders," said Laura. "You're a security detail, not a prison guard. You're just here to keep them safe."

"I will not be lectured about my job by a girl whose only qualification is that she hasn't died yet," Mr. Dour snarled. "No one in."

Okane's fist closed about his paper with a harsh crinkle. *"Excuse - - -?"*

As if Mr. Dour cared about qualifications. Albright might trust him to keep his mouth shut on this, but he was rude and belligerent and willfully ignorant. He didn't care to learn about Sweepers any more than what he'd heard from the newspapers.

"Then maybe I'll have you lectured by someone who does have qualifications," Laura said coolly. "Operator, there's a telephone downstairs, isn't there?"

The operator had been slowly retreating into the elevator throughout the interaction, and jumped at being addressed. "Ah. Yes, ma'am."

"Then I think you should bring us back down to the lobby," said Laura, not looking away from Mr. Dour's scowl. "I have a phone call to make to the police chief. I'm sure she'll have something to say about this situation."

For a moment, nobody moved. Mr. Dour continued to loom menacingly over them, trying to wait her out. If he expected her to back down and retreat, he was a bad judge of character. Okane glowered from over Laura's shoulder, and the operator glanced nervously between them.

"First floor, then, I suppose," said the operator, and reached to close the door.

Mr. Dour's lip curled. He reached out, and the door and grille clanged against his forearm.

"Sir, if you could please step back for safety," said the operator.

Mr. Dour snorted, shoved the door and grille back to their original positions, and skulked back to his spot against the wall. It was as graceful a defeat as he could probably manage.

"Thank you for your understanding," said Laura, though it sounded nothing like gratitude.

She and Okane left the elevator and walked down the hallway briskly, with their heads held high. Mr. Sour had watched the whole show over the pages of his book, but had made no attempt to rise from his chair for either party. Laura shot him a glare, daring him to say anything now, but he simply returned a cool look and went back to his reading. Laura stopped at the end door, number 307, and took a deep breath to calm herself. She didn't want to snap at the Rexians or let them think they'd caused her foul mood. Only once she was collected again did she rap her knuckles on the door.

"Good morning!" she called. "It's Laura and Okane. I hope you don't mind, we've come to visit you."

Silence greeted her. She and Okane exchanged a worried look. Had something happened? Mr. Dour had always been like this, but if something had happened to merit such stonewalling from the staff as well—A soft noise from the other side of the door brought back her attention. The lock clicked. Laura waited for a greeting, but none came; whoever had unlocked the door was now retreating deeper into the apartment. She pushed the door open herself, cautious not to hit anything.

"How are you doing?" said Laura. "Are you settling in?"

"Take a wild guess," said Zelda, who was indeed striding back toward the main room of the apartment. She'd forgone any semblance of presentation— she wore a ratty nightgown and her hair was a mess. She waved them to follow her, and Laura closed the door. The large apartment was sparsely furnished. It looked as if the last owner had moved out and left behind whatever worn items they'd disliked, rather than go through the hassle of disposing of it themselves. Bea sat on a sagging couch, geared up and rigid as if ready for an infestation at any moment. Ivo, for lack of another seat, had taken up residence on the floor with his own equipment. The room with its white walls looked overwhelmingly empty. This was not the look of a home. This wasn't the look of a meeting room, or even an office lobby the way the first floor had been. It was aggressively impersonal, like a punishment. Laura's anger stoked back up. They'd been living like this for a week?

"Want tea?" Zelda inquired, moving to the counter separating the living room from the kitchen; it was the only vaguely tablelike feature in the apartment. "I'd have to wash our only cup. Oh, but wait, we don't have tea! We'll have to settle for water."

Okane paused at the door, and from his heavy silence and narrowed eyes Laura knew he felt as livid as she did; possibly more so, given his experience with being displaced and mistreated. Of course, they witnessed this right after his vow to see the Rexians the way he'd been. Perfect, damnable timing.

"I'll get it," he said firmly, following her to the sink. "I can bring - - - more dishes, too. Clae left behind enough for a family, in the cupboards at my place. What did - - - mean when - - - said - - - can't get tea?"

"Mr. Dour out there said 'no one in and no one out,'" said Laura. "Do they seriously not let you leave?"

"No," said Zelda, shooting her a poisonous look.

"Truth be told, we haven't tried," said Ivo. "The officers are a barrier. We'd rather stay here and be quiet than risk agitating them and making our situation worse."

Okane twisted the tap a little too hard. The handle made an ugly clunk, and the whole faucet shuddered. He stayed still, whitened knuckles gripping it as if tempted to rip the entire fixture out of the wall, and Zelda eyed him with trepidation.

"Do you mean to tell me," Laura growled, "that you're willing to literally starve yourselves rather than be a bother?"

"That's a childish way of putting it," said Bea.

"We thought of it more strategically," said Ivo. "Going without food for short spans of time wasn't uncommon under Rex."

"For Sweepers, maybe," Zelda grumbled.

"Oh, this is bullshit," said Laura. She squatted next to Ivo and held up the box in front of him. "Eat some of these to hold you over. I'm taking you out for a proper meal."

Ivo gingerly took the box and opened it. "These are . . ."

"Cookies." Laura flushed. "My aunt and I made them as a housewarming gift for you."

The gesture seemed overwhelmingly trivial now that she saw their living quarters.

Ivo held one of the cookies up reverently. "Then this . . . is sweet?"

"It should be. Do you not like sweet? I guess I should've asked before we made them," Laura fretted. "I'm pretty sure my aunt knows other recipes that are semi-sweet, or maybe we shouldn't have even made cookies . . ."

"I will soon find out," said Ivo, turning the cookie over.

It was like he'd never even seen one before. What did he mean, he'd soon—Oh, no. She'd eaten Sweeper fare in Rex, and it had been barely palatable mush in a can. She'd thought that was just rations for crusades. Did Rexian Sweepers eat that all the time? She pressed her hands against her eyes to keep from screaming. Every time she interacted with these Rexians, every damn time, she found another thing to be horrified about.

On the plus side, Ivo seemed to like sweetness; he took a bite of the cookie and his eyes lit up. No sooner had he done that than Zelda descended on the box to snatch six cookies at once. While they busied themselves with food, Laura stormed back to the door. She looked out at the officers in the hall and said, "Get ready to go. We're walking until your feet fall off."

Mr. Dour and Mr. Sour didn't reply, but they both radiated displeasure. They knew full well they were being horrible—they knew these people lacked food and necessities—but they had no regrets. Oh, Albright would definitely hear about this. If Laura had her way, she'd get them chased off the force entirely. Why were they even police if they didn't have basic empathy?

"We're going with or without you," she told them, and ducked back into the apartment. "Is everyone getting ready?"

A loud noise from a side room told her that Zelda was getting properly dressed. Ivo had another cookie in his teeth as he buckled on a harness studded with amulets. Bea remained on the couch, ready to go but unwilling to stand yet. She was eyeing the cookie box with an unreadable expression.

"Did you get one?" Laura asked her. "We'll get something better soon, but—"

"No," said Bea.

"Well, here, let me get you the box, and you can pick—"

"Are they nutritionally balanced?" said Bea, her tone short and sharp.

Laura paused halfway through picking up the box. "Uh. No? They're desserts."

"Then there is no point to eating them," said Bea.

"You've never heard of enjoying what you eat?" said Laura. Bea leveled a hostile glare at her, and she decided that no, that had not been among the Rexian ideals. "Well, this isn't meant to be totally filling, either! Just to keep you from starving on our way to a restaurant. That's where you can get something nutritious."

"All the more reason not to eat them," said Bea.

"They're good," said Ivo, having fastened his harness properly and hidden it under his jacket. "The flavor and texture are unlike anything we were presented in Rex."

Bea's expression twisted. It was so small, so fast that a blink could've missed it, but Laura suddenly understood why Okane had been suspicious. That was definitely kneejerk hatred on her face.

"No," said Bea, and her tone was final.

Ivo deflated some. "All right. I trust - - -r assessment," he said, and moved off to see what Okane was doing.

Bea remained very still on the couch, her eyes fixed forward and her mouth taut as if nothing and no one was around her. It looked very lonely.

"Don't pay too much attention to her," said Zelda, coming up behind Laura. "She's always been like that. More importantly, where are we going for food? I don't know what's good in Amicae. Where's the best restaurant?"

Laura forced herself to look away from Bea, and to focus on Zelda's excitement. It was a little easier to smile as she said, "I don't know about the best restaurant, but I do know the Sweepers' favorite."

The Averills' restaurant had always been one of Clae's regular haunts as head Sweeper, which meant Laura and Okane came along frequently and were very familiar with the menu. It offered a wide range of good-quality dishes at an affordable price, so Laura immediately made a beeline for it. Oddly, it was closer to walk to from the apartments than it would be to reach it from the shop. As they all made their way down the crowded streets, Laura's head spun with memories, and she chattered about how Dan Averill tended bar and liked to get in on community bets, and how Peggy Averill, the waitress, could "peg" your desired order at a glance. Bea followed along just as surly as their police guard; Ivo listened to the stories with polite interest; and Zelda clapped her hands in glee at the idea of finally going to a restaurant where she could freely speak to the waiters instead of stealing their trays.

Laura's mood was much improved up until they reached the door, where she stopped at the threshold. She hadn't realized how long it had been since she visited. The bar and the jumbled tables lay before her like something divorced from reality. The only way it could be real was if Clae were to walk in front of her to their usual table, or his coat were thrown over an empty chair. She realized, with a ridiculous but sickening jolt, that she'd never come here without him being present in some way.

"Laura?" Okane rested a hand on her shoulder. "Are - - - okay?"

"Fine," she replied. She shook herself out of her memories and strode to a large table.

"Long time no see!" said Peggy Averill, hurrying over with a smile and her eternally handy notepad. "How have you been?"

"I've survived," Laura chuckled. "But look! I've brought the next generation of Sweepers to see you."

Okane and Peggy had already met at Clae's wake back in November—they exchanged a friendly nod—and so Peggy turned her full attention on the Rexians.

"Hello, welcome, welcome! I'm Peggy Averill, that man behind the bar is Dan, and we pride ourselves on being the Sweepers' number-one favorite restaurant in all of Amicae. I don't suppose any of you are interested in lasagna?"

Ivo sent Bea a dumbfounded look.

"Let me know if you've got questions, or whenever you're ready to order!" said Peggy, and she hurried away again to tend to other patrons.

"Don't worry about catching her later. She always comes back when you need her. She's like magic," said Laura, sitting down. She didn't need the menu herself, but she picked one up from the stand in the center of the table to make sure the others could see where to find them. "And don't worry about pricing. I'm paying. Order anything you want."

Ivo took a menu himself, but leaned to see the table at eye level. "If she is like magic, is there an amulet implemented in the table to alert her to our needs?"

"You mean like in banks? Oh, no," said Laura.

"I think it's all just observation and experience. She's quick on her feet," said Okane.

"I wonder just how quick on her feet," said Zelda, flexing her fingers as if eager to use her magic again after all. Laura raised her brow, and Zelda laughed, "Oh, come on, I'm not going to do *that*. There are too many people watching anyway."

Mr. Dour and Mr. Sour had sat at the table as well; Mr. Dour scowled at Zelda as if certain she'd shoplifted, while Mr. Sour made a big show of checking his pocket watch to show how much time they were supposedly wasting. Laura rolled her eyes at them. They could pay for their own meals.

As everyone settled, Laura studied them all. Zelda perused her menu with great delight, holding the page in one hand, chin in the other, hunched over it like a treasure map; it would probably be novel for her to get the dish she actually wanted instead of looking for the most easily stolen. Ivo sat straight and still, surveying the listings with a quick but bright eye. Bea, on the other hand, didn't read it. She looked blankly at her own menu, eyes not moving to follow any of the words. Her grip on the page was sure, her back straight, expression blank, but it all tripped Laura up. It felt like an act.

Laura leaned close enough to Okane for their shoulders to bump, and covered her mouth with her hand to whisper, "Should we help Bea at all?"

"It might be better for the others to do it," Okane murmured back, ducking his head to mimic her. "We already know she doesn't like strangers or interference, and for this of all things . . . I think she'll get very mad."

"But I don't want her to struggle . . ."

"Her pride's all she's got at this point. Maybe it's all tied up with Rexian ideals, but weren't we just saying we wanted her to feel safe and come out of it on her own? Bruising that pride so easily won't help anything."

Bea's eyes narrowed. She gripped her menu so it crumpled and snapped, "What are - - - two saying about me?"

"Nothing!" Laura said quickly. "Really, it's not—"

"If it were nothing, then - - - wouldn't speak at all," said Bea. "Or do - - - simply adore the sound of - - -r own voices?"

"There's no need for that," Ivo scolded, but Bea didn't look at him.

"What were - - - saying?" she demanded. "Do not lie to me."

Okane groaned and buried his face in his hands. Laura couldn't see any way out of this but the truth, so she admitted, "I may have wondered . . . whether or not you could read."

Zelda arched a brow. Bea looked livid; her fists came down onto the table with force enough to rattle it.

"I didn't," Okane cut in, before anyone else could speak. "It was one of the ways I was kept . . . under control. If Rex wanted - - - subjugated, they might've tried the same thing. We don't want to assume what - - - can or can't do and essentially leave - - - stranded."

"We are able to read," Ivo said evenly, again the blessed neutrality. "It was determined to be more of an impediment if we couldn't follow through with all orders. Our subjugation was forced elsewhere."

"I can read well enough to know I'll have the teccinia," said Zelda.

"I trust Zelda's sense of taste. I'll have the same," said Ivo, tucking the menu back into its holder.

Thank goodness they hadn't been offended. Laura looked at Bea and asked, "What do you feel like eating?"

Bea had not been placated in the least. She dropped the menu, lip curled as if it were a filthy rag instead of paper and ink, then planted her hand atop it and shoved it back to the center of the table.

"- - - should have something," Ivo said reproachfully. Bea gave him a cold look; he drew back and shook his head. "Have it - - -r way."

"You're not going to eat something even though you've gone days on limited food?" said Laura. "I told you, I'll pay—"

"I want no part of it," said Bea.

"If it's because of the reading thing—"

"Don't argue," said Zelda, waving a hand. "It's really not worth it."

"But—"

"Trust me, it's not - - -r assumption that's bothering her. Well, it is, but not in the way - - - think it is. She'll have to work through that mess on her own."

Laura and Okane exchanged a perplexed look. It felt too early in their acquaintance to push any issues, and Laura definitely trusted Zelda, but Bea hadn't taken any cookies. What else would she possibly eat if they weren't willing to face the policemen and go out for supplies? Luckily Peggy proved just as magically punctual as Laura had remembered: she'd avoided the initial outburst to minimize awkwardness, and now doubled back to get their orders and effectively derail the lingering tension. Her eyes lingered on the crumpled menu, but she made no comment. When she'd left again, Laura pulled that menu over to her side and ran hands over it to smooth the paper out again. She tried her best to smile and steer onto new topics.

"So, we haven't really had the chance to talk to each other as people instead of just as Sweepers—"

"There's no need for that," said Bea.

"Remind me why - - - insisted on bringing her, again?" Zelda grumbled to Ivo. "I couldn't even count the ways everything would be easier if she weren't mucking everything up for us."

"Bea, we brought - - - here so we could all be human," said Ivo.

"Yes, we are human. And our role is Sweeping. No additional detail is needed," Bea said flatly. Her gaze stayed fixed on the menu holder.

"We are not in Rex anymore," said Ivo, exasperated.

"*Clearly*," Bea bit back.

"So we do not have to decry our own humanity—"

"I have never claimed otherwise."

Their voices dipped down to angry whispers, and their argument continued inaudible and heated.

Laura cleared her throat and tried again, "What's something you're hoping to do here in Amicae? Is there something you want to try? Something you haven't had in Rex?"

Ivo seized on this. "I don't have much to go off of, but I'd like—"

"Privacy," Zelda said dryly.

Ivo looked tempted to strangle her.

Full stomachs did not improve anyone. Laura and Okane tried bringing up other topics, but it always turned into an argument. Ivo expressed interest in films, while Zelda despaired about talentless actors and Bea looked revolted by the very concept. Zelda drew comparisons between Rexian monuments and Battle Queen squares; Bea considered and Ivo showed offense. Mr. Dour and Mr. Sour seemed both vindicated and amused by the proceedings, respectively.

This uncomfortable lunch set the stage for the rest of an uncomfortable day. Laura vowed to take them shopping to supply their empty apartment—after all, Bea would have to eat at some point—but she wanted to cringe throughout the errand. She and Okane had long since stopped attempting conversation, but the others seemed more than happy to bicker with each other on topics of their own design. The worst part was, both Zelda and Ivo tended to agree on things. It was only Bea's sharp and short replies that got one's hackles up and derailed anything positive.

As they left the final grocery store and Bea needled Zelda for having given them names at all, Laura stepped closer to Okane to mutter, "I'm so sorry for dragging you on this trip."

"Don't be. I'm glad I came. It's not something I'd want to avoid." Okane held his shopping bags with a weirdly familiar, weary smile. Ah, that was the expression Aunt Morgan wore when Cheryl got particularly excitable in public: the *yes, I know, I don't want this to be happening any more than you do, dear passerby, but I have no control anymore* look. "I hate the idea of them not getting what they need. It isn't right. I can't say the company's been pleasant, but it was a good errand."

"No, I suppose the company hasn't—" Laura winced as Zelda squawked indignantly.

"I put a lot of thought into - - -r names!"

Bea pulled a turnip out from under her arm and pointed it at Zelda like a weapon. "Ill-conceived thought."

"Excuse - - -?"

It really was like dealing with a bunch of angry children at this point. Laura could feel her sanity slipping.

"Have I ever been this bad?" she asked. Okane politely did not answer.

"Names were unnecessary. *Ivo.*" Bea's face scrunched as if she'd tasted something bad. "It is foul."

Zelda threw an apple at her. Ivo rushed to admonish them both. Laura wondered if this was what Morgan felt every day of her life.

"We have a better idea of their personalities, at least," Laura grumbled, searching for a silver lining. Not that they hadn't before, but it was always good to see how someone acted outside of the job, right?

"Although, I do take offense at that surname they gave us!" Zelda had turned away from Bea to storm down the street, the others hurrying to keep pace. Bea did not keep pace, out of pure spite. "Kingsley! The nerve! Why would we want anything to do with kings? And it sounds awful with all of our first names!"

"Zelda, - - -'ll get lost if - - - go too far ahead," Okane called.

"Maybe I want to get lost!" Zelda glanced back, caught sight of the policemen's expressions, and groaned. "I'm joking! Is all of Amicae made up of such bakeheads?"

Okane's smile twitched, just like Morgan's would. Laura patted his shoulder pityingly.

As they trekked back, the sunset cast the street in reddish light and cast the surrounding windows in a harsh glare. It felt surreal, like the liminal rooms, or the time Laura had dangled from Rex's quarter wall. It had her feeling oddly introspective. They paused at an intersection on Fortore Street to let an automobile pass by, and her eyes caught the street sign. She'd started today planning to show them the armory, hadn't she? She stopped in her tracks, shoulders slumping. She wanted nothing more than to crawl home and hide her head under a pillow.

How did Clae manage this? He'd run himself into the ground and become a magical crystal out of stress before reaching the age of thirty—clearly not the best role model, but she had no other examples. If Clae were here, he'd send her a glare and say something about how they'd come here for a reason, and they were going to get it done.

Laura heaved a heavy sigh. "Everyone? We're taking one more detour."

"What? Why?" said Zelda.

"I wanted to show you the armory. I got sidetracked earlier, but it's close. Maybe a few blocks at most."

Okane tilted his head, as if to ask, *Should we really do that now?* Laura shrugged. When they were this close, it felt like a sign to get it over with. Thankfully, no one complained, and they changed course.

The armory stood as it always did: forbiddingly black until one noticed the stained-glass windows in the second floor, the gingerbread trim along the eaves detailed to look like black lace, or the floral design tangling the railing of the wrought-iron staircase. Rex had broken in months ago, but beyond the dents in the garage door, it showed no signs of damage.

"This is the armory," Laura announced, feeling much like a tour guide. "Anything that's not contained in the Sweeper shop is stored here, including our Kin system."

"So, this is where Amicae's magic got stolen from." Zelda held a hand up to shade her eyes as she squinted up at it. "I'm not surprised. It doesn't look like it has much defense to start with."

"It has more than - - -'d think," said Okane. "One of the Sinclairs' Magi predecessors put together a system of magical traps inside. It actually—"

He broke off. Zelda eyed him suspiciously. "It actually what?"

"It killed one of the invaders," Okane said quietly. "It shouldn't have, but he had hemophilia. It gave the others a lot of trouble."

The Rexians' steps slowed.

"Will we be recognized as unwelcome?" said Ivo.

"No," Laura said firmly. "You know the Amicae Sweeper rings I gave you this week?" She waited until all three of them glanced down at their hands, where new golden bands marked "S.S.Am." winked on their ring fingers. "Those mark you as part of the system. It might close partially since you don't have a key, but you don't have to worry about being attacked. If you ever need to get in and you can't reach me, just stop in the apartments next door and ask for Amelia Huxley. She used to be a Sweeper, and she takes care of the place now."

The staircase clattered under their feet as they climbed it. Laura stopped again at the landing. The heavy, mechanized door stood ajar, and the colored lanterns inside sent light through the crack. Someone was inside. She reached out, pushed it further, and peered down the hallway. She released a held breath.

"Hey, Amelia. Didn't expect to see you today."

Amelia was in the main room. She'd hiked her skirts up high and swung her prosthetic leg onto a table, and appeared to be fighting the hinge. A grin spread fast over her scarred face when she realized who'd arrived.

"Laura Kramer!" she laughed. "I knew you couldn't get enough of me! Speaking of, well, *enough* and *me* . . . could you fetch me the pliers from the toolbox over here? I've just got this pinned, and if I move now it'll all fall apart again." Laura hurried to do so. Amelia took the pliers gladly, but rather than set to work with them, she eyed the people who'd followed Laura in. "And who might these be?"

"Our new Sweeper recruits," said Laura. "We're trying to show them around, so they've got a feel for everything."

Amelia's gaze lingered on the Rexians' tattoos. She wrenched the metal brace of her prosthetic back into line, winked, and said, "Welcome aboard. By the way, cops, what's up with the closings on the Tiber? I hear about bombings in the paper every day."

She caught the policemen's attention in full, giving Laura a little more freedom to point out all the kin weapons here. There were quite a few. Where the Sinclairs used the shop as their front and home, the armory was their hoard. The kin-powered staffs, guns, gauntlets, and more in just this room could arm a small army. They glittered in heaps, gold and shedding rainbows from the windows and the lanterns, so they looked like a dragon's treasure. The Council might mandate that Amicae's companies produce a certain number of bullets and Egg shells for them, but Laura doubted elaborate works like these could be commissioned anymore.

Other cities had no problem with such supplies—the Rexians moved deeper into the trove with appreciation but no surprise. Bea lifted a gauntlet and weighed it; a similar gauntlet of Rexian design had scarred Okane's face.

"We didn't get trained in techniques beyond Eggs and guns," Laura admitted. "Most of this is useless to me or Okane, so if you like any of it, feel free to use it. Which leaves . . ."

She glanced surreptitiously at the police, then gestured at the ceiling. It took a moment for them to understand, but they all moved to the stairs.

The topmost floor of the armory formed a single room. Amelia had taken to using it for storage; excess Sweeper equipment was stacked along the sides, while cloth-covered furniture loomed between the piles. Laura had dragged some into a rough rectangle to corral the Kin setup. The structure dominated the floor in a glassy maze, all clustered around the massive tub that held the crystals and Gin. A hood had been fashioned for it, supposedly to keep in the magical haze during production but far more useful for shielding Clae and Anselm from a casual glance. Laura lifted the hood.

"So," she said, pretending nonchalance, "to those of you who haven't had the pleasure, meet Clae Sinclair. We're not convinced he's fully dead."

With Magi and their descendants, the loss of magical control was a very real and imminent danger. During the Falling Infestation, Clae had lost control of his own magic, and been converted entirely into it. What lay in the tub was a statue: Clae Sinclair as he had been in life, from the waves of his hair to the laces of his boots, rendered in golden crystal. His depths glittered in odd fractals from the crystal structure, but at his core something dark thrummed. He was now a magical strain, capable of producing magic to be used in their kin recipe, the way his brother had been for eighteen years. He couldn't speak or move. The presence of his magic was the only thing keeping them from believing he was fully dead. But his fingertips were clouding over. Laura didn't know what that meant, but it made something twist uneasily inside her whenever she saw it. Anselm lay beside him in the tub: Clae's nine-year-old twin, a mellower yellow and curled up as if sleeping soundly in the tank.

Zelda had not only seen Clae during the Rexian escapade, she'd seen the kind of magical damage he'd done to people he wasn't magically acclimated to; she averted her gaze.

"That's what Rex stole. The Wrath of God." Ivo trembled at the sight. Laura supposed she couldn't blame him; Clae had frozen while falling to his death, and his expression remained none too kind. "What kind of precautions have - - - taken to contain it? It's highly volatile from what I've heard. If Rex couldn't control it—"

"*He* gets along just fine with the right people," said Laura.

"He's more . . . aware than regular Gin is," Okane agreed. "He's as possessive and stubborn as a magic strain can be."

Zelda's brow furrowed. "Meaning?"

"Meaning he spies on us through Eggs." Laura held up one of her own to demonstrate; it thrummed with the same color as Clae. "He's infected almost all the equipment here so it gives off the same feeling, and it fluctuates sometimes based on what you're doing or saying."

"Like a scolding," Okane added helpfully.

Once she'd realized that infected kin had awareness, Laura had been thrilled. She'd tried having a conversation with an Egg the way she might with an amulet, but it had been an exercise in futility—Clae's essence remained steady and surly and gave no indication of hearing her.

Ivo backed away from the tub. "Then we shouldn't be here. I've seen the effects of his 'scolding' and have no wish to participate in it."

"That's why I brought you here, to introduce you," said Laura. "You introduce Gin during transfers, so—"

"Rex doesn't do transfers," Zelda retorted.

"Well, Gin doesn't hurt what it's familiar with, and from what we've seen Magi crystals act the same. If he knows you he won't hurt you. Okane and I will act as the mediators."

Laura rested one hand on Clae's shoulder and reached with the other. None of them reached back. Ivo and Bea remained expressionless, and even Zelda, who'd handled the crystals already, seemed unwilling to get closer. Laura withdrew her hand and awkwardly drummed her fingers on Clae's shoulder. She'd hoped letting them see and interact with Clae would be a good show of trust—not even her family knew about him—but maybe this was too much too fast.

"Okay . . . We don't have to do everything at once. We can hold off until you're comfortable."

Okane mercifully took attention away from her. "Did any of - - - have any questions about the distilling process or equipment?"

Bea tipped her chin up haughtily. "We have worked with better setups."

"Oh? Um, then maybe - - - could show us what they did to streamline?"

"Don't bother," Zelda scoffed. "Bea can claim all she wants that Rexian kin was better, but - - - all saw how underpowered the Rexian equipment was compared to Amicae's."

Bea glowered. "The Kin system was superior. Simply because there were fewer strains—"

"Rex has stolen dozens of Gin strains, and even that much power didn't match Amicae's—what is it?—*four* strains."

"A stray knows nothing of—"

"And neither would - - -, Miss High and Mighty. - - - were never assigned to Kin detail, and I could walk in whenever I wanted."

Very quickly they'd forgotten all about Clae, too busy verbally going after each other's throats. Okane lowered onto one of Amelia's couches and shook his head in despair. Ivo tried to worm his way between the two other Rexians, suggesting that maybe they tone this down a little, but they pushed him aside and talked over him until finally he lost his temper. He forced them away at arm's length.

"Enough!" he cried. "Can - - - see how unprofessional - - - look?"

"She started it," Zelda grumbled.

"Then - - - should've known better," Ivo retorted. "We are all tired. Bea has not eaten. We are in no state of mind to make any kind of decisions, or provide any kind of advice. Miss Kramer, I beg - - -, let's postpone this discussion until Monday. We won't bother - - - any further today."

Laura didn't know whether to be relieved or not. "If you're sure . . . I suppose it has been a long day. Do you want us to help carry your grocery bags back to the apartment?"

Zelda and Bea were already glaring at each other. Ivo looked very tired. "No, thank - - -. I do not wish us to embarrass ourselves further. We will need some time to unwind alone."

"Don't worry about it. I understand."

Laura and Okane replaced the hood on the tub, and they all returned to the lower floor. Amelia finally backed off from where she'd been hounding the policemen, who immediately turned their attentions to the Rexians. Their destination was relayed, and they all turned to the door. Zelda tapped Ivo's arm and bobbed her head as if in reassurance; Bea looked at the others as if confirming they were all well before moving on; and somehow, despite all the arguing of the day, they walked out in perfect stride together.

Okane watched them, eyes half lidded and face lax beneath the scars. It was a new layer of exhaustion, and it plucked at something horribly lonely in Laura's heart. For a moment she was convinced he would disappear. Okane jumped as she seized his hand.

"Sorry," she said, two beats too slow. "I thought I saw—Are you feeling all right?"

"Fine," said Okane, and his voice was rough. He cleared his throat and continued normally, "I hate to do this, but Mrs. Keedler was trying to rope Acis Road together for dinner tonight. Are - - - all right to—"

"To go home by myself?" She scoffed. "I know this city better than you do. Are you sure *you* don't need a chaperone?"

He laughed, and the shade of that uneasiness finally fell away. "We'll have - - -r family over for one of these dinners at some point. Mrs. Keedler is dying to know Morgan's work schedule."

"I'll see if I can get next month's timing down." Laura paused, then, "Do you think Mrs. Keedler would invite the new Sweepers sometime too?"

"I can't believe - - - even have to ask."

"You're right. It's just a matter of time."

Okane's smile slipped somewhat. "Of course, whether they accept the invitation is another matter."

They'd underestimated Bea's stubbornness, at least.

"Next time maybe we should ask Ivo or Zelda how to go about it. I'm sure there's some way to invite Bea out somewhere without her getting upset. Ah, but we'd still have Dour and Sour along . . ."

"One of these days - - -'ll have to call them by their actual names."

"Well, maybe if they'd been decent enough to introduce themselves instead of ranting about how we're traitors and stowaways, maybe I would."

"- - - are so petty."

"I've never claimed I wasn't."

Okane looked amused again. Mission accomplished. "I can ask Mrs. Keedler for advice, too. She's a champion at bringing introverts out of their shells."

"That's true. You'd never believe how standoffish Mr. Brecht used to be before she opened the bakery."

"I could even ask him. He'll be at dinner, too." He checked his pocket watch. "I should get going if I want to make it there on time. I'll see - - - later."

Laura watched him leave through the colored windows. On the street corner Okane turned and waved. She returned the gesture, even if he couldn't possibly see it. She stayed there at the window for a long while, worrying her lip with her teeth.

"What's eating you?" said Amelia.

"Nothing," said Laura.

A great clatter drew her eyes from the glass. Amelia had dumped her prosthetic on the table Laura was leaning on, and hopped up beside it to keep hacking at an increasingly bent bracer.

"Laura, I speak Sinclair," she said, unimpressed. "I know *nothing* means *everything's wrong and I'm letting it eat me alive.* You can't fool me any more than Clae could."

Laura snorted. "Really, I'm fine."

"More lies."

"Amelia—"

"If we were in a situation where we were looking for the remotest possibility of something wrong, what would you point at?"

Laura frowned at the prosthetic for a while before admitting, "I'm worried about Okane."

"Is he hurt?"

"Not physically." He'd long disappeared from the street outside, but Laura's eyes went there anyway. "He's been off for a while. It's hard to see, and most days he acts completely normal, but other times he goes quiet, and it looks like he's watching something far away . . . or his voice gets sad, all of a sudden. He did it again today, when the others left."

"Is it because of your new recruits?" said Amelia.

"I don't think so. Not directly, anyway. He's been like this since the Rexian invasion."

"Did something happen, back then?"

"He had a little breakdown. The invaders didn't—that is to say—"

Laura slumped. She couldn't say *Okane's dad has been stuck inside Rex's breeding program, so some of the people trying to kill us were his blood relatives.* That wasn't her secret to tell—not the Magi portion and not the program. Amelia hummed and looked back over the room.

"You know, this is where he died."

"What?" said Laura.

"The invader. Remember how Rex broke in here? They left one Sweeper behind. He got caught in a trap in this room, and bled out. I was the first to find him, and for a moment I thought he was Okane. I knew he wasn't as soon as he opened his mouth, but it was uncanny. I'd even call it a sibling resemblance."

She gave Laura a pointed look. She might not be in on the secret, but she clearly had her suspicions. Laura's mouth opened and closed uncertainly. Amelia turned to her prosthetic again.

"I'm not trying to accuse Okane of anything," she grunted, cranking hard as if to vent all the frustration that wasn't going into her words. "I'm just saying, if he saw people who looked like family dying, that's the sort of thing that has you facing your own mortality." She paused and wiped her brow with a sad smile. "When Anselm died I had a full-on existential crisis, and nobody would ever accuse us of having a blood connection. It's rough."

"I'm worried that's what he's feeling," said Laura. "But more than that . . . He's always been kind of lonely, and Rex Sweepers look more like him than anyone else. I'm afraid that instead of thinking they're like him, he'll think he's like them. I'm worried it's impacting what he thinks he should be."

"Okane's not that soft in the head," said Amelia. "You ought to talk to him about it, though."

"I'd rather he tell me what he's thinking when he's ready," said Laura.

Amelia gave her another skeptical look. She was very good at skeptical looks. "If he's anything like Clae, that would be never."

"He's not like Clae," Laura insisted. "He tells me everything, once he's had time to think it all through."

Amelia gave a disbelieving hum. "And yet, you worry."

And yet she did.

"On another note." Amelia lifted her prosthetic to eye the hinge, apparently satisfied with her work. "I wondered if you've gotten anything from Gaudium?"

"Not in a while. Why?"

"My pen pal's not replying."

Laura frowned. "Sorry, but why would I know anything about your pen pal?"

"Because she's a Sweeper." Amelia sounded flippant as she worked to fasten the prosthetic to her leg again. "Her name's Gina Hunter. We were both apprentices around the same time. I have loads of pen pals that I met during Gin transfers, but I was keeping an extra-close eye on everything she was saying, since Gaudium's having the same monster drought as Amicae. I haven't gotten anything from her in a while. I thought maybe it got routed to the head Sweeper by accident."

"I don't know about any Gina Hunter. My last letter from Gaudium was technically from their head Sweeper, but an apprentice named Ellie wrote it out." She smiled at the memory of Ellie's note. "That was a little over a week ago, though. It's . . . been a bit of a long time since that last message came."

Amelia looked up from her leg. "Longer than normal?"

"Yes." Laura thought back. "Since we're so close, the mail's usually very fast. I tend to get replies a day or two after I've sent something, even if it's as short and simple as an all clear. I've heard there's some kind of holdup on ERA trains recently, though. Rerouting, or something. It's all pretty vague, but that might slow down the mail."

"A week, though." Amelia leaned back in contemplation.

"Do you think something's wrong?" said Laura.

"I'm sure it's nothing." Amelia slid off the table to stand on both legs. "I can poke around a bit and get back to you. You just focus on your little Okane problem."

"It's not a problem."

Amelia gave her yet another skeptical look.

"You practice those in the mirror, don't you?" Laura grumbled.

Amelia laughed.

4

A WATERY GRAVE

Monday morning started slow. The Rexians showed up on time, and thankfully weren't interested in arguing so early. Zelda read through an old newspaper, Ivo tinkered with the harness holding his amulets, and Bea sat on a stool looking steadily out the windows, as if waiting for action. If any visitors did come this morning, Laura was sure they'd run screaming from the sheer intensity radiating off of this woman.

Laura leaned closer to Zelda and whispered, "I take it things didn't get better over the weekend?"

"Hm?" Zelda glanced over the newspaper before going right back to the article. "It's not that things didn't get better. Bea is Bea. There's no point looking for any improvements because she doesn't believe she should make any. She likes Ivo, but no one and nothing else. That's all there is to it."

"But she's so—" Laura gestured uselessly.

"Yeah. She's Bea."

"You can't be telling me she's always been like this."

"No, usually she just *thinks* nasty thoughts at - - -. Ivo finally convinced her to *word her feelings* . . ."

"But the intensity?"

"That's what the handlers loved about her."

"She seems specifically angry."

Zelda lowered her newspaper slowly, annoyed. "Look. Laura. I have been stuck with that woman for a month and a half now, and I knew her in Rex besides. If she's mad, it's because something's not sitting inside her fancy little box of a worldview, or because the breeze this morning hit her wrong. She snaps over little things, and she gets hissy if - - - so much as breathe something like compassion toward her. Don't start poking at her, or we'll all be suffering the consequences."

Laura was quiet a moment. "Did she at least eat?"

"*Do - - - think she'd really be sitting here if she hadn't—*"

Zelda was cut off as the shop door flew open fast enough for the wind chime to clatter. In a moment everyone was on their feet, primed and ready for trouble. A girl with a dirty uniform skirt and backpack stumbled into the shop, her ashy-blond hair windswept and her face red with exertion. It was the very last person Laura expected to see here at this hour.

"Cheryl?" she gasped, circling the counter. "What are you doing here? Aren't you supposed to be in school?"

Cheryl's eyes were wide with panic and her chest heaved; she must've run the entire way.

"It's in the canal!" said Cheryl. "The Sylph Canal!"

Laura's shoulders slumped. "The Sylph?"

"A monster! Laura, there's—I saw a monster!"

"But in the *Sylph*?" said Laura.

Okane looked between them, clearly perplexed by Laura's lack of urgency. "What's wrong with the Sylph Canal?"

"It's an urban myth," said Laura. "People say it's haunted. The grate has a face on it, and one Underyear someone thought they heard a weird howling noise come out of it. Ever since then schoolchildren tell stories and dare each other to jump in or ask it questions like it's a demon."

Laura's old classmate had always claimed that if you walked to the middle of the bridge over the canal at midnight, turned three times, and spat into the river, the spirit would climb up and ask you riddles. If you got the riddle wrong you were drowned. Mary Sullivan had been found floating in that very canal. Cheryl's class had gone crazy after that. *The sylph got her,* Cheryl had told the family very seriously.

"I have proof!" Cheryl dug into her schoolbag. "I'm supposed to give it to you. Here!"

She held up an Egg. It wasn't Sinclair style. A little too round, with heavier metallic ribs across the casing and kin more the color of melted butter than the gold Laura was used to.

"Where did you get that?" Laura asked sharply as she snatched it from Cheryl's sweaty palm.

"The man at the canal." Cheryl fisted her hands, watching anxiously as Laura turned it over. "He said you'd know."

Laura had never seen an Egg like it, and knew of only one group in Amicae whose equipment she hadn't seen up close. Cheryl must've found a mobster.

"Was he wearing a bowler hat?" She'd never seen Haru Yamanaka without a bowler hat.

"No! He had red hair, and—and eyes!" Cheryl gestured at her face, unable to describe them.

Laura thought back over the mobsters she knew of. She hadn't met many, but one stood out. Back when Juliana MacDanel had first arrived, they'd met a Mad Dog at the gun range: a tall redhead whose eyes were dark and manic.

"He had a Mad Dog tattoo, didn't he? On his right hand."

Cheryl nodded furiously. "I saw the monster, and it saw me, and I couldn't move until he pulled me off the bridge! He told me he couldn't help because he had an appointment about, um, an investigation? He said they usually have enough people but they're all tied up, and would I *please* ask Laura to take care of this. He knew my name already. And he—" She went quiet and admitted, "He gave me change for the trolley fare."

"He gave you an Egg and trolley money?"

"Was he really a mobster? He looked scary but he wasn't very mean," said Cheryl.

"Don't trust that," said Laura. "He was probably nice to you because they still want to be on my good side."

"We can't just ignore an infestation, though," said Okane.

"Of course not." Laura glanced back at the others. They looked prepared to leave as soon as she said the word, but . . . "Zelda, can you take Cheryl over to the bakery down the street? I think she needs to stay somewhere safe, and I know Mrs. Keedler will help her get home. And one of you"—Laura gestured at the policemen—"can you go with them? You can call in the infestation on the bakery's telephone and then meet us there."

Mr. Dour and Mr. Sour looked about as happy about that as their nicknames implied, but they didn't argue.

"Why do I have to be with the Keedlers?" said Cheryl, frowning.

"They want to get Morgan's schedule so they can invite us all over for dinner," said Laura. "You remember her schedule, right? Help them set it up, and let them know what you like so they'll be sure to have it. I'm counting on you, okay?"

Cheryl of course wasn't fooled by this—*I'm counting on you* was always Morgan's trick phrase to make her stay out of the way or do as she was told—but she went with Zelda and Mr. Sour anyway. Zelda shot a gleeful look over her shoulder as if to say, *That's right! I got out of this assignment without any effort!*

Once the door closed, Okane said, "Mrs. Keedler will probably keep them at the bakery for the whole day."

"I'm sort of hoping for that," said Laura. "Let's get the equipment."

There wasn't much to grab, so they were out and running in short time. Laura wished their police escort had come with a police vehicle, but that was clearly too much to ask. Riding the trolley would mean bumping shoulders with shoppers and regular businessmen without any significant gains for speed, so they ran the short distance toward the Sylph Canal. Laura took some mean pleasure in hearing Mr. Dour's wheezing as he tried to keep up with them. She was, indeed, very petty.

"Stop!" Mr. Dour panted. "There is—Stop, damn you, or I'll have you all reported!"

They slowed to a halt just a few blocks from the canal grate, and Laura turned to look back with her hands on her hips. "There's an infestation, sir. We need to get there as soon as possible. Can this wait?"

"No," Mr. Dour snapped, and waved.

From one of the side streets came another police officer, though not one Laura had seen before.

"Officer Dows!" cried the newcomer. "I didn't realize you were on this assignment!"

"What assignment?" said Mr. Dour. "Why are there so many of you over there?"

"It's bad business, sir." The newcomer tipped his helmet back to wipe his forehead. "It's the mobs again. The Mad Dogs."

"Aha!" Mr. Dour glared at Laura, as if she personally were to blame for him missing any Mad Dogs back at Club Toulouse. "Have they announced a target?"

"Not exactly, sir, but they're getting real heavy in this area! Swarming, even! We had a report that a Mad Dog envoy was assisting an unknown party in breaching the city wall southside, down by the bay. That was this morning, and we've been chasing them up through the Quarters ever since. Rumor has it the Mad Dogs boss has his lair somewhere by the interior wall here, so we think the outside group's coming to meet with him."

"Who are the outsiders? Rexians?" Mr. Dour said sharply.

"Not as far as we can tell," said the newcomer. "Sweepers, sure—they're attacking with magic weapons—but they look like regular city folk, or maybe even Rangers."

"You're sure they're not Rexians?" said Mr. Dour, glaring even harder at Laura.

"Fact is, sir, I don't think they're Rexian because they're just too tall."

Well. Valid. Ivo was the tallest Rexian Sweeper Laura had ever seen, and even he was a little shorter than her. Mr. Dour wasn't pleased by the answer.

"Are you here to assist us, sir?" the newcomer asked hopefully.

Mr. Dour looked between the Sweepers and the officer, warring with himself. Mobs and glory apparently came before the chief's orders, because he pointed at Laura and said, "All of you stay here. We're going to seal off the perimeter. If mobs have been sighted, they can't be allowed to interfere. Don't do anything until I get back."

With no other warning, he and the newcomer sped off back to their larger police squad. The Sweepers watched him go, flabbergasted.

"Well," said Laura, "I hope you all know that I'm not waiting for shit."

Ivo frowned. "But he said—"

"The longer an infestation is moving, the more casualties we'll have. Let him do his job, and we'll do ours."

Ivo looked to Okane to see if this was normal or even wise, but Okane jogged after Laura with zero hesitation, and the Rexians quickly took that cue to follow.

Canals in Amicae operated in a labyrinthine cascade from First to Sixth Quarters. How they moved inside the interior walls was a mystery to most people, and even Laura, who owned a map laying out all the passages, found herself stumped by how it actually worked. The stretch known as the Sylph began at the inner wall of the Third Quarter's west side. Buildings were packed nearly flush to the wall, save for a thin walkway tracing its edge for cleaners and pedestrians. The canal itself spanned fifteen feet across, deep enough for small boats carrying supplies. It branched off farther into the Quarter, but here, at the start, it ran wide and straight, with rippling waves dancing across its surface. The water issued from a grate of the same size: a yawning black hole covered with a metal frame. A twisted metal face sat in its center, its mouth open as if shouting and its curling beard crossing over to hold the other bars in place. Those bars had been warped and mangled like the uneven teeth of a beast. Over the years repairs had been made, the older sections tarnished by the constant flow while newer parts gleamed, but the face looked menacing enough through the wear. No wonder the Sylph had ghost stories. Laura eyed it distrustfully as they stood at the side of the canal.

"How do we get in?" Okane asked, surveying the grate and its jagged bars. "I'm hoping it's not as straightforward as climbing through the grate, but - - - told me that - - - went down a chimney once . . ."

Ivo looked ill. "Is there no other way in?"

"If breaking in is - - -r intention, I may help with that," said Bea, drawing her blade.

"No! Put that away. I know where the door is," said Laura.

She stepped up to the wall beside the canal and passed her hand lightly over the surface. She knew it was here, so it was just a matter of . . . aha. Her hand stilled. Something there tugged, ghostly, at her skin. She unclipped the Gin amulet from her belt and passed it over the section. On the first pass, the wall shimmered like a mirage. On the second pass, a line became clearly discernible. On the third pass, the illusion melted entirely and she could see the full edge of the door. She pried it open and gestured grandly at the others.

"Shall we proceed?"

"How did - - - know how to find it?" said Okane.

"I've got a map of the canals," said Laura. "Every canal has a door for maintenance. They just cover it up so people who aren't supposed to be there can't get in."

She entered first, shaking an Egg as she went. A walkway had been built on either side of the canal's path, wide enough for walking but not wide enough for comfort. The light slid easily over its wetly glinting stone, highlighting the smooth wear of the water. This made the walkway a hazard, and Laura kept one hand on the wall to keep from slipping. The canal went fifteen feet before branching off in two directions. Laura held the Egg high. As far as she could see, the walkways were identical on both routes. Both stone, both banking smoothly off into darkness. Then she noticed something on the opposite wall: indentations, barely discernible in the dim lighting, and the walkway below it bowed enough for the water to lap up on to its surface. Whatever had been there had come and gone long ago for the canal to weather it like this. Still, it might be a clue.

"I think we should go this way," she whispered, gesturing right.

"Have - - - seen something?" said Okane.

"There's damage on the other wall."

"An Egg," said Ivo. They all turned to look at him and he shrugged. "There were similar markings in the wilds of Zyra. Old impressions of Egg blasts while fighting monsters have scarred the rock there. This is very close, but presumably from more recent if the canals rise very high."

"So, another infestation was down here before?" said Laura.

"It seems so."

She faced forward again and frowned. "Great. Maybe we're on to some mobster stash. Would it have killed them to take care of their own mess?"

Maybe the Mad Dogs were gathering around here for supplies, not just for a meeting with the boss.

They slinked down the right passageway. On and on they walked. The farther they went the darker it became, but the Egg's glow kept them from any missteps. It highlighted more damage. The wall ahead was fractured as if hit by a cannonball. The crater continued to the floor, where the walkway was almost completely destroyed. More marks like Egg blasts scarred the walls, but in the crater, something glittered gold. It looked almost like the inner wall was made of Gin, but that was impossible. It was nowhere near the right color. It just sparkled.

"That's not right," Laura murmured.

She reached out one hand. Okane opened his mouth to protest, but before he could, Laura's scars burned. Blackness engulfed her so completely she almost thought the infestation had descended, but she felt nothing beyond the damp canal air. Light sparked behind her, accompanied by the tinkling of rolling glass.

A lone Egg bumped over the stone on the opposite platform, followed by a pair of grasping hands. A boy Cheryl's age chased it, wavy black hair matted against the blood on his face, his every breath a sobbing gasp and his eyes wide with terror. Hot on his heels came an infestation. The boy fell on already-skinned knees and made a desperate grab. His fingertips caught the Egg, but that brush sent it skittering out of reach and he had nothing else. The infestation cascaded like a wave toward him. The boy screamed. He was going to die. He was going to die and it was her fault, because he wouldn't be here otherwise, her fault *my fault my fault he's going to die no please Clae I can't oh god help help I can't I can't let it don't take him away I can't—*

Light flooded her surroundings again as arms caught her around the middle and heaved her back. She'd made to jump toward the other platform and Okane had stopped her. Why the hell had he stopped her? She tried to elbow her way out of his grip and heard a grunt of pain. The Egg she'd been holding dropped, cracked on the walkway, and fell into the canal. Their light dimmed. Where was the boy? She had to do something! She kicked and writhed, desperate.

"Let go!" Laura snapped. "I have to help him!"

"Who?" Okane coughed. "Laura, there's no one—Hold still! I'll show - - -!"

She didn't have time! Laura screamed.

Okane cringed. He pinned her with one arm, and used the other to shake another Egg into glowing. The Egg cast a dim light over the opposite platform. It was empty. It was . . . it was . . . Laura stilled.

"Where did he go?"

"Where did who go?"

"Him! I swear I—Ow!" Pain lanced through the branching scars on her arms, almost as if she'd pressed against another massive magic strain. She shook her hands but the sting stayed lodged under the skin. "Someone was there! I saw it! There was a boy with an Egg, being chased by an infestation!"

"We're the only ones in the tunnel," said Okane. "No one else saw anything."

"You don't understand, he was my—" Laura paused as she realized what she was saying. "My . . . my brother."

Okane eyed her with concern. "- - -r *what*?"

"I don't have a brother," Laura said faintly.

"- - - hadn't mentioned one before, no."

"Why did I think I had a brother?"

Now that she could see the opposite platform and her heartbeat began to slow, she felt foolish. Still, she couldn't shake the dregs of terror still clinging to her mind. For a short time, she'd been utterly convinced . . . But the more she thought, the more she realized that panicking voice hadn't been her own. It had been another child's.

"Is this like Toulouse? The lattice gallery? Am I getting some kind of magical overdose?" she asked. "I don't even know what's here that could affect me."

"This location does shows magical influence. It may be possible that there is an amulet nearby inflicting a vision or feeling to any trespassers," Ivo agreed. "A frightening vision may serve as a deterrent to maintenance workers or outside agents. Perhaps it is a ward of the mob's."

"They flash an image of a kid getting chased by infestations and expect people not to talk?" Laura scoffed. "Even if someone runs away they'll report it, and then the mob stash is swarming with police investigators. It doesn't make sense. Besides, this . . . this felt personal." She hadn't wanted to run. She'd wanted to stay, as useless as she'd be, because losing that person and living would be worse than dying. She stepped back and squinted at the wall again.

"I don't think - - - should touch that again," said Okane.

"You think a giant magical crater can be in here and not be related to an infestation?" said Laura. "Besides, I don't see anything else in here that could be interfering with me."

She braced her fingertips against the stone. Her skin smarted, like static up her scars, but she didn't have another vision. She pressed her hands flat against it and only then did she feel that impression again—not quite there in reality but the distinct feeling that a child was screaming. Little boy in distress, Eggs, infestations, Sylph Canal . . . realization hit her like a brick. She pulled sharply away from the crater and eyed it with mixed horror and wonder.

"Underyear 1215," she whispered. "It's so obvious."

Eighteen years ago. Clae would've been nine. Anselm died at Underyear, aged nine. A howling noise in the canal . . . When Clae shifted to crystal in the Falling Infestation there had been an awful howl, too. Anselm was the Sylph Canal's ghost.

"This is where Anselm changed," she said. "All those stories, it was about Anselm dying. The crater here was made when he crystallized. If Clae crystallizing had a magical output enough to wipe out a partial swarm of infestations, Anselm could've done a number on a wall."

"- - - mean—" Okane pressed his hand against it too. "- - -'re right. This feeling, it's fear."

"I thought Magi crystallized under anger," said Ivo, tentatively touching the stone. He pulled his hand back quickly. "Neither crystal felt like . . . like this."

"That's because the crystal is an independent magic source. The Anselm - - - saw in the armory changed from his original crystal shape. He used to be so afraid. But then he came in contact with Grim, and it soothed him." Okane gave a sad smile. "This crater here . . . it's like initials carved on a tree. The people who carved it may not be together anymore, or even alive, but the mark of that time remains—their changing doesn't remove the mark or the memory. So now we can see what Anselm was, at that time, regardless of what he is now. Of course, this is just a faded impression. When I first met him, Anselm as the crystal was still experiencing this moment." His smile slipped, and his voice went quieter still. "He was so much worse."

They stayed there awhile in silence, weighed down by the knowledge of what had happened here.

Laura wondered if Anselm had known he was dying. He'd destroyed the infestation, certainly, and Clae was able to escape . . . but how had Clae reacted? What had he done? The only time Clae had mentioned Anselm's death, it hadn't been detailed at all; he didn't like sharing anything too close to his heart. But it was the event that caused everything in the Sinclair family to fall apart. Had Clae ever hated Anselm for dying? Had he ever stood by the Kin tub's side, begging crystal to answer him?

"We have more to do than admire the mortar," said Bea. "Is there not another infestation here?"

Her tone was so flat and bored, Laura could hardly believe it.

"Yes," said Laura. "But—"

"Then we should move." Bea strode ahead of them without a second glance, and Laura scowled at her back.

"She really doesn't care, does she?"

"Rejection of emotion makes it easier to engage," said Ivo. He hesitated, then set his hand on Okane's shoulder. "I've never succeeded in it, and it feels a betrayal to those people even to try. Children don't deserve to die."

He dropped his hand again and hurried after Bea. Okane watched him go in confusion.

"Why did he say that as if he was convincing me—"

He snapped his mouth shut. Okane's father was trapped in Rex. How many little silver-eyed children had Ivo seen in the crusades?

They moved forward, tension running high. Laura was tired of so much stress; she was trying to come up with some words to calm them all down when she realized another conversation was going on in the tunnel beyond them.

"Do you hear that?"

"Workers?" Ivo guessed.

"It can't be mobsters if they're all bullying the police outside," said Laura. "Though if there are regular workers who see your Rexian numbers so deep in a restricted zone . . . How about you get behind us, just in case?"

They shuffled into a new formation. Laura held her new glowing Egg high, but she couldn't glimpse anyone else in the gloom. Surely if someone were here they'd carry a lantern of some kind? The voices went on, hushed by distance and cascading water. She couldn't understand what they said but it sounded like a group of men. She slowed as they neared a corner.

To the left the canal went deeper into the city. A wall separated them from the source, but the water came in through a grated pipe and formed a short waterfall to the main flow. Otherwise it seemed a dead end, but the voices came from within it.

"Hello?" Laura called.

The voices went on without pause. Either they didn't hear her, or those weren't real voices. She stopped and waited. The voices continued, near and far at the same time and utterly indecipherable. Her paranoia from the liminal room and the crater resurged. Were those even voices, or was this just another spell settling on her?

She forced herself to concentrate on it the same way she did with the Magi "you." Under scrutiny, it wavered. She couldn't determine the language. It wasn't real. It was a sensation in her own mind, prattling on in mimicry of humanity. But there was no second crater to be found, and why would someone set up a nonsense-whispering amulet so far in a canal where no one would reach it? This one she was sure had to be related to their infestation. None of the others looked at her, and none appeared to be trying to communicate at all. Were they even noticing this?

"Don't trust it," she whispered, pulling down her goggles, and the others copied without speaking.

Laura threw a flash pellet into the dead end. Light flooded the space, glinting harsh off of the gushing water and slick walkway. Nothing else moved under it, and when the flash faded it looked darker than ever. Her first instinct said an infestation would've reacted and given itself away, but the hive mind was tricky; they might know better than to flinch under simple light.

"What is our plan and formation?" said Bea, drawing her blade.

"Find it first," Laura murmured, "but I think it's trying to draw us in."

She threw another flash pellet to the other wall of the dead end, as if that might catch the monster where the first hadn't. Still no response. If it didn't show itself they'd be forced to get close to investigate, and possibly be trapped. Laura shuddered at the idea.

"We require bait." Bea strode forward without hesitation.

"What are you doing?" Laura hissed.

"Bea is used to this," said Ivo. "She's very fast. Don't worry."

He remained tense as Bea entered the dead end. She held her glowing blade aloft, sweeping it slowly back and forth as she inspected the walls and floor. It was the absolute worst possible light. Infestations could sometimes be spotted by the reddish glint off their bodies; under the Rexian red glow, every surface gave off that ugly sheen. Laura bit her lip, certain at any second that the infestation would surface, but the seconds ticked by without change. Bea stepped carefully, taking in every detail. The "voices" didn't alter. The water didn't discolor. Nothing appeared. Bea reached the far wall and gave the grated pipe an annoyed look. The others crept in slowly, looking around for anything she might've missed.

"Maybe it's not here after all?" Ivo whispered, uncertain.

Laura wasn't convinced. Was it attempting to ambush them all at once? Where could it be, so close and still hidden? There were no nooks or crannies out of sight. The only place that remained indistinct . . .

"Up!" she shouted, backing up fast. "It's on the ceiling!"

The blade's reflection fluctuated overhead as the infestation expanded. A thick curtain of blackness dropped at the dead end's mouth to trap them inside, and sludge roiled down all the walls. Laura cursed herself for approaching this stupid dead end in the first place. She pulled out an Egg, but Bea and Ivo beat her to the punch. The pair of them laid into the infestation's attempted wall, and it split under the seething glow of their blades.

"Out!" Ivo snapped. "Before it reinforces itself!"

They charged through the gap before the monster could repair it, and dashed back toward the Sylph's entrance. The infestation rumbled in annoyance, bunched itself together, and threw itself after them. As she ran, Laura clacked the Egg against her amulet and threw it. Okane had the exact same idea, and Bea lobbed her own red Rexian Egg. The volley smashed behind them, flashing mixed light over the tunnel walls and sending up a spray of water and magic. The whisper intensified, closer to real sound, closer to language. It pressed hard on Laura's mind with the overwhelming sense of revulsion. The infestation broke through the cascading water without hesitation. Under its two detested elements it appeared to be dissolving—smoothness reduced to clumping, kin sparking all over its shapeless bulk—but that wasn't enough to stop it. Laura took out her second Egg, but she didn't get to arm it before the monster lashed out with whiplike limbs. To make matters worse, those limbs splattered blackness in great arcs across the tunnel.

When the sludge hit the walkway and walls it smoked like acid, and the discoloration spread rapidly through the mortar. Laura skidded, trying to avoid one such patch, but her feet slipped on the wet stone, and she lost her balance. She veered into the wall scrabbling for a grip, and dropped her Egg in the process. It hit the walkway hard enough to put a crack in the glass, then overbalanced into the canal. And then . . . it rolled away.

"The canal has! Um! A strong current!" she called, indignant and impressed by just how fast the water carried her glowing Egg toward the Sylph's mouth.

"Do - - - think if we submerge the monster we might be able to take advantage of that?" said Okane.

"It would only send our prey out of reach," said Bea. "Be grateful it has made itself such a large target!"

As another limb swept for her, she sliced it apart with her blade. The spatter missed her entirely, and the severed limb splashed into the water along with all the dripping tar from the main mass. Ivo shot at the beast one-handed, and the Rexian bullets blossomed ugly and red on its squalling form. Okane threw another Egg, which pulverized the left side. The infestation shrieked. It dunked itself entirely into the canal water and came up spiraling, spattering all the more blackness over them, but it had somehow rinsed off all the magic. It heaved the main body of itself to the right side of the tunnel, where Ivo was; he hopped back, faster and nimbler than a human should ever be, chopping apart the infestation's limbs with the blade in one hand and taking shots with the gun in his other whenever he had a slim opening. Laura threw flash pellets in an attempt to spook the infestation away from him, but that flash highlighted a new issue. With all the dripping and submersion, the infestation had turned the waters black. Tar floated on the surface of the canal, and as Laura gaped at it, clumps started *wiggling toward her.*

"Oh, no. Shit, no, that's disgusting!"

She retreated fast, but the clumps followed as if they could see her. Since when could pieces move apart from the main monster? They rose up like snakes and lashed toward her. Instinct told her to kick them, but that was a terrible idea. She hopped aside instead. When the clumps hit stone they spattered into nothingness, but the stain they left behind seeped into the mortar much faster than before. The mortar began to crumble into blackened sand, and the stones shifted in the wall. If they didn't act fast, it would bring down the whole tunnel.

Laura aimed her next Egg at the canal itself. It plunked into the black-ness. For a moment the clumps continued to writhe over the surface, but then the Egg detonated and almost blinded everyone. The explosion threw the whole infestation toward the ceiling. The clumps writhed and squealed as they rained back down amid glittering tar to smoke on the walkways. The mortar darkened faster, and some of the walkway's stones dislodged to tumble into the canal. The mess had stayed stagnant on the water's surface before, but whatever hold it had now vanished; anything that landed in the canal again—infestation, kin, brick—was swept downstream at a tremen-dous pace. What was with this selective current?

Laura squinted after it and realized it wasn't actually going to the Sylph's mouth. The only light was gold, and it had all bunched up in the water below that glittering crater. She should've been able to see the entrance's light from here, but she couldn't get a glimpse of sunlight. She threw a flash pellet to the ceiling to confirm her fears, and it burst on a surface that was far too liquid and clumpy. The infestation had surrounded them in the dark while they were distracted. Everything beyond the crater was cut off.

"It's still on the ceiling!" she called. "It's gotten over and behind us to seal off the entrance!"

"Insolent monster," Bea hissed.

"Daylight may be beneficial. Should we attempt to fall back toward the entrance regardless?" said Ivo.

"Please," said Laura.

They dashed back the way they'd come, and the infestation came barrel-ing after them.

"Okane and I will hold back the main portion," said Laura. "Ivo, Bea, you've got those blades. Try to break through the entrance the way you did at the dead end. Shout when you're clear."

"Right," said Ivo.

He and Bea ran on while Laura and Okane stopped before the crater.

"Are you okay?" she checked; Okane's brow was furrowed in something like pain.

"I feel like it's shouting at us," he said. "Or maybe a deficit of shouting?" He clacked another Egg against his amulet and threw it. "It's doing some-thing magical, and I don't like it."

"It's also tearing through our equipment too easily," said Laura, throwing her own Egg.

The infestation slowed but kept coming. How could it still be coming with so many direct hits? Was this an old monster? Something imported from the wilds for an assassination, maybe? Why such a beast would end up in the canal interiors, she had no idea. She looked back to check the Rexians' status. At the other side, they'd started slashing at the monster's blockade, but it had grown smarter. Rather than a simple solid wall, it had begun spinning what appeared to be giant three-dimensional spiderwebs from it: thin enough to be easily fixed after every swing, insubstantial enough that attacking it did little damage to its source, encroaching steadily with every failed attempt to pass. Bea threw an Egg at it instead, and the web untangled just enough to smack the Egg into the water. It burst with a subdued effect, and the web kept growing.

"It's branching!" said Okane, because now their end had started creating webs, too.

Laura's hand went to her bag again and skimmed over her last Egg. She didn't want to waste it if the infestation was just going to deflect it into the water. There must be an answer. An idea occurred to her as she spotted red magic drifting *against* the current now. The liquefied kin of Bea's Egg had come to congregate with the rest by Anselm's crater, eddying at the outside as the lost Eggs and glittering tar made the water downright boil. Her scars hummed again. At the edge of her awareness, she could hear Anselm's wailing again: *My fault my fault I can't I won't no no NO YOU WON'T TAKE CLAE AWAY—*

"I have a plan," she breathed.

Okane backed farther away from the encroaching monster. Whatever "shouting" it was doing, it had a bad effect on him; he visibly wilted, and sweat beaded on his forehead. Still, he looked at Laura undaunted. "What's the plan?"

"We get Anselm's help." Laura braced her hands against the crater again. "Come on," she whispered, "Please, please, please!"

Magic glittered under her hands, there but uncomprehending.

I WON'T, it screamed, inaudible. *HE'S MINE I WON'T LET YOU TAKE HIM AWAY!*

Okane's confidence cracked. "But it isn't Anselm, just an echo!"

"But the echo still has power! He's here, we just need to figure out what he needs! The Gin on the train—"

"It's not Gin, either!"

"Neither was the Pit, but that activated just fine! Come on, Anselm, please!"

Okane gaped. "- - - won't get anywhere like that! - - -'re just bringing it back to - - -rself, not—ugh." He shook his head and leaned in to join her. "Let me try." He pressed his forehead against the crater and closed his eyes.

Ivo and Bea retreated close to them. The webbing had grown enough to force them this far back, and was coming even closer.

"Eggs and blades are having no effect," said Bea. "The blade auras are also proving insufficient."

With Okane's head still pressed against the wall and no change in the magic levels, Laura doubted they'd get help from there. She looked around for another solution. The infestation had draped itself fully around them now, cutting off any escape even into the water. The bricks in the wall trembled, their mortar eroding fast. Laura had been hesitant to use some equipment in such close quarters, but she couldn't see any way around it now.

"Bijou," she said.

"That will bring the tunnel down on us," said Ivo.

"It gives us better options than letting the infestation come down on us instead," said Laura. "We activate the Bijou, and as soon as we see any kind of opening we go for it, no matter what direction it is. Are we agreed— Okane? Okane, you have to be in on this!"

Okane's expression pinched, and then his eyes snapped open. He stepped back with teeth bared, spread his arms wide . . . and a scream echoed around them. It was Anselm but warped—a shriek, a howl, pain and fear and malice wrapped in a horrible unearthly sound, and it wailed like a siren without stopping. The glitter of the crater dimmed and then intensified as those little chips of light morphed into blinding stars. They ripped out of the stone with force enough to tear chunks loose. From the crater, from the nearby wall, from the walkway and even the canal channel they rose, until it seemed a thousand burning Bijou filled their little circle. Okane angled his arm, and all that magic screamed outward toward the infestation. It caught together, bounced off the webbing and walls. The infestation screamed in surprise and drew back, flattening into the canal and the far wall, and the light followed with all the vitriol and ramming force of cannonballs. Smoke issued so thick they could hardly see through it, and the already-unsteady tunnel shuddered.

"Let's get out of here!" Laura shouted.

Ivo and Bea vanished into the sparks and smoke. Okane took a step, and all the strength went out of him. Laura heaved him back up but his head lolled.

"Okane? Hey! This is not the right time to pass out!"

His eyelids fluttered and he stumbled to try standing. Almost as soon as he did he sagged again.

"Okane!"

"Got . . . me," he mumbled. His head jerked up again and this time his eyes were wide. "He's got . . . me! He's pulling . . . me . . . too!"

Anselm as a crystal had yanked the magical influence out of someone before, and Laura doubted Okane would survive it as Grim had.

"One of you get back here!" she cried. "Amulet harness needed!" Ahead she heard the crunch and clatter of metal, and behind her came the cacophony of the caving tunnel. "Help!"

Ivo appeared again. He took in Okane's pallor and didn't ask any questions, just heaved the other man over his shoulders like a bag of grain and ran. Laura did her best to keep up, but even without Okane's weight she only had two amulets' worth of speed. The tunnel shook. The walls were falling. They bolted through the still-open door and veered left toward the outside buildings. They barely escaped. Water burst out with force enough to knock the grate entirely off and send spray and debris twenty feet into the air. It was discolored with kin and sang an echo of the still-reverberating scream. The sound was muffled here but the outer wall shuddered, the thunder of collapsing stone reached a breaking point, and then . . . it stopped. The scream ended as abruptly as it started. The kin-influenced wave crashed over the Sylph bridge and flooded the banks so the cement glittered. In its wake the canal ran shallow.

"Cave-in," Laura whispered.

She hoped all those fireworks had killed off the infestation—they certainly seemed potent enough—but how could she tell when the infected amulet had to be buried under all that rubble?

"Okane, are you feeling better?" she asked.

Ivo had set him down once they got clear. Okane shook but forced a smile. "The drain is gone. I can breathe easier now."

"I've never seen a technique like that," said Ivo.

"I think there's a reason - - - haven't." Okane laid himself flat against the ground and closed his eyes. "I thought I'd die for a second there."

A loud gasp made them all look up. They'd had a one-man audience for their escape: a young policeman, alone and gaping at where the Sylph grate had been.

"The Sylph!" he cried. "It—It's been—"

Laura winced. "I'm so sorry about that, sir. There was an infestation, and it was big—"

"You've damaged the interior wall!" He looked down at them now, and his shock changed to fear. He fumbled with his gun holster. "And those—Rexians!"

"They're not Rexians!" Laura said stupidly. "These are ex-Rangers!"

"They are! I know what they look like! They're here to attack Amicae again, and you let them in!"

The others were tense with panic, Ivo and Bea ready for a fight, Okane still sprawled on the ground but watching with wide eyes. This was the worst outcome. Laura knew the truth couldn't be shared on a grand scale, but couldn't Albright have given her department some kind of heads-up? Where was Mr. Dour when she actually wanted him?

"Look, sir," said Laura, stepping forward. "Whatever you think is happening, you've got the wrong idea. I promise—"

"Stay where you are!" he barked, and wrenched out the gun. Laura froze when he turned it on her.

"We're not fighting you," she said slowly, raising her hands and trying for calm even while that trigger rested in far too shaky fingers. "We just—"

"Shut up!"

Okane tried to push himself up off the concrete. "Wait! Please! This is a misunderstanding!"

His arms buckled under him, and he fell back with a grunt. The policeman looked down, the gun followed his eyes, and Laura's stomach lurched. She stepped over Okane and snapped, "Hey! Cop! You're looking at me!"

"Laura," Okane said warningly, and she ignored him.

"Who are you really interested in, the boss or the lackey?"

The gun went back up. Good.

Bea adjusted her grip on her blade. "Shall I take care of him?"

"- - - are making this worse!" Okane hissed.

"I know who you are, Laura Kramer. I knew you were a traitor since the day you framed Miss MacDanel," said the policeman.

"I didn't frame anyone for anything," Laura retorted.

"Words from a traitor! MacDanel cared about this city, not what it could give her!" The irony had Laura rolling her eyes, and the policeman became even more agitated. He pulled back the safety. "I'm taking you in!"

"You can't be serious," said Laura. "Albright—"

"You can't hide behind the chief this time! I'll tell her everything! I'll tell everyone everything! Everyone will see you cuffed along with your Rexian partners!"

Laura had no doubt that Albright would fix this—she couldn't afford the truth spreading either—but what would happen in the meantime? Even the police specifically in on their secret treated Zelda and the others like trash, and other officers had no reason to treat Rexians any better. Would they abuse them? Would they shoot them, claiming the Rexians tried to resist? The MARU had done that with mobsters; it was what got the mobs organized and angry. Even if by some miracle they were given basic dignity, the press would snap up Rexian involvement and the city would riot; the Council would swoop in for that fake trial and execution, or otherwise start a manhunt. Running away now was the safest route for them, even if it did look incriminating. That way the policeman could cry wolf all he wanted, without any proof. If an investigation rose after that, Albright would quash it. Yes. They had to run. If only Laura could signal the others, and if only she could get rid of that gun . . .

"Why don't we get this settled right now?" she said. "Call Albright. Bring us to the closest police box or pick any of the shops around here for the telephone. If you say it has to do with Sweepers, Albright will talk to you immediately. Then you can have all your questions answered, and we don't have to go through all the hassle of transporting us."

The policeman scoffed. "You're just buying time for the rest of your criminals to get here!"

As if waiting for that cue, someone appeared in the alley behind him. The newcomer was tall, thin enough to snap in a breeze, hair red and eyes sparkling dangerously. It was the Mad Dog Laura had once seen at a shooting range with the MacDanels, presumably the same one who'd met Cheryl earlier today. His steps were sure but quiet, and he held a Sweeper weapon—a staff—tight in one tattooed hand. Laura had a very, very bad feeling.

"Hey," she said, but the policeman kept talking.

"I'm not going to fall for that! I'm not giving you any chance to talk your way out of the truth! The rest of my team is already on their way—"

"That's great, but I think we're in bigger trouble here," said Laura, trying to subtly point with her raised hands.

"Don't say 'we'! We're not on the same side!" said the policeman.

Still the Mad Dog stole up behind him, smile widening, both hands on the staff now. Laura's heart beat fast with trepidation.

"Sir," said Okane, face pale.

"Shut up!" barked the policeman.

"Look behind you!" said Laura.

"I'm not letting you escape! By the end of today, Amicae will know the truth!"

"Just turn around!" Laura cried.

The Mad Dog clicked his tongue. The policeman turned. He barely got a glimpse of the Mad Dog before the staff caught him across the face. The gun discharged far off course from anyone, and the policeman fell with a strangled cry. The Mad Dog followed, flipping the staff about, and drove the larger, sharpened end into the policeman's mouth with force enough to pin him to the concrete. The Mad Dog flashed his teeth, and the world went white. The staff had activated. The spilled canal water flashed in time with one, two, three vicious spikes of magic. Laura still wore her goggles, so while the bursts were bright, they didn't fully blind her. She saw the policeman's limbs flailing. She saw the Mad Dog twist the staff, as if to grind his victim further into nothing. It ended in seconds, and in the after-math, thick vanilla fought burning flesh for dominance in the air. The policeman didn't look human anymore. His head and shoulders were twisted and blackened, burned skin peeling and glittering in the lingering magical shock. The bared bone of his jaw split, and kin seethed through the crack. Laura had thought that Lester MacDanel's injuries after facing Clae in Rex looked bad, but this man was utterly, magically ruined. His bare hand and wrist bore branched lightning scars now, just like Laura's. The Mad Dog wrenched the staff back out. Its point sizzled with drying blood.

"Disgusting," said the Mad Dog. "The more I work my way up in the world, the more I'm brought back here, to taking out the trash. I suppose he makes for a good warning, at least."

He stuck the staff point to the ground and smeared a perfect MARU circle around the corpse. The ugly rasp of wood on concrete normally would've caused a shiver down Laura's spine, but she shook too much already for that to matter.

Laura had always known the mobs were dangerous. Anyone who lived in Amicae, who grew up with tales of the MARU's annihilation, knew not to overstep their bounds. Laura had been cautious too, but while the Mad Dogs claimed they wanted her, they'd operated like ghosts on the periphery of her life. They'd never been personal, never been a direct threat. She'd never really seen their brutality in action. There had been no pressing need to fear them, but now, face-to-face with a mobster and a freshly mutilated corpse, she felt all that neglected terror clogging her throat. Would he turn on her next and try to force the Sweepers to do the Mad Dogs' bidding? Would he target them even as fun, or as another warning?

The Mad Dog caught her eye and smiled as if he knew what she was thinking. He rested the staff on his shoulder in smug nonchalance and turned to face them fully. "Good afternoon, head Sweeper. I hope you don't mind the mess."

Laura couldn't think of a damn thing to reply. Her mind was content to run in panicked circles until Okane caught her leg. He'd tried to push himself up again, and lost balance. His lips pressed thin, and he shook worse than Laura. By instinct she caught him under the arm and helped him straighten, and she saw Ivo silently supporting him on the other side. Right. She had no time to be worried for herself. She pushed all thoughts of Okane, Ivo, and Bea to the front of her mind, and dredged up the memory of Juliana and the train depot. She hadn't backed down there, had she? This shouldn't be any different. She still had people behind her. She had to protect them. She squeezed Okane's biceps, half trying to build her confidence, half prepared to flee and drag him with her. He leaned just a little closer, ready to follow whatever choice she made.

"I thought you had other business to attend to this morning," said Laura.

The Mad Dog clapped slowly, mockingly. "So your little cousin passed along the message! What a good girl."

"Don't you talk about my cousin," Laura snapped.

"When I'm the one who saved her from being snatched off the bridge this morning? You wound me, Miss Kramer."

"You don't look wounded," Laura grumbled.

"Oh, no, trust me. I bleed with shame," he purred.

Laura suppressed a shudder. "What are you doing here?"

"Following up," said the Mad Dog. "Do you think I'm so unprofessional that I'd leave loose ends? My other business is finished, so I returned to see if you needed any assistance."

"I don't need any assistance from mobsters," Laura spat.

"No. No, you don't." The Mad Dog's eyes narrowed in resentment and his fingers flexed on the staff. For a moment he exuded such malice Laura stepped back for fear of a staff to her own face, but the moment passed; he was back to oily familiarity before she could fully comprehend what happened. "I'm afraid I'm at an impasse, Miss Kramer! As you know, I think you'd thrive under the Mad Dogs, but new information has just come to light . . ."

Coldness pooled in Laura's stomach. "*You* think that?"

"You didn't know?" said the Mad Dog—no, the Mad Dogs' *boss*. "Didn't Clae tell you about his old friend Renard? Of course he didn't. Knowing about me would give you another option, and he couldn't allow that."

He stepped forward. Laura wanted to step back, but Okane didn't budge. She forced herself to be still and steady with him even as Renard slowly approached.

"Even if you want to properly join us at this time, we wouldn't be able to give you the grand welcome we'd planned," he said. "The investigation that finished this morning tells us that there will be significant changes: very fast, and very relevant to our interests. Depending on how and what changes are made, we need multiple options in place to ensure we can close on the best opportunity. Drawing you fully into the mob would be putting all of our eggs in one basket. We'll need you to continue working for the Council and getting all that official correspondence and funding. You may end up holding the key to Amicae's survival. Any idea that we're linked should be erased. Any witnesses"—he glanced back at the smoldering policeman—"eliminated."

"Does that mean you'll stop writing about me in the *Dead Ringer*?" said Laura.

"Stopping would confirm your joining better than any article," Renard replied. "Now, that isn't to say we reject you from joining us. If you've finally seen the light, we will of course admit you. It would work well to your advantage. Even working separately, we could feed you information and collaborate to make sure no trace of monsters exists in Amicae."

He stopped very, very close. Okane leaned even more, losing strength or trying to cover her, Laura didn't know, but it was good to have some distraction from the eyes currently trying to pick her apart. Renard's gaze turned on Ivo and Bea, and his smile curled wider.

"I could also take your new recruits back with me. They'll be far safer among the Mad Dogs, and in much more familiar company. No one would be able to touch them with us."

And abandon them to another bunch of killers?

"Not a chance in hell," Laura seethed.

Renard barked with laughter. "You are a Sinclair, aren't you?"

"I am," said Laura. "And I'm not interested in changing that."

"Maybe not now, but I'll wager you'll be very tempted very soon." Renard pulled a business card from his pocket. A business card for a mobster. It was almost laughable. He held it up at Laura's eye level. "Memorize this number. You can use it to contact us once you realize just what's going on."

Laura didn't look at it. She focused instead on the lurid ink of Renard's tattoo, the claws and teeth of a rabid dog splayed over his knuckles. Renard snorted in amusement. He touched the card to the point of his staff, and it went up in golden flame. He held it out, watching it burn in detached wonder.

"Let me fill you in on what's happened today," he said. "Your cousin found an infestation. She escaped it by sheer dumb luck, and went straight to the city's Sweeper authority to report it. You came to exterminate the monster. In the process, you ran into mobsters. Being good, god-fearing citizens, you immediately called for police, who engaged the mobsters and told you to return to your offices to keep you safe. You did not speak with any mobsters. You were long gone before the man behind me *heroically* died to protect you. There has been no collaboration today. You're still the Council's dogs. Do you understand?"

He was giving them an out. It was an out with expectations, but one without real ties or any injury, and Laura took it. She tugged Okane away and said quietly, defeatedly, "Come on. We shouldn't be in a place with mobsters."

Okane nodded, and the three of them silently followed her. She glanced over her shoulder to see Renard watching them go. He flicked the burning card into the canal, and gestured with his freed hand. From the other alleys came more people: mobsters toting Sweeper weapons, some crisp as if they'd spent the day gambling in ritzy clubs, others tattered and dirty as if they'd really just crawled out of the wilds. Haru walked up to Renard, more relaxed than Laura had ever seen him.

"Your orders, boss?"

"Half our group needs to work around the back to access the Sylph, while the rest should prepare for a clash here in front. We have a police squad on their way, and I'd like to welcome them," said Renard.

"With fanfare?" Haru checked.

"Of course."

Haru bared his teeth. "Then blood we will have."

He barked orders to the other Mad Dogs. They fell out of sight as the Sinclairs rounded a corner, and Laura forced herself to face ahead. The police had already known there was mob activity around here; if the Mad Dogs wanted to get the drop on them it wouldn't be easy. She shuffled along, uneasy and disgusted, until they reached more familiar streets. Ten minutes into their trek, Okane stopped. He turned in to Laura, wrapped her up in a hug, and laid his chin on her head. His hair tickled her nose, and he smelled just like the shop: a purer, untainted vanilla. He was normal and solid, and for a moment Laura went boneless against him. This was a mistake, as she'd been his only support. They teetered dangerously until Ivo planted a hand against Okane's back and pushed them back to equilibrium. Laura buried a mortified laugh into Okane's bandana.

"Are - - - okay?" Okane asked quietly.

She most certainly was not.

"Fine," she mumbled. "Are *you* okay?"

"Mad Dogs are kind of old news for me," said Okane.

Of course. He'd lived in the Sullivan mansion while the old bastard was in league with the mobs. He might even have known who Renard was before Laura did. He'd been far more scarred by mob experiences, and he dealt with it with dignity. She could do the same. Laura inhaled deep and pulled away.

"Ivo, Bea, how about you? How are you holding up?"

"I am mostly confused," said Ivo. He cast a furtive look over his shoulder, even though the mobsters were far behind them now. "Violence is nothing new to me, but I can see why - - - worried about mob involvement, now."

"Why didn't - - - take the card?" said Bea.

"What?" said Laura.

"The card," Bea said slowly, as if speaking to someone particularly stupid. "The card with that Renard's contact."

Was this a joke?

"Why would I take it? He's a mobster," said Laura.

Bea cocked her head as if in question, but her eyes were accusing. "Clearly, because it was the best option."

"How was that a good option? He murdered a man in cold blood!" said Laura, incredulous.

"To prevent - - -r folly from starting a scandal."

"Folly?" Ivo echoed, brow furrowing. "Are - - - saying her acceptance of us was folly?"

"It was," said Bea. "The costs far outweigh the benefits. I would imagine someone willing to make that decision would be prepared to handle any developments, but instead we have - - -," she shot Laura a scalding look, "who will allow others to do - - -r dirty work and then have the gall to complain about it." Laura's mouth opened and shut, the words clogged in her throat. Should she be indignant or just plain worried? She didn't get the chance to decide. Bea continued, "Besides, it was evident to me that this Renard of the Mad Dogs is Amicae's true head Sweeper."

"He is *not* our head Sweeper," Laura hissed. "The mobs move illegally, and their Sweepers are just as deep in crime as the rest of them—"

"But they are the ones with the most members, and they are the reliable force that protects Amicae while - - - struggle," said Bea. "- - - bowed to them very easily just now."

"I left because that was a threat," Laura said bitterly.

"I do not fault the decision," said Bea. "They are clearly the best hands to leave this situation in."

Ivo watched this back-and-forth with clear discomfort. "Amicae's mobs are not the Black Guard. This isn't a proper solution."

"No. They are Amicae's true Sweeper guild, even if they don't get the credit," said Bea.

"No, they're not. Sweeping for them is just a side business," Laura insisted.

She couldn't let Bea think the Mad Dogs were good in any way. They were instigators, killers, and cheats. They made the Falling Infestation. They killed Clae. They shouldn't be given any kind of heroic status.

Bea leveled her with a very blank but very hostile look. "Ivo chose to leave the Rexian crusade because the handlers degenerated into vainglorious fools. It was a sensible action. Our handler of the time could never have assured us victory. I advise - - - not to make the same mistake, or - - - will not have us under - - -r command much longer." Her chin jerked upward in contempt. "I have memorized the information from his card. I will provide it to - - - once - - - realize how badly - - -r pride blinds - - -."

She stepped past Laura and kept walking toward the shop without so much as a glance behind her. Ivo hurried after her, whispering, "Bea, that isn't—"

Laura shook with rage. "*My* pride? Mine? Maybe she ought to look in a mirror sometime!"

"I'm sure she'll come around," Okane said wearily. "Let's just . . . Let's just go home. It's been a long day, and it's not even noon yet."

They made their slow way back to the Sweeper shop, and almost as soon as they crossed the threshold, Laura called in to the police. Albright was predictably unhappy that they'd managed to ditch Mr. Dour and Mr. Sour so easily.

"We didn't know where to find them," Laura lied over the phone. "When the mobsters showed up, the other officer on the scene decided to prioritize our safety. The recruits never left my sight, no one's hurt, and we're back at the shop waiting for your orders."

She felt sick to follow a Mad Dog's plans, but she couldn't think of a better way to resolve the situation.

Albright made no mention of the Mad Dogs' mischief or any police altercation, even though she must've known about it in order to set up so many police to catch them and fights must be happening even as they spoke. Albright didn't scold her. She just sounded tired. The guards were less than amused by the proceedings. While Mr. Dour stayed gallivanting with his squads against the Mad Dogs, Mr. Sour returned to the Sweeper shop to escort the Rexians home early.

Okane had regained strength on the way back to the shop, but the popping noise of healing magic remained conspicuously absent and his face stayed pale even after their coworkers had left.

"Are you feeling any better?" Laura asked.

Okane shrugged. "Empty, mostly. Sort of . . . ungrounded."

"Not in pain, though?"

"No. I wondered, did - - - ever feel . . . Never mind."

"Go on," said Laura. "Feel what?"

Okane frowned. "When - - - were affected by the Pit, back when Rex attacked in the mines . . . What happened afterward?"

Laura sat on the stool beside him. "I got knocked out, for one. And once I woke up, I was numb. I mean, I had glass in my hand and I didn't feel any of it."

"But not empty?" said Okane.

"Maybe? You could probably call numbness empty. Grim said that when I conducted the Pit's energy, it ripped all of my natural energy out with it, so he was scared to start treating me until I'd recovered a little."

Okane nodded slowly. "I think that's what happened today. Anselm's power was trying to pull more energy than what was actually stored inside the echo, so since I was the one directing it, it tried to fuel itself with me."

It *what*? Laura sprang up from her stool so fast it clattered to the floor. "That's horrible! Do you need to go to a hospital? A doctor? I'll take you now if you need it! I'll call right—"

"No!" He held up a hand, and she stopped halfway to the telephone. "No, it's fine. I'm just tired. If - - - recovered after some sleep, I'm sure it'll be the same with me." He lowered that hand and clasped them both tight on his lap. "It's funny. I told myself I could put that Magi curiosity away, but I feel like I'm up on that rooftop again, without knowing what I can do."

Put away? Okane had been quiet recently about his heritage, and she hadn't caught him experimenting with his magic either. Was that linked to the oddness she felt from him, since the Rexian invasion?

"Are you afraid this will happen again?" she ventured.

"I felt like, once all that magic was airborne, I could do anything with it," he murmured. "Thinking back on it scares me, because I felt strong. What else could cause magical drain or backlash? Is there a right way to use magic, to make sure it doesn't hurt - - -? Am I doing everything wrong? I just don't know."

"Do you want to try experimenting again?"

"- - - wouldn't like that, would - - -?"

"I don't like you jumping off of buildings without any safety measures," Laura said bluntly. "That's downright stupid. But if you've got someone with you to watch for danger and help you out . . ."

"I appreciate the offer, but what can - - - do to spot danger when neither of us know the warning signs?" said Okane.

A good point, but he was settling down into a sad kind of sulk and Laura wanted to pull him out of it. If this was linked to the breakdown, to his identity, she had to help. Her first thought was to ask the Rexians—they'd certainly know their abilities after being trained for crusades so long—but Rexian teachings were part of what he feared; even if they approached it kindly, Okane would see Rex's mark in every lesson. Bea would want that to be the lesson entirely. Who else could help?

The answer, when it occurred to her, was stupidly obvious. "Grim!" she cried.

"What?" said Okane.

"You should talk to Grim!" said Laura. "Don't you remember? He knows how Magi work. He talked about their hideouts and knew how to disable one of their cache traps in the wilds. He probably knows more about the Magi than anyone in Amicae!"

Okane looked surprised at first, but his brow furrowed in consideration. "The cache trap was definitely magical, yes. He understood their spells.

And since he's made of Niveus, he can probably gauge magical safety levels, too . . ."

"Right? It's perfect!"

"Do - - - really think he'd talk about them? He and Cherry were against it, back when we first met."

"Only because they were worried Magi might overhear them. Since we're in a city instead of any Magi's territory, it should be just fine. It wouldn't hurt to ask, right?"

Okane's eyes lit up, but just as quickly, doubt pulled him back down. He slumped in his seat. "Right. It's just . . ."

"Just tell him the truth. You're trying to figure yourself out." When he still looked uncertain, Laura took his hand in both of hers and said, softer, "I guarantee it. He won't say no."

Okane was quiet for a while, slowly considering his options. He squeezed her fingers in thanks for the gesture, and his mouth turned up at the end.

"- - - know what? It is a good idea. I will ask him." To her relief, some of the confidence returned to him and Okane's back straightened. "I will! Not today, though. I don't think I could even make it to the Keedlers' right now, let alone Toulouse. Tomorrow, though. It would be nice to spend time with Grim again."

"Not even to—Are you sure you're okay?" Laura fretted.

"I'm fine, Laura." He rolled his eyes. "I doubt we'll be called in for another infestation today, so I'm going to go take a nap."

"Do you want me to stay?" said Laura.

"I'd feel guilty for not being able to entertain - - -," he chuckled. "Besides, Cheryl's gone home, hasn't she? She'll be eager to see - - - after the Sylph Canal."

"Good point," Laura sighed. "God, I hope she didn't say anything to Morgan about this . . . but she must've, if she came home early from school. If I get there fast enough, maybe Morgan won't have convinced herself I'm dead yet. I'm serious, though, if you need anything, just call."

She lingered until she was sure Okane had made it up the steep stairs without trouble, and only then left the shop. She was a little proud of herself, she admitted as she locked the door. Yes, most of the day had been a disaster—she couldn't count the Sylph infestation as really being dead, and she'd witnessed a murder and been threatened by a mob boss—but she had made some kind of progress with Okane. She hadn't actually solved anything, but something that complex couldn't possibly be solved in a day. She'd at least been able to point Okane at someone who could help him along. She really hoped Grim would be willing to do it.

She turned to step off the stoop and jumped at a shout. "Think fast!"

She caught an incoming object by reflex.

The item was a small ceramic dog. Laura puzzled at it a moment before she recognized the feeling. This was an amulet, and judging by the warmth and the magical surge it was following an order.

Laura's world tilted.

She had the distant feeling of falling, and then . . . nothing.

5

NOT HER

Laura was sitting in the Sweeper shop. The sudden change had her blinking at the black drapes before grounding herself. The new scenery jarred her, but there was something more. This was wrong. *Okane's not here,* she thought, casting around, and then, *The Kin is back.* The tubing and glass had taken up its old place on the counter to hiss and steam, clouding a room darker than she remembered it. The clouds billowed, silvery, liquid, curling around the ceiling and down the windowpanes.

Beyond the windows there was no street.

Laura sprang up, knocking her stool to the floor.

All she could see outside was black as if the shop lay at the bottom of a lake of pitch. Her ring burned, her arms itched, and the Eggs in her bag felt hot. She tried to control her breathing, tried to figure out what the hell was going on, but—

"Not her."

She whirled around and the breath froze in her lungs. "Clae?"

Clae rose from his old haunt behind the counter. He looked strange, hyperreal like he'd been under Gustave's Moon, but harsher somehow. He glowered.

"Not her," he said again.

"I—What?"

"Not her."

He stepped forward. The Kin and counter swirled away into the same mist, and with a shudder the walls of the shop did the same. It all clouded, pressing in closer and closer.

"Not her," he repeated, but something else thrummed under the words. A separate voice.

Wake up.

"What?" said Laura. "Who are you talking about?"

"Not her!"

Wake up!

"Not! Her!"

For god's sake, Laura Kramer, open your eyes!

And her eyes must've been closed, because they snapped open now. She sucked in a large, shuddering breath. The clouds and phantom shop were gone, replaced by cold and stink and cobblestones. She sat on a hard chair with her hands bound behind its back and her ankles to its legs. On her lap was the small, carved dog, and she could feel the tremble of fading magic from it.

"That shouldn't have worn off so soon."

Laura looked up at the strange voice and regretted it. Headlights pointed directly at her, blinding and bobbing with the hum of a vehicle. A figure stepped in front of them.

"Maybe you do have some tricks up your sleeve. That would explain why the boss wants you so bad. God knows, it's not for anything else." The stranger leaned in, gripping Laura's chin hard enough to hurt and forcing her to look directly into her captor's eyes. "You've got a rotten personality, your looks are subpar at best, and you like making trouble for anyone who tries to help you."

This close, Laura could make out her features. The stranger's face was gaunt as if her skin stretched over bone with nothing beneath, and her needlelike fingers matched the severity. Her matted black hair shaded but didn't hide the tattoo: a twisted dog made of crimson cloud, its teeth on her brow, claws on her cheekbone, tail sweeping her jaw. Mobsters with facial tattoos were the most dangerous. These were the fanatics who struck in broad daylight and menaced both police and Silver Kings with bombings and shootouts. They didn't care if they were recognized.

Had Renard changed his mind so easily? Had he sent his minions to force her to submit to the mobs?

"Mad Dog," Laura ground out. "I used the story Renard gave me. Is that not enough anymore?"

The stranger laughed. She drew back and shouted over her shoulder, "Blanche! Blanche, she thinks we're here about the cover story!" She didn't wait for a reply but sneered at Laura. "Oh, no, little Sweeper. We're here on our own. You've read so many articles, but haven't you always wanted to meet the real power behind the Mad Dogs?"

"Can't say I have," Laura grumbled, and yelped when the stranger kicked her. God, that hurt! Laura bent double, arms straining and breath hissing sharp through her teeth. She wanted to grab her stinging leg, but couldn't touch it in this position.

"*Such* a rotten personality," the stranger repeated. "All the better for me, though. See, we're here to give you an ultimatum."

Sweat trickled down Laura's back even while she kept up a glower. She had miraculous luck so far with the Mad Dogs, but only because Renard had nebulous reasons for keeping her alive and active. If Renard hadn't changed his mind on the cover story for the Sylph Canal, and this mobster was really here on her own, Laura had no protection. Things could go south very fast. She could easily end up like that policeman, charred to death. Her scars ached at the thought. She never wanted to go through anything like the Pit strains again, but the alternatives weren't any better. She had to try to de-escalate. Limit the damage.

"What do you want?"

"What do I want?" The woman squatted down to her level. "*I* want what the boss wants. The problem is, he's so brainy! He comes up with plans upon plans until there's no room in his head left over for what he actually wants."

"And . . . what does he actually want?"

"Not you."

Considering all the work and contacts Renard and the Mad Dogs had made, that didn't seem entirely likely. Maybe she was missing something, or maybe . . . Laura ventured, "So he wants . . . you?"

The stranger clapped in delight. "Exactly! What he needs is a tried and true mobster! Someone to commiserate with! Someone to cheer him on and bury his bodies and make the city shake at the simple thought of her!"

"A . . . partner?"

"Yes!"

Laura recoiled. "He wants me to be a *partner*?"

She'd thought he just wanted another tool, but the woman's description sounded far more like an ally or confidant; a willing participant who would have power in the mob regime. It didn't fit in Laura's mind at all.

The woman's eyes flashed. Laura gave an undignified squeak as her chair jolted backward. The stranger kept it on a precarious two-legged balance even as she pressed a gun barrel to the underside of Laura's jaw.

"You think you have any right to demand that?" the woman snarled. "You little—"

"Minnie!"

Someone heaved the woman back with such force she staggered. Laura's chair crashed back to all four legs, and Laura hissed at the treatment. The newcomer—presumably Blanche—shoved Minnie further back so she bumped into the vehicle's grille.

"What do you think you're doing?" she spat.

Minnie's posture sagged and she kicked the ground like a petulant child. "The captive got mouthy."

"Our *guest*," Blanche corrected. "And was she mouthy or just confused?"

Minnie didn't answer. Blanche clicked her tongue and looked at Laura. She had a massive burn over the left side of her face and appeared to be missing that eye as well; side by side with Minnie, it looked like an echo of the Mad Dog tattoo. Did people go that far to remove ink?

"Are you aware of why you're here?" said Blanche.

"An ultimatum, apparently, without your boss's permission," said Laura.

"That's right." Now that Blanche focused on Laura, she . . . wasn't very focused. She was far more interested in locating and pulling something slowly out of her pocket. "If the boss were to learn about this—which he won't, because you're smart enough not to go tattling on mobsters, aren't you, Kramer?—he would be very upset.

"He has preferred tactics when it comes to Sinclairs. The problem with those tactics is that they work very well on new apprentices, but if you use them on the head Sweeper, it's like talking to a wall. The boss spent over a decade trying to recruit Clae Sinclair, with no result. He took Sinclair's refusal, and didn't punish him for it. He was too sentimental.

"I don't know that you understand how mobs work, Kramer, but allowing someone to disrespect us without consequences was very bad for the Mad Dogs. We lost confidence. We lost respect. We lost power. Since Sinclair's death our boss and the mob's reputation has been recovering quickly, but you . . ." She pulled hard on Laura's hair, forcing Laura to look up. "You're the same stock as Clae Sinclair, and for whatever reason, the boss has decided he needs that. He will continue to approach you, and he'll continue to let you go as long as you say no. The rest of us may have let that slide with Sinclair, but we know better now. Say no, and you will face consequences."

The object she'd withdrawn from her coat was a large pocketknife. She eased the blade out with delicate fingers, and its sharp edge glinted under the headlights. "Haru Yamanaka has tried the standard peaceful negotiations, but it's becoming obvious that won't work on you. Tonight, we decided to give you a taste of the alternative. Some people act brave and say we can't break them, but we're creative. If you won't break, your friends and family will. What's your aunt's name again? Morgan? And there's that little cousin named Cheryl."

Laura gritted her teeth, furious and suddenly afraid. Blanche cracked a smile at the reaction.

"We could go for your coworkers, too," she purred, running a finger over the flat of the knife blade. "From what I hear, that Okane gives up *fast* under a knife."

"You touch a hair on his head and I'll—"

"You'll what, Kramer? You're powerless here."

Laura shook with rage. "Do you only talk big when you can't get hit for it?" she snapped.

"Told you she was mouthy," said Minnie.

"It's all part of the process," said Blanche, watching Laura with an unblinking eye. "Rage and rage, little Sweeper. We're bigger than you. Anything you try will be given back tenfold. Now that you understand your position, know this: Yamanaka will try making you one more offer, and only one. You'd best accept it."

"Kill her," said Minnie.

Blanche whirled on her. "Convincing her to join us was the entire point of this!"

"I'd rather kill her than work with her!"

"The boss wants—"

"Renard can do better!"

Blanche marched so close they were nose-to-nose, and her voice dipped dangerously low. "Don't you dare try putting words in the boss's mouth. You know he wants every Sinclair we can get, and the head Sweeper sways all of them. You don't get to decree what his wishes are or that he can do better, especially when your own interests go against it. Until we hear it from Renard himself, we are recruiting them. If you interfere we will remove you as an obstacle. You don't get special treatment just because he saved you once."

That last sentence was barely audible. Minnie scowled and averted her gaze; Blanche clearly held the power here.

"Then at least let me knock her around a little. You can't have a kidnapping without a little tough love."

"Today is a warning, not a punishment."

"But—"

"Would you like to tell the boss tomorrow why his person of interest is bloody and bruised?"

"If I hit her around the chest, nobody will see it under her clothes," Minnie said slyly.

Laura doubted Minnie would do anything but beat her to a pulp, and thankfully Blanche knew it just as well. Blanche rolled her eye. "Minnie, I would sooner trust you with kittens."

"So I can—"

"*No*, Minnie." Blanche looked back and said, "Will you be joining us, head Sweeper?"

Laura almost gave an incredulous laugh. "One of you wants to kill me for holding out, and the other wants to kill me if I join. I'm not seeing a winning option here. I'll just wait for Haru."

"Then you'll be waiting awhile," said Blanche. She flipped her knife closed and gestured with it; Minnie sulked back into the vehicle. "Remember, you only have one more chance. After that, we'll be just as much at war with you as we are with the Silver Kings."

"Wait." Laura wiggled as she realized Blanche was retreating too. "Hey! Aren't you going to untie me?"

"I did say you'd be waiting awhile," Blanche drawled.

She slammed the door behind her and the engine revved. The vehicle reeled back, turned, and roared off into the night. Laura tipped her head back against the chair's metal and groaned. A dark clouded sky spread overhead, tinged by the glow of other Quarters even while no lights shone in any of the buildings around her. If she judged these shabby houses right, she'd been dumped in a random alley in the abandoned Ranger district. With the usual residents evicted, it would be morning before anyone ventured here. She didn't know if anyone would come at all.

Frustration welled up in her throat and her eyes stung.

Okay, she thought, *what would Clae do in this situation?*

He'd be free from this damn chair already. Laura tested her ties, but her wrists and ankles were bound fast; she couldn't do more than wriggle.

"Perfect," she spat, twisting her arms as if will alone could snap rope. "I get my ass handed to me this morning, kidnapped this evening. That's just more of the same these days!"

She kept struggling, but no one was there to hear or help her. Her breath started to rasp. She wished more than anything that Clae were here. Her being here in this chair felt like the crowning of all her failures.

Clae wouldn't have let Amicae get away from him.

He wouldn't have allowed this distrust of Sweepers to take root.

He wouldn't have been bullied by the mobs.

He wouldn't let his recruits get anything less than their due, and he would've made them feel protected.

He'd be that Magi grounding for Okane that Laura couldn't be.

He'd know what to do.

Something crashed in the distance. Laura jolted out of her self-loathing and listened. Another crash came closer, followed by barking. She knew packs of wild dogs roamed the lower Quarters, but this was the last place she wanted to witness them. The noise came from barely a block away. She redoubled her efforts to get free. Something moved at the alley's entrance, but—

"Laura Kramer?" A lantern rose, showing not a dog approaching, but a woman with braided black hair and a wide-brimmed Ranger hat hanging down her back.

Laura stared. "Cherry? But how—"

Cherry cupped her face, looked into her eyes, and said seriously, "Who hurt you?"

Only then did Laura realize she'd been crying. "I—No, they didn't— Well, they kicked me once, but this is just because I got really frustrated."

Some of Cherry's worry drained, but now she mostly looked angry. "Good. Otherwise I'd have to teach somebody a lesson. Not that I'm not tempted already. Who kidnapped you?"

"How did you even know I'd been kidnapped?"

"Just look at you! I may not have any warning here, but it's not hard to put two and two together." Cherry deposited the lantern and set to Laura's bindings with a knife. "Since this district's been emptied, mobsters have been using it as a base for their goddamn kidnappings. I came down to look for some supplies at our old haunts, and knew one must be happening when I saw the automobile go past. I never thought you'd be involved! Those Mad Dogs are going to lose their minds when they find out someone laid a hand on you."

Laura gave a short, humorless laugh. "They're the ones who kidnapped me."

Cherry groaned. "Why is my instinct so *off* when it comes to you? I didn't notice your last head Sweeper was crazy, and I was so sure the Mad Dogs wanted to win you over the nice way! I don't even have the excuse that I'd never met them, because I'm a bouncer at Toulouse. I see those bastards all the time."

"Technically it didn't sound like their boss sanctioned it, but—"

"Oho, then vengeance is just around the corner. I'll drop a few hints at work, and their boss can skin the bastards alive."

"I'm pretty sure they threatened to murder me if I tattled in any way."

"Then I won't say I heard it from you. Maybe I just saw you stumbling out of the Ranger district and came to my own conclusions."

"But—"

"Don't worry, Laura. I know my way around a rumor mill. I'm not about to drop any information unless I know it's going to be beneficial. Now come on. Let's get you out of here."

Laura's hands came free. She winced as she rubbed her rope-burned wrists and followed Cherry a few blocks away, to another vehicle. As Cherry drove her out of the abandoned district, Laura pulled out her pocket watch. The clock face read 7:51 P.M. Cheryl and Morgan would be worried sick. Cherry was silent the whole drive, a contemplative expression on her face, and when they reached the Cynder Block she sent Laura a wan smile.

"Hope you don't mind if I walk you to the door."

Honestly, it was a relief. The two of them walked up side by side in silence. No one waited to delay them on the stairs, the halls were as bright as always, and Laura could hear the murmuring of neighbors through the thin walls. It was all normal, but Laura couldn't shake her restlessness. They paused in front of her apartment. Cherry knew very well where they were—she'd been here before—but she remained silent even when Laura didn't move to open the door.

"The Mad Dogs knew their names," said Laura. "The two that kidnapped me, they talked about using a knife on Okane in the same breath.

And before I met you, a different mobster showed up right here to threaten me. They know exactly where to find my family. This place isn't safe."

Cherry laid a steady hand on Laura's shoulder. "Can you talk to your police chief? Maybe they can assign some guards for your family the way they did for your new recruits."

"But this . . . It's the Cynder Block, Cherry. You can trip and fall through to the next apartment here. I wouldn't call this place secure in a million years. Even if we had police watching over us," and she shuddered at the thought, knowing how their current escorts treated the Rexians, "they couldn't lock this place down."

"Then maybe you should stay with us," said Cherry. "Weaver Mateo's letting us stay in the rectory with him. There's plenty of open rooms."

"I don't think that will—"

"You don't think that's enough protection? The two best headhunters in Terual, *and* a priest? I told you before, nobody messes with mourners and priests. No mobsters would touch you at that place."

"You have too much faith in mobster ethics."

"Well, even if they did throw away morality and attack, I'd be there to put a bullet between their eyes. You can get a police guard on top of our protection. Our place is definitely easier to secure than here."

Laura shook her head, tempted but disbelieving. "Good luck convincing my aunt to move. She'll take familiarity over safety any day."

"We'll see about that," said Cherry. Since Laura didn't seem interested in moving, she turned the handle and opened the door to call, "Hello!"

"Hello? I'm coming! I'm coming!" Morgan hurried into the apartment's entryway to meet them, and perked up at the sight. "Laura! And Miss Cherry? Welcome back! Cheryl's been dying to talk to you again, something about horses . . . Would you like some food? I saved some dinner for Laura, but there's more than enough."

"I ate with Grim, but thanks," Cherry laughed as they were ushered inside and the door closed again. "I would like to ask you for something else, though. Just to consider something for me."

Wow. That was fast. Laura stared at Cherry, impressed and skeptical about the lack of lead-up.

"Oh? What's that?" said Morgan.

"With the mobs getting more active, I'm worrying about you," said Cherry. "There's not much to stop mobsters from causing trouble around here. Besides that, weren't people convinced Laura was a Mad Dog for a while? If that's still the case, you might even have to worry about how your neighbors will react."

Morgan's smile dimmed. "Charlie *has* kept spreading rumors. The neighbors know us better than that, but . . . well . . ."

But she was still the angelina on the floor, and for all her kindness she'd never won over the neighbors' love or loyalty.

Cherry nodded, sympathetic. "I'm not asking you to decide anything now, just to consider a temporary change. Do you remember the priest who came with me when we first met? Weaver Mateo? He's got a nice little guesthouse for visiting priests. Since there's not much intercity travel right now it's sitting empty, so he let me and Grim stay there without charge. There's enough room for more people. It might be a little crowded, but you'd be there with friends. I'd definitely rest easier if I can check in on you every day."

"That's very kind of you, but we can't possibly—" A loud thud interrupted them, and Morgan winced. "Cheryl, no throwing balls in the apartment, you can practice for sports tryouts at the park tomorrow! I'll consider it, Cherry. Really, though, wouldn't you like something to eat? You can't refuse a professional cook without offending her."

Cherry laughed. "Don't tempt me! Maybe a little food. Just a little. And I'm sorry, but could I sleep on your couch for the night? They're repainting the guesthouse, so—"

"Of course!" Morgan cheered. "Cheryl, come here and help me find the spare blankets."

Cheryl popped her head out of the other room and said seriously, "The Sylph Canal?"

The canal felt like forever ago. Laura gave her a thumbs-up. "Cleared."

Cheryl flashed a smile, said, "Of course it is," then hurried after Morgan to locate the elusive spare pillow.

Laura led the way to the table, where the leftover food sat cool but ready. It was set up for a single person, but Laura pulled out a plate and utensils for their guest.

"I can't believe Morgan even agreed to think about leaving," Laura said as she sat. "I thought she'd shut it down right away. Either you're a real smooth talker, or she really likes you."

Or the situation at home was much worse than Laura thought, which she really hoped wasn't the case.

"Maybe it's both," said Cherry. "Can they still hear us?"

"No. Why?"

"I had another question for you." Cherry was quiet for a while, picking at her own nails for a moment before apparently resolving herself and leaning across the table. "Leave Amicae with me."

Laura had been ladling out food, but the spoonful plunked right back down into the dish as she gaped at Cherry. "What?"

"Leave Amicae," Cherry repeated. "You know what's going on outside these walls, right? Abandoned rails, Sweeper retreats—"

"Of course I know about the backlash. I'm the head Sweeper," said Laura. "I've been in contact with all the neighboring Sweeper guilds. I know where the spikes have hit hardest, but around here? Between us and Gaudium, we've got an infestation drought. That gives us time to fortify, not reason to run."

Cherry glanced back, as if expecting Morgan and Cheryl to return any minute. "The Rangers in Terual are going to Ruhaile."

Rangers made their home in the wilds for years on end, facing dangerous animals, infestations, and other violent human competitors, with hardly a batted eye. For them to leave the area around Amicae, let alone the entire country of Terual, something must've gone very wrong.

"What do you know that I don't?" said Laura.

"Something's happened in the south," said Cherry.

"Yes, you just said, the railroads—"

"Something *big*," said Cherry. "It happened almost two weeks ago, but we haven't been able to get any details on it because ERA's cutting us off now, too. I thought they were just rumors from some picky Rangers, but I checked in with the train depot. For two weeks, ERA's been rerouting all south and westbound trains away from Amicae. It's not an official announcement, but the trains just aren't coming in. It's not just in Zyra. This danger is close, and Amicae's defenses are already rotted. Talk all you want about how you haven't seen a lot of infestations recently, but here's the thing: when the ocean goes away, you don't go looking to see where it went, you run as far as you can and get to higher ground. What's normal and usual vanishing—that's the first sign of a tsunami. Maybe the monster levels are down right now, but they're going to come back fast and hard. You got lucky with that Wrath of God stunt, but you don't have a good shot now. You could be the most talented Sweeper in history, but you're one person. You can only be in one place."

"No." Laura's voice climbed. "You can't just tell me to leave! You can't just tell me to let Amicae die!"

Cherry scowled and leaned further, hissing, "It'll die even if you stay!"

"But I can't—"

"Clae wouldn't want you to stay."

Laura reeled back in surprise. "You . . . you knew Clae?"

"No," Cherry said bluntly, "but you *do not* shut up about him. Think about that man. Think of how he died, and ask yourself if he wanted you to share that same fate."

It was silly, but Laura felt a little cheated. She scowled. "He wanted me to learn by example. Clae Sinclair knew the world was against him every day, and he never gave up on it. Any shit he got he gave back twice over, and he kept this city afloat alone for over a decade. If he could hold out that long, I can hold out until the end of this spike."

"Even if you're facing the hive mind?" Cherry challenged.

"Don't try to scare me with—"

"Believe me, I *want* to scare you, but I'm not going to lie to achieve that. There really are rumors that it left the bottom island."

Laura's blood went cold. "That can't be. It's been five hundred years. It can't cross water. It can't have moved."

"Rex uses boats to reach Kuro no Oukoku," said Cherry. "Not all of them die in the crusade. Some officers return for reports. And even beyond that, if an infestation is smart enough to turn weapons against Sweepers, why can't it be smart enough to push a boat offshore and float?" She closed her eyes in pained resignation. "The Rangers, we talk a lot. I'm one of the few that's managed to stay in Amicae, so I'm the connecting point for a huge amount of information. We have our own records. We know the wilds. And things *aren't normal*. The infestations are gathering strategically. Normally they all derive what they want from the hive mind and go their separate ways, but what we've seen in the last few weeks are exclusively swarms. They're traveling in recognizable patterns, like pieces on a chessboard instead of their typical chaos. They're strong. They're fast. They talk."

Laura cocked her head to the side. "Talk?"

"Phantom talk," Cherry clarified. "The old stories tell how the hive could speak with select people, while others couldn't hear it. A pack of Rangers near Vir experienced it—half of them heard something talking, the other half didn't, and then a swarm swept in that ate all but three of them."

"That doesn't mean anything," said Laura. It couldn't mean anything. "I heard something like that myself, today."

Cherry looked at her with horror. "You did?"

"Yes, but it wasn't—" The false whispering in the Sylph Canal hadn't been caused by an amulet like the liminal rooms. Laura had doubted it, but Okane had confirmed that the sounds had all come from the infestation itself. *I feel like it's shouting at us. A deficit of shouting? It's doing something magical, and I don't like it.* "It wasn't actually talking. Infestations scream and make noises all the time. This one just figured out how to mimic talking noises, but it was incomprehensible."

"How do you know it wasn't just a language you didn't understand?" Cherry asked quietly.

"It wasn't," Laura insisted. "Look, I'm new to the experience, but I know exactly what happened to those Rangers who heard something talking. They had a magical overdose. People who are sensitive to magic get affected easily, and experience a different depth to whatever spell is being cast. I experienced it in Toulouse already. You've been there, so you should understand—"

"But this wasn't Club Toulouse. It was the wilds outside Vir. There were no amulets. What spell was being cast on them? Where did it come from?"

"They may have heard the infestation's . . . existence. Its digestion. Something."

"You don't actually know, though."

Laura set her jaw. "It wasn't the hive mind. And even if the hive mind does come to visit, I'll exterminate it. I won't abandon my home."

And she wouldn't. She was sure this hive mind rumor was a bluff. The idea of facing the original infestation terrified any Sweeper with half a mind, but even if she knew the beast was truly knocking at the door, she'd stay put. Amicae was her world. She wouldn't abandon all these people. She wouldn't abandon what she and the Sinclairs had fought so hard for.

Cherry eyed her a while longer before sighing and leaning back in her chair. "Both you and Grim," she grumbled. "You're both idiots."

"Grim? What's he done?"

"He's set on defending this stupid city to the death." Cherry rubbed ruefully at the back of her neck. "All my instincts are telling me to run, and call me cruel, I don't care about this city . . . but I can't leave behind the people I do care about. I was hoping if I could convince you I'd get all the others in one fell swoop. I should've known better."

Morgan and Cheryl bustled back into the main room, and this noise saved Laura from having to form any response. Cherry smiled at them and complimented the food she hadn't even eaten, but there was a strain to her expression that made Laura's stomach twist.

Leaving was never a possibility, she reminded herself.

But what had happened in the south?

Why hadn't Gaudium warned her of anything?

When Laura slept that night she dreamed of the phantom Sweeper shop, just as she had under the amulet's influence: windows black, Kin steaming and bubbling on the unblemished counter. She knew this didn't exist in reality, but she'd never felt such clarity in a dream before. Clae was there, of course. He sat on a stool, bent over the counter to rest his head on crossed arms. Laura couldn't see his face, but she knew he was listening.

"And then she asked me to leave! She knew how far I've gone in the past for this stinking city! How could she think she could possibly convince me to leave everything behind?"

Clae said nothing. He'd said nothing throughout the story of Laura's day, but still, he listened.

"But what if something has really gone wrong, and I made the wrong decision? What if I can't do anything? What if Amicae gets destroyed, and Morgan and Cheryl die, and it's my fault for not listening and getting them out when I could?" She looked at Clae. "You got through this kind of danger before, didn't you? Is it possible for me, too?"

Clae shifted his head just enough that she could glimpse one eye. "Is it possible?" he said, in Laura's own voice.

Laura crossed her arms and glared. "I'm asking you."

"I'm asking you," he replied, again in perfect mimicry.

"I'm not the one with the answers!" said Laura.

"I'm not the one with the answers!"

"Ugh."

Laura sat heavily on the stool across from his and laid her own head on the counter. The texture mocked her. Not cool, not glassy; this dream had conjured only the idea of an obstacle and tricked her brain into supplying the rest, just like a stubborn amulet. As she stared listlessly at the countertop it faded in and out with her belief. It wasn't really there, but she wanted it to be so badly.

"I wish you were actually here," she murmured.

She reached out one hand and set it on Clae's head. This time, it didn't fade out under scrutiny. That was definitely hair. Her grip tightened on instinct and she looked up in alarm. Clae's eyes narrowed in annoyance, but he didn't shrug off her grip. Their surroundings wavered. He didn't.

"Are you actually here?" she whispered.

"Are you actually here?" her voice echoed back.

They held eye contact for a long, tense minute. The irritation gradually drained from Clae's expression.

"I'm lost," she admitted. "I can't tell if this is a nightmare about reflections or if I'm talking to Clae Sinclair. And don't repeat what I'm saying."

Clae had opened his mouth, and now closed it with a sour expression.

"Do you have any words of your own?" said Laura.

"Not her," said Clae.

This time she definitely heard his voice. It stirred the fake steam above them like a breeze.

"What does that mean?" said Laura.

"Not—" Clae raised a hand and set it on Laura's head, mimicking again but too warm to be a dream. "—her."

Her memory sparked. Like an amulet, he drew flashes of images and sounds, scents, emotion.

She remembered the pictures of Sinclairs from Clae's wake. Impossibly, she remembered chasing a laughing twin and crashing straight into Rosemarie's skirts when Anselm took a corner too fast. She remembered Helen Blair making lasagna in a tattered apron and filling their home with off-key humming. She remembered Martin Sinclair's crooked smile. And then she remembered losing all of them. The stink of the Sylph Canal and gold crystal under small hands. An awful Partch mattress stripped of sheets and occupant after sickness. Nightmares of a train pulling away from the station despite wailing for it to stop. A tired father leaving home one morning, only for police to return with *I'm so sorry but*—She remembered apprentices, too: injured or dead but forever out of reach. She saw Amelia laughing before her injuries; a much-younger Renard stealing amulets; Okane fresh out of the Sullivan house but finally safe enough to break down *hard*.

And then she saw herself.

"Not her," said Clae.

Not her, too, whispered the magic behind it. *I won't lose her, too.*

When Clae died, he hadn't been angry at his own fate. Afraid, yes.

Desperate, yes. But he'd met the same end as countless others he'd known, and a fate he'd tempted all his life. What made him angry was remembering the apprentices he'd left behind—both inexperienced, one scared of everything and the other too reckless. Laura had chased him into a felin's jaws once before; she could easily try again, and then she'd be dead like everyone else.

Not her, too, he'd thought. *I won't let either of them die!*

And that became his mantra.

Not her too.

Not her too.

"Not her," Clae said quietly.

6

CRACKED PIPES

On the morning of March 31, Laura went straight to police headquarters rather than the shop. She went with her jaw set and her back straight, and tried to add extra steel to her voice when she arrived at the front desk and said, "I'm looking for Chief Albright."

"Ah," said the elderly receptionist with the massive glasses, far too casually considering the fearsome look Laura was trying to pull off. "The chief's expecting you."

Maybe someone had witnessed Laura talking to the Mad Dogs boss after all. The idea made her queasy, but it should be easier to talk to Albright if she already had some idea of the situation, right? If she were in real trouble, she'd be led in here in handcuffs, or at least be given a stink eye from the officers present. Laura took the familiar route down the hallway to the back office, mentally telling herself to be calm with every step. So what if she was about to admit to lying over the phone yesterday? She was going to be up-front now! She'd follow any orders Albright had, even if that meant getting a Mr. Dour assigned to herself, too. It would be okay.

Albright was smart. Albright would understand.

Chief Albright sat at her desk, pen in one hand and head supported by the other as she studied a heavily notated map of the city. She glanced up, and once she realized just who stood in the doorway, she drew herself back up to her usual height. The movement was unsteady, and drastic bags pulled under her eyes. Laura was stunned speechless for a moment. It had only been a week and a half, and it looked as if Albright had aged years under sheer stress.

"Oh my god. Are you okay?" said Laura.

"You don't have to worry about me," said Albright, blatantly not answering the question. "Come in. I know why you're here."

"Oh. That's . . . good to hear."

Laura edged closer and sank into the chair before the desk as Albright opened a drawer. She slid three cards across the map. Laura blinked down at them, and found Zelda's visage looking back. It was an ID card, with only one star. Wait. Was this . . . She slid Zelda's card aside, and found matching IDs for Ivo and Bea. Huh. She hadn't expected these for a month, at least.

"But this isn't—"

Albright held up a hand. "I won't hear any arguments about the clearance levels of their stars."

"That's not what I was going to say, but that is a good point," said Laura.

"I am willing to be flexible, but not too flexible," said Albright. She pointed at the IDs with a frown. "Tell me, are you sure about these people? Absolutely sure?"

"Of course," said Laura. "I've trusted them with my life."

Albright's brow stayed furrowed as if she was warring with something, and then she said, "I'm taking away your escort."

"What?" said Laura, flabbergasted.

"The tracking devices will remain, as will their limited number of stars," Albright continued. "I may be deferring to your trust at this point, but I'm not letting them run wherever they please without some form of supervision. At any other time I'd want to keep the physical guard on you, but your recruits have behaved so far, and the mobster affairs . . ." Her brow furrowed even more, not in her usual anger, but in genuine worry. "They are getting out of hand quickly. I need all the people I can get for this."

Laura fisted her hands to hide her nerves. "Are the mobs making a move?"

Albright hesitated. She stood jerkily from her seat and made for the door.

"Oh. Um, I can get that if you—"

"I am not fragile, Laura." Albright peered through her window to make sure no one was around outside, drew down the blinds of her office so no one could see in, and locked the door. Only then did she return to her chair, and she fell into it like an old woman. "This isn't information to be shared with the public."

"I understand," Laura murmured.

"To the public eye it looks as if the Mad Dogs and other mobs have been lying comparatively low, but that is not the case. They've been going for stealth rather than showmanship. While we have been able to catch certain movements, we're not able to paint the whole picture. I told you before that the Mad Dogs were pressuring smaller mobs to take sides; with loyalties established, they appeared to be drawing more drastic battle lines between themselves and the Silver Kings. Byron previously predicted that they would go from scattered hits to street warfare in weeks, maybe days. But those predictions have shifted drastically. They appear to be shuffling their hands. The strongholds they'd formed for the inter-mob fighting have been emptied."

Laura frowned, wary. "How long ago did the predictions shift?"

"Yesterday. I'm aware this is a very short amount of time, but since yesterday morning none of the mobs have been operating within expectations."

The investigation that finished this morning tells us that there will be significant changes: very fast, and very relevant to our interests. It must have to do with whoever the Mad Dogs had pulled in from the wilds. Whoever they were, they'd given Renard some very important news. Stranger still, he must've shared it even with opposing mobs like the Silver Kings. *We need multiple options in place to ensure we can close on the best opportunity.* He'd determined the route of mob warfare to be inconvenient. What kind of news could avert a crisis that had been building up for months?

Albright was too tired or too focused on her own words to notice Laura's worry. "We don't know what their new objective is yet, but you shouldn't concern yourself with it. As Sweepers you should be safe. The Mad Dogs and Silver Kings both want you alive and working. If there are any changes in the political landscape, I'll give you forewarning so you can stay out of trouble."

Safe? After Renard killed that policeman in front of them, and Minnie and Blanche kidnapped her? Laura almost wanted to laugh. Instead, she asked, "Did something trigger this? There were a lot of police running around yesterday, and a lot of Mad Dogs besides. I heard something about people coming in from the wilds?"

Albright laced her fingers together, eyes narrowing. "That is correct."

"So maybe those outsiders said something to them?"

"They weren't outsiders. They were also Mad Dogs."

Laura blinked in surprise. "Wait. So . . . the Mad Dogs have put together a Ranger squad?"

"Considering they carried mostly Sweeper equipment, they'd be badly suited for real deployment in the wilds," said Albright. "From what we gathered, the Mad Dogs sent this group into the wilds sometime about a week ago, so we can't believe that an outside force is manipulating them—this is wholly a Mad Dogs operation."

"What were they sent for?"

"Clarification, likely." Albright frowned deeper. "There's some kind of news from the south."

"Ranger rumors? I've heard those already," Laura sighed, irritated. "Closed rails, disappearances, talking infestations—"

"Talking?" Albright considered a moment before shaking her head. "This isn't a rumor, and it's not from Rangers. The news reached me on official lines. ERA made the initial report, but Coronae's taken over authority on the matter, and they're now limiting the spread of related information."

"Coronae? The *capital* took control?" Laura gasped. "When's the last time they enforced regulations?"

"Thrax."

Laura sank back against her seat in horror. "Is Rex coming north? The crusade should've—"

"We don't know anything solid," said Albright. "We know an incident has occurred in southern Terual. The Mad Dogs appear to know more than we do. Byron reports that they keep saying they 'won't let that happen here.' Until Coronae releases its hold on the information, we're in the dark about the mobs' motives. Even if we weren't, they're mobs. Even pure motives get twisted with them. The guards I'm removing from your detail will assist in patrolling the Fourth Quarter districts where the Mad Dogs have settled. If we can prevent the violence from happening at all . . ."

She looked tiredly down at the map. Laura twisted her hands. She'd come to admit she'd talked to Renard and to ask for more protection, but what would that accomplish? Albright already knew that the Mad Dogs were changing tactics, and Laura had learned nothing beyond what she'd already known, so the report would only cast herself further from trust. Asking for more guards would only take bodies away from the real issue.

This way, Albright could stop the mobs before they interfered with Sweepers at all. This way, Zelda and the others didn't have to feel so imprisoned. Cherry had already offered Ranger protection, and a safer place for the family, hadn't she? That would work. It had to work.

So Laura forced a smile, and said nothing about yesterday. "We'll be fine without the guard."

"Good. I'll have them brought back right away," said Albright. "In the meantime, if you notice anything strange, tell me."

"Right," said Laura, and didn't.

She left the police headquarters feeling almost dizzy. That hadn't gone the way she expected at all. Had she done the right thing? She didn't know. The new IDs weighed heavy in her pocket. The lack of clearance was annoying, but workable; so long as the Rexians teamed up with either Okane or herself, then their higher star clearance would allow anyone in the group to pass anywhere they needed. It was more the principle of the thing that stung.

While she wandered back toward the trolley stop, heavy with stress, she noticed a large yellow sign: COMMERCIAL TELEGRAPH SERVICE. Of course there would be a telegraph office near the police. Laura almost ran inside. She had to wait behind a suited man for several minutes while he argued with the clerk over pricing of his own message. Laura bounced anxiously on the balls of her feet, craning her neck for any sign of another clerk, but it seemed there was only the one. Much angst, wringing of hands, and exchanged argents later, the suited man stormed back outside. The clerk already looked worn, but he took a deep breath to fortify himself and said politely, "Hello and good morning, ma'am. Are you here to send a telegram?"

"I am," Laura said firmly, stepping up to the desk. "I need to send something to Gaudium."

"Gaudium," the clerk murmured, pulling out a form. He turned it so Laura could read it all properly and pointed to the sections with his pen. "Don't worry about the information in the upper left. That's the details for the sending and receiving offices, nothing to do with yourself or the recipient proper. If you want the recipient to be able to reply to you, please write your address here and we'll deliver any response to you. Their own address should go here. Be sure it's clear and complete, especially with another city—it's easy for them to get all turned around, and you don't want it reported as undeliverable. The last box here is where you write the contents of the telegram. You pay the fee of ten words even if you only write one, and any word you add over ten has a by-word charge."

Laura took the offered pen and set to work. She'd written so many letters to Gaudium's head Sweeper she knew the address by heart, and within a few minutes she'd slid the following message back to him:

TWO INFESTATIONS FOUND STOP HAVE NOT RECEIVED
YOUR LETTERS STOP PLEASE ADVISE ON SITUATION IN
SOUTH STOP PLEASE RESPOND QUICKLY

The clerk reviewed it, brow furrowing. Laura half expected him to comment on the odd contents, but he simply set the page back down and said,
"That's seventeen words total. As for your fee . . ."

Laura handed over the argents; she'd heard enough during the suited
man's argument to know exactly the fee, and had calculated it for her message while still in line. "How long should this take to arrive?"

"A telegram can travel the length of Orien in a single day," said the clerk.
"With something as close as Gaudium, your recipient may even have it
within the hour. It really depends on their delivery service."

Good. If the trains were really being held up down south, then Gaudium's head Sweeper might be sending letters without any knowledge that
Laura wasn't receiving them; she might even be getting antsy the way Laura
was now. Had Ellie ever seen Laura's response? She hoped that it hadn't
gotten lost somewhere. In any case, the head Sweeper was always quick to
answer anything, so Laura should have an update tomorrow or the next day
at the very least.

Laura thanked the clerk and left the office feeling a little bit more put-
together. She had more things to work on today.

It didn't take much to pressure Morgan into leaving the Cynder Block.
If Laura weren't so relieved, she might be concerned; for Morgan to be so
willing to even temporarily leave her home of fifteen years, those rumors
Charlie spread must've been really damaging. Okane, Grim, Cherry, and
Mateo all showed up to help move the most important possessions out of
the Chandler-Kramer apartment. This was made still easier with Cherry's
automobile, which saved them multiple trolley trips. While Mateo apolo-
gized for the lack of space in the rectory guesthouse (Laura planned to
store any overflow in the armory), Okane approached Grim about magical
experimentation. She didn't know what they said, but Grim listened and
nodded, and Okane straightened with excitement. It must've ended well.

It would've *been* well, if they hadn't decided to blow everyone off for the
next few days.

On Wednesday, Cherry caught her as she was leaving to say Okane was
with Grim and might be late to work. He didn't show up at all. On Thurs-
day, Cherry said the same. On Friday, Laura was ready to pull out her hair

because she didn't like dealing with the Rexians alone, and in all their bare year of acquaintance she'd never gone so long without seeing Okane. He was gone before the shop opened, returned long after everyone left, and didn't even leave a note. She shouldn't be worried—he was with Grim, after all, and Cherry saw Grim at work to confirm that yes, he'd been with Okane, and yes, Okane was perfectly fine.

She almost wished he weren't fine. That would at least be an excuse.

"Trouble in paradise," Zelda sang on Tuesday.

Laura scowled at her over the latest *Dead Ringer*. "That's not accurate."

"No, I suppose that implies Amicae was a paradise to start with, doesn't it?" Zelda hummed.

"So - - - admit to its flaws," said Bea.

Zelda rolled her eyes as her own complaint was thrown back at her. "It might be a paradise if *someone* would stop doing all her noisy workouts in the middle of the night!"

Bea sniffed in disdain. "Someone will be caught unprepared here, and it will not be me."

Ivo looked tempted to bang his sleep-deprived head against the counter.

The rattle of the mail slot caught their attention. Laura perked up as quick as a dog. She threw aside the *Dead Ringer* and hurried to snatch up the envelopes.

Letter from Terrae, letter from Laus, letter from Aevum. Nothing from Gaudium. She threw the door open and cried, "Wait!"

The mailman stopped on the pawnshop's steps. "Yes, ma'am? Did you have a letter to send?"

"No, I just wanted to check with you. Are you sure there aren't any letters for me from Gaudium? Not even a telegram? I've been sending messages for weeks, but no one's gotten back to me."

"It's not just you," said the mailman. "There's no mail from Gaudium at all."

Laura's grip tightened on the other envelopes. "What do you mean, no mail?"

"It's all the trains," he sighed, shaking his head. "There was some kind of accident on the lines, I think. All the mail going to Gaudium is piling up while we wait for the go-ahead that everything's resolved, but until that's fixed, nothing goes, and nothing's able to come in."

"What about telegrams?"

"I'm afraid I don't know enough to say, but telegraph lines are close to the rails. If there was a train accident, it might've taken out the telegraph wires."

"Right," Laura said dully. "Train accident."

"It's reached such a state that I hear rumors about the Mad Dogs crossing the bay for mail. That's a laugh, eh?" The mailman tipped his hat. "I'm sure it'll be solved soon. Have a good day, ma'am."

Laura stayed there on the stoop, dejected. She'd counted on Gaudium's reply a week ago. This didn't make any sense. Wouldn't ERA be quick to fix anything in such a charged atmosphere? The cities couldn't afford communication or train routes failing with the spike happening. Was something bigger happening down south than she was aware of? Communication still held down there, because even the *Dead Ringer* had published something up-to-date about Vir's upcoming election and Canis's continued relief efforts for cities beyond Rex.

Gaudium, Okane, and the mobs. Laura wanted to scream. She felt stagnant and useless. She had to do something.

"You know what? That's enough." She strode back into the shop and threw the envelopes onto the counter unread. "If Okane's going to skip, we'll move on without him! Come on, there are places I haven't shown you yet."

"Didn't - - - say this and the armory were the only Sweeper locations?" said Zelda.

"The only Sinclair locations," Laura corrected. "We have Amuletories for recycling. I'm going to show you which you can use and which are traps."

Laura decided to start high and work their way down. The First Quarter had the highest percentage of amulet users out of all the Quarters, but it also had limited space and a lot of snobs, so maintenance businesses like Amuletories crowded the Second Quarter. Laura led them to multiple storefronts, offering Clae's original recommendations and her own observations: this one only treated you as well as you looked; this one was a front for the Blackwater mob; this one had an employee who wouldn't take your amulets until she'd talked your ear off about her side business selling vacuum cleaners.

They were taking the main circuit to reach one of the larger Amuletories when a commotion caught their attention. A large crowd had gathered, some milling in the street while others strolled in and out through the gates of Amicae's Grand University.

Many levels tall and built of dark stone, the Grand University didn't look like the smaller, blocky colleges and universities Amicae had to offer; it deserved the "grand" in its name. If anything, it looked like a stripped-down version of the official Council building of the First Quarter. Its center section bore a dome at every corner, framing what had once been a central rotunda but now served only as a staggered plinth for the statue of Queen Terual IV in a racing chariot. The building continued with wings on either side, descending into grand hallways and sloping roofs before jutting back up again with dome after dome, and its wings thrust forward at the end to wrap about the edge of its massive plaza. Its many windows and soaring arches made it seem even bigger. It was beautiful and imposing and far too large to only contain a school. Its northern wing was dedicated to a museum, one of the finest in the city. Laura had once visited it and seen a complete miniature model of the ruins of Thrax in its upper galleries. The museum had always been a draw, but a banner on the surrounding fence declared the entire building free and open to the public today for a technology fair. Laura's steps slowed.

Once upon a time, she'd desperately wanted to go here. During school recruitments at the end of high school, she'd attended an open house and been waylaid by an engineering student. *Good brains aren't determined by gender,* he'd said with a wink, and gave her the school brochure and a map of the canal workings of the interior. The map was fascinating and apparently very illegal; his faculty advisor came charging onto the lawn to confiscate all the copies, screaming something about *Armand you damn fool,* but Laura fled with hers and added it to her collage at home. It was how she'd known where to find the maintenance door of the Sylph Canal.

"Do you want to take a look? We could use a break," said Laura.

"We have a mission," said Bea.

"It's not like we could see every Amuletory in a single day. We can take it easy," said Laura.

"We could if - - - were not so easily distracted."

"Now we *have* to stop. I don't care if it's the most boring fair in the history of the world. If it annoys Bea, we have to attend," said Zelda.

"This is pointless. Let us move on," said Bea, turning to Ivo.

Ivo's gaze lingered on the banner. "Advances in technology may improve our Sweeping protocol."

Bea considered this. "Is this the ideal location for reconnaissance?"

Laura latched on immediately. "Of course it is! We can speak directly to the inventors. I'm sure they'll be happy to help us. If we find something usable, we can pitch it to the Council and land them a contract! They'd be thrilled!"

Bea hummed to herself, still hesitant, but for once she didn't dig in her heels, and Ivo steered her onto the university grounds without a fight.

The technology fair had drawn in not only the Grand University's students, but scholars from seven other of Amicae's highly ranked schools. Each representative and corresponding project was color-coded to show where they'd come from. Students and observers milled inside the wide hallways and classrooms. The largest area was an indoor gymnasium, the sports boundaries completely obscured by a flood of tables bearing inventive projects. In one section, a squat metal contraption rattled out a Spiritualist hymn while simultaneously spewing printed telegrams; on another, students demonstrated a tool for efficiently planting grain; on another, an audience applauded while a dainty robot poured a pint of beer. Zelda was utterly thrilled with the robot, but it reminded Laura a little too much of Charlie. She'd seen him working on such humanoid machines so often, it had been as natural as his uneven haircut. She knew he was far from the only person hoping to make it big on . . . androids? She couldn't remember the word. The association wasn't logical, but she had trouble separating the two in her mind. When she looked at that robot, all she could think about were Charlie's stupid rumors and how relieved Morgan had been to leave home. She left Zelda oohing and aahing over the robot's superior table service, and ambled down the aisle for more interesting projects. Two tables down, she found Bea inspecting ten pairs of rectangular boxes with collapsible antennas.

"The *ear-wit*?" Laura read the label aloud.

"Yes!" said the student opposite her, a red tag marking him OSCAR— INVENTOR, GRAND UNIVERSITY. "The Interactive Radio Wave Transmitter!"

"Does this replace a microphone for radio shows?" said Laura.

"And the cords, and the radio itself!" Oscar scooped one up to display proudly in hand; the ugly box barely fit his grip. "This beauty is a multiway radio! We all listen to radio shows at home, but that's like reading the papers—already done! Finished! No feedback! The IRWT lets you speak back and forth like you would over a telephone! First you dial it to a frequency nothing else is on, and then it will both send your voice and receive other people's voices on that same frequency! You don't have to be tethered to a wall! So long as you take this broadcaster with you—"

"Is it a locked frequency?" said another attendee, on Bea's other side.

Laura did a double take. The attendee wore a silver tiepin. That wasn't incriminating, but Laura had been attacked by a Silver King mobster with a similarly plain silver hair clip. Could it be a mob tag? Was there some kind of mob action planned here?

Oscar was far too excited about his invention to notice anything remotely suspicious. "Unfortunately, no. It's like a radio station. If anyone tunes in to your frequency, they'd be able to hear you. But if they're using a regular radio, they couldn't interfere with your conversation! They could only talk with one of these!"

Bea's tone remained flat, her expression Rexian-still, but her eyes were bright with interest. "Is it possible to install a headset, so no one else around me could listen to what I'm receiving?"

"Like on telephone operators?" Oscar scratched his head. "Sure. That could be an easy addition."

"Good." Bea nodded her satisfaction. She must be *really* impressed to compliment something instead of just choosing not to insult it. But— "Discussing formation by radio would be useless if our prey could hear it."

Oscar paused. "Our . . . what?"

"I don't think saying *our prey* is great in conversation," Laura groaned, rubbing her temple.

"But it is accurate," said Bea. "Inventor. When is - - -r demonstration?"

"I'm . . . uh . . ." Oscar glanced at Laura and the other attendee for help. "I'm scheduled for two o'clock?"

"The invention's aptitude will be measured then. I will be watching." Bea turned on her heel, showing off all her equipment (Oscar paled when he spotted the sheathed blade), then strutted away. Laura had not realized Bea could strut. She gaped after her.

The other attendee frowned at Laura, said, "Such odd company you keep," and left with far less drama.

That *was* a Silver King, wasn't it? Laura shut her mouth and looked closer at the crowd, but in this bustle, she couldn't make out much. The Grand University wasn't involved with mobsters, and did nothing to draw their ire. Hopefully this single man was a coincidence.

A shout and sudden movement caught her attention. Oscar dove to shield his inventions with his body, while Laura got a face full of beer. The robot two tables down had malfunctioned and was flinging cups of beer at anything in range. Its inventors rushed to shut it down, but the robot squalled and waved the emptied bottle like a drunkard. Zelda had escaped the spill herself, but spotted Laura wiping her eyes and began to laugh. Oh, did she laugh. She dissolved straight into hysterics. Laura actually had to catch her elbow to keep her from overbalancing.

"Are you okay?"

"- - -r *face*," said Zelda.

Laura couldn't help but snort. "Yeah, whatever. I'm going to wash this off."

Zelda clung, wheezing, to Laura's sleeve as she walked away. She managed to get her breathing back under control, just in time for Laura to catch sight of her own beer-drenched visage in the washroom mirror. Her expression was apparently too much; Zelda propped her elbows on the edge of the next sink down, buried her own face in her hands, and cackled.

"You're having too much fun with this," Laura grumbled, turning on the faucet.

"It's just so stupid," said Zelda. "I can't look at - - - anymore. I'll suffocate if I do."

Laura felt a smile pull at her lips. She'd seen Zelda amused, of course, had heard her laugh on occasion, but those had been short bursts and varied in authenticity. She'd never heard this kind of unrestrained glee before. She splashed water onto her face and said, "So, you're one of those types who likes pranks, aren't you?"

"How did - - - ever guess?"

"It seems pretty in character already. I mean, do you remember when we first met? You kept taking trays from the waiter. I'd love to have seen his face when he realized everything he was carrying disappeared."

"That kind of reaction is always golden. This magic is good for something, isn't it? But if - - - think waiters' reactions are entertaining, - - - should've seen the reactions on some of Rex's handlers."

She started talking about an extended prank she'd pulled on a handler who'd been particularly hard on Ivo. Laura kept scrubbing at her face and tried to dab herself dry with her bandana. She still smelled embarrassingly like beer, but at least it was bearable now.

"And he started screaming all that in time for his superior officer to walk in, and the officer thought he was talking about her! He was fired. Served him right." Zelda looked up, and her smile faltered. "Why are - - - looking at me like that?"

"Like what?"

"Like . . ." Her eyes darted away. "Like - - - look at Okane."

"No reason. I just think happiness is a good look on you," said Laura.

Zelda stared at her for a moment, then scoffed and turned on her own faucet. "*Happiness?* Is that what - - - think this is?"

"Maybe. You just looked really genuine in that moment," said Laura. "It made me happy, too."

Zelda opened her mouth to retort, then snapped it back shut. After a moment, her irritation melted away again and she shook her head. "Ugh. I keep having to remember that - - - actually mean things like that."

"Was that embarrassing? Sorry, I—"

"Don't be. I'm sorry for being the prickly one," said Zelda. "I'm not used to anyone caring about something as silly as happiness, and especially not when it comes to me."

That echoed Okane far too closely for Laura to bear.

"I care," she said, a little too sharply. Zelda frowned, and she bulled on, "I want you to be happy. No matter what happens, I'm here for you, okay?"

"Even if I murder someone?" said Zelda, trying for a joke.

"Depending who it is, I might thank you."

Zelda laughed again, quieter but still genuine.

Laura didn't have much time to feel relief. Heat seared at her back, and her bag jolted as if something were trying to escape. She recognized the accompanying aura instantly. Anger. One of the Clae-possessed Eggs had reacted. The faucet Zelda had neglected still ran water, but something stringy and dark came out with it. It slowly congealed before her eyes.

"And what's that expression?" said Zelda.

Laura tried very hard to smile. "Could you do me a favor? Could you go find the others and get them in here, then see if we can evacuate the building?"

"Why would—Oh, for the love of god, there's an infestation behind me, isn't there?"

"Maybe."

Zelda swore and hurried for the door. "I'll get them as soon as I can."

The door thudded shut behind her. Meanwhile the faucet water had gone totally black and bubbly, staining the metal.

"Of course," Laura spat, pulling an Egg from her bag. "Just my luck. I try to make a nice connection with someone, and I get interrupted by an infestation."

The faucet shuddered. She circled, watching, but the infestation seemed happy to pool itself in a twitchy, sodden mess in the sink. It protested in little plinking noises, flicking minuscule legs to shed water. Infestations hated water almost as much as sunlight. It was the reason Orien's main island survived while its southernmost neighbor had been overrun. Why in hell was an infestation in water pipes?

A horrible shriek split the air, loud enough that Laura ducked and the monster squawked in surprise. The emergency alarm. Muffled noise rose from the hall beyond, growing stronger still as the door opened again and the Rexian trio appeared.

"Where is the infestation?" Bea demanded.

Ivo was right behind her, but stopped short. "The sink?"

"I don't know any more than you do," said Laura. "Maybe someone lost an amulet ring down the drain. Maybe there's some amulet-based patchwork in the construction. Whatever it is, we need this eradicated. Any good ideas for tackling this?"

"Its structure appears distorted, but given the creature's cunning that could be falsified," said Ivo.

"So a trap."

"They are fond of traps."

Might as well gauge its aggression. Laura banged the sink's side and backed away fast.

"Down!" Bea barked, but even before she spoke they'd all ducked.

The infestation snarled. Its visible form coiled and lashed like a whip. Blackness flew in a wide arc to spatter across the walls and stalls. Almost immediately the discolored surfaces smoked; the stalls' metal groaned and warped as if hit by acid.

Laura clacked an Egg and lobbed it. It cracked on the sink's edge and blew. The infestation squalled at the sudden heat and thrashed, spewing more and more blackness like a noxious fountain as the kin raged around it. Another squeal and it retreated. It sucked back into the pipes and the kin went with it; its angry light glowed dim even through the walls as it presumably chased the infestation along the system. They heard muffled cracking and gurgling as whatever lay inside the wall was ripped apart. The glowing and snarling went up, left, down, backtracked and surged so far to the right Laura couldn't make it out anymore. A hideous crash came from that direction. Laura ran to the window. The infestation had punched straight through the outer stone wall. It flung sloppy tentacles into the sunlight as if the kin might have its same weakness—fortunately, the magic seethed on undaunted.

Unfortunately, however, this side of the building faced the plaza and the main street beyond it. Everyone evacuating witnessed the destruction of the front wall. The infestation flailed a bit more before trumpeting its annoyance and retreating back into the building. The thuds and cracks of its passing faded. The alarm came to a grating halt as if to punctuate its passing.

"Wow," said a strange voice in the sudden silence, and Laura jumped. A woman in maintenance uniform stood in the doorway with a mop and bucket; she looked over the ruined stalls to the bubbling tar on the tile. "I heard there was a situation in the toilets, but I think this is a little beyond me."

"Who are you?" said Laura.

"Dorthea. Building staff," the woman replied. "Was that what I think it was?"

"Yes," said Laura. "I don't suppose you know where these pipes go?"

Dorthea giggled, then went quiet as Laura waited impatiently for an answer. "You're serious."

"To exterminate it, we have to find and pin it down. The water system might be complex, but if you have any information we could narrow it down."

Dorthea stared blankly at them for a minute before a wide smile spread over her face. "Oh, I knew this would work someday! The campus is segmented!"

"It's what?" said Laura, confused. "But doesn't plumbing come off the main city's water flow? You can't possibly have your own reservoir. It must be tied into the main lines."

"It is. It's just specialized. Follow me. You'll understand when you see it!"

Dorthea took off, and the Sweepers ran to keep up. She led them deep into the university to a hidden stairwell, and down into the basement. Once there she took a hard left into a room labeled MAINTENANCE. The room looked as old as the city itself. A color-coded blueprint of the university sprawled across one wall, and on the other, a multitude of switches resembled a hedgehog's back.

"Fun fact," said Dorthea, seizing two switch levers. "Back in the day when the Council branches were scattered through Amicae, *this* was the city archive." She heaved the levers down with a thudding, forbidding sound, and something glowed red through the blueprint. "As a government building, it's got the same precautions as the main Council location, which for some reason can seal itself off." Two more levers. Two more segments shined red through the paper. "Maybe the Council anticipated being under siege, or maybe they wanted to be sure they had enough resources to put out any fires—"

"No," gasped Laura. She reached up, unhooked the blueprint, and pulled it down. The wall beneath was a single solid veneer of stone, carved painstakingly with the floor plan of the building at its origin. It was a massive Gin amulet, its reddening sections corresponding to orders and traps the same way the armory did. "The city was created with magical precautions. These are Sweeper fail-safes."

The only way the Wrath of God stunt had worked was because Amicae's builders had considered the possibility of an infestation swarm in the interior. They'd built the fountain Laura had used so that future generations could quickly produce massive amounts of kin and send it straight down to the interior without braving the darkness inside themselves. Once upon a time, maybe it had been truly efficient, or been part of a larger network to better target attacking monsters. The Sinclair family once had countless traps and fail-safes like that built into the city's framework, but as the years passed and the Council started ripping out Sweeper equipment, pulling it all apart under the wall policy and replacing old buildings with new, only the unnoticed or the hard to move managed to survive. Most of what Laura had discovered were fragments of original traps, their purpose completely lost. This time, though, the trap appeared to be fully intact.

Amicae's original government buildings must've been rigged to prevent or trap spreading infestations. If monsters could enter mines, they could enter pipes. It was clever of the builders to take that into account.

"Really?" Dorthea grunted, pulling down the last few levers. "Then Armand was right."

The name struck a bell.

"Wait," said Laura. "Wasn't there an Armand here in the engineering department? The man interested in the canal workings?"

"Exactly!" Dorthea looked immensely pleased at the recognition. "He stayed with us after graduation because he was fascinated with how these contraptions worked. We all had theories about the segmentation, and he swore it must be some pre-wall magical installation. The dividers are heavy-duty amulets."

Zelda looked over the blueprint with some admiration. "It's a good system. This keeps any infestation here from escaping into the city pipes."

Dorthea went to the third, otherwise unremarkable wall, where a telephone hung. She cranked and waited for a connection. "Hello, guard station? This is Dorthea in Maintenance. The alarm went off for an infestation, but you might've seen it already. We're working on solving the problem. Can you get Armand on the line?" She went quiet for a moment. "What do you mean, he isn't out by you? He has to be—Never mind. Oscar was his assistant this semester. Can you send him in to the Maintenance office? We'll update you as we proceed."

In short time, the same Oscar who'd so proudly showed off his radios joined them.

"No Armand?" he said. "I thought he'd be here with you if he wasn't outside."

"There's no sign of him yet, but I'm sure he'll turn up," said Dorthea. "Have you got any information about these amulet divides in the piping? We're counting on them to be blockades, but I want to make sure we're not missing anything."

"Not that I know of," said Oscar. "It's pretty straightforward. You get in this room, and you control the whole system. There's no sort of authorization needed, and no secondary system."

Dorthea nodded and turned to the building diagram. "Okay, so the monster was sighted in the women's toilet on the first floor." She rapped her knuckles against a section labeled 1-38. "What are we looking for in here to locate it?"

"That's tricky," said Laura. "Infestations expand and reshape themselves, and they've been known to leave trails up to a mile long. The water might ruin its solidity, but it's not a countermeasure. Even if it surfaced in one area, it could've come from anywhere in the system. If you've really got amulet dividers, though, they might've chopped the infestation apart in the pipe and killed off the branches already. That'll make it easier to track back."

"There is also the amulet itself to think about," said Ivo. "Infestations don't go into water on their own, so the amulet must have been placed in a spot it could not viably escape, beyond utilizing the pipes."

"We're looking for a spot in the system that saboteurs could access, with the width to hold an amulet without stopping the water flow." Laura unclipped the Gin amulet from her belt and held it up. "Let's say it's this size."

"The easiest accessible spot in I-38 is here," said Dorthea. She pointed to what had to be a storage closet inside the section. "It's a hot-water tank serving the labs."

"It's big enough," said Oscar. "None of the other pipes would be able to hold something like that, or we'd have found a blockage."

"But there are multiple tanks for the multiple sectors," Dorthea mused. "Just because we saw something in I-38 doesn't mean it originated there. It could've come from the other side of the building and been cut off by the dividers."

"Let's check that sector first, then expand our search," said Laura.

And so they did. The Sweepers and their guides took the basement's hallways. Oscar regaled them with the details of each room as they passed until they ascended a second set of stairs, and while climbing switched to pitching his invention again.

"Working with Dorthea and Armand is actually what inspired me to create the Interactive Radio Wave Transmitter! It's so troublesome to try coordinating with a team over a distance. Let's say I'm trying to reach Armand about a pipe breach: the only option I have right now is to either physically look for him, or try calling him on the telephone. But the university telephones are few and far between, and you don't know which he'll be at, or even if he is near a telephone at all! On top of that you've got to get through the operators and possibly be put on hold, which makes everything a hassle. With an Interactive Radio Wave Transmitter—*henceforth dubbed IRWT, patent pending*—we could all carry a transmitter easily, and the transmission is almost instantaneous! This allows for much easier coordination—"

"It's faster if we shortcut through the labs," Dorthea butted in.

Oscar changed direction without pausing in his pitch. "—and faster responses to all issues! I mean, if Armand had an IRWT right now we'd be able to correspond with him so much easier instead of going ahead without potentially critical information! It would make life so much . . . easier . . ."

He paused halfway through the lab door, eyes wide with horror.

The infestation had surfaced here. The monster hadn't lingered but left marks of its passing all over the room. Water sprayed from a large broken sink—faucet missing, basin lopsided and stained almost beyond recognition—to the already-flooded floor. The nearest tables, blackened to match the sink, lay sprawled and fractured. Sodden papers squelched underfoot as they entered the room.

"No survivors," Bea announced.

"No sign of the infestation, either," Ivo added. "It fed and moved on."

"Moved on?" Laura looked around, incredulous. "Why would it *move on* back into the pipes?"

The infestation had searched for an escape route. If it found easy food and an exit . . .

"If it left, we would encounter its roots connected to the piping." Ivo skirted the room's edge as he spoke to check for traces.

"And you can't feel it anywhere?"

"Only the remnants of its presence. It's not even in the nearby pipes."

They warily spread to search the room. Laura went straight to the sink. The ruined basin and wall resembled the wreckage of her encounter in the toilets, but when she squinted underneath, she found odd silver wire twisted around the pipe. She carried an almost identical wire in her bag. She reached out, pressed a finger to it, and felt the same familiar spark. Kin equipment. Sweepers had been here.

"Keep an eye out," she told everyone. "Mobster Sweepers coordinated this attack, whatever it is. If they're guiding it to a goal, we might end up in the cross fire."

"Mobs? But we're just a school!" said Oscar, alarmed. "Sure, we're Second Quarter, but we didn't have anything they could use, right, Dorthea?" He looked to Dorthea, but her attention was focused on lifting a broken pair of glasses from the floor. "Money, maybe, but our funding is all in the bank, not on site!"

"Or maybe it's tied to the event?" Zelda suggested.

"The inventor's radio project is intriguing enough to be used for Sweeper purposes," Bea agreed.

"Or for a mob war," said Laura.

If a mob war was even happening anymore. The mobs had stayed very quiet after the Mad Dogs' clash at the Sylph Canal. But just because the Mad Dogs were waiting for policy changes didn't mean any of the other mobs were. They could still easily be active.

Oscar looked faint. "You think my invention's a target?"

"You did have a Silver King looking at it, earlier," said Laura.

"But I wasn't able to take any of them with me! We weren't supposed to bring anything out with the alarm or there'd be a bottleneck— Oh, no, my prototypes—"

If that was the case, the mobsters only needed the monster to be visible without damaging anything. Perhaps this lab had been the first attempt at staging chaos, except the monster proved itself too efficient. The mob Sweepers had beaten it back into the pipes and directed it somewhere more populous, where witnesses might possibly outnumber casualties. Bile rose in Laura's throat.

"They might be using the infestation to evacuate the building and leave the area clear," she said. "Can you get to a telephone? With the alarm you might be getting emergency services arriving, and if they bring any police, we'll want them in the gymnasium. If it is an attempt to steal an invention, they might catch the mobsters in the act."

This was prime time for Oscar to make some comment about how his IRWT would improve the situation, but he was too caught up by the idea of them being stolen; his mouth opened and shut like a dying fish's.

Dorthea elbowed him and said, "Go make the call, then get out of here. I'll see you at the front."

He nodded dumbly and hurried away. As Dorthea watched him go, she folded those fallen glasses with shaky hands.

"Will he be—"

"He'll be fine," said Zelda. "We're the ones walking into a monster's lair."

It wasn't kind, but it goaded Dorthea into certainty. She tucked the glasses into her uniform pocket and made for the opposite door.

"Then we'd better hurry."

Luckily, they didn't have far to go. Upon leaving the lab, they found themselves looking down a long hallway that ended in a crossing hall. There, at the center of the T formed by these paths, stood a closet door.

"There it is," said Dorthea.

Laura didn't know much about water tanks or plumbing, but even she could tell where Dorthea meant: the closet door had been broken open. Someone—or something—had pushed it back to closed position, but it hung weirdly on its hinges, the wood scarred as if someone had hacked the lock apart. Laura pried it open. The water tank stood innocently in the center: a metallic cylinder with two pipes sticking out the top, taller than Laura and twice as wide.

"It looks pretty mundane," she muttered.

"It is a basic design," Dorthea replied. "Dip tube pulls in cold water, displacing warm water which goes out the other pipe. It's heated by an amulet, rather than electricity or gas."

"Is there a way in?" said Laura.

"Of course. We have to switch out the amulets," said Dorthea. "Just let me drain it."

"Be careful that the infestation doesn't come out with the water," said Laura.

Dorthea turned a valve that shut off the intake, then knelt down to a little spigot on the heater's side and twisted it. Water gushed out to pool and gurgle down the drain in the floor. Laura kept a close eye on the water, half expecting the monster to send feelers with it, but that didn't happen. More than likely the infestation heard them and understood what the draining meant. It knew they'd be opening its prison soon.

The Sweepers took up positions. Ivo and Bea hugged either side of the doorframe, using the wall as a shield. Laura shook an Egg in one hand until it glowed. Dorthea backed out of the closet and started poking at the tank using a thin metal stick with a hook at the end. When the spigot's flow reduced to drips, she tugged on a panel with the hook and deftly twisted a few latches. She caught the handle and pulled. The seal broke with a sickly, sucking noise, and the panel flopped open. They glimpsed the shine of an amulet just inside.

"Nothing's there," said Dorthea, disappointed.

"Not so fast," said Laura. "Is that your standard-issue amulet?"

"From here I can't really tell."

Dorthea made to lean closer but Laura caught her arm; the Rexians were far too tense for there not to be trouble.

"Shame for there not to be anything here. Dorthea, could you go back and let the others know we've got the wrong tank?" Laura followed up with a really obvious wink. "We'll need to"—wink—"figure out the right one." Wink wink.

Dorthea's brow furrowed with incomprehension. "Okay? I'll let you know what I find?"

She retreated back down the hallway. Zelda shook her head pityingly, as if to say, *You really think a monster can be fooled by such an obvious ruse?* Laura gave a shrug.

"May we dispense with the foolishness?" said Bea.

"If you know what you're doing, have at it," said Laura.

"I shall," said Bea.

She stepped to the middle of the doorway and shot the amulet dead center. Laura didn't need Magi instinct to know this would not end well. She dove aside as the infestation surged into the hallway, splintering the doorframe. It thundered down the length of the hall, sprouting new limbs across its surface: not hands or tentacles but sharp protrusions curving in every direction. It climbed and moved like the swarm had in the Falling Infestation. It shredded the walls, shattered windows, squalling, snarling—

"This was - - -r plan?" Zelda screeched.

"It is a target now," said Bea, and threw an Egg.

Laura followed her lead and threw another. Despite the doubled attack the infestation didn't seem to care. It continued its ascent to the ceiling and broke through. Cracking sounds issued down the branching hall.

"It's going to bring the ceiling down!" Ivo called from out of sight, presumably on the infestation's other side.

"This place is centuries old. I don't trust its structural integrity," said Laura. She threw two more Eggs, but even with Clae's influence they didn't seem to affect it. From down the hall came the hiss and stink of dissolving wood. "We need to get rid of it fast!"

The infestation filled more of the area, lashing out with scythe-shaped limbs. One missed Laura by an inch and hit the floor so hard its point broke through the wood. Blackness seeped between the floorboard cracks. A fourth Amicae Egg sailed into the main body, but sank out of sight without a sound as the infestation closed around it. For the infestation to shrug off attacks using four different magic strains when usual weapons only used two . . . It had to be old.

"We need new tactics!" she called.

A red light flashed. Ivo had drawn his blade. An eerie afterimage hazed its edges, but as Ivo gripped it tighter the haze grew, expanding until it wreathed him in a bloody cloud and the blade at its core blazed forge-bright.

"Bea! We trim it!" he said, and slashed at the monster's side.

It shrieked and a mass of limbs twisted to face him. Ivo ducked under the larger ones, and the smaller dissolved into smoke upon touching the red cloud. He scored another blow to the infestation that made the whole beast shudder.

"Bea!"

But Bea seemed not to hear him. She'd swapped back to gun and bullets, and aimed at strategic points farther down. Ivo struck a third time, and the infestation reacted violently. A ripping sound announced the destruction of the ceiling, and Ivo vanished as he dodged tar and plaster. The infestation turned, rolling, reaching for the greatest threat.

"Hey!" Laura screamed. "Here! Aren't you supposed to be smart? I'm the head Sweeper, you should want me dead first!"

She had the rest of the Sweepers with her, while Ivo stood alone; she didn't like his chances with a focused infestation.

"Bea!" Ivo cried, more desperate, and when that didn't work, "128!"

Bea whipped out her own blade and jumped. Between her Magi ability and her amulets, she tore a gouge down the infestation's side with blinding speed, crashing one foot into the wall next to the closet to check her momentum. Her own red haze hovered like a blood trail, splitting the monster in two. She pivoted with teeth bared as it gave a piteous wail and sliced into it again. The infestation bucked. More red flashes told them Ivo had resumed his position. The two of them hacked at the infestation's base. The monster panicked. Its limbs couldn't reach them through the red fog, so it groped for a new target. Half of its bulk swerved toward the others.

Laura realized in a split second that it was headed for Zelda. Zelda had no weapons or gear, and her magic wouldn't protect her. On instinct Laura leapt, but she knew even as she did that it was going too fast. Neither of them would clear the infestation's path in time. She caught Zelda, forcing them both to duck as if it might by some miracle go over them. The Eggs in her bag seared again, and somehow this echoed the blades enough for the infestation to veer wide before wrapping back to circle them in seething blackness. It fluctuated, screaming at all the magic sources. Somewhere in the noise, Laura thought she almost heard a voice.

Wrath? Wrath? Mother, it is wrath?

The darkness around them shifted to smoke. Laura didn't know what that meant, but she'd seen what smoke could do in the wilds and had no intention of repeating that.

"Out!" she coughed, and heaved Zelda with her. Once they escaped the cloud, she asked, "Are you okay? Hurt anywhere? Breathing normally?"

"Fine," Zelda rasped.

Laura looked back and called, "Ivo? Bea? Are you all right?"

A crackle came from the smoke screen. It billowed and parted under the slice of a Rexian blade, and Ivo jogged out to join them.

"Exterminated," he said. "The creature pulled its remnants back into the amulet and carried all the kin it had swallowed with it."

"They're stupid enough to do that?" said Laura.

"It wouldn't have done so if we hadn't forced it back into a defense. It was attempting to consolidate itself for a fresh attack."

"And Bea?"

"Whole and healthy." Ivo looked from Zelda to Laura, perplexed. "- - - covered her."

"More like pinned me," Zelda grumbled.

"- - - could've died," said Ivo. "I have not . . . Protecting each other is not common on Rexian expeditions."

"I noticed," Zelda said icily. When Bea followed them out of the cloud, she said, "What was that all about? Why didn't - - - help Ivo earlier? - - - weren't pinned down!"

Bea's step faltered.

"Zelda, there's no use in pointing fingers," said Ivo. "We destroyed the infestation. We succeeded."

"Results aren't everything!" Zelda hissed. "She specifically didn't pull attention away from - - - until - - - called her by her damn number! What happens next time? Will she let - - - die unless - - - go back to Rexian standards?"

She and Ivo squabbled. If Bea really had held out until Ivo defaulted to her number instead of name, she was the sort who'd make a point of saying so when the action died down; Laura hadn't known her to bottle up her opinions before. But now she stood off-kilter, face blank but eyes wider with barely discernible surprise, and Laura wondered if she'd even realized what she'd done. The Rexians hadn't been here with their new names long, and if she was drilled to react to a number for twenty years of training and fighting . . .

"Give her a break," said Laura. "You haven't needed to coordinate in a fight with your actual names much, right? There haven't been many infestations here to practice on, and you've got years of calling each other by numbers before that. It might be a little harder to transition for her, but that doesn't mean she meant anything malicious."

"Precisely," said Ivo, perking up. "I understand the confusion myself."

Laura turned back to Bea, hoping this smoothed things over, but it hadn't.

Bea clearly didn't like being caught in such a truth; her face flushed red with anger. "Protecting each other is folly," she spat. "All it means is decreasing our chances of success and survival. If a Sweeper is so weak as to fall into trouble, it is their own fault and they should atone for it, rather than drag someone who *is* strong with them."

"So - - -'re saying Ivo should've atoned?" Zelda growled.

Bea shot her an acidic glare. "He has proven himself strong on many occasions. - - -, on the other hand, are useless. No efforts should've been wasted on - - -."

"Wait just a minute," said Laura, but Bea rounded on her with fire in her eyes.

"- - - are also useless! - - - dare to call - - -rself a head Sweeper with such feeble abilities! I had thought Okane was worthless, but the truth is that - - - are the useless one, and drag down anyone with talent! On this assignment - - - could only shout and pretend to be a hero over someone still more worthless. - - - are nothing without him behind - - -, and Okane knows this! Where has he been this past week? - - - are slow, and smug, and shameful! Unless - - - can accomplish a mission with - - -r own hands, - - - have no right to speak to us of Sweeping!"

Laura was sure this was all just Bea lashing out from her own embarrassment, but that cut deeper than she'd expected. Resentment hung bitter on her own tongue as she shot back, "It sounds to me like all you care about is accomplishing the mission."

"It's true," Bea said without hesitation. "The mission is all that matters. No matter what I have to throw away, I will accomplish it!"

"- - -'ll even throw away Ivo," said Zelda.

"Stop," Ivo said firmly. "If the mission is truly all that matters, this one is accomplished. We have more pertinent things to worry about."

They all backed off, but the animosity remained.

The amulet in the water heater was clearly a planted one: it was the black bishop piece of a chess game. That had far too much in common with the pawn of Toulouse. Laura doused it in kin and packed it away to present to the police.

As planned, they reconvened by the front doors, and Laura was relieved to find old, reliable Officer Baxter talking with Oscar and Dorthea. Oscar had hunched over in misery, and Dorthea rubbed his back in a vain attempt to cheer him up. That was a bad sign.

"Any luck catching the mobsters?" she asked.

"None, unfortunately," said Baxter, fretful and sweaty as ever. "Just as you suspected, they took this young man's inventions. We've set up a search, and the chief is considering offering a reward for information, but . . ." He shook his head.

"You're not confident you'll find the thief?" said Laura.

"It's like they disappear," said Baxter. "One moment you're chasing them down a street, and then you turn a corner and all you see is the canal. The only ones you can catch are the young and inexperienced, and they either don't know anything, or they know better than to betray the mob."

As he spoke he walked out onto the front steps. From here they had a good view of the gates, the street, and the plaza. The infestation's earlier attack had ripped deep gouges into the ground and left an ugly smear of black ringed by broken cobblestone. Most people in the street gawked but couldn't get closer due to the ring of police vehicles around the entrance. Black uniforms ran between them, leading arrested mobsters, making reports, and hurrying up and down the stairs to check for clues in the university. One of the latter pulled Oscar aside to ask for more details on his invention.

Laura sighed. It was good to be out in sunlight again, even if the air wasn't particularly warm. She glanced back to check the others and realized that with Oscar distracted, Dorthea had deflated. She looked downright miserable.

"What's wrong?" said Laura.

Dorthea pulled something from her pocket: the glasses she'd picked up in the lab. "I recognized these right away," she murmured. "They're Armand's. He's blind as a bat without them. If they were really dropped . . ."

With infestations, there couldn't be any more damning proof of someone's death.

"I'm sorry," Laura whispered.

Dorthea shook her head. "You're not the reason he's gone. I'm just . . . It's nice to have closure, but at the same time, if I hadn't found them, I might not have to mourn." She gripped the glasses tighter, enough that the thin metal creaked under her thumb. "I could pretend he took an unscheduled vacation. I'd be able to convince myself that he'd come back. I don't have that anymore."

Laura opened her mouth. Even after a year of Sweeping she hadn't figured out how to talk to survivors, and had no idea what to say now, but she couldn't just leave it like this.

"Hey," said Zelda, laying a hand on Laura's shoulder. "Come here a moment."

"But—" Laura glanced between Zelda and Dorthea.

"That's why I'm saying *come here*." Zelda towed Laura a few paces away and whispered, "Leave that woman alone. There's no right answer, and no consolation for her."

"I can't just say nothing," said Laura.

"Silence *is* the answer. Look, I understand - - - want to help, but that just makes everything awkward. She doesn't need a stranger's empty words. Leave her healing to the people who matter."

While they spoke, Oscar trudged back over. He and Dorthea slung arms around each other's shoulders in a hug, and more university workers crowded in to ask what had happened. Dorthea forced a weak smile. They could support her best right now, but Laura still felt guilty for being so inadequate. Guilty for feeling useless, after all.

7

BAITING

Laura went to the armory in a foul mood that evening. She balanced a box that contained the canal map, her old Coronae book, and the remnants of Clae's Underyear candle, mixed in with Cheryl's knickknacks. She'd hoped to keep it in the rectory guestrooms with all their necessities (she'd be damned if she left these in a place the Mad Dogs might trash), but she'd tripped over the box no less than five times just after returning from work today. Morgan had gently suggested that they face the facts, so Laura had trudged out as the streetlights started coming on.

She grumbled as she climbed the armory stairs and propped the box on her hip as she fit the key in the lock. It didn't turn. Laura frowned before realizing the machinery had already disengaged. Someone was inside.

"Amelia?" she called, pushing the door open. But it wasn't Amelia who waved at her from the main room.

"Laura!" called Okane. "- - -'re here! Come in!"

"Oh," Laura said flatly. She kicked the door shut behind her. "It's you."

Okane looked like a frantic and jubilant mess. His hair was uncombed, his shirt untucked, and the bags under his eyes showed he hadn't gotten much sleep. Still, he moved around the room with a spring in his step, pacing a well-worn circle he'd clearly moved equipment to allow. Grim sat cross-legged on the floor with a tight ring of Niveus amulets clustered around him. The room was overly warm. They must've used the Kin at some point.

"Is this where you've been this whole time?" she asked, dropping the box on the nearest table.

"Laura," said Okane, as if he hadn't heard her. "We've had a breakthrough."

"I hope you did."

"And it was so obvious! I don't know how we never guessed it!"

"We were just too slow to notice," Laura said bitterly.

"I wouldn't say slow. Just inexperienced," said Grim.

Laura sent him a poisonous look. Just because he was listening didn't mean he was exempt from her irritation.

"It all goes back to Magi! Grim, infestations," Okane continued, pacing faster.

"Not everything has to be Magi," said Laura.

"The whole world as it is, it's Magi—"

Laura watched him go, and Bea's words crept unbidden into her mind. - - - *are the useless one, and drag down anyone with talent.* Maybe it was Laura's fault that he didn't figure things out sooner. - - - *are nothing without him behind - - -, and Okane knows this! Where has he been this past week?* He didn't seem to have noticed her absence at all. Laura pressed her lips shut hard, trying and failing to stamp out her resentment. Bea's words had a little truth to them, didn't they?

Thunk, went something upstairs.

"Finally, we have answers!" said Okane.

"Great," said Laura.

"And - - -! And - - -!"

"Okane," Grim said warningly.

The Eggs in Laura's bag radiated heat and anger and *Clae,* and the resentment hit its peak.

"Why does it have to be Magi?" she snapped. "For god's sake, Okane, what does it matter?"

He stopped to blink at her. "But . . . Magi's the whole reason why I—"

"I don't give a shit about Magi!" Laura shouted, and it wasn't true but she was caught up in rage and misplaced adrenaline and they kept making her chest hotter and hotter, and her stupid arms itched so much they burned. "You're letting this idea of them run your life! But if everything is Magi, where are you? You're the only part of this that matters to me! But we've been together almost every day for a year, and now it's been a week of nothing! You couldn't even let me know you're alive! If you're so fixated on Magi, you were using your magic here, weren't you?"

His guilty start made the anguish worse.

Thud-thunk-crack.

The amulets around Grim began to tremble. Grim sat up straighter in alarm, but Laura barely noticed.

"What if something happened? What if it got to be too much? What if you changed like Clae? Grim can't stop something like that! What if you were gone over something that doesn't matter? What if I lost you?"

Okane's mouth hung open. Laura sucked in her breath for more, but—

A thunderous crashing came from the stairwell, as if someone had heaved the entire Kin system down the steps. Steam gusted under the door even before it broke open, and then billowed out into the room. The pieces of kin equipment began to hum and bubble; their magical components glowed gold, and something in the cloud raged to match them. *Thud. Creeee, hiss, thud.* It crossed the threshold, steam roiling off of it, and its glow intensified. Clae stood before them. His crystal shimmered, fractals dancing at his impossible movement, and his core throbbed bright and dark like a vicious heartbeat. His crystal eyes were blind. He took another heavy, rasping step forward. The crystal somehow bowed to match, crunching hideously but re-forming so he stayed intact. Kin tubing had been wrapped around his leg, and dragged broken glass across the floor behind him. The equipment around them quivered in time with that step, and magic pulsed through the air.

"I understand telling someone who is upset and in pain to calm down is ill advised," said Grim, "but please, Laura, *calm down.*"

How could she calm down, seeing that? Clae stumbled over the kin tubing. He rammed an elbow against the doorframe for balance. A crack split the air and the frame buckled, wood blackened as if burned. He seethed with the horrible, overwhelming stench of vanilla. With every throb of magic the steam shifted faster, from mere water to an oppressive cloud of kin. Laura remembered Rex trying to tame him, the burns on Lester Mac-Danel, the policeman Renard had killed . . . Okane caught her arms and stepped to block her view.

"Look at me," he said firmly. "- - -'re okay. Everything's okay."

"How?" she squeaked.

Okane dialed up his magic, and she felt the nonverbal shout again: "(*You*)'re okay. (*You*)'re okay."

Grim caught her by the wrist, and his own influence leached under her skin. She had an autumn breeze inside and heavy assurance on the outside. Her arms stopped itching, and somehow, slowly, her breathing evened out. Everything went quiet again. The golden cloud faded from the air. The equipment dulled but didn't fully deactivate. After almost a minute, Okane asked, "How are - - - feeling?"

"Do you really want to know the answer?" said Laura.

"Ah. Understandable." He ducked his head in embarrassment. "Let's rephrase that. Are - - - going to freak out?"

"Maybe a little."

"A little?" Grim said flatly.

"You can't expect me to just be okay with this!" Laura shrieked. "I mean, look at that! Did I just imagine it? Did I just imagine my dead ex-boss coming down the stairs to fry us alive?"

"He wasn't going to fry us alive," Okane groaned.

"He was absolutely going to fry us alive!"

"Calm," said Grim.

"I am calm!" Laura took several deep, hurried breaths. "I am. Calm. It's not a big deal. I've just seen him kill and grievously injure people like this before. Why aren't you panicking?"

"Because he's not here to fry us alive," said Okane, his voice exasperated but still damnably even. "Look at me. I can tell when something's here to hurt me, remember? Instinct? And I'm definitely tired enough to be paranoid."

Laura focused on his eye bags again. "Yes. God, you look almost as bad as Albright."

"That bad, huh?"

"This is—" Laura sighed. "Okay. All right. I trust you. I'm not . . . okay, but I'm not going to panic."

"- - -'re sure?"

Laura simply raised her eyebrows. Okane huffed a laugh. He let go of her and stepped aside so she could see the damage again. Clae had stalled at the doorway. He hadn't gone dormant by any means, but he'd dimmed.

Laura tried to swallow her nerves. "So, if you're not scared, you must have some idea of what's going on. Why is he down here? How did he move in the first place?"

"Whatever you felt just now, it resonated with the memory of his death," said Grim. He pried his fingers off her one by one, and cradled his sparkling hand close as if suffering frostbite. "You've successfully baited him. Many Magi would be jealous."

"I've what?"

"It's part of the breakthrough I mentioned," said Okane. "Do - - - want to sit down? We can explain."

Laura all but collapsed to the floor. Grim was none too pleased by the resulting disturbance to his circle of amulets. He sorted through them one-handed, flicking the newly broken ones out of the formation and gathering the intact ones into a tighter circle. Laura followed one of the broken ones with her eyes, and saw it roll under a table and into a pile of other broken Niveus amulets. When had those gotten here? Okane settled beside them with far more grace than either of them had managed and said, "Grim's seen crystals like Clae before. Magi call them sentinels."

"Sentinels are the guardians of Magi havens," said Grim. "They are Magi who've fallen prey to their own magic. When they are overcome with uncontrollable emotion, it leaps out of its constraints and changes them wholly. They're no longer human this way, but they are still alive."

"Like Gin is alive?" said Laura.

"Gin has no understanding of human emotion. Sentinels are the dregs of it. When the sentinel was human, they created human connections. If that connection with someone was deep enough, they would be able to un-consciously recognize that person's strain of magic. They could understand the fluctuations of mood or health, to an extent, but once they change to a more heavily magical state, they sense the other strain with higher accuracy, while everything else becomes nil. The fact that he felt *you* just now made him move where nothing else has. He doesn't have a human's rational mind, but the leftovers of the human's thoughts are there, and the sentinel will act on them."

Laura glanced at Clae, still frozen in the doorway. "But if that's the case, why didn't he move before?"

"The connection wasn't fully established." Grim bowed his head. "Not all sentinels move for their human ties. Of all Magi that become sentinels, I would say only about twenty percent are capable of moving, even for their dearest relatives. The whole process—from crystallization to waking and all in between—is very emotional and subjective, which makes it hard to connect. You may think of it this way: the feelings must match on both ends. But even if you both feel grief over the same loss, the nature of your grief may differ, and that prevents the connection. Because this is so personal, and because it changes with every person, it's not something that can be taught or reliably recorded. The approach used to wake one sentinel will not wake another."

"Magi are apparently bitter about that," Okane muttered.

"But if crystallization's so rare, I can see why they wouldn't—" She paused when Okane shook his head. "It's . . . not rare?"

Okane had looked sleep-deprived before, but only now did he look truly tired. Softly, he said, "They do it on purpose."

"They *what*?" said Laura. Clae made a low, inhuman sound, and they both hurried to comfort her again. Laura knocked their hands away and demanded, "What do you mean, they do it on purpose?"

"To shore up their defenses, they forge sentinels," said Grim. "The most common way is to threaten a child, and force the parent to shift under stress. The shared trauma of the experience is what allows their connection, so the child may later 'bait' their parent into place."

"They fucking what?"

Laura surged back to her feet. She didn't know what she'd do, but she was livid enough to throttle someone. To hell with the Magi. This whole time she'd thought they were kind, oppressed people, but then they did this to each other? What kind of sick society did they live in to willingly murder their own family members? No wonder Grim and Cherry had been so unwilling to talk about them! No wonder—

She paused. Clae's crystal gaze was fixed on her. He couldn't see, but he was looking at her. A horrible thought came to mind. Laura's hands fell limply to her sides, and she felt very, very cold.

"Did they let it happen to Anselm?" she whispered. "Did their parents— Clae's father knew about Magi. Did he let them go and get hurt on purpose? Did . . . did he want Clae to bait Anselm?"

Helen Sinclair abandoned us, Clae had told her. *My father told her why I was able to get away, and she didn't take it well.*

When Clae was a child, the Sinclair Sweepers had already been in dire straits. His father might've gotten desperate. Maybe Clae's mother hadn't abandoned him for some bigoted opinion on her husband's bloodline. Maybe she'd found out what Clae's father planned to do to her children. Too late to save Anselm, knowing he wanted Clae alive if only to have him there for baiting . . . No wonder she got scared. Maybe she planned to take Clae with her when she ran. And maybe, still uninformed about most of Magi society, she'd thought Clae's connection to Anselm had a chance to save him. Maybe that was why she left him. Maybe that was why she left without a word.

She should've taken Clae.

She should've taken Clae.

"I don't know," said Okane. His head was bowed, forehead resting against his hand. "There's no one left to ask, is there?"

Laura sank back down, eyes stinging and hand over her mouth.

"Back in the wilds, when we found that courier hideout, - - - were right about that one as well," Okane continued miserably. "The crystal that kept us warm that night was a person. The Magi baited that person to a location and built the hideout around them, and then they left. We don't know anything about that person anymore, because they were just thrown away."

Laura pressed her knuckles harder against her lips. "How could they do that to each other? What kind of horrible place . . ."

"For Magi, it's as simple as survival," said Grim.

Clae had once worried that people might take advantage of Magi, to change them on a large scale. This was worse than his fears. Magi cannibalized themselves.

And if they wanted people to be crystals . . .

"It's true then, isn't it? They never come back," she whispered.

"I would not say that," Grim said carefully.

Laura looked up at him in surprise. "There is a way?"

"I would not commit to that, either."

"Then what do you mean?"

"It's the root cause," said Okane. "The breakthrough. The truth of crystallization, the truth about Grim, and the origin of infestations . . . we think that they all came from the same place."

"It is not proven," said Grim.

"But we spent the last week figuring it out," said Okane. "It's . . . complicated. Grim, could - - - try starting from the beginning?"

"Yes," Grim said solemnly. "With 'you.'"

"Laura, do - - - remember back in Club Toulouse, when Grim started acting so strangely around Ivo at the end?"

Laura nodded slowly. "Yes? You went totally silent for no reason. It was a little awkward."

"It rattled me," Grim admitted. "Ivo referred to me not with a word but a magical implication. I have of course heard Okane use such a thing to speak to me before, but Ivo's struck me differently. It reminded me of the time I was born. It is a memory I thought long gone or otherwise useless, but it makes sense now. I was born in Thrax, in the wake of its destruction. I was born at that time because I'd taken too long to form. In truth, I was meant to be born to the city as it fell. I was to be a new version of the infestation."

Laura recoiled. "But that can't be. Infestations are anti-magic, but you're—"

"I am not magical. Not in the sense of being the infestation's opposite," said Grim. "Long ago, when the Magi and Wasureijin faced the ends of the crusades and feared for the survival of their people, they needed something that fit their purpose: something to destroy the magic the mainland invaders used against them, at any cost. I believe they created the infestation as they created me. If that is the case, they prayed for what they needed."

"I thought you said you wouldn't pull the religious card on us," said Laura.

Grim hummed, considering. "It isn't so much the prayer itself that had impact. It was more about who was praying, and how they did it. The Magi's 'you' hides no lies, and carries all sincerity. It is not a word, but a suggestion and a determination at the same time. When Okane says 'you,' he defines your existence to both of you. You 'hear' the word because he has thrown forward his impression, or definition of you, and you accept that definition to allow it to register in your mind. If you pay suitable attention while he speaks, you can understand his definition of himself. For example." Grim and Okane looked each other in the eyes. Neither of them spoke, but Grim's eyes closed in contentment. "When Okane speaks to me, I can feel the familiarity and respect he feels for me. It is the same subjective, emotional power that could one day forge him into crystal, but projected onto another person. Do you understand? Definition? Crystallization?"

"The prayer . . . defined you?" Laura said slowly.

"Yes," said Grim, as if he'd been waiting all his life for someone to realize it. "Imagine it: the whole of a population screaming *you,* and in that word implying who or what they desired. That word held all their anguish, all their pride, the knowledge that they would soon fall to callous invaders but desperation not to pass without leaving a terrible mark upon the world. A single Magi's word is nothing but an implication that can be discarded by the listener. But every Magi speaking at once . . . that is not an implication, but a command. They commanded something to serve their needs, and since nothing existed that matched, a new being was created to answer them. The Magi's foe was magic, and so this being became magic's enemy. The Magi wanted the invaders to die in fear and pain, so the being became clever and malicious. But because it was the whole of these people commanding, there was no single direction it could follow for shape or even its limitations. As a result, it became boundless and uncontrollable. The infestation's hive mind is exactly what it was born to be."

"Were you meant to fight it?" said Laura.

"No. I say that I am its successor, but my birth was more of an accident. You are aware that Thrax dealt heavily in Immortalist teachings?"

"It's one of the reasons no one tried to help them."

"One particular Immortal they enshrined in that place: Aster, light in the dark, soother, healer, and heavily associated with the Niveus found so abundantly around the city. They had a massive statue of Aster formed entirely out of solid Niveus. When I was born, I woke in this statue's lap. And I have realized," he ran a hand down his face, "that I share its likeness. It is my belief that when Rex attacked the people begged their patron deity for help, and there were enough Magi in that population to form the command. I am different from the infestation, because the people who created me had a solid focus on what they were summoning. They spoke as if to Aster, when their words reached only the stone. The Immortal either does not exist or deigned not to come, so the stone itself decided to answer them. I answered them. I am Niveus masquerading as the Immortal Aster, with the sole purpose of protecting Thrax from Rexian invaders. But by the time I was fully formed, the battle was over. There was no Thrax to protect."

"I'm sorry," Laura whispered.

"The old purpose has served me well. My dislike of Rexians has saved multiple Rangers in the past. I suspect it's also the reason I resurfaced after touching Anselm: a city being invaded by Rex, needing protection? My very existence balked at the idea. And so I returned." Grim looked up to meet Clae's crystal gaze. "Those who were re-formed in stone instead of born from it are more difficult to understand. If I could be called out of something that never lived, it makes sense for that which wishes to live to answer a call as well."

"By baiting?" said Laura.

"No," Okane said bitterly. "Baiting is just our convenience. That would just be using Clae as another piece of equipment."

"Though the concept is not entirely flawed," said Grim.

Laura bristled. "You think we should be happy using him like this?"

"I meant speaking and expecting a reaction," said Grim, unperturbed. "If you call sincerely enough, something will surely answer. The way Magi call, they are answered by what they expect and wish for: a dead guardian. If instead you call and expect a specific person, the response changes to fit." He cocked his head, studying Clae for a moment more. "Something is inside this shell and responding. Is it your friend? Is it something else believing itself to be your friend? I can't say. I doubt anyone will know until it gains enough consciousness. You may even end with an amalgam—personality without memory."

"So Okane just has to speak to him?" said Laura.

"He moved for - - -, not me," Okane pointed out.

"But I'm not Magi," said Laura. "I can't make a magic command like that!"

"You're not creating a being. You're addressing what's already there," said Grim. "It responded to you rather than Okane, so it sounds as if you've already reached it. It is already molding to the implication you've given by reaching out to it. All that's left is to solidify that, and the being will essentially dig its way out. Just keep speaking. It will follow your voice back to the light."

"Like an Underyear candle," said Laura.

Grim gave a small smile. "The tradition started for a reason."

Laura hesitated, then stood again. She approached Clae slowly.

"Not her, huh?" she murmured. "It's okay. You're not losing me yet."

Clae gave another sighing sound, and the crystal dimmed. He turned and retreated back up the stairs, trailing the tubes and broken glass with him.

"Amazing," said Okane.

"The amazing part of this is that only three amulets broke under his presence," said Grim, glancing at his pile of broken Niveus. "I'll need to replace them before I risk coming back. Between your magical testing and an active sentinel here, I'll stand the risk of breaking otherwise."

"Sorry, Grim."

"I knew the risks of success." Grim gathered his amulets together and stood. "My shift will begin at Toulouse soon, so I'll need to leave. I'll return when I gain new amulets, or when I have news on the tattoo removal for your recruits. Whichever comes first."

He bid them good-bye. In the following silence, Laura rubbed at her arm and said, "Okane, I'm sorry about what I said before, about Magi not mattering. I didn't mean—"

"I know - - - didn't," said Okane. "- - - weren't entirely - - -rself."

"I don't know why I got so angry so fast. I know I was worried about you being gone so long, but that's not an excuse."

"I . . . actually meant that literally. - - - weren't - - -rself."

Laura stopped short. "What?"

"- - - have a normal presence, as a magic strain. When - - - got angry earlier, it wasn't - - -r strain anymore. It was Clae's." Okane's brow furrowed. "I wonder if maybe channeling the sunk Pit affected - - - more than we realized. When - - - said it ripped out all - - -r energy . . . maybe - - -'re still a little empty. That would explain why - - - were so susceptible to the magic at Toulouse, and Anselm's echo. - - - were conducting again."

Laura snorted. "Like a bootleg Magi ability?"

"Put crudely, yes. But - - -'re not built to handle that kind of energy."

"Neither are you," said Laura, glancing back at the stairs.

Okane opened his mouth to argue but thought better of it. He simply sighed and held out a hand. "I'm sorry, too. About going so long without telling - - - what was happening. I didn't mean to worry - - -."

Laura smiled and took his hand. "It's okay. We're in this together, right?"

"Right."

As they made to leave, he stepped closer in a playful nudge and said, "I did find a few useful non-Magi things while experimenting in here, though."

"Do I even want to know?"

"It might come in handy. Did - - - know that if - - -'re using one of those staffs, or something that makes an aura like the Rexian blades, - - - can manipulate the aura?"

"Liar."

"It's true, I swear! It's not by much, but if - - - think *really* hard about it being hot—"

"Or maybe it just was hot already?"

"Ha, ha. If - - -'re going to scoff at my discoveries, why don't - - - tell me what happened to - - - today?"

"Well . . ."

"Ah. I missed a lot, didn't I?"

"It's nothing I can't catch you up on."

8

HOOK LINE AND SINKER

Amicae *Dead Ringer*, April 1, 1234

AMICAE GRAND UNIVERSITY ATTACKED

In the midst of Amicae Grand University's Alternate-Automate Convention, the building was evacuated due to an infestation. Good on you, Silver Kings! This is surely an opportunity to gloat about how skillful you are compared to Mad Dogs. The Second Quarter pisses itself in fear of your greatness. More importantly, rumor has it that this was staged to cover up theft of one of the event entries. Which entry remains a mystery, as the participant list is now classified. Will it help uphold "balance" in the city?

As always, many thanks to Head Sweeper Laura Kramer and her tireless workers, who ensured that the infestation didn't spread and thereby saved hundreds of lives. No one else will likely acknowledge you, but your bravery is not lost on us.

The *Dead Ringer*'s article crumpled as Laura stuffed the paper under one arm and hopped down from the trolley. She was doubly frustrated with their stinking writers today. Why did they constantly have to sing her praises and ruin her reputation with the public? This was exactly what got her in trouble so easily when Juliana MacDanel started her plans. Sure,

Renard had a point about it being suspicious to not write about her, but still. Life could be so much easier. More importantly, she'd read every copy of the *Dead Ringer* from front to back ever since the Sylph infestation, and hadn't found a trace of whatever "news from the south" the Mad Dogs had been so worked up over. It was just like them to be so eye-catching and secretive at the same time.

"One of these days," she grumbled, striding down Acis Road, "I'm going to corner one of those Mad Dogs and force the truth out of them."

"Could you really?"

Laura froze. She turned her head slowly, mortified. Renard leaned against an alley wall, out of sight from the street and primed to flee into the residential sprawl behind him. He smiled with amusement.

Really? Renard himself? Hadn't Minnie and Blanche said Haru would be trying to recruit her next? No, there was no need to panic. They'd also said that Renard was lenient with Sinclairs—he'd accept any refusal and be on his way without any trouble.

Laura sucked in a deep breath for courage and said, "What do you want?"

"No 'thank you'?" Renard rolled his eyes. "I suppose that would be too much to ask for in a Sinclair of any type."

A thank-you, after threatening them? How arrogant. Some of Laura's fear ebbed for actual annoyance.

"What are you doing here?" she asked.

"Looking for you, of course. Come here."

"I'd rather not."

"Oh? Either you come here, or I'll go out to you and make ourselves truly obvious to anyone at the trolley stop."

Laura stormed over to him, ignoring his laughter.

"You are *just* like your old boss."

"Who hated you," Laura recalled.

"Most people do," said Renard, still smiling.

"What do you want?" said Laura.

"Many things. For now . . ." He held out a paper shopping bag. When Laura didn't immediately take it, he waved it from side to side. "Come now, it's not dangerous anymore."

Laura took it gingerly and looked inside. The object there was a familiar shape. On her first wilds experience with the Rangers, they'd found an amulet forged in the shape of an old sword hilt—an original high-magical piece. This looked the same size and shape, though part of the cross guard must've snapped off. She couldn't confirm it because the whole object was wrapped tight in the same wire she used to light Bijou.

"The amulet you buried in the Sylph," said Renard. "We recovered it and got rid of what little infestation remained, but it does your goody-goody little heart well to see we followed through, doesn't it?"

Honestly it did, but Laura leveled her flattest look at him.

"If you're looking for a thanks or a pat on the back, you really shouldn't—" She broke off. She'd been warned against mentioning the kidnapping to him. Maybe Renard would let her go, but she had a feeling Minnie would hunt her for sport at the slightest excuse. "Never mind."

The Mad Dog's smile vanished. "I apologize for the kidnapping."

Laura blinked in surprise. "You knew about it?"

"Not at the time, but Minnie tends to brag even when she shouldn't." At Minnie's name his expression soured; as much as Minnie had raved about him, her adoration must not be reciprocated. "It's been made clear that Mad Dogs should respect your decision, whatever it may be. They shouldn't have tried coercing you that way."

Laura eyed him shrewdly. "So you'll respect my choice even if I say no?"

"Why, of course! We'll treat you as a respected enemy just as we did with Clae, and the Silver Kings."

"That doesn't reassure me."

"It's not meant to. But perhaps this will: we are both Sweepers. We are both fighting for the same cause: to protect our home from that."

He gestured at the bag and the amulet inside. Laura was quiet a moment, then asked, "Did you plant it?"

Renard raised a thin brow. "Are you accusing me of threatening the public with infestations?"

"You planted the Falling Infestation, didn't you?" said Laura.

Renard threw his head back and laughed. He didn't answer the question.

"All of them that I've seen in this drought were related to you," Laura pressed. "The first appeared in a property that pays protection fees to the Mad Dogs. The second one was the Sylph Canal"—she shook the bag for emphasis—"and the one at the Grand University showed traces of other Sweepers steering it. The only other Sweepers in Amicae are the mobs. It all leads back to the Mad Dogs."

Renard sneered. "What a pretty little web you've drawn."

"What did your investigation tell you that day? What's the news from the south that has people so scared?" Laura demanded.

"Luckily for you, Coronae's lifting its ban on the information today." He smiled again, thin and mocking. "I'm sure you'll be briefed on it in a few hours. It wouldn't do well for you to know the information going in, or the Council may really suspect a link with the mobs. Ah . . ." He tipped his head. "But I believe someone's here to warn you already."

"Laura!" someone called. Was that Amelia?

"Best to listen to her fear," said Renard. "Best to understand the consequences. Learn just what path will really save you."

"Laura!" Amelia cried again, frantic.

Laura had never heard Amelia afraid. She instinctively moved back toward the street, but halfway out the alley she stopped. She looked him in the eye and asked, "Do you think the hive is in Terual?"

"Who can tell? There's been no precedent to say what the hive's presence looks like. At the same time, it can't be disproven, either." He pushed himself off the wall and turned to walk away down the alley. "Try to stay intact. We may need you in the near future."

"Laura!"

This last shout came far too close to her ear, coupled with a body slamming into her back. Laura almost toppled over entirely before righting herself. It was indeed Amelia, out of breath and cupping Laura's face to inspect it. Laura glanced to the side, but Renard had vanished.

"Did he do anything to you?" said Amelia; she must've seen him leave.

"No," said Laura. "What's wrong? Why are you here on Acis?"

"I followed up on my pen pal." Amelia's voice broke. "It's—It's—Laura, there's no more letters coming. There will never be another letter. Gaudium is dead."

The words passed over her like air.

"What are you talking about?" said Laura, because that couldn't be true. The infestation spike might be happening everywhere else, but Gaudium had the same infestation sightings as Amicae did and had many times the number of Sweepers. There was no way a single piddly monster could overpower an entire city. Amicae would've gotten an SOS, or a messenger, or seen something. There would have been warning. Their closest neighbor couldn't just slip out of existence without Amicae noticing.

"Everyone is dead," Amelia whispered.

"How?" said Laura. If it wasn't an infestation . . . "Did Rex get past—"

Amelia shook her head. "It wasn't Rex. Monsters took over the city."

Laura tottered back against the wall and slid down it, gripping the wrapped amulet as if that could bring back reality. Amelia sank to the ground in front of her.

"The only notice was a telegram sent to Spei, but no one could make any sense of it. When Spei tried to hail Gaudium for clarification, there wasn't any answer, so they reached out to cities like Avis to help with an investigation. But when the representatives arrived . . ." Amelia gestured uselessly. "They couldn't even get close. It's teeming with monsters. There's total silence on the radios, the telegrams, the telephones. They don't think anyone survived."

"The satellite towns?"

"Gone with the city."

Laura could hardly comprehend it. Gaudium's newspapers had reported on the Falling Infestation. Their head Sweeper had been so punctual with her letters, her words clipped but kind. That apprentice, Ellie, had written her such an excited note. Ellie was dead. Laura would never get to visit them for a Gin transfer. She'd never be able to see the girl who wrote with such choppy, energetic handwriting. She'd never be able to thank her. The realization made her feel sick. "How could that happen?" she whispered.

"I don't know." Amelia's voice was barely audible. "No one's left to tell us."

Laura held the amulet closer to her chest. If it weren't wrapped, she'd likely cut herself on the pieces. "We should've done something. We should've gone to help. Why would they contact Spei instead of us?"

"Laura, you're four Sweepers total. They knew you didn't have anyone to spare."

"But I would've helped them."

"And sent maybe one person. What could you really have done?"

"Something!" Laura cried, clutching the bag so hard it began to tear. "I don't know! I never know! But I can't just—Ellie is—Why couldn't I have done anything for Ellie?" Amelia slid to sit beside her and wrapped an arm around Laura's shoulder, pulling her close as her breath began to rattle. "A-are you sure? The whole city? It's not a joke?"

"I'd never joke about something this big," said Amelia.

"All of them, though?"

"Every man, woman, and child. It's—" Amelia's breath caught too. She had to choke out the words: "It's been too long. If anyone had survived the first wave . . . they still wouldn't have lasted to now. They're all gone. Ellie, and Gina . . . and everyone else." She pressed her face against Laura's crown, as if trying to prevent herself from crying. "Coronae's made it official."

Laura tended to operate on what was in front of her. She dealt with the people assigned to her, complained about her encounters, but she had a hard time seeing the forest for the trees. Her mind kept catching on *Ellie, Ellie,* but this had been all of Gaudium. It wasn't a personal event. It was a catastrophe for all of Orien. A little piece of her—the head Sweeper, the inner Clae—kept trying to galvanize her toward action, but that was an entire city. It was too much to bear.

"What do we do?" she whispered, petrified. "What should—Is there anything we can do?"

"There's always something we can do," said Amelia.

Yes. Yes, she could . . . Laura braced herself as if to stand, but just as quickly her strength failed her. She had four Sweepers. How could she possibly defend Amicae? She didn't know what to do! If only Clae were here. If only someone could tell her how to fix this.

"I have to find Renard," she said absently.

Amelia's head jerked back up. "What did you say?"

"Renard!" Yes. It was perfect. He would know. "He already knew about Gaudium. He's already putting together some kind of plan. He's a Sweeper, too, he'll know how to—"

"No!" Amelia rumbled.

Laura gaped at her. "But—"

"No," Amelia repeated. "Don't you dare go chasing down that path. The Mad Dogs might have numbers and equipment, but they've also got ulterior motives. Once you sign with them, it's not some friendly alliance that lets you talk back or step out if you're uncomfortable. They will *own* you. They won't play nice with the Council or other Sweeper guilds, either. You want any shot of intercity help or a strong front against infestations, you have to stay above them. You have to be Sinclairs."

"How does being Sinclair possibly help us?" cried Laura.

"The name has power," said Amelia. "Sinclairs are the height of Sweeper romance—this is the Sweeper city! You need to milk that for all it's worth." She seized Laura's shoulders and gave her a gentle shake. "Help will come. You don't have to rely on Renard for anything." She gave a rude gesture where Renard had disappeared, then pulled Laura back to her feet. She fit Laura under her arm and guided her toward the shop. "Renard isn't any better than the rest of the mobsters. I knew him all the way back when his voice was cracking and his face was full of pimples, but even then, he was a fanatic. You know why he was fired as a Sinclair apprentice? Clae found him stealing amulets out of storage. He'd been rotating out infestations for the Mad Dogs to use, because he figured more infestation activity would force the Council's hand about the wall policy. How many deaths do you think he had a hand in? He didn't care who got hurt as long as he accomplished his goal, and he's the same way now. He's not someone you should put your trust in."

Laura nodded, but she could only think of Ellie and Gaudium. She didn't know if she had the luxury of trust at this point.

In a gap between buildings, she caught sight of the horizon and the bay. Gaudium sat there on its other side, a lonely, distant husk, and it was very quiet. It always would be.

Avis *Wings*, April 9, 1234

GAUDIUM HAS FALLEN

With great distress, we must inform you that the city of Gaudium is destroyed. The first sign of trouble was reported at 7:45 P.M. on March 18, when Gaudium's head Sweeper sent a telegram for assistance to the city of Spei, which read simply, "TALKING WALLS." Gaudium's communication by telegram and telephone continued at this time, before cutting off at midnight.

With no further clarification on the message and normal levels of intercity calls beyond the Sweeping department this was considered unremarkable, but nevertheless Spei's Sweepers deployed to investigate. Communication did not resume the following morning and hails from the incoming Sweepers were not answered. Investigation teams slowed their approach, and discovered that Gaudium had been overrun by infestations. A joint operation by Coronae, Avis, and Spei encircled the city and advanced through the equally wrecked fifteen satellites.

While Gaudium itself remains impenetrable, attempts at reconnaissance and eradication have led Coronae to issue the official proclamation that the city is lost. No survivors or remains have been recovered. If Gaudium's Sweepers put up a fight, they were not able to issue further distress calls, and too much time has passed to hold any hope of their continued existence. Avis's head Sweeper Florian Wiles, whose sister was highly ranked in Gaudium's guild, remains unavailable for comment. The inciting incident remains unknown.

Lux *Beacon*, April 9, 1234

CORONAE CALLS FOR HEIGHTENED DEFENSE

Following the declaration of Gaudium's loss, Coronae has outlined preventative measures for all cities to adopt against a new wave of infestations. These measures include increased lighting in all districts and the dedication of an emergency Sweeper line (turn to page 5 for a full list, and direct any questions to your local police or Sweeper office). In addition, Coronae has ordered Gaudium be cordoned off, both to prevent anyone from interfering in their investigation of the city's demise, and to ensure that the infestations breeding there do not overflow to threaten nearby Amicae.

In the past year Amicae has experienced much tribulation in their Sweeper department, leaving only four persons employed. If Gaudium's infestations grow, we are certain to have lost two cities. This will compromise trade, travel, and communication, and potentially cripple Terual's southern support. As Coronae has stated, "We must not allow monsters to take root in our land or in our thoughts. Together we will hold our ground, and together we will fight for tomorrow."

Amicae *Sun*, April 13, 1234

COUNCIL ISSUES EDICT ON GAUDIUM'S FALL

Last week it was announced by Coronae that Gaudium has been destroyed. Amicae's Council secluded themselves to deliberate how best to protect the city in the wake of such a disaster. After receiving reports from head Sweeper Laura Kramer, representatives of the Ranger scouting force, and Coronae's own investigators, they have reached a decisive conclusion. While Gaudium is currently infested with monsters, their original telegram alert spoke specifically of talking walls. "Gaudium's destruction was clearly by some interference," says Councilman Raymond Burke. "The rest of Orien is so paranoid about monsters that they haven't considered the truth of human sabotage." Amicae has already dealt with Rexian interference during the Falling Infestation of November

1233 and the invasion of the mines in January of this year. Rex has made no secret of wishing other cities harm, and the recent upsurge in monster activity provides them cover and force in attacking their targets. The status of Rex has been a mystery since ERA abandoned its southernmost rails, but the Council believes this is further evidence of their hand in Gaudium: infestations have mainly been harassing Zyran cities, and historically their activity level loses steam while traveling northward. For such a sudden and vicious spike to occur so far beyond the observed line shows that it was planted and nurtured for such an effect.

The Council will now be enacting measures to prevent any further Rexian aggression against Amicae.

Canis *Trekker*, April 15, 1234

AMICAE TIES ITS NOOSE

Amicae's Council has announced they are rejecting Coronae's list of preventative measures. While every other city in Terual and Zyra has adopted these measures, Amicae states they are "unnecessary," as they believe Gaudium was destroyed by Rexian extremists. Canis Sweeper Basil Garner wishes to remind everyone that, even if it is planted by Rexian design, an infestation is still the ultimate enemy we face; Coronae's measures are valid safety precautions no matter where or how an infestation is introduced.

Amicae's Council decision was unanimous in the court but contested on the ground. Even the city's mobs have lobbied alongside anxious citizens for Coronae's anti-infestation measures to be adopted in addition to the Council's anti-human protocols. The Council has declined, stating their current stance will prevent any infestation from taking root. This echoes their earlier "wall policy," previously debunked in November of last year. The correlation has sparked fear and concern among their neighbors. Travelers and foreign workers have been advised by their home cities to evacuate Amicae immediately, but while Amicae's rule may be dangerous, it isn't so easy to leave.

Over a telephone call Miss Dolly Cosetta, teacher at Amicae's Rutherford University, admitted, "As much as we fear being trapped and dying inside Amicae, we fear leaving it almost as much. ERA has blocked off routes near Gaudium, leaving only the northern rails. For a native of Vir like myself, I would need to travel the width of the island and back again for us to round the mountains and reach home. I shudder to think of those poor citizens of Avis, whose commute was once manageable but would now take them three times their usual distance; and poor Spei can no longer be reached by land at all. This is a long way in wilds that were already dangerous, where even city walls and a full Sweeper guild were not ample protection. There is no illusion of safety. Few people are secure enough to face such a journey, and most people are resigning themselves to die in suitable comfort."

Amicae *Dead Ringer*, April 16, 1234

TO WHOM IT MAY CONCERN

We did not expect any better from you, Council, but know this: We will not allow our city to die for nothing but the pride of old men.

Amicae *Sun*, April 17, 1234

AMICAE COUNCIL TARGETED BY MOBS

The painted circles which once terrorized the MARU have reappeared: every Council member who voted not to adopt Coronae's anti-infestation measures woke to find circles painted in their homes or on frequented routes.

While the MARU functioned, such circles were used as targets to threaten victims, though they were gifted in much subtler ways. Unlike that time there is no overarching mob alliance, as the police report Amicae is currently split between the Silver Kings and Mad Dogs mobs. It is believed that the Mad Dogs faction is responsible for this resurgence of threats. The Council has described these actions as childish and repugnant; they have vowed that the previously voted decisions will remain in place. Amicae's police force has been granted increased authority in order to bring the Mad Dogs to justice.

Laura was no stranger to dreaming of strangling politicians—she'd done quite a bit of that while the wall policy was in place—but even she was a little surprised by her own resentment when she opened up the papers this week. If Clae had been here to read the news, he'd have stormed off to give the Council a piece of his mind, but they'd clearly learned from their dealings with him. Sweepers had been forbidden from attending their meetings. Laura had to make her "report" through Albright, who then turned over all that information to Councilwoman Victoria Douglas. As much as Douglas fought for Sweepers, she was only one voice in the whole of the Council, and they hadn't yet hit election season; the same people who'd so aggressively upheld the wall policy were still the ones making decisions, even when Rexian spies weren't filling their pockets. In retrospect, Laura really shouldn't have hoped for much.

To Laura's argument that infestations could get past walls, the Council replied that they would prevent infestations to start with by blocking the Rexians . . . because that kind of approach had worked *so well* even without a human enemy.

To Laura's argument that "talking walls" could mean infestations instead of people—she'd heard the whispers in the Sylph, and the voice at the Grand University—they informed her she was hysterical.

To make matters worse, Laura had gotten the news about Gaudium before Coronae's official announcement. Amelia had received the warning from another pen pal, an Avis Sweeper who'd been involved in the initial investigation, and Laura had immediately reported it to Albright. She'd been up-front about where she'd heard it, and her source was legitimate, but the Council still somehow seemed to think she'd gotten her information from somewhere shady. It didn't take a genius to connect her lead to the Mad Dogs who'd already been working with such knowledge. Most of the Council had already believed she was a Mad Dog sympathizer, if not a full member, and with the Mad Dogs' recent activity, this made them extremely unwilling to deal with Laura or any of her protests.

The Council's anti-Rexian protocols doubled as anti-mobster. Barricades went up at every ramp to other Quarters, and even blocked off portions of the major circuits. Anyone who wanted to pass had to provide not only their identification but also written permission for them to leave their Quarter; it was an absolute nightmare for anyone who commuted across Quarters for work or shopping, made still harder because any suspected mobsters or protesters were immediately arrested at the blockades. Even Weaver Mateo, who'd shared Coronae's measures with his parish, was warned that he'd been added to the list of undesirables. Satellite citizens and those with faulty IDs like Grim and Cherry had to lie low and ask other people to do their grocery shopping. If their locations were shared with the police, raids were carried out. The gunfights and protests reached the level they had after the chaos of the Falling Infestation. Honestly, it had only been a few days and the jails were already overflowing.

It was worst for the Rexians themselves. Just hearing all of this suspicion had to make them paranoid, and on top of that they had the tattoos on their faces. A clearer target couldn't be drawn. They'd taken up Albright's original suggestion—to find a Spiritualist interpretation for the tattooed numbers—and took it a step further by painting the pattern of the accompanying Spiritualist weave over them every morning, The design had come courtesy of Mateo, who'd happily told Laura that this was common practice among the more zealous Spiritualists in his sect. It might have hidden the tattoos but was even more blatant.

"Honestly, we may as well draw one of those circles on ourselves," Zelda grumbled as she read the mob article and scratched irritably at her nose. She'd spread a number of different newspapers on the Sweeper shop's counter, as if to fact check that the situation really was as bad as it appeared. "It's only a matter of time before someone asks us to wash this all off, and it's not like people could've missed us before."

"The people who saw you before also saw you moving with a police guard, so they ought to keep their mouths shut," said Laura.

"In this climate? I'm surprised we haven't got an angry crowd kicking down the door. Imagine the torches, the pitchforks—"

"Luckily for us, all pitchforks are being used as traps in the satellites," said Okane.

Zelda looked up, clearly unsure whether to laugh or not. "Was that a joke? It was a pretty terrible one."

"Not entirely." Okane held up another page of the *Sun,* which outlined the steps satellite towns were taking for safety. "It sounds like they're using a lot of farm equipment for blockades and traps."

"As if that's going to help at all," Laura groaned.

"- - -'re sure Amicae's Council won't reconsider their decision?" asked Ivo.

Laura shook her head in resignation. "They'd rather dig their own grave than admit they've made a mistake."

"What happened to overturn the wall policy?"

"An entire evacuation of the city, the fireworks show of the century, and outright riots from the mobs," Laura drawled.

Okane sadly nodded along. "Can't be reproduced."

"Hopeless," said Zelda, and Ivo looked worried; he probably wondered whether it would've been better to stick out the Rexian crusades than come to Amicae.

The telephone rang. Laura winced at the sound. To her knowledge the police had rerouted any Sweeper calls to headquarters to ensure only legitimate contacts reached the Sinclairs, but a few incorrect ones had been patched through since the Coronae announcement went public. She really, really hoped it wasn't another person calling to berate her for being a Mad Dog.

Laura lifted the earpiece and said, "Hello, Sinclair Sweepers."

"There's an infestation in the Fourth Quarter." The voice came fast and hushed. "How soon can you be here?"

Ah, so it wasn't a complainer. She didn't know whether to be relieved or horrified at her first real infestation since the announcement.

"Where in the Fourth Quarter?" she asked, pulling over her notepad. "What's the extent of the infestation? Any casualties?"

A pause, then, "You won't be bringing policemen with you, right?"

Laura almost laughed. "Sir, I would if I could, but the police are a little too busy chasing Mad Dogs to be tailing us right now."

"Good. If police were on the premises, we'd never live it down."

"I'm sorry, but if you're in illegal activities, then maybe it would be better for you to chase down the Mad Dogs yourself."

"Legality isn't the issue," the man rushed to assure her. "You see, it's a meat-packing plant. If news of an infestation were to get out, our employees would never feel safe there again. Besides, even if it's a ridiculous notion, if our competitors got wind of it they'd employ the trashy news to spread rumor of us canning essence of monster or something. No matter how unrealistic it is, it would catch the public's imagination, and especially in this climate . . . Oh, we'd be sunk."

"What information do you have about this infestation? What have you seen of it?"

"It got my coworker while we were doing inspections. There's no way to fake something like that. Slimy thing."

Okay. This man was far too calm for someone who'd seen his coworker die. Yes, he sounded nervous and shaky, but still . . . maybe he was in shock? "How long ago was this?" she asked.

"W-within the hour."

Not *just now*? No panicking about the escape, or even a range like *twenty minutes*? She didn't like that kind of vagueness.

"Is the building in a crowded district, or is there ample space around it? Has the sunlight been able to pen it in?"

"Yes, we're set apart from most of our neighbors. There are trucks and rails around us, but as far as buildings go, we're alone. I don't believe it's escaped."

Laura kept asking questions, narrowing down the location before assuring the man they'd be there as soon as possible. She hung up the telephone, ripped the notes from the pad, and announced, "We've got to get going. It sounds like this one's active."

Okane had been standing rather close, and he looked between her and the telephone with trepidation. "- - -'re suspicious about something."

"Honestly? Yes. He sounded way too even. But I can't claim that everyone's reactions to this sort of thing would be the same, and besides, we can't just let a potential infestation sit," said Laura. "I mean . . . Gaudium is *dead*. What if their end started like this? Just one little monster that got out of hand?"

The knowledge made her freeze up a little again. Panic bubbled in her chest, suffocating. She closed her eyes and breathed deeply through her nose. If she could just focus on something else, then *an entire dead city* wouldn't be pounding through her head at every moment. It would just hang high above her, like a guillotine blade ready for whenever her mind was suitably unoccupied. Needless to say, she hadn't been sleeping well.

"That's true." Okane's shoulders hunched at the reminder, but he shook himself back to the situation at hand. "I don't think we can all go on this one, though. If someone tries to reach us to report a second infestation, we need to have people ready to respond to it."

"Okay, we'll split in two. One half stays here for any news, the other goes to the confirmed infestation."

Laura, of course, was going. While her instinct was to drag Okane with her, she couldn't just leave all the Rexians alone—what if someone came in and called the police on them? They might have another Sylph Canal debacle. No, Okane would stay with Zelda. Ivo and Bea were used to fighting in tandem, so they went with Laura.

Of course, descending to the Fourth Quarter meant passing by a blockade. "Stay close to me," Laura told the other two as they approached the line of soldiers. "I've gone through something like this before. Have your IDs out and ready, but don't make any other sudden moves."

"Identification," the nearest soldier demanded.

Laura and the others held out their IDs. Once upon a time they'd have shown their Sweeper rings, but those weren't recognizable enough outside the police department and no police officers were here to intervene for them. The soldier looked over their cards closely. Luckily the photographs were too small to make out what exactly was on the Rexians' faces.

"What's that you're carrying?"

"This?" Laura patted her new holster. "This is an axe. It's Sweeper equipment, the same as anything else I've got on me, but it looks a lot more threatening than a few glowing beads, doesn't it?"

She didn't know how to use it, but she'd picked up the axe from the armory in an attempt to look a little scarier. It wasn't foolproof, but mobsters would be less likely to try kidnapping her if she could swing a sharp instrument around. From some basic testing she'd found it had similar properties to Rexian blades.

The soldier didn't look impressed. "Openly carrying a weapon is against the safety protocols."

"You'll find I have stars enough to allow it," Laura said sweetly.

The soldier scowled. "Your friends don't."

"My *employees* are in my care, and also carrying Sweeper gear. If you'd like us to demonstrate the weapons' magical properties, we can do that. But they *have* been cleared by the police chief, the same as I have."

"What's this?" said another soldier, squinting at Ivo's face. "They've got marks on their faces!"

Bea stepped between him and Ivo, and gave him a withering look. "I advise - - - to keep - - -r rude observations to - - -rself."

"We're looking for Rexians with face marks!" said the second soldier. "Where did you come from? Are you Rexian?"

"We were originally Rangers based in a satellite town near Terrae, and were recruited to serve as Amicae Sweepers," Ivo replied. For all the tenseness of the situation, his tone was crisp and cordial . . . but Laura noticed he'd fallen into something very close to parade rest position. He was definitely channeling some old Rexian behavior right now. "We were promoted to our current posts by the chief of police on March nineteenth, so our lower clearance is evidence of our short time here. If - - - need at any time to confirm our identities with Chief Albright, we will of course be happy to comply with - - -r investigation."

"But you'll have to be the ones to tell the chief why you stalled the only official Sweepers in Amicae when they were on their way to an infestation," Laura cut in.

Clearly neither soldier was pleased at the idea of facing Albright. The second one pressed, "But your faces—"

"They're Spiritualists, idiot," said Laura.

"We are members of the Three Child sect. Normally we would wear our chosen weave in our clothes, but Sweeper uniforms are not issued in such a design," said Ivo. "My weave is that of harmony, and my friend Bea's is the weave of strength."

"They could be hiding markings under the paint," said the second soldier.

Ivo reached a hand to his face in false distress. "This is something sacred to me. If - - - insist, I'll wash it off, but I hope - - - will provide me the paint to replace it. I wonder, do I look so Rexian to - - -?"

He didn't look Rexian in the least.

"The girl, though," the second soldier said, halfhearted.

"I've known Bea since we were infants. We grew up together," said Ivo.

And bigoted Rexians surely wouldn't raise their own children alongside Wasureijin, would they? The second soldier backed off, grumbling.

"And where are your orders to leave this Quarter?" said the first soldier. "If you're working on the police chief's orders, you must have a note."

"A note?" Laura tapped her foot irritably. "You think we have time to wait around for *notes* when infestations move as fast as they do, and the police are busy as they are right now?"

The first soldier sneered. "No orders, no passage."

"Call Chief Albright," said Laura. "I see a call box set up in your little bunker over there. Call her right now."

"I'm not about to—"

"You'll answer to her sooner or later. It's best for you if you get it done now and let us do our job."

They must be fairly new at this, because they were easily bullied. The first soldier waved irritably for the second to go to the call box. He left the door ajar, so while they were too far away to hear what was said, Laura definitely saw him jump in fright when he finally got Albright on the line. After a brief conversation the man returned and said, "Chief says we let the Sinclair Sweepers through, no questions asked."

"Thank you," said Laura.

The soldiers returned their IDs and waved them on through. Once they were out of earshot, Laura dropped back between Ivo and Bea and said, "How are we doing? Are you two okay after that?"

"We've dealt with far worse," said Ivo.

Bea seemed not to notice. She seemed weirdly vulnerable: a far-off look in her eyes, one hand up to brush fingers over her jaw as if her skin were fragile as porcelain.

"- - - painted the weave of strength on me?" she said.

"I did," affirmed Ivo.

"But it was supposed to be based on the number." Bea's brow twitched ever so slightly, with what might be puzzlement on a normal person. "I thought it was a match for 'attentiveness.'"

"It's only a line in a weave. Just because it matches one pattern doesn't mean it will not match another at some point in the design. - - - didn't appear pleased by 'attentiveness,' so I took the liberty of looking up a more agreeable match." Ivo cocked his head. "I believed it fitting. - - - are the strongest person I know."

Bea's eyes narrowed as if in pain, and her hands fisted.

Laura frowned, unable to see what could be causing that distress. "What's wrong?"

"I don't want to talk to - - -."

Bea's tone was bland, but there must've been something hidden in her "you," because Ivo leaned in, concerned.

"Bea? If - - - don't like it, I can look up another—"

"I do not wish to speak," Bea said, harsher, and this shut him up.

She walked ahead of them, as if she couldn't bear to look at their faces.

Laura looked between them, totally lost. "Am I missing something here? Usually she's mad at me, but this time it was more like she was shaken up."

Ivo frowned at Bea's back. "Bea has been facing some frustrations lately," because when was she not, "but I'm afraid I don't know the cause right now either."

Bea stayed clammed up during the rest of their trip, and not even Ivo's renewed fascination with the cable car could peel her gaze from the toes of her boots.

The cable car trundled them all the way down to the warehouse district of the Fourth Quarter. Apparently, the barricades at the cable car stations above and below were enough security in the military's opinion, so no one awaited them at the stop to demand identification or letters. No one awaited them at all, actually.

Normally there would at least be an attendant in the station to monitor the mechanisms, but when they coasted into place, Laura saw nothing beyond the window. They opened the car door on their own, and stepped out into the Fourth Quarter.

The warehouse district was just as shabby as the Ranger district had been, though its buildings were definitely more permanent. The Sweepers strode past storehouses, factories, and holding pens as they approached the outer Quarter wall. Maybe it was due to all the issues with the blockades, but activity here seemed nonexistent. The stink, though? That was certainly present. No wonder all these factories were out so far; it kept the smells from bothering residential neighborhoods.

They knew their destination when they heard squealing and the smell got worse. Laura's nose rebelled at the stink of unwashed, sunbaked pigs and their droppings. She pulled up her bandana, breathed deep from the kin-infused fabric.

The meat-packing plant was a complete mess of buildings across a wide area: some squat, some tall, some sprouting smokestacks taller than the Cynder Block, all broken up with tracks for easier movement of the products. On the far side of the buildings lay a sea of holding pens, all filled to the brim with snorting, slathering pigs. It was enormous. Pigs, as far as the eye could see.

Ivo's eyes watered, and he pulled on his own mask. "What is this smell? There is something in addition to the pigs."

"Dead meat?" Laura said dryly. "Decay? Pickling chemicals?"

"- - - sound thrilled by the idea," Ivo observed.

"I've got to say, I've never wanted to set foot in a packing plant." Laura checked the ground as she walked closer. With this many pigs, they must've been herded in at some point, and the stench of their droppings was bad enough without it being on her shoes. "I've heard terrible things about them. The Council passed a bunch of laws for food safety and worker rights, so everything should've been reformed, but those horror stories linger, you know? One of my other Cynder Block neighbors has an uncle who worked in a meat-packing plant, and his hands were *pickled*. Regular factories have workers losing fingers or hands to the machines, but in packing plants entire people fall into the machines and die." Something occurred to her. She looked up at the pigs. Even if the factory was closed for inspection today, someone had to be minding the livestock, if only to make sure no one stole it all. Her voice came slower, more contemplative as she tried and failed to locate any workers. "I've heard rumors that some of the smoked meats ten years ago contained bits of lost child workers. I don't think it was ever proved, but—"

"I assure you, Miss Sweeper, you are in no danger of falling into the hopper," said a man, approaching them from the direction of one of the shorter buildings.

He was dressed as plainly as she expected a plant worker to be, but he walked with a certain ease that didn't match a potential crisis for his company.

"Are you our caller?" said Laura.

"I am," said the man, but elaborated no further. Laura's suspicion rose.

She glanced back at the pigs and said, "It looks like the infestation hasn't gotten out yet. If it had, you'd be down a lot of livestock."

"Yes, I believe it's been hiding in the holding rooms. I've asked the guards to monitor the doors and windows but not to enter."

"Has it made any other attempts at attacking you?" said Laura.

He shook his head. "Out of sight, out of mind, apparently."

"That or preparing for an assault," said Laura. "What's inside the holding rooms? Anything that it could make use of?"

"It's a brainless monster." The man coughed out a laugh. "What could it possibly make use of?" When they simply stared at him his mouth flattened out again. "Meats are held there before being transferred into the freezers. There are no machines beyond the conveyors and hooks."

"Is any meat left in there?" said Laura.

She wasn't worried about a pig's corpse coming off its hook to chase them; it had long been proven that infestations couldn't use dead bodies as amulets. She was much more concerned with the idea of hunting something through a forest of carcasses; the scenario seemed nightmarish. If she'd wanted to see something's insides she'd have chosen a different profession.

"Some, but it's all cleaned. There are no foreign objects inside," said the man.

"Comforting."

"I'll bring you to the doors," said the man. He seemed suddenly shifty again, looking between them all before asking, "None of you are involved with the Scrooge Packing Plant, are you?"

"We're from a satellite town," said Ivo. "We have no link even with - - -rs."

"Excellent."

Still, he hesitated before leading them away. They skirted the first few buildings, past the initial entry for the animals, past the presumed areas of dismantlement and machinery. The man kept assuring them that the infestation had been isolated, that the holding area itself was isolated, but Laura couldn't see how that could possibly be the case. Factories had to be somewhat encapsulated, right? It would be counterproductive to trolley meat to a separate building and then right back into processing, no matter how many conveyor belts or days of amazing weather they might have. As they walked she looked around, and the doubt worsened in her mind. Still she found no one keeping an eye on the hogs, and no people there to guide the supposed inspector. She couldn't even spot the aforementioned guards.

"Hey," she whispered, lagging behind so she could lean in toward Ivo without the man's notice. "Do you feel anything off? Any sort of threat? Okane's picked up on hostile humans before."

"Do - - - expect hostility right now?" Ivo murmured.

"This is all rubbing me the wrong way," she admitted, still looking around for anything suspicious. "I may have jumped on this too fast. It didn't sit right with me on the call, but with Gaudium—I didn't want to take chances. For starters, who would be here about an inspection? Whatever inspector has to be impartial, right? Probably a city worker, a representative of the Council. If a Council worker discovers an infestation in the place he's inspecting, he's not going to try hushing it up. He'd call the police immediately, and we'd have heard it through them. The police are taking all our calls before forwarding the legitimate ones to us, so I assumed it was fine, but maybe this was something a police officer should've been on the call for, too. Or maybe they were even supposed to take the notes and then report it to us to be worked? They weren't really clear when they explained the new protocol. They might've been able to explain the situation to us better."

"I'm not sure how to interpret the police involvement, but perhaps it's the Council's man who was eaten?" Ivo guessed.

"If that's the case, then this person's trying to cover up the Council man's death. What does he have to gain from that? If they skim over the infestation's presence entirely, all that's left is to use the excuse that he died in the machinery here and there was too little of him left to identify. That's hardly better for the plant's reputation."

"Perhaps they'll claim the inspector never arrived," said Ivo, but he didn't appear convinced.

"We report our infestation sightings to the Council every other month," said Laura. "It wouldn't go unnoticed then, even if it bought them some time here in the present. So what's he playing at?"

"He may not be aware of that Sweeper tendency."

Laura glanced to check that the man wasn't hearing any of this. No, he was too busy fussing over the lock to the back door.

"I am not sensing any infestation presence whatsoever," said Bea.

"We may be too far beyond the walls to sense it, or it may be dormant," said Ivo, "but I agree. There is something unnerving about the situation. We'll have to be on our toes."

The man opened the door and gestured for them to follow. Yet another warning sign: surely a man who'd really seen an infestation here would be reluctant to even enter the shadow of the plant again, but he showed no hesitation.

"You see the staircase to your left? That's where the monster was when I saw it last."

"It could've moved," said Laura, watching his reaction. "It's been a while, and they tend to spread rather than stay put when there's any kind of activity around."

"You are the expert, Miss Sweeper," said the man. "I've seen no evidence of it moving, so I'd still start there, but please feel free to move through the rest of the plant as you see fit. Simply keep in mind that the equipment may be dangerous for those unused to its operation."

"We will." Laura jerked her head at the darkness spreading beyond them. "I don't suppose you could turn on the lights, too? That's the easiest way to keep infestations from spreading, and gives us the needed visibility to hunt them. Maybe you're trying to hide your machines, but all you're doing by leaving these off is hindering us in taking care of your problem."

"Of course," said the man. "The light switches are in another location, though. Please, allow me to put them on."

He slinked away. Ivo tracked him as he went, but once he was out of sight, looked forward again.

"Still not sensing anything?" Laura checked.

"No," said Ivo. "Could this really be a trap?"

"I'm not sure what it is," said Laura. "I mean, I don't think it is? I've already been kidnapped once. The Mad Dogs have more than made their point, and they've got bigger things to worry about right now."

At the mention, Ivo's eyes narrowed. "If they attempt such a thing again I'll make them regret it. That said, this situation seems a bit beyond a simple prank. I'm also leaning toward trap. Why and how, I don't know."

Something occurred to Laura, and she tensed, surveying the darkness before them with a sharper eye. "You don't think this is about you, right?"

Ivo frowned. "That man didn't pay any special attention to us or our faces."

"If this is an ambush to catch Rexians, they would not leave us so idle for so long," said Bea. "They would set upon us immediately, to limit our response."

She had a point.

They stood there a long while, the minutes dragging. Where had that man gone?

"We're not moving until you turn on the lights!" Laura shouted. Her voice echoed back in an ugly distorted waver. No one replied.

Bea pulled her blade from its sheath with a hiss. "If they will not seek our response, we shall seek theirs."

Ivo unsheathed his blade as well, and Laura pulled her axe from its holster. Together they climbed the flimsy, grated stairs. The sound echoed across the unknown length of the room. How big was this place, really? How many hiding places were in this gloom? She gripped the axe tighter and ordered, *light*. Its inlaid, twisting design hummed with the sense of fading sunlight; its hazy aura shone off the metal rail and dirty grates.

These stairs were too thin and flimsy to be for workers or transporting products. Sure enough, at the landing they found an office with large windows facing onto the floor for observation. They skirted this, and the light caught something on the nearby wall. A lever. Ivo looked around—a useless gesture—before seizing the handle and forcing it down. It went with a screech, a pop, and then light flooded the area. It was cold and impersonal, an ugly, white light that hummed overly electric and cast the room in a winter chill. Worse, it illuminated the length of the room: a half mile of dirt-covered floor, four long rails along the ceiling wrought with bands and gears to pull along the chains and hooks suspended from them. From these hooks dangled pigs: headless, footless, split open down the middle so the ribs, spine, and every muscle were sickeningly visible.

"Oh, right." Laura grimaced. "It's been *cleaned. No foreign objects*."

Luckily only the outside rails were stocked. Rather than slink through a forest of meat, they walked down the center with the pigs like a grisly honor guard.

"If this is 'some' pigs, I shudder to think how many they must go through in a normal day," said Ivo.

"They're not even refrigerated in here," Laura grumbled. "Do they just let meat hang here and fester on their days off? Disgusting. Remind me never to buy anything packaged here."

"Still no sign of infestation," Bea reported.

At the end of this room was a thick canvas curtain, dotted in stains just like the floor. Laura gripped her axe tighter in one hand, reached out, and pulled the curtain aside. The sight made her freeze.

This section of the room was a dead end, with no hooks along the side but one hanging directly in the center. The body there wasn't a pig. Laura sucked in a breath and averted her gaze, but the bloodstained shirt and lolling head were burned into her mind. That was a human. A human hanging from a meat hook. Her breath shuddered out as she whispered, "Oh, that is one hell of a way to go."

"He's not a worker," said Bea. "The clothing indicates upper-class status. Such an outfit is ill-suited for this environment."

She and Ivo ventured farther in and stepped around the corpse to inspect it.

"There's no way this was an accident," said Ivo. "His entire right arm is missing. Besides, look at the spatter on the floor. He must've been swinging."

"Swinging," Laura said faintly.

"Someone was pushing him. This was torture."

Laura forced herself to look back. Blood had been spattered all across the cement, but around its edge it had been smeared like a giant dark circle. For a while she focused only on that, breathing determinedly in and out. She looked higher.

The man on the hook had been through hell. His once-crisp clothing had been dirtied and torn, soaked in the blood of his mauled stump of an arm and the wicked hook punched through his left shoulder. Worst of all, she recognized him.

Good brains aren't determined by gender.

"Armand," she groaned.

"The Grand University worker?" said Ivo.

Dorthea had found Armand's glasses and thought he must've died in the infestation. Maybe that infestation hadn't been a cover-up for stealing an event entry. Maybe it had been placed to cover a kidnapping.

"Welcome to my office, head Sweeper. You've been overdue for a visit."

All three of them started. The canvas curtain shifted, and in stepped a familiar man. Haru's sleeves were rolled up, but that hadn't saved his shirt from blood splatter.

"What is this?" said Laura.

"This is one of our interrogation rooms." Haru kept walking, gave Armand's body a shove as he passed so it swung. "I am a negotiator, Miss Kramer, and I negotiate with all techniques I have access to. How far I have to use them is up to my client."

"Did you set up the call to the Sweeper shop?" said Laura. There were always policemen in the mobs' pockets; that was a fact of life. One of the crooked ones must've taken the Mad Dogs' call and sent it through to the shop without approval.

"I did," Haru confirmed. "As you can tell, there's no infestation here. You've just been invited for a talk."

"So, this is the last offer that Blanche and Minnie mentioned?" said Laura. "You're trying to recruit me to the Mad Dogs again?"

"You rejected our gentle offer, so I thought we'd try something a little more threatening," said Haru. "Blanche and Minnie's little escapade made for a good warning, but it wasn't quite official, and it happened before you learned about Gaudium. So, allow me to start again. Our boss wants to recruit you as a Sweeper for the Mad Dogs. He's partial to Sinclairs because they operate in similar ways to his established system, and we know you're quality workers. We're working to protect Amicae from infestations, which aligns with your own goals. It's not a large leap to transfer over to us. You'll be far more effective, and better supported. For the time being you won't even have to work with us directly, simply collaborate for the greater good. What do you say?"

Armand still swung from the hook, and Laura's lip curled.

"I'll tell you the truth," she said. "I was tempted, when I heard about Gaudium. I almost chased after Renard to ask for help. But someone reminded me that the mobs don't care who gets hurt as long as they get what they want, and what you've done to Armand here makes that much more real. I'm not going to help you hurt people, no matter what you pretend you're fighting for. I'm not throwing anyone away. That's not how Sinclairs work."

Haru shrugged, in no way disappointed. "I thought you'd say that. Renard's entire interest in you is because you react so much like your old boss, and that was the great recurring argument they had. I never anticipated you actually agreeing to join. It was kind of you to bring our other candidates with you, though, so I'll open up the offer."

From the corner of her eye, she saw Ivo and Bea stiffen.

"We know you two are Rexian Sweepers. You of all people know how dangerous the enemy is," said Haru. "It must be frustrating, being limited as you are with the Sinclairs. Wouldn't you like the freedom to act as you need to?"

His voice was sweet and smooth as silk. For a moment, Laura was afraid. She could understand if they were tempted to leave. The Council's current position on Rex was scary. Angry citizens spat on Rex's name and vowed to maim or kill any Rexians they came across. The manacles remained on their wrists, proof that even the people who wanted to use them didn't trust them, and they'd been stuck following a head Sweeper with only a fraction of their own experience. It must be intensely frustrating. But at what cost would they turn to the mobs? It was a step closer to Rex's hold, no matter what kind of pretty packaging Haru tried to wrap it in. She had to think of an argument, a good one and fast, or—

"No, thank - - -."

One step brought Ivo close to Laura's side. She gaped at him, but he rested his own cool gaze on Haru. "I came to Amicae because I didn't believe in the idea of throwing people away. Laura has proven to me that she shares that ideal. - - - speak of saving people, but the man behind - - - shows that is a lie. Laura is my head Sweeper. I will not have another."

Laura pressed her mouth shut, and her throat clogged. He hadn't so much as hesitated.

"Thank you," she whispered.

He looked back at her, and a faint smile lit his face. "- - - gave us a chance where no one else would," he murmured. "I am eternally grateful for that. We will save Amicae, and we will save it properly."

But where he stepped back, Bea stepped forward. "- - -r mission," she said. "Tell it to me again."

Haru tipped his head, the act melting into true amusement. "To fight infestations. To keep our city alive. Miss Kramer can talk all she wants about saving everyone, but that's not realistic. Either select people to die now to ensure Amicae's safety, or they will die with all the rest of us when the city falls."

"Sensible," said Bea. "Yes, I've always known some things must be discarded for success."

In the silence that followed, one could've heard a pin drop. Ivo stood frozen. Laura stared, first in disbelief, then in growing rage. Was Bea blind?

Could she not see the innocent man hanging from a goddamn hook? The torture? The murder?

"You can't possibly think this is the right path!" Laura snarled. She gestured viciously at Armand's body. "Look at that! Look at what they did to him, and this bastard's not even batting an eye! He literally admitted that he does this for a job! Is that what you want to do? Just hurt people?"

Bea looked at her with cold indifference. "The right path is the path of survival. I told - - - before that - - - were weak, and - - - can blame this 'Sinclair attitude' for it. - - - cling to the dead, and forget what's needed to live."

Ivo took a shaky step toward her. "But how is the other path living?"

"It is survival," Bea insisted, eyes still on Laura instead of him.

Ivo took another step, his voice breaking. "All this time, - - -'ve been rejecting everything that makes an existence life!"

"I have not."

"In thoughts, in tastes, in experiences—"

"They are unnecessary," Bea snapped.

By now Ivo was directly in front of her, arms wide and reaching, expression beseeching. He looked like he wanted to embrace her, to hold her close and safe, but Bea would never accept that kind of gesture. She stood still, arms at her sides, as if Ivo and his worry didn't exist as long as she didn't acknowledge them.

"- - - don't need to turn back to Rex!" he whispered, desperate. "There is more to this existence than their chains! - - - don't have to trample others to live! - - - don't have to reduce - - -rself to nothing!"

Only then did she look at him, and her face was filled with loathing.

"I have not reduced myself," she spat. "- - - may be complacent enough to welcome death when it comes, but a bright future exists for me. That dawn will come, even if I have to drag it into existence!"

She turned back to Haru.

"Stop!" Ivo lurched forward and caught her hand in both of his. "Bea, please. - - - don't have to do this. *Please.*"

Bea froze. Ivo shook. As they all stared, he fell to his knees and pressed his forehead against the knuckles of her trapped hand.

"Please, my sister. Please. Don't throw away the person I love. She is only just beginning to live."

Bea's mouth opened, but nothing came out. That odd vulnerability she'd shown after the barricade was returning. Her lip trembled, and she averted her gaze.

"I . . . I . . ."

"I see what's going on," said Haru. He stepped back toward where he'd come from, a scheming smile on his face. "No need to say anything. I understand."

"Where do you think you're going?" said Laura.

Haru shrugged again. "It's the end of the negotiation. There's no point in me staying around, is there? The Mad Dogs here and I are pulling out. You can call the police for poor Mr. Armand if you'd like. After I report my findings to the boss, we shall take . . . appropriate action."

"Appropriate action" sounded like a threat.

"If the Mad Dogs really have the city's safety in mind, you won't do anything to us," said Laura.

"Keep thinking that if you'd like." Haru disappeared behind the canvas curtain, and they were left alone.

"Bastard," Laura spat.

Ivo looked up to see him gone, then turned his relieved eyes back to Bea. "Bea—"

Bea's expression contorted. She wrenched her hand out of his grip, ignoring the hurt on his face, and glared at Laura. "- - -r orders, *Head Sweeper*?"

Laura was just as angry at Bea, but she was mature enough to reel that back in for Ivo's sake. She crossed her arms tight over her chest in an attempt to crush her resentment and said, "We'll call the police. I don't like it, but let's not touch Armand. They might be able to get more information if we leave the scene as it is."

"Then I will call them."

"Maybe Laura should call them," said Ivo. "- - - and I, we'll guard the body."

He clearly wanted to speak with her more, but . . . "Do - - - not trust me?" Bea challenged.

"We are partners," said Ivo. "We have always worked together, haven't we?"

"- - - do not trust me at all," said Bea. "It's a wise choice."

They retreated to the Sweeper shop.

With the threat of "appropriate action" hanging overhead they all opted to stay the night in the old Sinclair home. *It was meant to hold five people in the first place,* Okane reminded them, and sure enough it did. Okane and Ivo shared the old twins' room; Laura and Zelda used the large master bedroom; and Bea, who'd opposed being with any of them, took the grandmother's room.

Zelda was already snoring, but Laura couldn't get comfortable.

This is Clae's room, she thought, staring at the 1:00-A.M.-dark ceiling. *I don't belong here.*

She wouldn't be surprised if the bed swallowed her up for daring trespass. Clae's bed. Clae's blankets. Clae's coat hanging from the metal frame. Clae's family photos stuck up around the walls. She had his title, too. Laura groaned, rubbing her face with her hands.

"You're thinking way too much," she told herself, but it didn't help.

She didn't have many times like this, where Clae's absence rang in her head. Lately she'd been too busy to linger, too focused on actual threats to think on much more than how he'd have done this better. Here, he was inescapable.

You wanted to be a great Sweeper, whispered a little goblin in her head. *Aren't you glad you have that title? Maybe you're glad he's dead.*

She rolled over in a huff.

Maybe you're no different than Juliana MacDanel.

She rolled again, the movement sharper. Zelda made a loud, annoyed sound, and Laura stilled. She waited until Zelda settled again, then slipped out of bed. She felt the chill of the floor through her socks and shivered. Stooping, she dug through her bag, and pulled out an Egg. The angry kin glowed without prompting. It warmed her hands like sunshine, leaching under her skin and burning along the lines of her scars. It grounded her like nothing else in this room. Her next breath came easier.

"Hey," she murmured. "I made the right choice, didn't I? It's not worth allying with the Mad Dogs, even if Gaudium is gone."

The kin bubbled away, silent inside its glass casing.

Not.

Her head jerked up.

—er.

Clae's voice came like a breath at the edge of her senses, like someone shouting from far away.

No—er—

The Egg glowed brighter. Zelda flipped off the blanket and sat up to glare. "Put that out!" she hissed. "I can't sleep a wink with—"

The Egg shone even more, lighting the room as easily as electricity and washing *angerangerwarning* through Laura's hands. At that exact moment, she heard the distinct sound of wind chimes. The shop's chimes didn't move without a breeze. They needed an open door. She and Zelda caught each other's eye, and they both hurried out of the room. Down the stairs they went, and emerged into the shop just in time to see the front door swing closed. Bea's shape flitted across the window.

"Where is she going?" said Laura, making to round the counter. "Doesn't she know it's dangerous out—"

"Don't," said Zelda.

"She's going to get hurt!"

"She made her choice."

"But—"

Zelda looked at her without any anger or bitterness, just resignation. "- - -'ve seen how she is. - - - can't convince her to stay."

"Aren't you worried?" said Laura.

"Honestly, more relieved." Zelda looked tiredly at the window, as if Bea had left ages ago and this were just a memory. "I always knew she'd leave at some point. Ivo insisted on taking her with us, but she's not looking for the same things we are. Better to have her go now than keep guessing when she'll ditch us in the future. I'm going back to bed."

Zelda retreated up the stairs, but Laura couldn't bring herself to abandon this so easily. Not after Ivo had been so desperate to keep her. She threw the shop door open and stood out on the stoop.

"Bea!" she called.

Bea paused partway down the street, and looked back with an unpainted face.

"The mission is all that matters," she called. "No matter what I have to throw away, I will accomplish it. I will throw Ivo away, too. That is my protection."

She jogged to the bend in the road, where Haru waited. He tipped his hat to her, and the pair left without so much as a glance behind them.

9

THE BOMBING

Ivo was inconsolable.

Laura had predicted that, but it was one thing to think, *He'll be upset;* it was another to see him pale at the news the next morning and run out onto the street as if Bea were still there to be stopped. He stood out there like someone utterly lost, his nightshirt soaking fast from the rain. Zelda waited for him in the meager shelter of the doorway, arms crossed tight over her chest and expression caught somewhere between annoyance and grief.

"He should've known," she said, when Laura stepped out to join her. "After what - - - told me about that encounter yesterday, it was obvious she'd leave, and even before that, he knew her well enough to know it was just a matter of time."

"It's still awful," Laura murmured.

If she were in his place, and Okane up and left without warning, she wouldn't know what to do.

Ivo looked up and down Acis again, as if coming to his senses, and returned to the shop.

"Look at the state of - - -r clothes! - - -'re going to catch a cold," Zelda scolded.

"I'll get a towel," said Laura, but needn't have bothered.

While they'd been gawking, Okane had pulled out several towels and prepared tea. He offered Ivo a steaming cup in one hand, a towel in the other, and told him firmly, "- - -'re not alone."

He tried to load all his concern into the word the way Grim had described, and even Laura felt the weight of it brush over her awareness. Ivo gave a meek nod, and toweled his hair rather than face any of them.

"- - - should change," Okane said softer. "Otherwise - - -'ll be cold and miserable."

"And sick," Zelda added.

"I don't have anything here," said Ivo.

"- - - can use some of mine," said Okane.

He pulled a full outfit from his pile of towels, more thoroughly prepared than Laura realized. He didn't stop fussing until Ivo had properly changed and sat down, and at that point all three of them sat around him. Ivo looked up from his cooling tea and said, "I am not - - -r entertainment."

"Of course not!" said Laura. "It's just . . . I'm not sure how to help you."

"I don't need help. This is the way all things go."

"Damn straight," said Zelda, leaning in. "Look at it this way. Now that Little Miss Rex is gone, - - - can do whatever - - - want without her bitching over - - -r shoulder."

Ivo slouched even lower. "Right. Of course."

Zelda seized his arm and said, "- - - wanted to see the theater, didn't - - -? And uncensored books! And clubs! We can do that now, and actually experience them instead of dancing around Rexian sensibilities! We could start today!"

Desperate for some way to help, Laura nabbed yesterday's paper from under the counter and spread the entertainment section before them.

"What kind of theater?" she asked. "There's films, plays, orchestras—for that matter, what genre did you want? You could also watch a sports match, though the rain isn't ideal. Anyway, I've got times and locations here for the weekend. We'll have to keep it within this section because of the barricades, but . . ."

"- - - don't have to go," said Okane.

"What else is he going to do, sit and sulk?" Zelda scanned the listings and pointed at a film on the Tiber Circuit. "Let's do this one. It starts in two hours."

She wouldn't take no for an answer.

Maybe, Laura thought as Zelda towed them all out the door again, *she's afraid if he lingers too long on it, he'll follow Bea and leave her all alone.* It made sense. The Zelda they'd observed was always curious and talkative, but now Zelda couldn't seem to keep her mouth shut. She talked about the rain, the upcoming film, how Ivo should get one of these shirts because it looked good on him. All the while she clung to his elbow like an anchor.

They visited Brecht next door for his eclectic and uncensored bookstore; Brecht happily regaled Okane with the virtues of firedogs while the others browsed, and let them borrow some of his many spare umbrellas when they departed. The trolley ride to the Tiber was muggy and crowded, as was the theater. The film itself was artsy and near incomprehensible. Laura spent most of it glancing between Ivo and Okane to see if they gleaned meaning where she hadn't. Both of them wore poker faces until the end. Okane nodded along sagely afterward when Zelda chattered about *depth* and *theme*, but Ivo didn't engage any more than he had all day. To make matters worse, the sky grew still darker and the rain went from a sprinkle to a deluge. The crowds branched off quickly to seek shelter, leaving only a few brave umbrella-wielders on the thoroughfare. Laura and the others ducked under the awning of a flower shop, where a Ralurian man had wrapped himself up heavily in dark clothing.

Okane held out a hand to test the rain. "I think we'll be stuck here awhile."

"We may as well enjoy it," said Zelda. "Aren't there word games we could play? Like, we pick a theme, I say a word, - - - say another word in the theme that starts with my word's ending, and then the next person does the same—"

"I'm not interested," said Ivo.

"There's more we could do! Stories, or charades, or—"

"I don't want to," said Ivo.

"But—"

"Zelda. I don't want to," he repeated, almost begging.

A heavy silence fell over them. Okane frowned out at the downpour, shoving his hands in his pockets before saying, "Am I right, when I think - - - just want some silence for a while?"

"I understand what - - -'re trying to do with these distractions, but . . ." Ivo's head bowed. "Yes. I need some quiet. Some space. Some . . . time to mourn."

Zelda's lip curled. "There's nothing to mourn. She's not dead."

"But she's gone," said Ivo.

"Because she left us! She left - - -! Nobody twisted her arm. She didn't like us, and she left. - - - don't have to feel bad for her, because she's crawled away wherever she wants to be; and - - - don't have to feel bad for - - -rself, because she held - - - back!" said Zelda.

"She was my partner," said Ivo.

"And - - - deserved better! It makes no sense for - - - to—"

"It doesn't matter what makes sense! This is what I'm feeling!" Ivo hissed. "- - - wanted to hear Mr. Rexian Sweeper have some autonomy? - - -'ve got it."

Laura glanced at the Ralurian man in alarm. He didn't seem to have noticed the raised voices or the Rexian admission, just kept still as a statue.

"I miss Bea," Ivo groaned. "I miss being able to look at someone for answers. I miss how confident I was, how it felt because having her involved meant we could do anything. She's competent, and determined, and I've known her since basic training. She's always been there. For that matter, I miss Rex!" He gestured angrily, uselessly at the rain, face twisted in grief and self-loathing. "I hated it, but I had a place there! I knew what to expect, and I knew I was performing the way they meant me to. I don't have that, here. I'm mourning because I have no direction, and the people I'm turning to are just as lost as I am. I'm not confident anymore. Even what I thought was permanent, like her, it's all—" His hands curled into fists. "It's all . . . It's just . . . disappearing."

His hands went lax and fell back to his sides. The anger drained from his face, leaving only a bone-weary sadness.

Zelda looked suddenly very small. "I'm here. I'm permanent," she whispered.

"- - - weren't, before. - - - were there and gone. - - - had to hide, in Rex," said Ivo.

"We don't have to—" Zelda broke off.

"We don't have to hide anymore?" A halfhearted smile pulled at Ivo's smearing face paint, and his nails picked at the manacle on his wrist.

"We hide together," Zelda said firmly. "Wherever - - - go, I'm permanent. I'm not leaving - - -."

"That's what I tell myself." Ivo's fingers curled, trying and failing to pull the manacle loose. "But all the same, I feel overwhelmingly displaced. As if I am a cog fallen to the bottom of a strange machine, and the gears work smoothly above me. I'm alone, and even the broken gears above me—"

"Have more weight than - - - do?" Okane murmured.

Ivo looked around in surprise. "Yes. - - - feel that, too?"

"I never had a purpose to start with, so I'm a little jealous of - - - for that," Okane chuckled. "I've just sort of . . . floated."

"Like - - - didn't belong in the machine," said Ivo.

Okane nodded. "If it's a machine . . . I'm a cheap part trying to fill in for a real gear, and failing at it."

"But - - -'re already established here. I would've thought . . ."

"I don't know much about myself or where I came from. Most of what I hear about what I could be comes from Rexian Sweepers, or rumors about Magi in the wilds. I don't belong to either of those groups, but I'm not a normal Terulian, either. I'm thinking almost the opposite of - - -. While everything else is permanent, I'm ready to be blown away in the wind at any time."

"What is your machine for?" said the Ralurian.

Everyone else finally realized they had a stranger with them. They all went very still. The Ralurian pushed up his wide-brimmed hat and gave them a warm smile.

"Mateo," Laura sighed, shoulders slumping. "Don't scare me like that."

"My apologies," said Mateo. "I am, as they say, a wanted man. It's growing hard to move around in my usual uniform."

"What are you doing in the Tiber Circuit?"

"Visiting parishioners," said Mateo. "More importantly . . . the machine you believe you don't belong to, young man. What is it for? Every machine has a purpose."

Ivo pondered this. "The machine is society, and reality."

"It exists to allow the turning of the gears inside." Mateo mused. "I wonder, then, why you feel that you're a wrong fit or displaced entirely. I see four perfectly functional gears here, all turning together."

The others exchanged confused looks, but Laura shook her head in mock exasperation and said, "You're weaving."

"True," Mateo laughed. "Spiritualism has many sects. You're familiar with the Three Child testaments, correct?"

"I can't say that I am," said Ivo.

"That's somewhat ironic, considering you're wearing our design," said Mateo. "You see, with us, we don't believe there is a machine at all. Life is a cloth. It's not something cold or impersonal but something soft and warm, to wrap yourself up in and give you comfort. We believe that every person is a thread spun with great care by the Spinner himself. To exist at all is to be well loved by your creator. You speak of the world as a machine where you can be replaced or discarded, but the truth is that you are part of the Spinner's great masterpiece. You can't be replaced, and if you were to deny the truth of yourself, the masterpiece would be lesser for it. 'Harmony' in particular"—he pointed at the paint on Ivo's face—"is a complex creation that may look at a glance like mere blocks of the same color, but when you take the time to inspect it, you see the many undulating colors of the threads: all different, all binding, all precious to the whole. It is our job as humanity, the masterpiece, to work within our weave to better each other."

Ivo's brow furrowed, and he brushed his cheek absentmindedly. "If I come from a city that ruins - - -r weave, do I still belong?"

"As long as you exist, you are our thread to love. Where you came from is irrelevant," said Mateo. "'Harmony' is our dearest teaching, and one you seem to already be starting to understand. I'm glad it spoke to you."

Ivo's hand jerked away from his face. He looked at Mateo in wonder. "- - - don't care that I'm Rexian?"

"Not in the least," said Mateo. "I am proud to be woven into the same world as you."

Ivo's mouth opened, then pressed firmly shut again. He blinked against what might've been rainwater or might've been tears. "- - - are very kind, sir, but I don't think I can believe such a thing very soon."

"I understand. Belief is much more meaningful if you find your way there yourself," said Mateo. He spotted someone in the rain. "I'm afraid my host has arrived, so I'll be going. If you ever wish to talk more on the subject, I can always be found at the Three Child Church." He stepped out into the rain, but he turned back and said again, "You are loved," before hurrying away.

"What a strange little man," said Zelda.

"Oh, hush," said Laura. "He's really nice. He's letting my family stay at his church's rectory."

Ivo rubbed at his face again. "His ideas are intriguing, but I'm not sure I believe any of it."

"Maybe instead . . . Would - - - like an anchor?" said Okane.

"A what?"

Okane ducked his head and pulled an object from his pocket: a flattened canvas ball with a bell inside. Hadn't a pair of those been in the twins' room above the Sweeper shop?

"I don't know if I believe in something like the Spiritualist weaving myself, but this has helped me. I thought if I was an impostor, maybe I could anchor myself with the truth. I'm living in Clae Sinclair's old home, and this was his. It reminds me that he invited me in. That I do belong. I was given permission for that."

Ivo shifted in discomfort. "I appreciate the thought, but I never met Sinclair. A memento of his wouldn't have meaning for me."

"But it wouldn't be a memento of him," said Okane. "I meant from me to - - -. Something to keep - - - here, because I don't want - - - to leave. A physical proof that - - -'re meant to be here."

Ivo went very still. "- - - want me to stay?"

"Yes. - - -'ve already got people here—there's Zelda, of course, and she's a more effective anchor than anything I could think of, but if there's something - - - can hold . . . a piece of permanence . . ." Okane went very red. "This doesn't actually make sense, does it?" he said quickly. "Please ignore everything I just—"

"Please," said Ivo.

Okane glanced shyly up at him. "- - - don't have to bend to my rambling any more than - - - have to deal with us trying to distract - - -. It's okay if - - - don't want it. It is pretty foolish."

"I don't know if an anchor would help me in the long run. But if I had one, then it would help me remember this moment. It would help me remember the way - - - said that. I have . . . No one has ever said that word to me with such kindness or conviction." Ivo started to shake. "I always hated to hear '- - -' from myself, from all other Rexian Sweepers. But from - - -, I finally understand its sincerity. That's . . . If only I . . . I want to remember it."

He ducked his own head and took in a shuddering breath. Okane nudged him lightly and said, "I've got the perfect thing in mind. How about we go back to the shop now? We'll have a quiet night in."

Ivo nodded quickly. Okane opened his umbrella, and the two of them shuffled out under it. Laura and Zelda followed under their own umbrellas.

"How did he do that?" Zelda said in wonder. "I'd never seen Ivo so worked up, and then Okane just . . ."

"They understand each other," said Laura. "I didn't really get it before, when Okane told me. But it's nice to be known."

"I should've understood, too," Zelda murmured.

"Don't worry about it," said Laura. "Isn't there a saying about this? It takes a village, or something? You can't live life just interacting with one or two people."

"- - -'re part of the weave." Zelda closed her eyes and smiled. "- - - Sinclairs are such utter saps, aren't - - -? - - - *being happy made me happy too! Let me give - - - an anchor!* Pah. Don't - - - ever get embarrassed?"

"Oh, shut up," said Laura, but she was smiling too.

They took a trolley to Acis Road and headed back toward the shop with higher spirits. Laura was laughing at one of Zelda's jokes when the two in front of them stopped walking.

"What's wrong?" she asked.

"It's the shop," said Okane. "The lights are on. I remember turning them off."

Zelda squinted. "Didn't - - - close the blinds, too? What are they doing up?"

"Maybe Bea came back?" said Ivo, hardly daring to hope.

He moved forward, but Laura caught his shoulder to hold him back. Only one person stood on the street besides them: someone on the shop's other side, who stood in a solid stance with no umbrella, so drenched by the rain her suit stuck to her frame and her hair hung in clumps. The stranger lifted her head, and the lamplight caught the lurid tattoo on her face. Minnie.

"We have to get out of here," said Laura.

"What? Why?"

"That's a Mad Dog! This can't be good! We're going somewhere else, and we're calling the police—"

Minnie laughed loud over the rain.

"You made your choice!" she jeered, and threw up her hands. "Now it's open season, sweetheart!"

Light erupted from inside the shop. The sound was deafening. The windows blasted outward with a roar of flame. Glass and wood chunks flew thirty feet into the air. The walls bent, screeching, and the second floor collapsed into the first. The fire went yellow, sparking, popping, shimmering as the first few kin weapons broke. The following blasts put the first to shame. Eggs burst and Bijou ignited, engulfing the whole of the building in a shrieking inferno. More and more debris flew, smoldering wood and whizzing Bijou sailing to land on other buildings and sear neighboring roofs. The buildings on either side went up in flame and more creaked under the onslaught.

"Get back!" Laura cried.

She hardly noticed that she'd dropped her umbrella, just that they were in the danger zone and the others had all frozen. They reacted under her pull, and together they all turned tail and ducked into a side street. Zelda swore profusely, Okane was deadly silent, and Ivo kept glancing back for any sight of pursuers.

Minnie's laughter was far behind them, but it still rang in Laura's ears as she ran. Her eyes stung horribly. The Sweeper shop kept burning, an ugly blazing wreckage, and she felt like home was gone.

Within two hours, they'd settled into the armory, and a veritable battalion of police officers were running in and out.

"I can't believe this," said Albright, pinching the bridge of her nose as she and Byron stood in the makeshift parlor of the attic. "All the information we have on the mobsters said they wouldn't target you! They've been championing you this whole time! And with Gaudium—Why doesn't any of this make sense anymore?"

"Did you snub the mobs at any point recently?" said Byron.

"We told the Mad Dogs we wouldn't join them," Laura grumbled. "Does that count?"

"But they'd attack her *now*?" Albright threw up her hands. "They're the ones saying we need more Sweeper regulations!"

"They're also the ones pressuring the Council," said Byron. He looked just as tired as Albright. His habitual pipe was in his mouth, but unlit. Laura didn't think he'd noticed yet. "When you take a step back, you could consider this another way of forcing their hand. If the city's official Sweeper guild is knocked out, the Council would have to take up anti-infestation measures to serve as a poor replacement."

"Sacrificing a few for the ultimate goal," Laura said bitterly.

She wondered if Bea had been involved with this. Speaking of which . . .

"Where is your third recruit?" said Albright.

"Checking in with Amelia. They're fast friends," Zelda lied.

They couldn't tell her that Bea had turned traitor—it would just prove all her earlier suspicions and get Zelda and Ivo into hot water that they didn't deserve.

"But she's unhurt?" said Albright.

"She's right as rain," Laura grumbled.

Albright shook her head but didn't press any further. "If the Mad Dogs really want to eliminate the Sinclairs, we need to keep you safe. They've proven they can get into multiple high-security locations already, so we can't move you there . . . but I've seen what this place can do in lockdown. I want you to stay here under guard. No one in, no one out. I'll arrange similar protections for your family, Laura, but they'll be placed elsewhere."

"For how long?" said Laura.

"As long as it takes to get the Mad Dogs off your back," said Albright. Byron snorted.

"That could take weeks! Months!" Laura cried. "You can't keep us in here with the city in this state! Who'll fight any infestations?"

"If the mobs think they can do your job better, I'll invite them to do so," Albright snapped.

"So you're surrendering?" said Laura.

"I'm playing the long game," Albright corrected. "You Sinclairs are the ace up my sleeve. I'm keeping you off the board for now so the Mad Dogs don't target you. That way, when the crisis hits later, you'll still be around to protect the city. I don't like your chances otherwise."

"Considering the amount of time their boss wasted on you, I don't like your chances either," said Byron. "The Mad Dogs get very personal, very fast."

"Can you play the Silver Kings against them at all?" asked Laura.

Byron winced, but Albright said, "We won't deal with such a powder keg. I don't want to risk a full mob alliance like we had during the MARU. We have plans to solve this. Maybe not quickly, but we will solve this. The water in the taps here is potable. I'll have food brought in for you, and assign your detail. If you have any questions, don't hesitate to reach out to Byron on the phone lines. He'll be easier to reach than I will."

She retreated back downstairs. Byron, meanwhile, finally realized his pipe was out. He patted down his coat for matches and slumped when he found none. Zelda clicked her tongue and offered him a matchbook from her own pocket.

"Seriously," said Byron as he lit the pipe, "if you have even slight suspicions, call me. I'll keep you up to speed with any reports on my end, too."

"Is there anything new right now?" said Laura.

"The Mad Dogs put a wreath on the Council building's front gate," Byron said dryly.

"They put a circle *there*?" Laura drew back in revulsion. "Where are the Silver Kings? If they hated the Mad Dogs so much, and they love their balance as much as you said they did—"

Byron shook his head. "The anti-Rexian and Mad Dog precautions the Council's enacted have been mostly anti–Silver King. There are no Rexians, of course; the Mad Dogs have evaded the blockades almost entirely despite all their movement; the blockades are really only affecting citizens, and disproportionately affecting the poorer sectors. The Silver Kings draw heavily from Wasureijin and other minorities, so when the Council or businesses take aim at the lower Quarters the Silver Kings go up in arms. As much as the Council says they don't want the mobs getting stronger, they do like forcing them into closer alliances."

Laura groaned and buried her face in her hands. "I hope you can call us with good news, soon."

"I hope," said Byron. "For the time being, I need to work with Heather to limit our damage to the mobs. We might still be able to prevent full unification there."

As Byron left, Laura rubbed at her face and turned to the rest of the Sweepers. They'd all climbed onto the furniture surrounding the Kin, as if the Gin and crystals could keep them warm. By now they were well dried, and Amelia had happily fetched them all a change of clothes, but they couldn't shake the chill after the bombing. Zelda was preoccupied with picking at the tassels of a throw pillow. Ivo couldn't sit still, so had taken to pacing around the furniture circle. Okane had folded himself small and tight into an armchair and remained silent up to now.

His home was gone. Everything that was his, and everything that had been Clae's, was gone. No more steep stairs. No more awful Partch mattresses. No more stools or countertop or wind chimes. She ached with the knowledge, but at the same time, it didn't feel real. Maybe in the morning she'd walk back down Acis and see it standing as it always had. It wouldn't be. Still. She could dream of it.

Okane pulled the flattened ball from his pocket again. He ripped its canvas, took out the bell, and held it out. "Here."

Ivo stopped in his newest circle to stare at the bell in front of him. "What is this?"

"The anchor. It's not the one I thought of before, but—"

"No." Ivo pushed it back toward him. "I can't take that. - - -'ve lost - - -r home. I can't take anything else from - - -."

"I'm giving it freely."

"But it's - - -r anchor."

"I've still got half," said Okane, waving the canvas and its flattened frame. "What I said before is still true. I want - - - to stay, and I want - - - to remember my truth. Will - - - accept that?"

Ivo's wariness crumbled. He took the bell in shaking hands and said, "- - -'re too kind to me."

"Whether we're in a machine or a weaving, I don't know. And I don't know what our place in anything is, but I think we can find out together." Okane looked around at them all, a sad smile playing on his face. "Time, and buildings . . . those can be fleeting, but we can all be permanent. Right?"

Zelda grinned back at him. "- - - will be *annoyed* with how permanent I can be."

Laura sat next to Okane and said simply, "Right."

She was too choked up to form any other words, but Okane seemed to realize it. He opened his arms, and she wrapped him up in the tightest hug she could muster. For all the pretended calm he'd shown before, his breath was uneven and he clutched at her coat as if she too were an anchor he feared to lose.

"Together," she whispered against his ear. "We'll get through this together."

10

REMOVAL

The first day of their impromptu house arrest was boring as all hell.

The armory was not equipped for comfort, and had no kitchen to prepare food in. They sat on the hard floor and ate food out of cans, much like they'd been forced to in Rex. It brought the past to mind, and they ended up swapping stories about how each party had survived in the wilds to reach Amicae. Once that derailed (too much talk of Bea had everyone uncomfortable), they attempted parlor games. Zelda was very good at charades, while Ivo was utterly baffled by it. A few others were attempted, but didn't hold their attention long. Laura kept glancing out the window to check the police guard outside, and her hands itched for a newspaper. For all she knew, the Mad Dogs had assassinated someone already. Surely Byron would've called to tell them that, but still. She missed having daily printed updates.

Night had fallen and they were all winding down for bed when the visitor came. Laura went to the middle floor to turn out the lights, but when she reached the bottom of the stairs, she realized someone was standing in the equipment room.

"Who the hell are you?" she screeched, snatching up the nearest weapon.

The spike of fear shot warmth through the Eggs in her bag, and a crash sounded upstairs, followed by more shouting.

"Laura, make him stop!" Okane cried.

Was Clae moving again?

"Stop! I'm fine! Everything's fine!" Laura called. She dropped the weapon back in its stand and gave the visitor a surly look. "How did you even get in here, Grim? There's police outside and this place is on magical lockdown."

Grim blinked at her, as calm and casual as if he'd been invited inside for lunch. "The armory's traps are rigged for people. I am a rock."

Laura shook her head in resignation and waved for him to follow her upstairs.

"Grim?" Okane said when they'd reached the attic. "Why are - - - here?"

"I told you I would come to visit when I had news," said Grim.

Probably Magi information. Laura circled to the glass tub, where Clae had stood up and knocked over the cover. Zelda had drawn her feet up onto the couch and eyed him with wariness, while Ivo had a hand on his blade hilt. Laura patted Clae's crystal arm.

"Don't worry, it's just Grim. You've seen him before, right? He's a friend. I was just startled to see him."

Clae dimmed but didn't lie down again.

"We've managed to bring in the tattoo specialist tonight," said Grim.

Laura didn't remember what he meant at first.

Zelda sprang to her feet, all trepidation vanished. "Really? - - - mean we can get these stupid numbers off our faces tonight?"

"That's correct," said Grim. "That said, the specialist has a busy schedule and he's especially jumpy tonight. He feels safe in Toulouse, so that's where he will operate."

Zelda's shoulders slumped. "Then we're sunk!"

"I don't believe the police guard will allow us to leave for such an occasion. They may think it trivial, or otherwise treacherous, to remove our Rexian markings," Ivo agreed.

"Is there no way to convince him to come here?" said Laura.

"None." Grim glanced at the window. "But you may leave, regardless, if you so choose. Some may say it is an unwise choice, but it is possible."

"How did - - - get in?" Okane asked suspiciously.

"The door in the garage."

"No, you didn't. The garage door hasn't been fixed since the break-in," said Laura.

"A human door, not a vehicle door," said Grim.

Laura frowned. "I've never seen one down there."

"I believe it's meant to be secret."

It sounded like a horrible idea. Laura looked at the others for opinions.

Ivo's eyes were bright; Zelda's hands clasped tight, and she bounced on the balls of her feet. Ugh, how was she supposed to say no to such obvious hope?

"I'm going to regret this," Laura sighed. "You know what? Sure. Let's go."

Zelda cheered. "I'm saying good-bye to Rex for good this time!"

They all followed Grim down to the garage. As always, Laura saw only the damaged garage door, the parked vehicles, and a lot of emptiness. Grim angled toward the wall and opened what appeared to be a cupboard under the stairs, but Laura had never seen a cupboard with such a complex lock system. When it was undone he stepped inside, turned to the side forming the outer wall of the armory, and started poking at bare paint. Before their eyes, an invisible door popped open. Grim cracked it further, cast around, and then reported, "The guard has rounded a corner. We're clear," and pushed it wide. They all hurried out into the night air, and when the door closed behind them it was utterly indistinguishable from the rest of the siding.

"How did - - - find that?" Okane gasped.

"It is very well hidden, even from those with good sensing. But this place is a Magi building, and Magi *always* have an extra escape route." Grim gave a light shiver, as if reliving a bad memory. "Some of the fittings of that door were Niveus, as well. I have limited control over external pieces, so I was able to work the mechanism without use of an actual key or spell."

"Fascinating, but can we get moving?" Zelda hissed.

"If you please," said Grim, and they all hurried away before the guard could come back around.

Toulouse wasn't terribly far. They rounded Water Tower Seven and angled toward the red-light district. Despite the late hour, they found far more people on the street than on their last trip, and a scattered group stood outside Toulouse's door. Grim tipped his hat to the bouncer at the entrance, who gestured him and the Sweepers inside without a word.

Laura had only seen Toulouse dim and empty, but now it was anything but. Every seat in the house held someone in their flashiest clothing, most of them sipping alcohol and listening to the band as the singer belted one of the new Ruhaile tunes. A crowd milled in the back, waiting their turn in the liminal rooms. A thick swath of glimmering purple cloud obscured the ceiling, and the bottoms of birdcages peeked out, seemingly holding a collection of stars.

"Oh," Okane whispered as he stepped in. "I didn't expect it to look like this."

"I preferred last month's installation," said Grim. "Madame Toulouse had rigged the amulets to show an aurora, but it proved too difficult to use. The steady stars cannot be manipulated easily, but to keep a constant waver or movement like the aurora meant the magic was susceptible to outside influence. It kept picking up on the patrons' emotions, and reflecting aspects of the liminal rooms they experienced at the time. There was also the day with the bad singer. The aurora changed color to match the audience's irritation. Amusing, but embarrassing."

"I didn't realize existing spells could be affected like that," said Laura.

"It depends on the magic. The orders you use on your Sweeper amulets are instinctual and fast-acting, but more importantly, they are temporary and limited in scope. Since they focus only on yourself, the amulet itself must be manipulated to change the spell. If you had a cloud of it hanging around you to affect a large area and multiple objects, though, lingering as *potentiality,* that is a different matter entirely."

Grim beelined for the far side of the room. Another window of Toulouse's signature red glass glowed there, nearly hidden by cigarette smoke. This turned out to be part of a door, and Cherry stood beside it.

She winked at them. "I see our guests made it here in one piece."

"We're hoping to bring them back to the armory quickly," said Grim. "The specialist is inside?"

"And already fit to leave. He won't keep anyone longer than he has to."

Grim nodded and ushered the Sweepers through this latest door. The room inside was an office space, with a desk and filing cabinets toward the middle, but a little pink divan and coffee table on the side. A nervous man stood there, gripping a case with whitened knuckles. Laura vaguely recognized him; he was one of the pawnshop owner's friends, who'd watched the Underyear fireworks with the Acis crowd.

"Ju-Min?" she said.

Ju-Min jumped at being so quickly identified. "Do I know you?"

"Not really. We only met in passing."

"That works in our favor," said Ju-Min. "You've met me. You aren't suspicious of me. There's no need for any kindly banter or dancing around trust. Let's please finish this and move on with our lives."

"Are - - - all right?" said Okane. "- - - seem very jumpy."

"It will not affect the procedure," said Ju-Min. "Who is first?"

Zelda threw up her hand. "Me!"

"Lie on the divan."

Ju-Min set his case on the coffee table and started unloading large glass bottles of clear liquid. These were fixed with tubing and ended in a knob and fat needle. It looked something like those newfangled spritz-perfume bottles Laura had seen in a recent Puer film, but it couldn't be. She crouched and squinted at the nearest bottle. There seemed to be a stone dog inside that gave off the impression of vibration.

"Is that an amulet?" she asked.

"It is." Ju-Min twisted the knob on his chosen needle.

"Why?"

"It's how we remove the tattoo."

"And how does that work?"

"It's impossible to truly wipe out a tattoo. Most ways of 'erasing' are just tattooing over the first one with a new design. I'm using a magic-infused solution that will break up the ink in the skin."

"Will it look as if we never had the damn things?" said Zelda, practically throwing herself on the divan.

"Not that easy," said Ju-Min. "It kills color, but it's slow-acting. It'll take hours for the ink to vanish, and afterward some of your own skin color will blotch."

"Blotch?"

Ju-Min pulled up his left sleeve. There was no sign of the tattoo itself, but his forearm had slight discoloring from what must've been the lurid Mad Dog. By now it seemed more like a faint arrangement of clouds: already-pale skin gone truly white.

"That'll be on my face?" Zelda said dubiously.

"Not nearly so big, but with your skin tone it'll be more obvious."

Zelda was quiet for a while before settling back. "Better that than a Rexian fingerprint."

"Facial work will be very painful. Are you ready?"

Zelda fisted her hands. "I've been ready for years."

"Try to stay as still as possible."

He twisted the knob. The contraption hummed, and liquid swirled up into the tube. He leaned over Zelda, placed a hand on her forehead to keep her steady, and set to work prodding at the tattoo. Blood began to well up beneath the needle.

Okane made a retching noise and lurched for the door. The sharp movement made Ivo and Grim look up in alarm. Laura waved her hands to placate them as she left the office. Okane had retreated to the main room and stood over an empty table, holding the edge in a vise grip.

"Are you okay?" said Laura. "That's the fastest I've seen you move in a while."

"Fine," he replied, reedy.

"Did the blood get to you?"

"Not the blood so much. I'm used to blood. We've seen people shot, remember? Shot, cut, bludgeoned, exploded—It's just . . . the methodical nature. It's specific. It's so . . . Why is that so much worse than the rest?"

The edge of a scarred argent symbol peeked from under his sleeve.

"Premeditated is scary," Laura murmured. "But remember, he's not doing that to hurt them."

"It's just a side effect," he mumbled.

"Whoa, you look like shit," said Cherry, coming up behind them.

"Thanks," said Okane.

"I won't advise you of all people to step outside for air, but maybe you two should head upstairs."

"I don't think the liminal rooms will help," said Laura.

"No, but the catwalk above them is clear." Cherry pointed upward and gestured where the catwalk must be. "It gets warm up there, but it would get you out of the crowd."

"I think I'll take - - - up on that," said Okane.

"You were up there last time, right? The door's hidden by an amulet right now, but it's not locked. Head up at any time."

Laura and Okane left immediately. The door to the stairs was hidden just like the canal maintenance doors, so Laura had it open quickly. The walkway appeared to be suspended between sea and sky. The starry amulet fog hung low overhead, and the false ceiling of the liminal rooms wavered like clear water. The sound of the stage was distant here, and the liminal rooms themselves were insulated, too. As Laura walked across the divide between rooms, the clear conversation between two girls about antique clocks cut out entirely, replaced by the next room's chatter over Toulouse's menu. Okane leaned his elbows on the rail and quirked his head to listen to a couple in the water room.

"Feeling any better?" said Laura.

"Much. There's more room to breathe up here," said Okane. "It helps that no one's watching. I feel odd watching others, though."

"It's a little like watching a film," Laura agreed.

"Not so dramatic, of course."

"Are you sure?" Laura cast around and pointed at a woman in a massive hat. "That's a grand duchess on vacation from Coronae. Her grandchildren are clamoring for her money, so she suspects an assassin at any moment."

The woman chose this moment to look furtively over her shoulder, despite the fact that she was very much not a grand duchess.

"And . . . that's the assassin." Okane gestured as a man in a dark coat entered the room. "This is his last target before retirement."

"They're looking at each other, getting closer . . . Oh, sorry. I thought we'd found an inheritance drama, but it was actually a romance."

Okane snorted. His color was improving already. Laura looked around for other distractions, and spotted a patch of light. The liminal rooms wound together in a maze of doors, but one section had a buffer of unused, unlit rooms surrounding one functioning piece.

"What do you think that is?" she asked.

"Some mazes have goal points, right? Maybe if - - - reach the center of this one, - - - win a prize," said Okane.

"What kind of prize would this place give out?" said Laura. "A souvenir poster? That would be too cheap."

Okane grinned as he pushed himself back up from the railing. "- - -'d still take it for - - -r collage."

"Yes, but who else would?" Laura shrugged, unashamed. "It must be something fancy. This place has money."

Okane hummed as they fell into step beside each other. "Decorated fans, maybe?"

"An embossed coin?" Laura mimed a coin flip.

Okane tugged at his bandana. "Fabric, like a handkerchief?"

Curiosity led them across the walkway, directly over the room in question. If it was a maze goal, it was a disappointing one. The room was lit like a smoky parlor, with a pool table in the center. Four people stood around it.

"All the people are in place," said one man, aiming his cue stick. "From here, it's just a matter of timing."

"I commend you for your speed," said the other man.

He scraped chalk onto his own cue, and his bared hand showed a snarling Mad Dog. Renard. The man at the table was Haru. Minnie and Blanche waited their turn. Every single Mad Dog Laura had ever spoken to, here in one place.

"That's the woman who blew up the shop!" Okane whispered. "Is that—Laura, she's wearing Clae's coat!"

Minnie was wearing the dusty coat under a set of bandoliers. Laura felt some relief—she'd thought that coat burned with the shop—but mostly she felt furious.

"That *bitch*," she hissed.

"We could've moved even faster if Haru wasn't so particular about the Sinclairs," Minnie drawled.

"He was working on my orders," said Renard.

"But they don't even matter anymore!" said Minnie.

"Every Sweeper matters," said Renard.

"And we've gained the best of the lot." Haru sent the balls scattering and drew back to plot his next move. "The Rexian woman is already proving highly capable."

"Do you like her?" said Renard, looking at Minnie.

Minnie laid a theatrical hand over her heart. "I love her."

Renard snorted. "You only like what you know I won't."

With Haru's turn ended, Renard approached the table. Minnie pranced closer, her smile widening.

"I can't have anyone else stealing your attention! You're mine, after all, Renard. I'm the one who recruited you."

"You almost killed yourself with an infestation when we were fifteen. I wouldn't call that recruitment."

"But you saved me! And you listened. I'm the reason you're here. I know you better than anyone. And I do know what you like." Minnie sprawled atop the table and plucked at the coat's lapels. "Am I Sinclair enough for you now?"

When Renard spoke again, his voice was cold enough to raise goose bumps on Laura's arms. "If you disrespect Clae Sinclair in front of me one more time, I'll cut off your head and drop you in a canal."

After what he'd done to the policeman, Laura had no doubt he would. For some reason Minnie looked thrilled.

"Get off the damn table," Blanche snapped.

Minnie slinked back to her earlier corner, entirely too smug. Haru sighed and started corralling the billiard balls again.

"I wonder why we even bother playing this with Minnie around. She always interferes."

"We're bad at giving up," said Renard. "You said the Rexian meets your standards?"

"She's an excellent candidate. I'm sending her with you tonight," said Haru.

"That's high praise. I hope your faith has good foundation."

"Tonight?" Laura murmured. "What's tonight?"

Okane could only shrug.

Below them, Haru had brought the billiards into perfect order. Renard lined up his shot.

"Have the plans been distributed?" he asked.

"To those who need to know, yes," said Haru.

Clack. The cue ball rolled and broke the group at an angle. Two striped balls plunked into pockets while the rest wheeled slowly to a stop. Renard straightened again and turned to Blanche. "The plans are clear?"

"As crystal," said Blanche. "Armand's information about the piping was valuable. We'll be able to cut off the building easily."

Renard circled the table for his next shot. "Do we have the guard schedules? The codes?"

"All preparations are made to dispose of and imitate them," said Haru.

"Have we dropped hints about the raids?"

Haru checked his watch. "It could happen any minute."

Renard bent and lined up his cue stick. "And you pointed them to the Silver Kings' hole as well?"

"Renard, you wound me. Of *course* we have them involved."

Clack. Another striped ball in the pocket. Renard rose with a smile. "I don't doubt you. I'm just invested in pulling this off. Everything we've done in the past year leads up to this. The Falling Infestation, Clae Sinclair's death . . . we need to make it matter."

Laura and Okane exchanged a wary look. Below them a door opened, and Laura gripped the rail tighter as Bea stepped into the Mad Dogs' midst. She stood at attention and said, "The police are converging on the street. As predicted, they've cut the telephone lines."

"But our communications are still intact?" said Renard.

"Yes." Bea didn't look afraid or even gratified to be in the mob boss's presence. She simply tapped the IRWT clipped to her belt to get the point across.

The Grand University infestation had covered up a theft after all. But if the Silver Kings were the ones who stole those, then they must be far more firmly entrenched with the Mad Dogs now than Byron had realized.

Haru came to stand next to Bea. He sounded almost proud as he asked, "How are the other raid targets doing?"

"The police have been baited into attacking two Mad Dog fronts in the Fourth Quarter, and the Silver Kings' Sundown Hill."

Haru sent Renard a smirk. "I give it two hours before the Silver Kings create a formal alliance with us."

"If they offer you a decent contract, you have my permission to sign it." Renard's attention had gone back to the table.

Bea tipped her head back to where someone must be whispering past the door, and announced, "The police outside are taking position."

"Their attack is our signal," said Renard, unhurried and unbothered. "Minnie, Blanche, start the vehicle. We'll rendezvous with the rest of the caravan at the gondolas. Our agents in the Toulouse crowd will slow the raid, and they can manipulate the amulets here for a fight. Those few Toulouse workers we didn't give the night off will be evacuated quickly, so they shouldn't be in the way. There's no need for us to wait on anyone."

Blanche nodded; they must've covered this once before. "And the customers?"

Renard gave a cruel smile. "The police can decide how many innocent victims of theirs will be printed in the papers tomorrow."

Shit. Were they really on the site of the newest shootout? Okane tugged at Laura's sleeve, glancing urgently back the way they'd come, but Laura shrugged him off.

"If the police are here—" Okane whispered.

"They won't catch Renard," Laura retorted. "Look at these bastards, they already know— They'll get away and we'll be just as lost as we were before. I'm tired of not knowing what's going on. I have to find out what *tonight* means. You can go back and warn the others, but I have to know."

Okane pursed his lips but didn't leave.

"I suppose evacuating them too would give us away," Blanche mused, unaware of the audience.

"One last push," Renard reminded her.

"We'll make it count." Blanche turned and gestured for her partner to follow. "Come on, Minnie. We won't get anywhere if our ride is compromised."

The two of them left. Bea didn't so much as blink as they passed. Renard eyed her and said, "What do you think of our grand plan?"

"I will follow my orders," said Bea.

"I notice you didn't seem to care that your fellow Rexian escapees had their headquarters destroyed."

Bea didn't reply.

"And you're obviously blasé about killing the guards at our destination."

Haru frowned. "Are you going to ask her a question, or dance around it all night?"

"I'm searching for how she feels about all this," said Renard.

"If - - -'re looking for emotion, - - -'re asking the wrong person," said Bea. "I have no need of such things."

Haru smiled. "Spoken like a true Rexian Sweeper. You're dismissed. Wait with Minnie and Blanche for now."

Bea inclined her head and retreated. When she was gone, Renard scowled and turned back to the table.

"I knew I wouldn't like her."

"What did you expect, boss? She's clean, efficient, talented—" Halfway through his sentence Haru realized something. He became suddenly surly. "But she's no Clae Sinclair, is that it?"

"Clae was much less boring. He liked to argue. Keep you on your toes," said Renard.

Haru rolled his eyes. "Bea is valuable *because* she doesn't argue. We need her to follow orders. She's the most loyal—"

"You need a sense of your own self before you can feel real loyalty for another person," Renard sneered. "Say all you want about how easily she obeys, but she'll throw her life away on any old cause and leave us in a lurch without a second thought. She just wants purpose. She's got no loyalty to the Mad Dogs or our mission."

"Isn't that all the better? We can dispose of her when we need to," Haru said coldly.

"I don't like working with such useless people," said Renard.

"Clae Sinclair also died for nothing," said Haru.

Renard straightened. The move was subtle but he seemed to tower, the whole of his frame sharp and dangerous as a knife.

"Haru, Haru. For your own safety, I'll pretend you didn't say that."

Haru quailed a moment but drew himself stubbornly back up. "There's no use dwelling on dead men, boss. For the plan as is, we have to make sure everyone does exactly as they need to. Loose cannons like the Sinclairs would only sabotage or betray us. They can be toyed with after you're in power."

Renard gave a disdainful sniff.

The door opened again, and a Mad Dog ducked in to say, "They're charging!"

Almost exactly as he spoke, Toulouse's main door burst open. Laura couldn't see what was going on from this angle, but she heard shouting from the incoming officers and shrieking from the patrons. A glance back down showed Renard and Haru disappearing into the liminal maze.

"Let's get out of here," said Okane. "Trust me, - - - don't want to be caught in a raid."

The people in the liminal rooms kept drifting through the decorations, completely oblivious to the Sweepers running overhead. Laura had almost reached the stairs when the door swung open. She instinctively raised her fists, but forced herself to relax.

"Cherry! You scared me!"

"No shit," said Cherry. "Follow me. We're getting out of here."

"But Zelda and Ivo—"

"Grim's got them. We'll meet up back at the armory. Let's get out of here before we get shot."

She led them back across the walkway, to the far wall with its windows looking into the alley. She propped open a window and stepped out onto a thick outside ledge with practiced grace, as if she navigated this escape on her lunch break. Laura didn't question it as they hurried across the roof-tops. A weighted board spanned the gap between Toulouse and the build-ing across the alley; it was the same width as the ledge, but much more unnerving to cross without anything to catch their fall. Laura activated her amulets for balance, and Okane's magic popped nervously behind her. From this building's far side they descended a fire escape, and spotted Cherry's vehicle. They all piled in, and Cherry hit the gas.

"I can't believe we went through that and didn't even get the damn infor-mation," said Laura. "What is tonight?"

"Raids, obviously," said Cherry, but Okane knew what she was referring to.

"They specifically mentioned Armand and the Grand University's amu-let divides. Why would they want to seal the university? And why would the university have enough guards for the mobs to be wary?"

"Unless it's not the Grand University they're targeting," Laura muttered.

"But all of that was specialized to the university. Where else has that kind of divide in their piping?"

Laura groaned, trying to remember. "Dorthea said it used to be the orig-inal city archives, with the same precautions as the Council building itself. Are there any records from the old archives that they might've stored in the museum portion? Something the mobs might want?"

Realization dawned on Okane's face. "The Mad Dogs put a circle on the Council building."

Another old government building. Another building with magical divides. Laura's stomach dropped.

"Cherry, do you know if the Council is convening tomorrow?" said Laura.

"I think so? Something about an addendum to the city's defenses and reallocation of funds. That would need a vote," said Cherry.

Laura sank back, hands over her face. "They're planting something to kill off the Council."

"Wait, outright kill?" said Cherry. "Not threaten or convince?"

"They've been threatening the Council already!"

"If they're utilizing amulet divides in the pipes, that tells me they're using an infestation," said Okane. "A bomb could be defused, but a monster . . . Only a Sweeper could stop it."

"And they've so helpfully removed the Sinclairs from play," Laura growled.

On other occasions, if the Sinclairs couldn't reach an infestation it was hoped that the mob Sweepers could eliminate it themselves. But if every mob was finally rallying, none of them would bother stopping the Mad Dogs.

She gave Okane a determined look. "It has to be us."

"What? No. Call the police," Cherry chided.

"They can't stop an infestation! And if Renard wants the Council dead on such short notice, he'll bring a monster that's old and strong. He's not taking chances. If we report this to Albright, we'll still be pinned down— she won't want us running into the Mad Dogs' hands. But we have an advantage."

Okane met her gaze. "*All Sweepers matter.*"

Laura nodded. "They'll capture instead of kill us."

"What is it with you two? First Rex, and now this? You're downright suicidal!" said Cherry.

"We're doing this because we don't want to die," said Laura. "If the Council falls, there's a power vacuum. Amicae's organization would fall apart. If we can't coordinate anything, how can we protect against infestations?"

"You're still ridiculous," said Cherry.

Okane ignored her to lean closer toward Laura. "How should we do this?"

"We'll follow Renard's route," said Laura.

"How do - - - know where that is?"

"It's obvious." And it was. *One moment you're chasing them down a street, and then you turn a corner and all you see is the canal.* The Sylph, Armand, their evasion of the barricades. She couldn't believe she hadn't figured it out before. "They've been using the canal maintenance paths, in the interior."

"The canals," Okane groaned, smacking a fist against his head. "Why didn't I guess? But can those go from Quarter to Quarter? I know they connect sections of the same Quarter, but . . ."

"It's entirely possible to ferry yourself from Sixth to First Quarter without leaving the interior. It's slow and annoying, sure, but possible," said Laura.

"Can we navigate it?"

"Of course. The Mad Dogs aren't the only ones who got a map from Armand."

At the armory, Cherry pulled up behind another parked vehicle. With the engine off, she turned to glare at Laura and Okane.

"You're sure about this? Completely sure?"

"Absolutely," said Okane.

She groaned. "Fine. I'll drive you to the stinking canal."

"You're the best!" said Laura, hopping out. "We'll be right back."

She and Okane hurried to the armory's hidden door, where Grim and the others waited. Both Zelda and Ivo sported sterile dressings on their faces, obscuring where their tattoos had been blotted out.

"If you're coming with us, stock up," said Laura, and ran inside.

She ransacked the equipment floor until her pack was fit to burst with Eggs. She strapped an additional harness over her torso with more bags for Bijou, flash pellets, and Sinkers. And then—Aha. She pulled out the canal map from the box she'd dumped here after the move. Thank goodness she'd brought it over; even with it all spelled out on paper, the directions were complex enough to give her a headache. Trying to navigate the canals without it would've been a nightmare.

"- - -'re not serious," said Zelda, following her in. "Okane's not serious, is he?"

"I don't blame you if you don't want to come." Laura hefted up the axe, and it glowed in anticipation. "But we're breaking into the Council building tonight."

Clae liked this idea about as much as Cherry did. While the others dug up their own supplies, he stormed his way down to their level (scorching the stairs as he went), and no amount of wheedling or attempted calm would make him return to the attic.

"I think he knows what we're doing. He sees through the Eggs, remember?" said Okane.

"Then he should know he'd be a big, glowing giveaway," said Laura.

"We're literally storming a castle. - - - can't tell me he wouldn't do exactly the same."

"I can't believe you want to bring him along."

"We at least know he can't be stolen."

"No, he's proven difficult to subdue already." Ivo shuddered. He clearly hadn't recovered from whatever impression Clae left on him in Rex. "He'll do what he wants. We can't force him otherwise."

This proved doubly true when Clae followed them to the garage and straight out the door. Grim considered the sight for a moment, then turned to Cherry and said, "He's riding with you."

"It's for the best," Cherry muttered, flexing her hands on the steering wheel. "God, when did my life get to be like this?"

Okane sat with her in the front. He spent the drive watching in mixed amusement and incredulity as Laura attempted to share the back with a crystal man who couldn't comprehend how to sit. It was a relief when they finally reached the mouth of the closest canal. When they'd all gathered at the water's edge, Laura strode to the front and unfolded her canal map.

"Okay," she announced, "the interior has inner elevators and gondolas to ferry maintenance workers around—much more efficient than forcing them to navigate outside. The lines are color-coded like trolley routes. We're at the Nymph Canal, so we're looking for the red line first."

"Quick question." Cherry raised a hand. "Will the gondolas fit all of us?"

Okane blinked at her in surprise. "- - -'re coming?"

"What else do you expect me to do, go home and lie awake thinking of all the ways you could die?" she spat. "No thank you."

Grim nodded his agreement. "I will go too. Protection of a city is my reason for existence."

Zelda rolled her eyes. "We're all idiots." But she made no move to leave.

They all looked at Laura for direction. Laura sucked in a deep breath and said, "Let's move."

She opened the maintenance door as easily as she had at the Sylph, and they stepped onto an identical (if in better condition) walkway. Laura held the map in one hand, a glowing Egg in the other, while the others relied on Clae's ambient light. They followed the map almost ten minutes before reaching the start of the red line: a large control panel faced the water, and beside it floated a large, flat boat.

"I suppose they would have to move large equipment sometimes," said Cherry. "This'll fit us all."

They piled into the gondola, and Laura typed their destination into the control panel. The gondola was locked into the wall via rails to follow the red line's route; when Laura finished submitting information, the mechanism ground to life and heaved them forward at a decently fast pace.

"We're taking the red line in the Third Quarter, going up the elevator, going green, then orange, another elevator, and transferring from white to blue in the First Quarter. We'll need to change gondolas at each end point."

"Do - - - know what it'll look like when we reach the Council building?" said Okane.

"Not really, but both the Grand University and Council have canal lines going under them. I'm guessing that's for maintenance or accessibility, but if the original Sinclairs were paranoid about the plumbing, I'm sure they'd have blocks on anything a human could get through too. You might be able to sense the amulet divides as we get closer," said Laura.

"Have we got any idea where in the Council building they'd plant this monster?" asked Cherry.

"If the Mad Dogs are bringing so many Sweepers, they may also be intending to plant more than one," Ivo mused.

"Both good points." Laura slumped. "I've got no idea."

"Then it might be advantageous to split up," Ivo suggested.

Cherry hummed dubiously. "There's strength in numbers, though."

"Also slowness," Ivo pointed out. "We would be more noticeable in a pack, and make a larger target."

"We'd cover a lot more ground that way," said Okane.

Cherry sighed. "I'll trust that you know what you're doing. How should we split?"

"Keeping things even would be ideal." Okane looked around at their number. "There's six of us, so we could do three groups of two. At least one person on each team should be able to sense infestations, and at least one person should be able to fight them. Grim, would - - - like to pair with me?"

Zelda considered her options and said, "I call Laura."

"It looks like you're stuck with me," said Cherry, nudging Ivo.

They rode the gondolas from one track to another, rising with the elevators and zigzagging their way across Quarters on their way to the First. They ran into no other people, mobsters or otherwise, during this task, though Laura could tell someone had taken this path before them. She kept having to press the retrieval button to summon gondolas from the opposite ends of their tracks. It was a slow business waiting for them to arrive, and she spent every moment worrying about how far they'd fallen behind the Mad Dogs. For all she knew, they could be finished and gone already. At the end of the white line the group began to walk again, and Laura glanced from map to walls, trying to gauge how far they'd gone.

"We're approaching active magic," said Grim.

"Sweeper weapons?" Laura checked.

"Nothing that strong. It's just . . ." Okane sniffed. "A smell?"

As they rounded a corner Laura detected a hint of vanilla. Tracking the scent found them another hidden door, its fake bricks already warm to the touch. Laura unlocked it with her amulet. When it opened, out flooded a golden cloud. It buffeted Laura's hair and almost choked her with the smell.

"Active Gin," she reported, pulling up her bandana. "They must've deployed the barriers already."

Cherry wordlessly handed over her scarf, and Grim bundled himself up until nothing of him could be seen. Luckily the Gin's cloud preferred to swirl around Clae, but all this magic couldn't be good for Grim's structural integrity. They'd have to push through fast.

"Stay here," Laura ordered, pointing at Clae. "I'll call you if I need you."

She wouldn't, but hopefully that would keep him still. She pulled down her goggles and braved the fog. It was so thick she could barely see. There appeared to be three Gin sources all pumping out magic, and it took some fumbling to find a staircase. Up she went, passing more and more Gin until finally she stumbled out of what might've been a broom closet, and into the side hall of the Council building's massive round entry hall. The golden fog crept along the ground to cover half of the atrium's marble floor. While the others came up behind her, Laura took brochures from the gimmicky gift shop display and handed them out.

"These have the layout of the building, and show where tours go. It should help orient us, at least," she explained.

"They've got mob threats, and they hand out maps of the damn building?" Zelda scoffed.

"It's revenue, isn't it?" said Laura.

She unfolded one, and everyone crowded around her to view it. This map had the larger, basic parts of the tour highlighted: procession hall, portrait gallery, public offices . . . the rest was shaded in gray, leaving a good eighty percent of the place a mystery.

"Ivo, how confident are you in a fight?" said Cherry.

"Very," said Ivo.

"Good. Laura, Zelda, you take the west side, since that looks pretty straightforward. Okane, Grim, straight forward through the unknown—it's probably a honeycomb of offices, so you'll have lots of hidey-holes. Ivo and I will take the east side, since that looks the worst for ambushes. Between the two of us we'll make those Mad Dogs regret messing with us," said Cherry.

"Remember, any guards will be Mad Dogs in disguise," said Laura. "Is everybody ready? Okay. Break."

They split and ventured into the branching hallways.

Laura studied their portion of the map, biting her lip. "If you were a power-hungry mob boss, where in this section would you go?"

Zelda tapped her chin before pointing at the third level of the main hall. "That spot would give a view of the main staircases from top to bottom. One of the ways - - - stay in power is to see - - -r enemy coming."

"Gives us more opportunity to see them, too. If someone's keeping watch, they can lead us right to him," said Laura.

The main hall lay far on the west end; the tour route wound along the east and north of the building before reaching it, but presumably they could cut through the gray portion and arrive faster. They hopped a divider and snuck down a thin passage lined by doors with foggy windows.

As they walked, the darkness felt deeper. The silence felt sharper. Laura cast a muffle command on her amulets without thinking about it, but when she realized what she'd done she stopped in surprise.

"- - - feel it too?" said Zelda, barely audible.

"I feel something, but I can't tell what it is," Laura whispered. "Do you recognize it?"

"We've crossed into a territory." Zelda shuddered. "This is how the bottom island feels, all the time. There's an old infestation here. - - - can feel its weight."

Laura had anticipated Renard bringing a monster with serious power, but she hadn't expected it to be strong enough for a non-Magi to sense it. How old must it be? Years? Decades?

"Can you track the source?"

"That's like going into a dark cave and trying to find which wall a painting's on."

"So—"

"*No,* Laura, I *cannot* track it."

"So we can't tell if it's sneaking up on us?"

"No." Zelda gave her a grim smile. "That's why so few Rexian Sweepers survive the crusades."

11

THE PRIDE OF OLD MEN

They kept on through the hall, zigzagged twice, and found themselves facing a door. Laura opened it gingerly, dreading the idea of a mobster on the other side. She needn't have worried. The door opened under one of the main hall's grand staircases, out of sight and out of mind.

The hall itself was enormous, with a marble floor the size of a sports field. Decadent pillars sprouted to support first one, then two levels of balconies that led further into the building. The elegant curve of the main staircase connected each floor, though smaller flights ran from second to third floors. It was beautiful, and loud, and cold.

"We'd be targets out there," said Zelda. "There's no cover. Nothing to blame sound or movement on."

"It's too quiet. I don't know about infestations, but I don't think any mobsters are here," said Laura. "How do you want to do this? Keep to the sides?"

"I want a vantage point," said Zelda.

The only way up was the main staircase, pride of placement and painfully obvious to the eye. But infestations didn't rely on eyes. Zelda took Laura's arm and led her so close they were almost flush.

"Slow and quiet," she whispered, eyes flicking back and forth.

Climbing the stairs took an agonizingly long time. Laura measured every step and took shallow breaths, and Zelda's hand threatened to cut off her circulation.

Nothing changed. They might as well have been moving through a mausoleum. At the top of the stairs, the third floor, a mosaic spread over the wall. Glittering white and gold tiles formed a map of Orien, with Amicae boldly in the center. It was pretty enough that Zelda's eyes caught it, and her grip eased.

Laura averted her gaze and cast around for anything else of interest. Pillars, portraits, railings . . . and a coat. She took half a step, squinting. That was definitely Minnie, tugging irritably at the dusty coat's sleeves as she leaned to inspect the ground floor.

"There she is," Laura hissed.

She heard a sharp intake of breath from two paces too far. Minnie looked up, and she spotted Laura immediately.

"Mice!" she cried.

Laura turned to grab Zelda and run, only to find their path blocked. Blanche had a gun pressed to Zelda's temple.

"Impressive disappearing act," she said. "It's a shame you ruined it."

"Put the gun down," said Laura.

"Or what?" Minnie skipped over to press her own gun barrel against Zelda's head. "You try anything, and this one's deader than dead."

"Are you willing to risk your companion's life?" said Blanche.

Zelda said nothing. She looked off into the distance as if bored, but her fisted hands betrayed her nerves.

"Why are you here?" said Blanche. "To devote yourself to the cause? To sabotage our plan?"

Obviously the last one, but Laura couldn't say that and get away unscathed. She went for the middle road and simply said, "I want to understand."

Blanche looked contemplative. Minnie looked furious.

"You don't really believe she wants to *chat*!" Minnie spat. "We should get rid of her right now."

"It's not my place to believe anything," said Blanche. "The boss wants—"

"Renard doesn't know—"

"He gave specific orders—"

Minnie rounded on Laura, eyes flashing. "I've spent long enough playing second fiddle to even the *memory* of your boss. If anyone gets to replace that bastard for Renard, it won't be you!"

The next few moves happened very fast. Minnie turned her gun on Laura. Blanche noticed this and moved to intervene, knocking Minnie's arm down so her bullet hit one of the staircase's balusters instead. With no more guns at her head, Zelda ducked away and shouted, "Run!"

They both bolted. Zelda made for the stairs, but going past the mobsters would be dangerous. Laura sprinted for the lesser stairs on the other side of the hall.

The gun cracked again. A vase and plinth toppled and smashed. Laura heard running steps behind her. She'd be an easy target on the open staircase. She took a hard left into the nearest hallway, out of easy range and off the map. She had a vague understanding that she'd turned toward the building's center and the grand Council room, but she could only guess how many honeycombed offices lay between. She dashed down thin hallways, zigzagging as she met dead ends until she lost all sense of direction. All the while, Minnie's laughter rang behind her.

"Run as much as you want! You can't get away!"

Laura jumped into a random office and slammed the door behind her. The noise probably caught Minnie's attention, but the walls and door could buy her some time and shelter. She knelt on the floor of the dark office and swung the axe into her hands.

Don't glow, don't glow, she mentally begged.

It did glow, but dim enough to be passable. Hopefully the glass of the small window in the door was distorted enough to hide it, and Minnie would walk past. No such luck, of course. She heard only silence for a moment, then the sudden bang of a door being kicked open.

"Knock knock!" Minnie screamed into the room at the end of the hallway.

Bang went another door, closer this time.

"Do you think you can hide?"

Bang! Even closer.

"Hide from me? I'll blow this place to bits!"

At every kicked door, Laura flinched. The axe's light fluctuated and she had to concentrate on keeping that down even while Clae-infused Eggs burned at her hip.

"You may as well get it over with and come—Oh. Really?" Minnie's voice became a simper. "Did you really think your patron could save you?"

Baffled, Laura looked at the rest of the office. VICTORIA DOUGLAS, read a nameplate on the desk. The same name had been painted on the door's glass, and Laura hadn't even noticed. She scrambled to the side of the door and gripped the axe tighter.

Minnie's silhouette appeared at the window.

"No one's here to save you," she cooed. "Not Victoria Douglas, not Clae Sinclair. We've gotten rid of both of them, and nothing can change it!"

The door cracked open. Laura acted. All the light she'd quelled surged at once into the axe blade, and the whole thing shrieked like a Bijou as she swung it up at Minnie's face. Whatever Minnie expected to see, it wasn't that. She reeled back just in time. The axe pulverized the doorframe. Wood chips and plaster whistled and rebounded off the opposite wall. Laura stumbled with the momentum, then swung back the other way. The axe's glow dimmed and then surged white-hot in midswing. This time she punched a new window into Douglas's office, and judging by the resulting crash, the magical force behind it had been enough to flip furniture. But as much damage as those strikes did, they took too long to recover from. Minnie danced easily out of the way.

"So you've got some bite!" she laughed.

Distantly Laura felt the magic shifting in her weapon, withdrawing into itself in preparation for another blast. Whatever function she'd tapped into, it didn't work well in close quarters.

Go back to normal, she urged, and the magic evened out. The excess magic hissed out into a glittering vanilla smoke screen, heavy enough to obscure even the walls.

"Do you even know what you're doing?" said Minnie, unimpressed.

Laura didn't answer but backed away fast. It hadn't been her intention, but if she had a smoke screen she'd use it to escape. She could find Zelda, and maybe then—

"Amateur!"

A punch caught Laura in the arm and she staggered with a yelp. Minnie rushed out of the fog; she'd abandoned the idea of shooting and switched to only her fists.

"Absolute idiot!" Minnie spat. "Maybe that bullshit works on infestations, but not on anything with eyes! I know exactly where you are!"

Sure enough, the axe-head's glow remained distinct in the haze. Laura tried to fend off Minnie's attacks, but she was more blinded than her opponent at this point; when Minnie pulled back, there was no telltale kin weapon to pinpoint her. She circled left, circled right, striking hard and fast from seemingly everywhere and gone before Laura could retaliate. Laura backed up against the wall and laid about her with the axe, but hit nothing. A shape lunged from the left. Laura lifted the axe, but Minnie caught the handle with both hands. Laura tried to tug it away but Minnie held fast.

"Pathetic," she said, shoving back, and she had height and gravity on her side; Laura stumbled. "For a while I thought I was wrong, but it was a fluke. Any cleverness in you is just panic. Your strength is desperation. Your survival is sheer dumb luck. You're not worthy of our time."

She leaned harder, pressing her weight toward one end of the axe so it began to tilt. The burning blade wavered closer and closer toward Laura's side, and she had neither the stance nor strength to keep it away long. Laura's mind raced. She couldn't think of a way out of this. With her axe compromised, no hands free to use Eggs or Bijou . . .

The answer came as she wavered again under Minnie's press. This wasn't wholly unfamiliar. Back in the mines, she'd tried fending off a Rexian Sweeper with far more experience than her. He'd leaned on her blade almost like Minnie did now, but he'd been burning.

"Joke's on you. I've got you right where I want you," said Laura.

"Oh? Do tell," Minnie simpered.

"It wasn't luck when I drove Rex out of the mines." Laura's knee hit the floor. "It was magic, and I'm good at that."

"Magic," Minnie laughed. "I suppose you'll breathe fire at me now?"

"No. It's already in the air." Minnie's expression flickered toward unease. Laura flashed her most vicious smile and said, "I burned them with the kin in the air!"

A constant waver or movement like the aurora meant the magic was susceptible to outside influence.

Did - - - know that if - - -'re using something that makes an aura like the Rexian blades, - - - can manipulate the aura? If - - - think really hard about it being hot—

Laura doubled her grip on the axe and ordered it to *glow brighter, hotter, give me an aura like a fire!* And it did. The inlaid design blazed hot enough to hurt the eye, metal seared her hand, and the aura pouring out of it thickened and flickered in mimicry of fire. It couldn't really become flame, and it had nowhere near enough power to fry her enemy the way the Pit had, but all that mattered was that Minnie doubted. Minnie pulled back, and Laura lurched after her. She planted a foot on the hem of the dusty coat and tighened her grip for a swing of the axe, but Minnie had clearly escaped from such a predicament before; she ducked and slid out of the coat in a single fluid movement, and paused out of the axe's range. Her eyes flicked from the axe blade to Laura's arms. Laura's scars were glowing to match the cloud around them, she felt like her lungs were drowning in molten vanilla, and it hurt like hell, but Laura gritted her teeth and pretended all that pain was rage as she roared, "Come at me if you want to burn alive!"

Minnie's lip curled, and she stepped back to disappear into the fog again. Laura pulled out a Bijou, scraped it across her amulet, and threw it after Minnie. She scooped the coat from the ground, turned, and bolted. The Bijou blew, crashing through the flimsy walls and offices and shrieking to high heaven. In such close quarters, it had to have hit her opponent.

Try chasing me through that! Laura thought. She broke out of the fog at the end of another office hallway, spotted a larger door, and ran for it. She emerged into the second level of the atrium.

The temperature change made her shudder. The fog might not have become flame, but at the end there it had gotten at least as hot as a boiler room, and sweat beaded heavy on her forehead. She lifted an arm to swipe at it, but paused halfway through the motion. She'd been aware that her scars from the Pit were glowing back there, but the level of it was downright horrifying. It looked like her skin had cracked open along lightning lines to seep shimmering golden blood, the worst of it on her palms where she'd gripped the axe. She slid a shaking hand over one arm. No, her skin was sensitive and uneven but not broken. She wasn't bleeding. It was just . . . lighting up from the inside. Hadn't Lester MacDanel showed similar injuries after being attacked by heavy kin magic? Could this be what Clae had looked like as he was turning? Laura had to swallow bile at the thought. Maybe this was the real reason Minnie had backed off; she thought Laura might be contagious. Laura slung Clae's coat onto her shoulders and shoved herself into the sleeves, half for utility and half to hide her own arms. She stuffed the axe back in its holster, too. The last thing she needed was a glowing beacon for any other mobsters.

"Right," she whispered, trying to reassure herself as she pulled out the brochure and determinedly ignored her glittering hands. "On to the next piece of business."

She had to find Zelda. In retrospect it had been a terrible idea not to specify a rendezvous point in case of separation. She squinted at the map, trying to decide Zelda's most likely hiding place. She'd probably escaped easily, since Minnie and Blanche had focused on Laura. Blanche was unaccounted for, but she seemed more used to issuing orders than chasing people down, so that was a point in Zelda's favor. Not so pleasingly, Zelda's invisibility could be ignored easily by someone specifically looking for her. Blanche might have even ordered other mobsters into the search. Zelda's invisibility might be useless now.

One of the ways - - - stay in power is to see - - -r enemy coming. Where could Zelda go that kept her hidden while providing a wide view? Laura's finger traced the map before stopping on a location. The procession hall lay deep inside the building, a long stretch from end to end of the central portion. No one could set foot there without being seen at the other end, and since it was in Okane and Grim's portion of the search area it had the possibility of being in friendly hands. But it ran right next to the Council chamber. Everything in this building seemed to be built leading to that central point. She felt like she was creeping to the belly of a beast. She followed the map deeper and deeper. She didn't hear anything—no talking, no walking, not a single breath that hinted toward anything else being here. It was so quiet and empty, it felt like she'd never encountered anyone at all. But with every step, the sense of weight from the old infestation returned, and the feeling grew worse. By the time she arrived at the procession hall, Laura was shivering. She leaned close to the wall and peeked around the corner. The hall stretched for what seemed like miles in the dark, decorated only with oil paintings of Amicae's founding. Laura was free to run away now and get as far from this territory as possible . . . but where could Zelda be?

She chanced a glance back as if Zelda might be behind her, and screamed. Minnie's bleeding face was inches from hers.

"Thought you got the best of me?" Minnie snarled, seizing her by the throat. "That'll be your last mistake!"

Laura gasped for air and clawed at Minnie's hands, but her attacker only gripped tighter. Minnie laughed, and then—*Wham!* They rolled, and Minnie let go.

"Get off of her!" said Blanche, wielding a plank of wood. Where had she gotten that in the middle of the Council building?

"Traitor!" Minnie hissed, standing and cradling her ribs.

"You're the traitor here!" said Blanche. "We need to get Kramer to the boss."

"I told you, the other one can—"

"The other one's dead," Blanche snapped. "Jumped out the window. Now, unless you want to explain to Renard why we've killed off *two* of the people he expressly wanted brought to him . . ."

"Not a chance! I'm not letting this one anywhere close to him!"

Blanche's face twisted, and what was probably several months' worth of bitterness came out in one outburst: "How can you possibly expect him to love you when you pull all of this shit?"

"Ex*cuse* you?" said Minnie.

"You're not *cute*, you're not *passionate*, you're a goddamn maniac who ruins everything she touches! You pretend to agree with him and then foil all his plans! He has reasons for everything he does, and you don't respect those reasons or the man himself!"

Minnie growled, "Renard is everything to me!"

"Then fucking act like it!" said Blanche.

"Killing off these Sinclairs is for his sake!" said Minnie. "Have you heard the way people talk about him? About how soft he is on people who've rejected him for years? He's been losing respect across all the mobs! Even Haru's worried about it! Softness is what gets a mobster killed!"

"This isn't softness, it's protecting his own assets," said Blanche. "And even if it were, that's still his choice you're disrespecting." She closed her eye, breathed deep to calm herself, and said, much quieter, "These could be our last days. Do you want it to end with Renard cursing you, or do you want him to be proud?"

Minnie drew back with an ugly expression, and said nothing.

Laura was too caught up in Blanche's earlier revelation to care much how Minnie was reacting. Zelda, dead? It couldn't be.

"There was no sign of her in the hallway?" she whispered. "She really jumped out a window?"

Blanche gave her a dark look. "There's nowhere else for her to have gone."

Oh, thank god. Zelda must've given her the slip, and Blanche went with it to keep Minnie from murdering anyone. Zelda was still in here somewhere. Laura's relief left her as slumped as she would be at the thought of a death, so the fact that they needed to heave her up was entirely genuine. They shoved her down the procession hall toward the Council chamber. Laura wasn't comfortable with either of them at her back, but swallowed down fear and forced her back straight as she walked. *I'm getting out of this alive. I'm going exactly where I need to be,* she thought, but it still felt like a walk to the gallows.

The grand Council chamber dwarfed any hall or room Laura had ever seen before. It seemed larger even than the depot, filled with row upon row of blue-cushioned seats and long, curved desks, descending in a semicircle

like theater seating. At the very bottom lay the debate floor, hardwood discolored by the passage of 150 years of pacing and arguments.

On the far wall was the massive single desk of the Council judge, crowned
with a carving of Amicae's old government seal: a rising phoenix, wings
spread to form a perfect circle. In one set of claws it held a miniature sun—
symbol of the Sweeper city—and in the other a bushel of grain. Standing
there, looking up at the seal, was Renard. He had a staff strapped to his
back, and he tossed a chess piece—a black queen—up and down in one
hand without looking.

"Boss," said Blanche. "You have a visitor. The Sinclairs are crashing our
party."

"I thought they'd show up," said Renard.

I thought they'd show up, Minnie mouthed sarcastically.

Renard turned to look at them, and true to his word he showed zero surprise at Laura's presence. "Blanche, I want you to go join Haru. The Silver
Kings have proposed their contract, and I need someone with muscle at the
signing so they don't think they can strong-arm him into anything."

"They'd never be able to in the first place," Blanche scoffed.

"True, but if we can avoid their pettiness entirely, it'll be a much smoother
process."

"As you wish, boss." But she hesitated.

"No need to worry about Minnie," said Renard. "She won't kill your captive in front of me. Would you, Minnie?"

Minnie gave them a tremendous scowl. She stormed past Renard, snatching the queen from his hand as she went. Blanche breathed easier.

"I'll update you once the signing's done," she said, and retreated from the
room.

This left Laura alone and unbound. She could probably run away and no
one would try to stop her.

Renard reclined casually against the judge's desk and said, "What brings
you here, Kramer? Glory? Stupidity? A combination of the two?"

"I want answers," said Laura. "Are you really planning to kill the Council?"

"Yes," he said, without batting an eye.

"What, so you can call yourself the king of Amicae? All that talk about
protecting the city, and then you do this?" She gestured at the room in
disgust.

"This is for Amicae's survival," said Renard.

"And you just so happen to be the best thing for Amicae?"

"Oh, no. Not me. When the Council dies, it won't be the Mad Dogs taking over."

Laura's heart shot into her throat. "Rex?"

Renard barked with laughter. "You're not gullible enough to buy the Council's garbage, are you?"

"Who else is there?"

"Are you so out of touch with Amicae's politics? My Mad Dogs are Sweepers, not politicians. We couldn't govern our way out of a paper bag. The Silver Kings, however . . ."

Laura drew back in surprise. "You'll hand the city over to your rivals?"

"The Silver Kings are already most of the law in the lower Quarters. They have experience, vision, and most importantly, a coherent plan to keep citizens safe. They're Amicae's greatest chance at survival."

Laura cocked her head and frowned. Renard smiled, thin and menacing, like he knew exactly what she was thinking.

"How can you talk about Amicae's survival so much when you're the ones who set up the Falling Infestation?" she asked.

"Because that, too, was for our survival," said Renard.

"Amicae had to be evacuated. So many people died in the mines and interior—"

"And they would be dying with us now if that didn't happen."

"You can't know that."

"Gaudium has fallen," said Renard. "We're also going to fall, and very, very soon. Haven't you found it strange, how all of Orien is reporting the worst spike in history, and in Amicae we're all sitting on our asses?"

"Maybe the infestations are targeting other places," Laura said half-heartedly. "Gaudium had the same—It . . ." She faltered.

"You can't excuse our infestation levels when all the cities around us are fighting tooth and nail," said Renard. "*We* are the target. You're right that Gaudium also had a strange drop in infestations. They sailed smoothly for weeks before being suddenly wiped off the map. I believe Gaudium was a test to see just how low humans could lower their guard."

"Infestations don't coordinate like that. They swarm, sure, but they don't have tactics," said Laura.

"You think the hive mind could wipe out the Wasureijin empire without tactics?" Renard drawled.

"Do you really think the hive mind is in Terual?"

"I think the hive mind is in Gaudium right now, with its pretty little eye set on our trash heap of a city," said Renard. He pushed himself up from the desk and began to pace, his eyes never leaving Laura's. "We're facing the potential extinction of humanity in Orien. Potentially the extinction of all humanity, depending on whether Orien's quarantine was effective all those centuries ago. We don't have the luxury of waiting for the old men of the Council to die off or get over their pride. They hate Sweepers for taking away their 'good old days' where they could pretend everything was fine, and the days before citizens stopped them in the street to demand why they upheld such a treacherous lie. I've given them chances. I've lobbied like a good citizen. When that didn't work, I tried threats. It's time to follow through on those."

"You could still reason with them," said Laura.

"Reason?" he scoffed. "We left reason behind long ago."

"But with the threat from Gaudium—If you make your suspicions about the hive mind clear—"

"The Falling Infestation was the point of no return. It was the worst-case scenario: the entire population displaced, the interior overrun, the famed head Sweeper dead. That's the heavy dose of reality; that's the point where you need to change. And they didn't. They acknowledged the wall, and did nothing else. If the Falling Infestation didn't make the Council change, nothing will." Renard shook his head. "We planted it to create an irreversible change. We did it because we had hope that the Council could protect Amicae if they were confronted with that kind of proof. I don't have that faith anymore."

Laura fisted her hands. "You had Clae die on purpose?"

"I didn't order his death, but I should've tried harder to keep him alive," said Renard. "I suspect he'd join us now if he were still capable of the choice. He held out so long because he had faith in the Council, too."

"Clae would not have joined you," Laura spat. "He knew you'd sacrifice other people without a thought. He wouldn't approve of this."

She'd been angry at how he'd used Clae to dig at her, but her own mention cut deeper than she anticipated. Renard stopped short. His lip curled and he hissed, "Clae didn't have that spectacular moral compass you seem to think he did. What an idiot. I always thought I might've been in the wrong somehow, for him to refuse my help even when he was a child alone in the world . . . But where he refused a mobster, he would still use Anselm."

Laura recoiled. "You know about Anselm?"

"I do," said Renard, his bitterness palpable.

"Anselm?" Minnie said sharply. "What's Anselm?"

Renard ignored her. "Yes, I know all about Anselm and Clae and their daddy's sick little plots. I started Sweeping young, you see. I was the closest to their age. I knew them better than anyone. And I understand that you're taking advantage of Anselm, too." His fingers twitched as if he wanted to hold the staff again, wanted to bash another man's skull open to vent the hatred now hissing through his teeth. "Do you think a hypocrite like you can talk about sacrifice while desecrating him?"

"What is Anselm?" Minnie pressed.

"It doesn't concern you," Renard snapped, and turned back to Laura, eyes more manic than ever. "You're not better than me. Clae was not better than me. You're both stuck on dreams and the relics of your pride. This is the real world. If you want to save something, you have to fight for it and claw your way through any obstacles."

"You have to be a pain," Laura said faintly.

Minnie looked between the two of them, horrified by whatever understanding they seemed to have reached. She gripped the chess piece tight in her fist, then whirled to kick the judge's chair over with a scream. It must be a common enough occurrence, because Renard didn't seem to notice or care.

"I will save Amicae, no matter what blood I have to spill," he said. "I won't kill an enterprising young Sweeper. We'll need you working in the aftermath. And you will work, won't you? You'll protect Amicae no matter who's running the show."

Laura forced herself to breathe evenly. Okay. She had some answers for the past, but she should be focusing on the here and now. Gather information. Pretend she was on board with this after all. If she could get that information and then find the other Sinclairs, or even steal one of the IRWTs the Mad Dogs carried to broadcast the news . . .

"I'll do anything for Amicae," she said firmly.

"She won't!" Minnie shrieked. "She can't join, I won't let her!"

"She's not replacing you," said Renard.

"She never could!" cried Minnie.

"Then there's no reason for you to be upset."

"Her even existing undermines your authority," said Minnie. "Are you going to bow your head to another head Sweeper who doesn't deserve it?"

"If that's what it takes," said Renard.

"She should die instead," Minnie muttered, turning away again. "They should all just die."

"That chess piece is an amulet, right?" said Laura. "It was a pawn amulet in Club Toulouse, and a bishop in the Grand University. The pieces matched."

"That's correct. This is a complete chess set of amulets," said Renard. "Since white moves first, we used the first half for practice. The remaining black pieces have all been scattered through this building."

"Where did you put them?"

"Here and there. In the offices. In the storage rooms. Good luck trying to find them all now."

"And the divides were to keep damage to a minimum?"

"Precisely."

Laura sucked in another breath. "How can I help?"

"If you do want to help, the answer is simple," said Renard. "You and the rest of your team go back to the armory. Lie low until we come for you. You're useless here right now, and doing anything else will land you in very hot water with the public."

"You're sure you don't need anyone monitoring the planted amulets?" said Laura.

Renard rolled his eyes. "You can't hope for any kind of success when you're being that obvious."

The IRWT box on Renard's hip crackled to life.

"We've diverted the raid parties' reserve forces," said a man's voice. "You're sure we shouldn't get rid of them for good, boss?"

Renard held it up to his mouth and pressed the button. "We'll need them as early as tomorrow. Have you had any trouble with the military?"

"Ha! The barricades are good for one thing at least. Military doesn't give a shit about what the police are doing unless we get close to their posts. Like hell we're doing that."

"Continue as you are. We're almost finished." Renard clipped the IRWT back onto his belt and said, "Minnie, hand over your communicator. Kramer can have it for now, so she can hear when we call."

"Then how will *I* hear anything?" said Minnie.

"You'll be with me until we get you a new one. You won't miss anything," said Renard.

Minnie paused as if this were something out of character. The way she and Blanche had argued, maybe it was odd for Renard to easily go anywhere with her. She warred with her own irritation for a moment, then pulled off her IRWT and tossed it to Laura.

"No funny business," she said with a sneer. "If you think you can double-cross us, you really will all—"

A sickening sound cut her off. Like a squelch, or a rumble; something wet and distant and terrible. Minnie sucked in a sharp breath, eyes wide.

"Minnie?" Renard eyed her dubiously. "Minnie, what's wrong?" When she didn't immediately respond, he continued, "If you're so concerned about the communicator, you can hold mine."

Minnie was visibly paling. "That's not it."

Renard understood something was wrong. He shifted his stance, one hand going back toward the staff on his back. "What are you seeing?"

"The last infestation," Minnie rasped. "It's not in the amulet anymore."

"What do you mean, it's not—"

The sound came again, and her arm *bulged*. Her sleeve ripped, bone snapped, and she gave a scream of fright and pain. Her skin discolored, swirling black under the flesh. Black like an infestation. Laura backpedaled fast, and Renard yanked the staff from his back.

"Keep it held out," he snapped.

"I can't move it!" Minnie whimpered. "Boss, I can't—"

Renard swung the staff up. The infestation saw his attack coming, and was faster. Minnie screamed as it tore up her arm. The sick, squishing, rending sounds intensified as it ripped through muscle and vein. She jerked sharply as it hit her shoulder, and her arm dropped like a dead thing. The queen piece clattered to the floor.

"Minnie," said Renard, more urgently. "Where is it?"

She was crying now, and to Laura's horror those tears ran red. It took two tries for Minnie to speak, and when she did, she croaked, "Spinner, my thread ends."

It was the opening to Spiritualist last rites. Renard paled. "Too short this thread, but woven true," he whispered.

Minnie opened her mouth to reply, but all that came out was blood. Her torso wrenched, snapping her head forward and back with the motion. Laura backed up so far she bumped into the first row of desks. Minnie rattled in place. Finally, she heaved forward, bent double, and her stomach ripped open. Laura screamed and pulled herself atop the closest desk. Fuck bravery. She'd signed up to face shadow monsters, not things that spat someone's insides all across the floor.

Even with her organs steaming on the ground, Minnie's body kept heaving, spewing blood. Renard stayed rooted to the spot, his face ghost white. Minnie continued to move, arms swinging like dead weights.

Awful.

Laura's hair stood on end. Fear snagged the breath in her lungs, and her heart beat faster. Her amulets burned.

Run, the magic hummed.

Foul, said something else, not amulet, not magic, not human.

Friend friend see you danger run run far fast go—

Hideous.

Minnie lolled left, then right, then up. Blackness writhed in the hole left in her belly, glinting red in the light or red with blood. An eye opened in its midst.

Disgusting, the infestation hissed.

Even without the paralyzing eye, Laura couldn't have moved. Infestations were not supposed to talk. Infestations were not supposed to occupy bodies, not even bone. Even ancient creatures in the wilds had never shown such behavior. Either the mavericks had really gone rogue, or . . .

"Hive mind," Laura whispered.

Sound and feeling rose again, not words this time but a distinct pleasure at being recognized.

Not as stupid as you seem. Still repulsive. Too much noise inside you.

Laura wanted to vomit. Her amulets sang *danger, danger,* and even the Eggs in her bag were reacting to the threat. But they couldn't do anything unless she armed them, and there was no way she could. Not under that eye. She was doomed.

The infestation roiled still more, enjoying their dread.

The children were silly to fear you. Such a tiny creature. Wrathful, but tiny. I will silence you easily.

Renard took slow, measured steps backward, angling his staff while his eyes stayed toward the floor.

Or do you think you can really stand against the dark? There is no winning.

"There's no winning alone," said Renard, "but I've never tried doing this alone."

The staff came close enough to block Laura's vision, cutting the eye's hold. He took her by the biceps and urged her down from the desk. She wanted nothing to do with him, but she wanted even less to do with the hive mind, so she followed his lead. They both inched back toward the door.

"Do you have a plan?" Laura whispered.

"Get backup," said Renard, and the top of the staff glowed. "Seal the doors so it can't reach the canal system."

"Good idea," said Laura.

Minnie's body fell to its knees, the jaw hanging open and streaming black.

Think you can run? The hive mind sounded delighted. *Think you can hide? You can't. I've come for the Wrath of God, and now I've found it, I won't let you get away.*

More blackness seeped out the sleeves of her shirt and wriggled toward them on the floor. Renard lifted his staff and brought it clanging, point down, to the ground. The top gave a flash bright as lightning, the staff shuddered, and all its gathered energy surged out the bottom. A kin blast ripped floorboards from the ground and splintered the desks before them. A yellow fog obscured the air, and the hive mind hissed somewhere on the other side.

"Move!" Renard barked, and they both tore out the door.

12

CHECKMATE

Laura and Renard each went a different way down the procession hall, and judging by the sliding, crashing sounds, the hive mind followed. Most of Laura's mind was caught up in the running, but a small section remained entirely calm.

What can beat an infestation? it asked, sounding far too much like Clae.

She had magic, certainly; the charged Eggs practically sang in her bag, and she had equipment enough to bring the roof down on them if she wanted to. But so had every Rexian crusade. No, she couldn't let despair in. If the hive mind was truly the origin of infestations, it would be the same species as all its offspring; it would have the same weaknesses, if only to a lesser degree. The only reason the Rexians hadn't killed it before was because they never made it through the rest of the infestations to reach it. This was doable.

"Get all Sweepers to the Council building!" Renard's voice snapped from the IRWT still clutched in her hand. "The hive mind is loose, heading outbound from the Council chamber. We have one fatality. It's wearing Minnie as an amulet. If anyone runs into it, bait it to an open area where multiple Sweepers can reach and then radio in. We'll join you."

Open area. The main staircase would be ideal, if she could comprehend just where she was going. She'd gotten lost on the way here, and now that she was running pell-mell again she couldn't orient herself. Besides, she couldn't run all the way to the west end from a procession hall in the very middle of the building.

Where else nearby had a wide area that could support multiple Sweepers? She thought hard about the building, its domes, its many-leveled roofs . . . Wait. The roof?

A stupid idea, but the hive was gaining on her, she was almost on top of a staircase, and *shit*, it was worth a shot. Gritting her teeth, Laura dismissed the speed order on her amulets. Immediately she slowed.

Where do you think you're going, Sweeper?

She forced speed again, directly left instead of forward. She hit the wall, but it was better than where she'd been; a thick black arm had smashed into the floor there. It writhed, and expanded after her. The infestation punched deep into the wall, and if she hadn't ducked in time she'd have been decapitated. It sliced a painting in two and dropped to the floor. Laura kicked off—one, two steps—and she was level with Minnie again. Laura caught a glimpse of her fast-staining face, her open mouth leaking pitch, and if anything could scare her faster, that was it.

Laura twisted sharply to bound up the stairs. Her amulets whined with the increased draw on their power, and when she hit the next landing she skidded badly before correcting her course and dashing left. The hive slipped and slid its way after her. More floor. More doors. So much marble. Laura's every footstep rang loud as a bell as she searched for another staircase. She was on the fourth floor now, higher than most old, decorative buildings went. Rooftop access had to be nearby. She passed grandly carved doors, but there—an alcove. She'd never been so excited by a RESTRICTED ACCESS sign.

She dove for it. The flimsy door might have been locked, but it broke open when she hit it, and she stumbled into a narrow hallway. Plain walls. Tiny. No storage in sight. She tore down it, and the passage dead-ended into a cramped, winding metal staircase.

"Damn this architect," she wheezed, but climbed.

She glanced down through the grate, only to see the infestation winding up the path behind her. She bit back a curse and dug through her bag. Her fingers closed around a flash pellet, and she threw it down without stopping. Light cascaded through the stairwell, but there was no scream of bewilderment or hissing annoyance. A seething sound came from below; the hive was amused again.

Think that will hurt me? Silly thing.

The metal groaned and Laura stumbled. She threw another flash pellet, saw it burst on the infestation, but the creature didn't flinch. It just kept moving, sliding stick-thin fingers to wind branchlike about the metal core, through holes in the grating.

I know these tricks. Annoying. Not painful. Useless. Will you try again?

Screeching. The stairs were bending, groaning looser where they were bolted into the stone. Laura didn't have time to pause and watch.

Will you use true light? Burning, killing, detestable. No. You won't. Not where you would burn with me. Here you are powerless. You are nothing. You will be quiet!

The staircase wrenched. Laura lost her balance and snatched for the railing, heaving herself forward, faster. Metal rattled and screamed, and stone dust billowed. She launched herself onto the last stone step just in time. The whole staircase ripped out of the wall and shrieked down, gouging the wall in its plummet to the infestation's roiling mass. Laura threw her weight against the door and almost sobbed. It didn't open.

"Come on! Come on!" she screamed.

She had no room to build up momentum, so just kept hitting the door. On the third try, her arms burned. Light flickered again through the scars on her hand, and the lock on the door snapped. It swung open, and she almost fell through. Fresh air caught her face. She'd reached the rooftop.

The decorative architecture of the building meant multilevel roofs. Laura stood on the main straightaway: an evenly paved stretch of roof that spread out over the main halls before branching into shingled peaks and chimneys. The main dome with its white spire was visible in the near distance, blotting out the horizon. At the roof's edge she spotted little bulbs strung on wire, emerging from the mouth of a very large, very ugly gargoyle. A glance each way showed gargoyles all the way down. She guessed they held amulets, presumably sheltering them from weather damage. If Clae knew about these he would've had a field day, but Laura was thrilled. She knelt next to the closest gargoyle, clasped her hands around its grimacing head, and concentrated: *Are you there?*

There came a ping of awareness against her skull. This changed fast to the magic she was used to, pulsing excitedly.

Here, the amulet replied.

Here, said the next one.

Here, here, here, all the way down. Energy crackled in the split second before all the bulbs flared. Light engulfed the rooftop, so bright Laura was almost blinded even with her goggles on. The distant glow of the First Quarter was muted almost to nothing, drowned in false daylight. The hive recoiled into the tower.

Annoying, it spat again.

Here, the amulets sang. *Here, here. See me. See you. Happy seen. Look, look, strong!*

Only Niveus amulets clamored so much for attention, and that was a point in her favor. If she had to deal with any sort of amulet, Niveus was the closest thing to true Gin.

Laura pressed the button on the IRWT and said, "This is Laura Kramer! I'm on the Council building's roof, and I've got space, a shit ton of light, and a really angry hive mind! If anyone can help out, I'd really appreciate it!"

"All Sweepers, divert to the roof!" said Renard, but after that no one else spoke.

"No one can help you. You can't escape."

Laura whirled around. The hive had withdrawn entirely into Minnie's body.

Minnie looked as if she'd crawled out of a pool of ink; blackness dripped from her clothes, off her matted hair, from her chin. Her ruined eyes were wide. Worst of all, her jaw worked, and the voice that came out was hers, stained with the monstrosity puppeting her.

"Be resigned to your fate." She stepped forward. It was an awkward, stuttering motion, but while the inkiness smoked under light, the body continued undaunted. *"Run, run, but we will catch you. You cannot escape us. We are the natural state of the world."*

"Brighter!" Laura shouted, clutching the gargoyle so tight her hands hurt.

Niveus would break under too much magic, but she didn't have the luxury of pacing it right now. The lights burned brighter. She forced herself to stand and swing the axe out of its holster. Gripping this kept her hands from shaking, and it hummed reassuringly as it gave off golden fog.

"Natural state of the world, my ass," she said, with confidence she didn't feel. "The Magi created you. You're as natural as a machine."

The hive stopped. It snickered.

"From peace comes chaos," it said. *"From dark, light. Noise and light are fleeting things. We are eternal."*

"Just because you haven't died yet doesn't mean you're immortal," said Laura.

"Do you mean to make me mortal?"

"I can damn well try."

Minnie's arms spread wide. *"Then try, Sweeper! Know that any attempt is~"*

Crimson light blossomed at Minnie's right shoulder. Too bright for blood, and too loud to be anything but a bullet, the force made Minnie stagger. The hive shrieked in outrage.

Bea stood on the next walkway, a Rexian kin gun in her hand. She flipped back the safety again, and smiled wider than Laura had ever seen. She raised her IRWT to her mouth and said, "I have eyes on the hive."

"Good," Renard replied. "Pin it down but keep a distance. I'm sending you a gift."

A door at the straightaway's other end burst open, and Okane and Grim staggered through it.

"We heard - - - on their radios!" Okane called. "Where's the—oh my god."

Grim laid a hand on a gargoyle and said, "I'll try to brace the amulets here. You focus on the hive."

He didn't need to tell them twice. Bea was already shooting again, making Minnie stagger, and Okane pulled out his own kin gun to join in. Laura doubled her grip on the axe and charged. With such bright light, the infestation didn't want to leave its shell; instead Minnie's corpse dropped like a rag doll to avoid attacks, before catching itself in positions a human could never manage. It danced and twisted and rolled for her, and Laura did her best to try hitting it. Finally, as it bent backward, she found it suitably pinned.

She took another swing, this time for the tear in Minnie's stomach. Limbs surged out. The axe blade sliced through them but slowed to a halt an inch from the body, its entire head hidden in a wad of tumbling blackness. Laura could still sense its magic going, but as much as she tried to wrench it free, it wouldn't budge. The eye surfaced again, glinting behind an exposed rib.

Thought you could defeat me? It laughed. *Wrath is nothing before us!*

More limbs curled away, rose above her head, and sharpened like scythes. They were almost out of Laura's sight, close enough to dread and far enough that she couldn't confirm what it was doing. Her breath came shallow but she couldn't move.

Help, she begged the amulets, but that wouldn't work. It wasn't complete enough an order for the amulets to understand. The Niveus lights shot bright enough that one shattered and took out an entire wire's worth of bulbs, but the hive didn't flinch under them anymore. Past it all she could hear Okane swearing as he reloaded the gun, saw Bea jumping and drawing her blade, but help from there would be too slow.

Be resigned, said the hive, and its scythes descended.

Tiles smashed upward, accompanied by a shrill of energy. A horrible weight slammed into Laura's mind, like a felin's influence reversed. It sang along her scars, pulsed anger in her ears.

NOT HER!

A crystal hand had broken through the roof and caught Minnie's ankle. As the hive's eye swiveled down to look, more of the roof's surface bucked. A laugh gushed out of Laura's lungs, newfound feeling flooding through her limbs.

The hive screamed. Its scythes redirected, trying to rip away its tormentor. Clae's second hand sliced through them easily and caught just below Minnie's knee. His head surfaced in the rubble, eyes blinding and crystal teeth bared.

NOT HER!

The hive reeled.

But it was you? it howled. *I felt the wrath from you and it was tiny?*

In its fright, it lost its grip on the axe. Laura heaved it out with a sickly sound. By this time Bea had reached them; she slashed through the writhing scythes and gouged deep into Minnie's side. Minnie's torso flopped. Again, the hive screamed, half its own wordless pressure and half abusing Minnie's vocal cords. It wrenched itself away, dragging Clae up though the roof, and Laura realized it wasn't just the crystal.

Clae appeared to be wearing Renard's coat. He also appeared to be making a sizzling sound. Oh, no.

"Back up!" Laura screamed, already dashing for the next roof down. *"Back up, back up, back up—"*

Bea flitted away again, and the others scattered further. The Bijou loaded into Renard's coat pockets hissed for only a moment more before catching under Clae's magic. The result was thunderous. It sounded like sixteen fireworks going off at close proximity, and the flashes were bright enough to match. The Bijou shrieked and tore through fabric to bite at the hive, spewing sparks. Clae reached through the hailstorm of sparks without hesitation, trying to catch the monster. The hive's form fluctuated. It tried to throw up a tarry shield, but the magic kept penetrating it.

Laura caught a glimpse of Minnie's arms, saw a Bijou sear her pant leg, before all the hive's scythes cascaded back in on themselves. It grew into a massive, writhing pile of blackness and proceeded to roll, zigzagging across the roof. The tiles splintered and discolored under the monster. Whole chunks of the roof ripped out and fell as thick as hail. The hive careened over the roof's peak, down the slope, and almost off entirely before catching itself with a scythe-limb and veering back up; for all its sharp turns Clae clung doggedly on and the Bijou raced to catch it, leaving shimmering gold scars in the roof to seethe along the infestation's own trail. Finally, it swerved past one of the gargoyles, and Clae slammed into it. The stone fractured on impact, but it was enough of a hook that he was left behind, still clutching Minnie's shoe. Her leg had snapped at the ankle and ripped apart entirely, so there was a glimmer of red blood mixed in with the hive's trail. The hive came to a stop by the opposite door and plunged a scythe through the doorway, destroying that route for any backup.

Disgraceful! You lied about what you were! You will pay dearly!

Grim fled from the hive's shadow and hid in the lee of the cracked gargoyle as Clae stood. Bea touched down next to Laura and Okane.

"Nice to have you back, Bea," said Laura.

"If - - - think I'm here to assist - - -, then - - - are mistaken," said Bea. "I am here to destroy what I was born to destroy. There is no further meaning."

She launched herself forward again, blade at the ready.

Laura hadn't realized that she'd only seen the Rexians fight in close quarters, but they were wholly different with more maneuverability. Between the amulets on her harness and her own magic, Bea was *fast*. She sped left, right, backtracked, slid under flailing limbs and jumped to score injuries anywhere the hive possibly left unguarded. The hive was by no means slow—on several swipes Bea avoided capture by a hairsbreadth—but Bea made the fight look effortless.

The hive billowed black smoke and lashed out on all sides. The limb aiming for Laura and Okane was chopped apart, its remnants burned by the axe's aura; the limb that went for Grim and Clae was blocked by angry crystal and stomped into the roof tiles; Bea jumped to avoid the last one, but the hive flung out a new shape: a massive skeleton's hand that curled as if to cage her. Bea's jaw tightened. She must've given her amulets an order, because she was inexplicably drawn backward. She landed heavily on the roof, and sped away again on good footing as the tarry hand crashed down where she'd been. The hive's lumpy main body churned, and out of its mess came the shape of a skull. It didn't seem to know whether it was meant to be human or canid; all the teeth were shaped like jagged swords. The smoothness of its black skull began to bristle with these too, and it opened its maw to scream loud enough for all the Quarter to hear.

Bea loaded a new crimson bullet into her gun and fired. This one hit with twice the force and brightness of any other bullet, spraying sparks like a firework that surged back in to pierce the infestation's sides. Boils rose on the monster's surface, and then . . . smoothed out. The crimson light died in a heartbeat. The hive's teeth gnashed in a macabre grin. Bea froze. She turned back to Laura and cried, "Use a Sinker!"

Laura's first instinct was to say no—Sinkers worked by smashing root amulets to bits, and were only supposed to be a last resort—but what better time was there to irreversibly destroy a single infestation? The hive *was* a last resort. She pulled out the blue capsule, clacked it against her amulet, and threw. Midair the contents flared brighter, and it shot straight into the hive's bulk as if pulled by a magnet. Just like in the Falling Infestation, the hive bulged, but unlike back then, nothing else happened.

Satisfied? The hive laughed.

"I don't understand," Laura whispered. "That works. Sinkers are always supposed to work."

Silly, feeble Sweepers, said the hive mind, swaying back and forth with glee. **You think I don't understand weapons? Sinker is for amulet. I have no amulet.**

But that was impossible. All infestations had a root. They always had a place to be beaten back into, something that could be purified to actually kill them.

I am darkness! I am quiet! I am the world! And I am unrestrained! There is no key to destroy me, because I cannot be destroyed. If my shell breaks I find a new one. It is only convenience to have one. It is fate for you to die. Become quiet.

Okane glanced at Laura. "Is it possible to kill an infestation without an amulet?"

"We're about to find out," said Laura. "It's still reacting to other weaknesses. Just because we can't target that point doesn't mean we can't target others!"

The hive angled down, flooding under the roof's surface and vanishing from sight.

"Split up!" Laura cried, and jumped down the slope facing the building's front.

Okane made to flee the other way, but the roof cracked beneath him and threw off his footing. Blackness sprayed up through the shingles. Bea veered off her course just in time to snatch Okane out of danger. With his added weight, she couldn't balance herself quickly enough. Instead of the light landings and pivots she'd been managing before, she landed hard enough to send them both tumbling. A loud snap and cry of pain made Laura scramble after them.

"Clae, cover them!"

Clae planted himself beside them, issuing thick clouds of golden vanilla. Okane straightened without trouble, but Bea pushed herself up with a far more stilted motion.

"What happened?" said Laura.

Okane hovered over her, arms outstretched but unsure what to do. "It's Bea! She's hurt!"

"Is it her ankle?" Grim asked from just outside of Clae's range.

Okane reached to help steady Bea, saying, "I'm so sorry—"

"Do not touch me." She swatted him away with a poisonous expression. "- - -'ve *just* seen what a futile action it is to act for others in the middle of an infestation."

"But - - -r leg—"

Bea's right leg had broken. Her shattered tibia protruded through a hole in her pants, but she hopped determinedly on her good leg and gripped her blade tighter as if that could chase the paleness from her face.

"If - - - commit to a goal - - - must *commit in full*," she said, "and I am committed to killing this beast. I do not care what I lose."

She hopped once, twice, and with a pop of magic she sprang out from the curtain of Clae's aura. While still nimble, she couldn't brace or change direction nearly as fast.

"Get back here! Bea, that's not—Ugh. Okane, cover me. I'm going in to help her," said Laura.

She wasn't nearly as fast or experienced, but she could at least distract the monster. As she ran, Laura scraped an Egg against her amulet and swung; it fell into the hive's form, bubbled, and vanished like the Sinker. Okay, so single bursts wouldn't work. She needed something continuous, to keep eating steadily at its victim. Bijou would be best, but the roof was already heavily damaged by the hive's earlier rolling, and adding any more Bijou to the hissing number on the roof could wreck the very structure that kept them up. Otherwise . . .

"Clae!" she shouted.

She didn't need to explain her plan; while she veered left, Clae moved right, both of them pouring out kin clouds.

Bright, hot, burn like fire, she ordered, as she had with Minnie before. Unweaponized kin wouldn't burn a human, but it should still have an effect on the monster as long as it was airborne. The hive shuddered and grew larger. It reached for them with tarry skeleton hands, swung its sharp head, and let acidic discoloration seep and bubble from the mass at its base. Bea kept moving on the far side. Another *crack* split the air, and a golden bullet that wasn't Okane's hit the hive. Mobsters had reached the rotunda. Renard and Blanche leveled guns at the fight, and Laura was sure more of them would be coming soon. They couldn't do much, but the bullets were helping to drive the hive into a corner. Laura would almost feel accomplished at hemming it in like this if the beast weren't laughing the whole time.

Useless, you are useless, useless, useless~

It lurched toward Clae. One, two, three skeletal arms broke upon touching him; his core throbbed dark and bright again, and cracks ran up the hive's limbs in eerie echoes of Laura's own glittering scars. Before these could reach the main body, the hive released those arms and let them fall to shimmering ash.

You first, it said, reaching again with innumerable arms. Wrath will fall! It has no place!

Laura's first thought was panic, but she bit that back. Clae wasn't human anymore. He was stronger. The hive couldn't devour him. His mantra echoed along her scars—*Not her, not her*—and it wasn't a plea but a promise: the hive wouldn't kill anyone else today. Not this time.

"Don't let it take you!" she shouted. "We're not losing anyone this time!"

Clae's crystal flared even brighter. Magic crackled like lightning over his form, and when he caught the next of the monster's arms, that magic shot faster up its limb and streaked out the beast's back hard enough to make the whole of the hive jerk backward. The fog around him shivered, and the roof at his feet went up in golden flame.

NOT HER, he rumbled.

Fall!

NOT HER!

You do not belong!

NOT! HER!

Be still!

More of the hive's form seeped away. Now there was a thick, dripping rib cage below that skull, and inside it was Minnie, scorched and mauled by the Sinkers and Bijou. Minnie's head tipped back, her mouth opened far enough for them to hear the audible crack of bone, and the hive's eye appeared between her teeth. It looked straight at Clae, clearly trying to paralyze him, but he had no eyes of his own to be affected with.

"Okane, the eye in Minnie's mouth! Hit the eye!" Laura cried.

A kin bullet flashed and missed. God, that was such a small target. The mobsters at the rotunda probably couldn't even see it. Laura couldn't try to clear the ribs for an easier shot, because she was busy fending off the veritable moat of tentacles at the hive's base. Another bullet, another miss. The hive seemed to understand its eye wasn't working, because Minnie's mouth began to close.

"We're losing it!" Laura said in a panic.

A blaze of red caught her eye. Bea had launched herself with force enough to make her amulets scream. She was angled just enough to pass through the ribs.

Minnie's head turned to look at her. The hive shuddered in realization. Minnie's jaw sagged again as the eye drew back for escape. Bea roared at the top of her lungs and swung the blade with a *crack-crackle-BANG*. Crimson magic showered from the arc of her swing. Minnie's head came clean off. Bea had no maneuvering room in the rib cage, and slammed into its opposite side. The blade fell from her hand as the hive gave a horrible, piteous wail. Laura gaped at her, stunned by the audacity. Bea caught her eye. She smiled wide and vicious, like it was a victory. And then the hive withdrew. All of it—Minnie's body and head, and all of Bea—was sucked into the inky abyss of the hive's body.

For a split second all was still, and then the blackness exploded outward. Laura barely managed to keep hold of the axe as a wave of solid dark slammed into her and sent her flat on her back. It was wet and viscous, but couldn't seem to decide what it wanted to be; one second it shoved her as hard as if another human had tackled her, and in the next second it burst apart and around her like tainted sea-foam. Whatever it was, it eclipsed all light and writhed around her, stinking like rot and every inch of it shrilling in agony. Laura held the axe close, and its aura intensified. The foam burned before reaching her, and the waves curled away. It tapered and vanished, leaving Minnie's headless corpse staggering through the acidic puddles. The hive tried to speak, but its "voice" was distorted beyond all recognition. Whiteness winked in Minnie's stomach again. The eye blinked, but incomplete. Bea's strike had split it. Only half surfaced properly, torn straight through the pupil and weeping a mixture of ink and Rexian crimson; the other half winked in and out of existence, as if the hive was trying not to absorb its own dead pieces.

SEaaEEaE? it managed, pained and livid. *This is nOOOT VICtorY FOR you! It is! Useless!*

Laura scrambled to her feet and looked around quickly. Bea had not resurfaced. She hadn't been flung out with that wave. She was gone. Really gone. Minnie's body stumbled again, just as broken as the hive's eye—one of her legs ended in bloody, shattered bone at the ankle after Clae had caught it; and Bea's first blow had cut her almost entirely in half at the middle, so her torso flopped hideously at every movement. Ink spilled out these wounds like an unending fountain, and the hive seethed, *Useless amulet! Too noisy! Too fragile! Humans are useless in every sense! I will find a new one.*

It jerked around to face Okane and Grim, down by the gargoyles.

Come to me!

What was it talking—

"No," Grim said sharply.

Yes, said the hive. *You are an amulet. This is your purpose.*

"I am not an amulet. I am myself," said Grim.

No! You are stone. You are silent. There is no noise in you. We are the same, and we belong together!

"We may be similar in creation, but that doesn't mean anything to what we are now," said Grim. "I will not help you destroy this place, or these people."

The hive shook with rage. *It is not destruction! It is a restoration! We are the natural state of the world! We are all that belongs! The light and noise and wrath that poisons us both will be removed! This is Fate!*

More scythes surged from its body and tried to hook Grim, but he dove into Clae's fog and the scythes faltered.

YOU CANNOT ESCAPE! THIS IS FATE! FATE!

Clae caught the scythes and threw them off as easily as he had the skeleton hands, but more of them were growing, and they swept in from more and more angles. Laura hurried to help deflect them. Okane snatched up Bea's blade and moved to cover the other side. They backed up to guard Grim between them. Maybe he was as weak to magic as infestations were, but maybe an infestation housed inside such a large amount of Niveus could balance itself out to be stronger or more efficient, the same as regular magic. Laura didn't know, and she didn't want to find out.

"Don't worry," she said, glancing over her shoulder at him. "We'll keep you—shit!"

Grim was blistering. Being Niveus himself, he couldn't take much magical strain. He'd avoided Clae and the active amulets as much as he could earlier, but now he was in the very thick of it, caught right next to solid angry crystal. All his skin glittered, and the side that faced Clae flaked apart as if he were ready to crumble entirely. He cringed in pain, but took another staggering step toward Clae.

"- - - have to get away from the magic!" said Okane. "Laura, we have to make an opening—"

"No!" Grim snapped. "If I leave the magic, I am susceptible to possession. I would make the hive strong again. It cannot be allowed."

"But if - - - keep going like this, - - -'re going to die!" said Okane.

"It is as Bea said: we are committed," said Grim. He forced a smile through the pain and the spreading fractures on his face. "It is all right, Okane. Whatever you are, Magi or otherwise, you are worth breaking to protect."

Okane bit his lip, grip tightening on Bea's blade.

"Nobody else," he hissed, looking at Laura. "I don't want to lose anyone else. There has to be something we can do."

"The Eggs aren't working, the Sinkers aren't working, the flash pellets don't work for shit, and all these hand weapons only make temporary injuries," said Laura. "I can't think of anything else! It needs to be something continuous. I tried the fog, but it can't—"

"The fog," said Okane.

"Yes! I can't get it to do anything!"

"But I could. Like the Sylph! Clae. I could—"

"You said it ripped all the energy out of you!" said Laura, horrified.

"But I'm not drawing on an echo this time," said Okane. "This is real. And this is the end."

Laura pursed her lips. "Fine. But if it starts pulling too much, you pull from me too, okay? I'll conduct all the magic you want!"

Okane gave a sharp nod and closed his eyes. He fisted his free hand and ground his teeth. *Not her* reverberated around them again. *Not them. I won't lose anyone else.* And for a moment, it wasn't simply Clae's voice caught up in it.

"You're all connecting," said Grim.

The magic in the air condensed. It went from foggy shield to a dazzling array of stars, many times larger a swarm than what had appeared in the Sylph. Instead of lightning or fog it was stars rising from Clae's frame, from the axe blade, from Laura's scars and Okane's shoulders. As the hive attacked again, all those stars pitched themselves forward. The scythes broke. Smoke billowed even thicker than before as the hive shrieked with surprise.

"We've got an opening!" cried Laura, and ran.

The airborne energy was killing off the hive's limbs as fast as it could grow them, leaving it floundering with only Minnie for shelter. Laura aimed her axe at Minnie's stomach. The hive saw her coming and flung up Minnie's arm to block, almost severing itself at the forearm. Okane came at its other side and used the blade to take out one of Minnie's legs at the knee. The hive wheeled.

No! You cannot kill me! I am nature!

Laura tried another angle, and Minnie contorted to duck. It evaded Okane too, and backed toward the edge of the roof as if to escape. Clae caught Minnie under the arms and pinned the corpse against crystal. All the ink on her ruined clothes scorched, and the stars continued to bore into them. The eye flickered again in Minnie's stomach, looking desperately for an escape. Maybe it could leave amulets behind, but leaving Minnie meant leaving all of itself exposed. It trilled in anguish.

But they wanted me! They called for me! I am the nature and the silence they wished for! I am love and desire and the death of all enemies! I am all that is good!

Laura and Okane charged. The eye finally turned on them. Laura felt the tremble of paralysis in her limbs. Maybe the eye was too broken to make it work properly, maybe it couldn't figure out whether to focus on her or Okane, or maybe her momentum was already too much. A howl ripped out of her throat, and she swung the axe with all the strength she had. The axe and blade plowed into the eye with force enough to cut all the way through and ram against crystal. From the stomach down, Minnie's body crumpled. All the blackness poured out like water. The hive gave one last, long wail. Its dissolving body ate through the roof and everything below, billowing with the stench of dead infestation.

Laura watched the hole, panting hard. "What—What next? Is it still attacking?"

"No," Okane said blankly. "It's gone."

"Gone?"

"All the weight of it is lifted."

"Gone," Laura echoed. "It's . . . gone. The hive mind. It's destroyed?"

"Completely," said Okane, just as disbelieving as she was.

The realization came slow, bubbling from acceptance to downright giddiness. The five-hundred-year-old monster, the reason for Orien's quarantine, the vicious link between every monster in the world, was dead.

"Gone!" she cried. "We did it! We killed the goddamn hive mind!"

She dropped her axe and hugged him, laughing as if the world were ending. He hugged her back tight enough to hurt. Clae had not so much as dented after being hit by sharp kin weapons. He deposited Minnie's body with great care, and Grim ventured up toward them again as all the airborne kin faded from stars to shimmering dust.

"Laura!"

On the next roof over, where Bea had first appeared, the rest of the Sinclair group came through the door.

"See, I told - - - they were up here," said Zelda, ruffled but certainly not dead. "Thank god they're all—Ivo, wait!"

Cherry couldn't catch Ivo fast enough. He used his amulets to jump over to the straightaway and jogged up to them.

"I was worried when the infestation's weight vanished so quickly, but - - - did it, didn't - - -? - - - killed what Rex couldn't," said Ivo.

"Maybe Rex couldn't kill it, but Bea could," said Laura.

Ivo drew back. He looked around at all the damage, the lack of another Sweeper, the discarded blade still hazy with Rexian magic. For a moment he looked utterly distraught, but he pulled in that emotion quickly.

"I always knew she was strong," he said. "I always knew . . . she could make anything possible."

Laura pulled him into their embrace, and with her arm over his shoulders she murmured, "She talked big about throwing things away, but that's not what she was doing. I think this whole thing—joining the Mad Dogs, running into danger—was the only way she could figure out how to protect you."

He smiled shakily. "I know. She was kind, if - - - looked close enough to understand it. I'm glad she was able to act with confidence, at the end."

On the rotunda, Renard and Blanche watched them only a few moments more before retreating back into the building. Police sirens wailed in the distance. The sky broke from deep blue to the vicious red of sunrise.

South across the bay they could see the dark husk of Gaudium, and a fate that Amicae would not share.

THE CANDLE IN THE WINDOW

Amicae *Sun*, April 20, 1234

INFESTATION THREAT PERMANENTLY EXTERMINATED

Late last night, the Sinclair Sweepers tracked an infestation to the roof of the Council building. This was no ordinary monster, but the hive mind: the first such beast that came into existence, which produced all the other infestations that tormented Orien for the past five centuries. Despite its considerable strength, Amicae's Sweepers subdued and destroyed it, with only two fatalities (Sweeper Beatrice Kingsley, age 24; and a second yet-unidentified young woman). This is an unprecedented victory over the enemies of mankind. While infestations still exist, the hive's loss prevents them from communicating and spreading as easily as before.

"Amicae has always been known as a magical power," says Council treasurer Marcus Walz. "We are proud of our Sweepers, and have never doubted their dedication or bravery."

Coronae has stated by telegram that they will send a delegation to present Amicae's head Sweeper Laura Kramer and the rest of her workers with awards for service to humanity. This will be a public ceremony, and will take place at the Tiber Courthouse of the Third Quarter at 1:00 P.M. on Monday, April 27.

Canis *Trekker*, April 21, 1234

HIVE MIND DEAD

Despite interference by its own Council, Amicae's Sinclair Sweepers have destroyed the infestation hive mind. Reports state that the hive mind had entered Terual and destroyed Gaudium before moving on to Amicae itself. Canis Sweeper Basil Garner believes Amicae's "Falling Infestation" and the magical implementation referred to as the "Wrath of God" may have caught the hive mind's attention, hence its odd target. The hive mind's death was immediately noted yesterday, as infestations of the wilds suddenly failed to react against Sweeper tactics that had been used on other sides of Canis: this implied that the hive mind's connection between all its children had been somehow disrupted. Aggression levels have also dropped significantly. Previous theories that killing the hive mind would kill all infestations in existence have proven false, but investigations are under way to determine what further impact the hive's death may have on infestation behavior in the future.

While this is good news from Amicae, Canis officials continue to warn travelers and businessmen to avoid the Friendly City. Amicae has not recanted its earlier claim of Rexian interference, and the city remains under lockdown.

Lux *Beacon*, April 21, 1234

SWEEPER CITY SHINES AGAIN

Head Sweeper Olga Verbaun wishes health and happiness to Amicae's Sinclair Sweepers, who achieved the unthinkable by destroying the infestation hive mind. Verbaun had previously worried for Amicae's safety under their strange conditions, and was greatly impressed by their Sweepers' verve.

"This is a moment that will go down in history," says Verbaun. "Amicae may not realize the significance of what these Sweepers have done. The Sweepers themselves may not recognize the depth of their actions. But when I heard the news, I felt like the weight of death had lifted from my children's shoulders. I've seen people weep for joy in the streets. Telegrams have been sending nonstop as everyone rushes to assure each other that they are not

alone, and that this is not the end. The
Sinclairs have given us a new lease on

our future, and I am eternally grateful."

Coronae was coming. The knowledge was a blessing and a curse. In just a
matter of hours, Sweeper representatives of Terual's capital city would arrive
in Amicae, for the express purpose of seeing the Sinclairs. The ceremony
was tomorrow, sure, and today's meeting would be only a brief check-in at
the depot and rundown of what the ceremony would entail, but she would
be meeting people from Coronae *today*.

It was a dream come true.

It was the biggest honor in all of Terual.

It was terrifying, because Laura was in no way prepared for it.

"We have to clean up!" she cried, shifting boxes on the armory's main
floor.

For the past week she'd been thrown from meeting to meeting, reporting that yes, she'd broken into the Council building; yes, the Mad Dogs were
involved; yes, it was the infestation hive mind that wrecked a portion of the
building's roof, and it had paid dearly for that. Reactions all around were
jubilant but also extremely confused. It seemed like no one could believe the
truth for even five minutes before they had to call Laura back in and have
her recount the entire tale over again. On the third affirmation that the
hive was dead, even Albright had laid her head down on her desk and gone
totally unresponsive for two full minutes, worrying everyone but Byron before sitting up and issuing commands like nothing had ever left her control.
Laura had spent days run into the ground, barely able to process it herself
when her only free time was spent trying to get some shuteye back at the
rectory guesthouse or reciting the same story to Morgan and Cheryl (Morgan's reaction was much like Albright's, but with a lot more tears and a
lot more promises of celebratory recipes). That was her excuse for why she
hadn't checked in on the armory before now.

Nothing had happened in the armory, so it wasn't an issue until she realized just how much of a mess it was. She needed to whip this place into shape
before the Coronae representatives asked to visit. It was a useless fight; the
armory had accrued equipment over decades, and with the Sweeper shop
reduced to ash and blackened framework, they had nowhere to put the excess. All she could do was stack boxes and kick things under tables, which
was basically like Cheryl sweeping dust under a rug. She continued anyway,

increasingly frazzled, and it got bad enough that Clae had started to react to it. He paced fast circles around the middle table, pointless and honestly in everyone's way, but no one stayed in the crystal man's path for long, because right now he didn't seem to comprehend obstacles.

Ivo hastily hopped onto the table to avoid Clae's most recent circuit. He sprawled amid creaking boxes of kin bullets, and floundered a moment before pulling himself up and shooting Laura a weak glare. "Could - - - ask him to go back upstairs?"

"I've tried!" Laura snapped.

She had. With Clae down and active, all of the equipment here was primed to match him; all the kin glowed, a faint fog lifted from the heavier armor and staff pieces, and even the colored lanterns seemed to glimmer a little more ethereally than usual. It was also too warm. Laura wore an old pair of gloves to keep from hurting her hands while she tried to sort equipment, because all of it felt like metal in direct sunlight. She dumped the latest pack of magical arrows into a box and cast around for somewhere to put it. Why had the Sinclairs not installed any closets?

"I suspect this may be a hazard," said Ivo, looking pointedly at the lines of bullets bubbling inches from his face.

"I *know*," Laura groaned.

"Don't tell her that. - - -'re just making it worse," said Zelda. She'd sat herself down on a table near the front door, legs crossed and perusing a newspaper with the headline MAD DOGS MISSING IN ACTION.

"How can it get worse?" Ivo grumbled.

Zelda shot him a very judgmental look over the top of the paper. "He came down because she's stressed, and - - -'re making her *more* stressed. He's sensing her mood, not her looks. Even if she tells him to scram, she's not any calmer. It's like if I told - - - I was fine while missing an arm. - - - wouldn't just take me at my word."

Laura set down the box. She took a deep breath in, held it, breathed out. She turned to face Clae, arms wide as if to present herself: *Look! I'm calm! So calm!* Clae made another circuit of the table with absolutely zero acknowledgment. Laura snarled and made a strangling gesture at his crystal back. Ivo gave her a very sympathetic look, but in his current position draped among ammo boxes it came across more sarcastic than anything.

"Fine, circle around for all eternity," said Laura, returning to the arrow box. "It's not like I care whether you wear down the floor. You can go until—" She'd been hefting up the box, but a horrible thought occurred to her. She dropped it again, and the arrows rattled against each other. All the equipment in the room gave an ugly throb, and Clae whipped about to march back toward her. Laura hardly noticed. She turned to the others again, hands clutching her paling face, and screeched, "What if the Coronae reps see him?"

"Oh my god," Zelda said flatly.

"It's okay!" Ivo's voice was thin, eyes fixed on Clae, who'd begun to issue golden fog. "It's fine! No one's seen him!"

"But they will!" Laura wailed.

"- - - can bait him back upstairs!"

"If I couldn't convince him to stay away from the Council building, what makes you think I can make him stay put now? I can't stay up there with him, I'm the head Sweeper so they'll want to meet me, and they'll want to check out the upstairs anyway. This is awful! He'll barge in, and he'll scare them, and they'll ask questions, and I—Ugh!" She waved her hands, trying to fan the thickening vanilla cloud away from her face and coughing all the while. "You are making! This! Worse!"

"Should we just strap her to Grim's back?" Zelda asked conversationally.

Ivo clearly didn't get the joke. "I don't believe he has recovered enough from the hive mind to withstand contact with someone for long enough to sufficiently calm her."

The cloud was getting downright hard to breathe in. Laura stumbled away. She threw open the stained-glass window and leaned far through it for clear air.

"Tell me you have good news!" she begged.

Below her, Okane jogged away from the armory's garage door to stand with Grim, Cherry, and Amelia in the street.

"I think we've got it!" he called. "Amelia?"

Amelia held up some kind of device and clicked a button on it. The garage door, long ago damaged by Rexian invaders, now looked pristine, as if it had been newly installed. At Amelia's signal it shuddered into hopeful motion . . . and quickly began to screech like a metallic banshee. Grim stared at it flatly, pretending the noise didn't affect him; Cherry plugged her ears with her fingers; Okane's eyes squeezed shut as if not seeing it could make it all go away; Amelia nodded along as if the sound were somehow profound, and clicked the button again. The hideous noise stopped.

"I don't think we've got it!" said Okane.

The complex Magi-placed security protocols still seemed to think the

272 ∞ MIRAH BOLENDER

lower floor was in lockdown. Laura would be impressed if she weren't on a deadline. She groaned and slumped. The sill at her hip was the only thing keeping her from falling straight out the window.

"I really thought we had it that time!" cried Cherry, genuinely upset. "All the hardware's intact! Okane pieced together all the magicky bits, and Grim thought they lined up, too—"

Okane shook his head wearily. "I just matched what felt similar. I have no idea how the structure actually works."

"You may need to enlist an actual mechanic," Grim agreed, dropping a wrench into the toolbox at his feet.

"Maybe we could remove the entire door?" Cherry suggested.

"And make it even worse?" said Okane.

"If you can just rearrange it and then put it all back once you understand it, that should still end up plenty secure . . ."

Amelia snorted loudly. "If you think you can dismantle that sucker, you're in for a nasty shock. If it could be removed from inside, the Rexian intruders would've done it, and it's specifically built not to be dismantled from outside."

"And the Rexians were Magi. They'd sense the same way I do," said Okane, frowning. "There's not any specific Magi requirement. We need the basic knowledge."

Cherry folded her arms. "Do you really think a random mechanic would be able to fix it?"

"Maybe not, but they'll be better at it than a Ranger and a layperson. No offense, Grim."

"None taken," said Grim.

While the four of them went on discussing possibilities, Laura turned her head to look miserably up the street. Tomorrow the Coronae representatives would come by this exact road, expecting the trappings of the Sweeper city, and they'd find a three-story pigsty with doors that didn't even work. She could just die of shame right now.

There was a man in the road, several blocks down. It took a moment for Laura to realize it, but when she did, she straightened with a whole new sense of alarm. Renard? At this distance she couldn't be sure, but the shape was tall enough, thin enough. What could he want here?

As Zelda's newspaper had said, the Mad Dogs had gone underground. The move puzzled every journalist in the city, considering they'd made such a racket in the lead-up to their move on the Council building. A few scattered members had been spotted among the Silver Kings' ranks, but on the whole they'd gone totally silent, their business ties were unceremoniously dropped, and no more circles appeared at politicians' doors; the Mad Dogs had also exterminated all the other infestations they'd planted in the Council building that night. If Renard's boasting was true, that he only cared about defense against infestations, it made some sense. The danger, while not entirely gone, was far diminished.

The hive's death had caused a ripple effect across Orien. It hadn't spontaneously killed all infestations in existence (wishful thinking), but the connection between them had been broken. They had to rely on their own knowledge, rather than learning from each other. That would make exterminations much easier. Even better, reports were coming in from multiple cities that new infestations weren't forming—their birth had been tremendously slowed, perhaps even stopped outright. It was a massive victory, and the *Sinclair Sweepers* were being praised in every city. Meanwhile, the new Sweeper order had been spelled out: Sweepers would still exist, supported by the cities to defend against any old infestations, but the departments would be cut down due to fewer threats. Sweepers laid off by the cities could join the Ranger forces, who were enthusiastic about hunting down and eradicating the infestations of the wilds.

If Renard had been honest, then his pressing demands were met: the hive and oncoming swarms were gone, Sweepers were recognized, and the remaining threats were being hunted. The terrible urgency had lifted. Laura suspected the Mad Dogs were undergoing a shift in ideology. Would they still be so Sweeper-driven? Would Renard remain in charge? She doubted he'd relinquish control so easily, and she didn't trust that he wasn't interested in more power. The Mad Dogs would likely resurge in a different market, and go on to dominate the mob scene just as they had in the past. Renard had known about Clae and Anselm, how they'd been crystallized and cannibalized for the Sinclair magic production; could he be coming to steal them away for his own uses? He'd never made a bid for Anselm in all the time Clae had been in charge, and hadn't tried to snatch them away when Laura was still floundering in her new role, but did that really mean anything?

Renard seemed to notice her staring. He didn't call out to her, didn't make any other sign of acknowledgment. He turned and disappeared into the alleyways again. He'd been so indistinct that as soon as he was out of sight she started second-guessing that it had been him at all.

"Laura?"

She looked down to find Okane frowning at her.

"What was that?" she asked, pretending normalcy. "I thought I saw something in the road, but it was nothing."

Okane didn't believe that, but luckily Amelia was too boisterous to let him argue.

"You shouldn't even be worrying about this!" she shouted, strolling toward the stairs with the others trailing behind her. "Everyone who's anyone already knows the Council tried to sink the Sinclairs, so they're not expecting a palace. If anything, they're going to be even more impressed that you managed to do so much with so little!" The clatter of feet on the iron stairs covered up her continuing words. Laura slipped back and away from the window, leaning to see through to the front door. When Amelia arrived there she draped herself against the doorway dramatically, to emphasize a statement Laura hadn't caught at all. "Besides, they're *Coronae*. They don't *impose*. If you're really so worried about the garage door, just lie and tell them you don't want to take anything out with the traffic."

"But there's no traffic on this circuit. Not that I've ever seen, anyway," said Laura.

Amelia laughed. "You think you can have royal ambassadors here and not draw a crowd? You'll have traffic here tomorrow just by existing. Do you know how many new people I've seen walk by to get their bearings so they can swarm in the afternoon?"

"Oh, no," Laura moaned.

Coronae reps *and* a crowd of Amicae witnesses. She felt dizzy.

"Can none of - - - let this poor woman relax?" Zelda snapped.

"They're just Sweepers!" said Amelia, still jolly.

"Coronae Sweepers!" Laura slid down the wall to sit on the ground and wrapped her arms around her legs. "Oh, this is hopeless."

"We'll take it one step at a time," said Okane, ducking under Amelia's arm to get into the armory proper. "Laura, where can I help?"

"Make them reschedule," Laura groaned into her knees.

She couldn't see him now, but his amused voice came from much closer. "Don't think about the armory. Think of the ceremony."

"That's not going to help."

"Isn't it?"

She peeked up to find his hands outstretched and waiting. After a moment more of wallowing, she took them. He pulled her to her feet, and smiled down at her like the mess and the doors and the very obvious crystal man didn't matter.

"Head Sweeper Laura Kramer," he said, loud and ostentatious as a radio announcer, "it is with great honor that I present to - - - the prestigious King's Cross, proof of - - -r miraculous achievement and the salvation of all life in Orien, if not the world. Under - - -r leadership, - - - have made the impossible possible. We owe - - - our lives."

He let go of her to mime draping a medal around her neck. Laura couldn't help the amused curl of her lips. She gave him a gentle shove, and he allowed it with an even wider smile. Zelda caught on; she stood and cast her paper aside, grinning as Okane faced her next.

"To Zelda Kingsley—who may absolutely change her surname if she so pleases—without - - -r talent and cunning we would surely be lost. For - - -r bravery and selflessness, this award!"

When he mimed gifting the medal, Zelda played along and struck an all-important pose. Ivo slipped off the table in time to be caught next.

"Ivo Kingsley, who never let hope grow dim in his heart. This is proof of - - -r dreams, and a sign - - - can go still further. Take my good wishes into the future."

Ivo huffed out a laugh. Okane turned next to the empty air at Ivo's side, held out a hand as if presenting another award, and his smile became something much softer, much sadder.

"Bea Kingsley. The dawn - - - saw, - - - dragged into existence. - - - gave us a bright future."

The air grew somber. Ivo blinked, first in surprise and then more rapidly in grief. He looked to that empty place as if a ghost might truly stand there, and murmured, "Yes. - - - did. - - - didn't understand what this freedom meant to us, but - - - gave everything so we could have it anyway. I will never forget - - -r strength."

Laura curled her arms around herself. All her worries seemed very small and petulant now.

"You're accepting her medal, right?" she said quietly. "Have you thought of what you'll do with it?"

"Hang it here," Zelda said immediately.

She gestured at the walls: at the medals and ribbons of Sweepers long passed, the picture frames and the newspaper articles. Ivo followed the gesture, still slumped.

"A piece of me wishes to keep it with me to remember her, but—" He clutched his chest with one hand, and his brow furrowed as he tried to force confidence back into his voice. "Bea as she was . . . that's anchor enough for me. She would want to be honored as a Sweeper, among Sweepers. She would be happiest if it were hung here."

"Don't talk as if you can't come to see it in here," said Laura.

"But Sweepers are downsizing," said Ivo. "Zelda and I . . . we won't be Sweepers for much longer, if we can secure other employment. This is a Sweeper building."

"Maybe the Council won't recognize you as Sweepers, but I always will," said Laura, leaning back against the windowsill again. "You're always welcome here, no matter how long it's been or how far you go."

"I'll go *so* far!" Zelda held up her arms and twirled with excitement. "All the way to the upper Quarters, where the food is so much better!"

Ivo began to cheer up at the sight. He straightened from his slump and watched her fondly. "We will leave Sweeping behind us. For most of my life I did not allow myself the luxury of considering other possibilities in my future. The ability to do so now is . . . exhilarating."

"But you still have to check in with us!" Laura scolded. "Just because you won't be my employee anymore doesn't mean I won't still want to keep up with you."

Zelda stopped her twirling so fast that her skirt gave an audible swish. "- - -'ll hear from me whether - - - want to or not," she said cheekily. "- - - can't get rid of me that easily, Laura Kramer!"

"Why do you all have to act like you're saying your final good-byes right now?" Amelia sighed. "It's just one night, and then you'll all be stuck together in the afternoon for the ceremony again. And believe me, you two, just because you're job hunting doesn't mean you'll find anything soon."

Okane shrugged sheepishly. "It felt right."

"I think we'll be saying our good-byes for the night, actually," said Cherry, as she and Grim set their toolboxes down just inside the armory's door. "Our registration is due tomorrow afternoon, so if we want to make it to your ceremony we have to get everything arranged tonight."

"Registration?" Laura echoed, leaning to see them better. "Registration for what? You're not with those Rangers signing up for infestation hunts, are you?"

"A Rexian hunt, actually! We'll leave infestations to the professionals," said Cherry. "See, at this point no one knows if Rex is still intact, so a force is pulling together for reconnaissance and retaliation. If they're still around, they must be weak after all the infestations, so we should be able to free everyone they've taken as slaves."

"We also worry about their Sweepers," said Grim.

"If anyone could survive a surge it's Rexian Sweepers, but we don't know if they're still under the old leadership or if Rex is bending them to new uses," said Cherry.

"They're only worthwhile with infestations around," said Ivo. "We were never Rex's ideal. If our use is gone, they'll get rid of our ugliness."

"That's what I'm afraid of," Cherry muttered.

"If we find survivors, we'll evacuate them," said Grim. "I hope to find the Magi they imprisoned, as well. This may be the perfect time to free them."

Okane straightened with interest; while recent revelations about Magi had been pretty horrible, his father was still a Magi who'd been held captive as one of Rex's "paragon" stock, and had gone to great lengths to keep them safe during their brief stint in the city. "- - -'ll keep me updated?"

"Of course."

"Oh, the Magi will be around." Zelda waved her hand as if the very idea that they wouldn't was ludicrous. "If - - - don't find them in Rex, it won't be because they're dead. It'll be because they saw their chance and broke out. They're tough old bastards."

"How long do you think that Ranger registration will take?" said Amelia.

Cherry rubbed at her chin in thought. "An hour or two, maybe?"

"Then how about we all eat together tonight?" Amelia clapped her hands together with glee. "No more of this gloomy good-bye nonsense! You've had a victory, so we should be celebrating! And if we drop the fact that we're Sinclairs, you never know what restaurant might give you free drinks!"

"I wouldn't want to keep you too late," said Cherry.

Amelia blew a raspberry. "Nonsense! The more the merrier. Who else is with me?"

"I've certainly got nothing better to do," said Zelda.

"Company would be nice," said Ivo.

"That's great! But—" Laura looked around, her nerves flaring again.

"Laura and I will stay here a little longer to clean up, and then meet - - - there. How does that sound?" said Okane.

"Fantastic!" said Amelia. "Let's meet at the Averills' restaurant, how about that? It's close to the official expedition offices, and we already know it's good food. If Dan doesn't give me a free beer I'll eat my leg."

They all agreed, and went their separate ways. Cherry and Grim made for their expedition office, and Amelia walked toward the restaurant with an arm looped around Ivo's and Zelda's shoulders (they'd escaped early to avoid cleaning). It left the armory much quieter, and maybe Okane was still there, but maybe that was the reason Laura could actually relax. She stretched out her arms and heaved a heavy sigh.

"It's hard to believe it's been a week since all of that happened."

"Sometimes it's hard to believe the hive mind died at all," Okane agreed.

Papers from other cities wept over how amazing it was for the hive to be gone, and how drastically the world would change, but day-to-day life in Amicae hadn't truly shifted yet. The barriers were still up, the mobs (at least the Silver Kings) were still upset, and infestations still existed. In the long run, she'd notice. In the long run, maybe she'd be able to settle into it. There had never been a time in her life where the hive mind hadn't been menacing everyone from the bottom island, and she was looking forward to finding out what the differences would be. Although . . .

"Are you sure that you still want to be a Sweeper?" she asked. If she tried very hard, she could look and sound normal. "If we're downsizing, this is your chance to expand somewhere else. You can consider other possibilities, the way Ivo and Zelda are."

Okane didn't look at her. He looked instead over the armory's walls, and his expression was as warm as all the kin's glow.

"I thought about it," he admitted, "but it didn't feel right. I'm not ready to let go of this quite yet."

Thank goodness. The relief in Laura's chest forced a smile to her own face.

"Glad to hear it. So, partner in crime, let's get to work tidying this place up. Amelia can guess all she wants, but I'm positive Coronae will have some standards."

He laughed, and they split up to conquer more boxes.

"So," said Laura, as she finally stowed the arrow box in a corner, "we know what we're doing for Bea's medal, but what are we going to do about Clae's?"

Okane lifted a box that definitely wasn't Sweeper-related and started sorting through the contents as he replied, "We could probably claim it the way we're doing with Bea's."

"Yes, but this is Clae Sinclair. They know he died," said Laura. "I put his name on the list of team members, but what if they think that was a gimmick I made up to get more gold? What if they don't bring anything for him?"

"I don't think that'll be a problem," said Okane. "I'm listed as a Sinclair. They may assume 'Clae' is a family name, for another apprentice or something."

"Hopefully." Laura frowned down at the nearest ammo crate. "But it hurts thinking we did all that work, and it's all his life was leading up to, and now he can't get on stage and get acknowledged for it."

"Maybe not now, but if he wakes up, I'm sure he'd appreciate the medal itself." Okane paused. "He looks like he's doing well. Grim said the closer he is to acting human, the better his chances are to come back."

But Clae remained near the window, where Laura had been panicking earlier. He hadn't moved to look or follow them, and he didn't understand their words. Even Laura's odd dreams of the Sweeper shop had stopped.

"Do you think if Grim and Cherry find any Magi, they might be able to help him?" she said wistfully.

"Doubtful. Magi force the crystallization, remember? They don't want sentinels to recover. They never would've tried it. Besides, even if we had a Magi here, Clae wouldn't care, would he? It'd just be another stranger. They wouldn't connect."

A good point. It still hurt to think about, though. To keep her mind off of it, Laura hefted up the crate and turned. She found Okane holding a coverless book, his own box neglected on the table. It was her Coronae book, the one Laura had obsessed over since childhood. She made a shrill, embarrassed noise, and he looked up in surprise.

"The illustrations here are beautiful," he said, and his eyes went right back to the page.

Laura dumped the crate and hurried over to him, face red. "Don't worry about that! That box is mine, I brought it in for storage after we moved in with Mateo, but I must've forgotten it after that whole baiting thing! It's one of my childhood books, it's really nothing—"

But she stilled as she came up next to him. He had the book open to the passage on Sweepers: the image of an impossible man with the sun in his hand. It had always been her favorite. She'd wanted to be that man, and here she was. Head Sweeper of the Sinclair team that killed the hive mind. The realization made her a little light-headed. Maybe someday her picture would be printed like this. Maybe someday a bratty little girl like herself (or maybe, she thought with a twist, like Ellie) would read about *Head*

Sweeper Laura Kramer, and start to dream the way she had when she found that book.

Okane ran fingers gently down the worn edge of the page. "This book is well loved."

Laura nodded. "It was my favorite. It's what made me want to be a Sweeper in the first place."

He carefully folded it closed again. The book hadn't had a cover as long as she'd owned it, so the dirtied title page looked up at them, reading: *We Are Coronae.*

"Is this why . . . ?"

"Yeah," Laura said quietly. "Coronae was my dream for years. Having them come to me in reality is a little unreal."

She was the impossible woman, now. She was going to get a Coronae medal, and she'd hang it here on the armory walls, and she'd really, finally feel as if she belonged to this legacy.

"I'm glad - - - found this book, then," said Okane.

"What?"

"If it's what made - - - a Sweeper, I owe it a lot. Without it, - - - never would've found me. Or the others. And we'd still be plagued by the hive mind, so this is a very important little book."

Laura snorted and took it away. "You're getting sappy. Wasn't Amelia just saying we weren't doing good-byes? And you're not even leaving."

"I'm in a sentimental mood today," said Okane.

Laura shook her head fondly and set the book back in its box. It was indeed the same box she'd carried here the night Clae had begun to move. She sifted through the contents, confirming that everything was still there, but on one item she paused.

"Well, would you look at that."

"What?" said Okane, instantly alert. "Is something wrong?"

"No, I just—I forgot about this."

She pulled out the stub of a dust-colored candle flecked with gold.

Okane's brow rose in recognition. " - - -r Underyear candle?"

"Exactly." She carried it reverently to the window where Clae still lingered, set it on the sill, and pulled the shutter to half closed. She had matches on her somewhere, didn't she?

"I don't understand. Underyear was months ago," said Okane, following her over.

Laura lit the candle. This little stub wasn't near as impressive as the full taper of its original form, but it was still the candle she'd bought for Clae.

"Let me do something childish," she said quietly. "The candles at Underyear are supposed to be a beacon. They show we remember. They guide lost people out of the dark."

Clae remained still between them. The candle burned before him, but a crystal couldn't see; he faced straight to the window with no sign of noticing it. Laura took the hard crystal of his hand and said, "It's okay. You can come home, now."

After a moment of hesitation, Okane took his other hand and said, "We're waiting for - - -."

Clae did not look at them, or the candle. He was silent and still.

"Can I try something childish, too?" said Okane.

"Why not?" said Laura, trying and failing to smile.

Okane held out his free hand, and she took this, too. He gave her a reassuring squeeze and closed his eyes. She felt it in her scars as he pulled at his magic and tried to concentrate the energy around them again. He didn't pop or crack now, and he wasn't mining power from their surroundings either; the power eased out of him as steady and natural as the air itself. The candle guttered and burned higher. The kin equipment glittered behind them. Clae's dark core shifted, but not by much. Laura bowed her head and tried to focus her mind on the feel of that magic. If she could channel it herself, the way she'd channeled the Pit . . .

Come back, she thought. *Come back. I want to see you again. I want you to see everything I did. I want you to see that your time wasn't wasted on me. I want you to see that the danger's gone, and everything you worked for succeeded.*

I want you to see how tall Okane stands now, and how happy he is. I want you to meet Zelda and Ivo, because they're very special to me. I want to tell you about Bea, because I think you'd respect what she did. I want to tell you about all these people I've met, and all the things I've seen.

I want to see how all your neighbors would react if you showed up again. Amelia and Mrs. Keedler would probably cry. I want to know what you think a good lasagna is. I want to know what you look like when you're living with hope.

I miss you.

I miss you.

Fingers stirred against hers, and they weren't Okane's. Laura's head snapped up, and her heart lodged in her throat.

Clae looked back at her with human eyes.

ACKNOWLEDGMENTS

2020, huh? *Wow.*

Book three in a series is a fun challenge! Changing the narrative scaffolding in edits for book one means bigger changes in the structure of book two, which means the sandcastle of your book three has been overtaken by the tide and you've got one soggy tower standing from your original plan that still works. Needless to say, this last book in the trilogy needed a lot of help. Thank you again to my editor, Jennifer Gunnels, who helped me rebuild this castle (or Fortress, as it were) with enthusiasm for the work that I'm still thrilled and a little amazed by. Thank you also to my agent, Peter Rubie, who's never been anything but supportive.

Thank you also to the rest of the team working on this book: my copy editor with their eagle eyes; the people who formatted the book itself (I still want to cry a little bit every time I remember that I have a book with something as simple as page numbers); artist Tony Mauro, who worked on the last two amazing covers but topped them both this time; Natalie Naudus and the Macmillan Audio team for their fantastic work on the audiobooks; and everyone else at Tor who helped make this series a reality.

Thank you to my family, especially my sister and her husband, who had to deal with me during rewrites.

Lastly, thank you to everyone reading this. Without readers, I never would've gotten this far. I hope you enjoyed this final installment of the Chronicles of Amicae!